Journals of The

EARTH
GUARDIANS
SERIES 1

Journals of The
EARTH
GUARDIANS
SERIES 1

L.C WEBB

To order additional copies of this book, contact:
Xlibris
AU TFN: 1 800 844 927 (Toll Free inside Australia)
AU Local: 0283 108 187 (+61 2 8310 8187 from outside Australia)
www.Xlibris.com.au
Orders@Xlibris.com.au
793537

CONTENTS

"Secrets . . . are at their safest when you eliminate all who know."

CHAPTER 1

THE LAST ONE

Journal entry by Adela Eden

This story is not the fairy tale that most people want to hear about. This story is dark, filled with pain and lies.

It all began at the end of a dark car park in the bushes outside a shipping warehouse called Pack 'n' Send.

With dark green eyes peering from the bushes, I watched as a small bluebird flew from the rooftop of the warehouse and into the bushes where I waited for a "sit rep".

The warehouse door flew open as the last factory worker clocked off for the night, completely oblivious to the world around him, listening to ridiculously loud music from his phone. He locked the warehouse door while he danced and shimmied and began to whistle as he strutted to his car.

The bluebird chirped, and the leaves rustled as I shushed the bird to stay quiet. The factory worker stopped, pulling one of the headphones away from his ear, looking cautiously back at the bushes.

"Hello?" he shouted, now pulling the headphones fully away from his ears and resting them around his neck. He shouted again: "Is someone there?!"

He slowly walked towards the bushes, fearfully reaching into his pocket to retrieve his flashlight. He looked around the car park, his eyes following the shaking light of the torch.

"Hello . . . ?"

The bluebird startled the worker as it flew from the bushes and began to encircle him with low swoops. I stayed quiet, hiding in the bushes as my green eyes began to glow—just slightly—as I looked up at the sky, watching small rainclouds form over the factory car park.

The bluebird hurriedly flew back into the bushes as heavy rain began to fall, drenching the factory worker. Now frustrated and soaking wet, the factory worker scurried back to his car, attempting to cover his head with his jacket.

The small bluebird seemed to watch on from the safe cover of the bushes as the factory worker's car lights disappeared out of sight.

I saw the bluebird slowly hop towards the factory, then turn, glancing back at the bushes. "Adela," it whispered.

That's right—he can talk, and sometimes never shuts up!

He called out again—this time much louder, looking up at the grey clouds and shaking his wings profusely to loosen the water from his feathers.

I closed my eyes and the rain stopped. I stood up and climbed out of the bushes and pulled my hoodie up to cover my long brown hair. (To paint you a picture, I also have one red streak of hair from my fringe leading back into my ponytail—in my family, I'm the rebel!)

I looked down at the small bluebird and asked with a slightly annoyed tone in my voice, "Are you sure this is the right warehouse?"

The bluebird flew up and perched himself confidently on my shoulder. "Positive," he responded. "Now please stop stalling and continue with the mission."

I drew a deep breath, and I admit I was a little scared as I looked up at the warehouse rooftop. "Okay then, now it's just a case of finding out how to get in . . . any clues, Blue?" Unfortunately, I took a pretty good guess at what Blue's answer would be.

"Bluey!" the bluebird responded. "You are aware my name is Bluey. I do not understand why you insist on calling me Blue!" With a flutter, Bluey the Bluebird flew up onto the rooftop, disappearing into the dark.

I sighed in disappointment. "I was afraid you were going to do that."

I looked around the car park, walking to the far wall of the warehouse, and found a long ladder leading high up onto the rooftop, locked behind a large steel fence.

I couldn't help but smile smugly and rub my hands together before taking a running jump over the fence like it was a small playground hurdle.

Bluey was still waiting at the top of the warehouse, staring down at the empty car park. As I climbed timidly over the last rung of the ladder and lay down on the flat roof, holding on to the railing, I took some quick calming breaths. (If you haven't guessed, heights were not my thing, like . . . ever.)

Bluey chirped and asked if I was okay.

I nodded as I regained control of my nerves and got up onto my knees and vigilantly avoided to look up as I crawled slowly towards a rooftop skylight. Bluey tweeted back to me as if to say, Hurry up!

Angered by Bluey's domineering attitude towards me, I growled back at him, "Blue—seriously! One more tweet from you and I'll drop a giant snowball on your tiny head!"

Bluey, unshaken by my threatening remarks, snapped back, "Given that there is no snow, and that we are in Melbourne in the middle of summer, it is unlikely that you will follow through on that threat . . . so I will note that this fear of heights is irrational and—"

Before Bluey could finish his sentence, I looked up at him with glowing eyes, as suddenly a large ball of snow fell from the sky and covered him completely, silencing him momentarily. I smiled as I watched Bluey attempt to dig his way out of the snow.

"What would you know about fear?" I asked sarcastically. "You're half robot . . . you let a computer run your brain!"

I grabbed the side of the skylight and ripped the plastic sheeting and its bolts away from the roof, creating a large-enough hole to fit through. Just as I was about to jump happily off that roof and into the office below, I heard the sound of that shivering bluebird, failing to dig itself out of the snow. Letting out an unwilling huff, I reached into the pile of snow and lifted Bluey up and out of the cold and onto my shoulder. I jumped down into the office space below and smiled as I felt my confidence return and my fear disappear. I left Bluey in the safety of the office window, overlooking the darkened warehouse floor.

Walking out of the office and down a flight of stairs, I adjusted the small earpiece inserted in my ear, whispering, "Bluey, can hear me? . . . There doesn't seem to be anything suspicious here . . . I'm going to look through the back warehouse." I hoped that Bluey could hear me.

I stared into the almost pitch-black warehouse for a moment before I closed my eyes and took several slow deep breaths. When I opened them again, the outer rim of my iris glowed faint blue, and I looked around the warehouse again, now finding it much easier to see. (That's right—I've got night vision, baby!)

As I looked around, I spotted some piles of papers and a few stacks of boxes, and in the distance, I could make out a large shipping container sitting at the very front end of the warehouse.

"Curious . . .," I muttered under my breath. "Bluey . . .," I said cautiously, adjusting my earpiece, "are you sure this is the right warehouse? There's nothing here except boxes and an empty shipping container."

A large rat ran across the floor of the warehouse, and I jumped in fear as it sent shivers throughout my body (Yuk! I totally hate rats.). I looked over at the rat nibbling on some stale bread and whispered, "I'm starting to really regret leaving Alex behind . . ."

Warily, I moved to inspect the empty shipping container to find absolutely nothing inside. I was right to think Bluey had been given a dead lead. (I'd tell you what we were looking for, but that's classified.)

The shipping container was empty, I thought to myself. I began to wonder why only one factory worker was leaving this late at night from a warehouse with very little in the way of supplies and boxes, plus one empty shipping container. It kind of felt . . . off.

I snapped back to reality as I heard the sound of thick oozing mud exuding from the roof of the shipping container, wrapping around my feet and trapping me inside the container. I tried to run, but it was like the mud was alive—it chased after me and dragged me back into the shipping container, somehow slamming the door shut. All I could do was scream. "Bluey . . . Bluey! It's a trap! Run, Bluey . . . Run!"

That was all I remembered before everything went dark.

Journal entry insert by Agent Bluey

My name is Bluey—and yes, I am a bluebird with a robotic brain.

I was sitting at the office window watching in horror at Agent Adela being chased by what looked like mud. I heard the floorboards creak in the office, and I turned my head to see the factory worker from the car park standing behind me, holding a bag out ready to catch me. Remembering my training, I flew in a weaving pattern and clawed at his hand and face, then I circled the room, flying up and out of the hole where the skylight once was, and flew as fast as I could into the darkness.

I watched, perched high on a tree in the car park across the road from the warehouse. I saw a man step out of a parked SUV and stand in the shadows, watching as the shipping container (presumably with Adela still locked inside) was loaded onto a truck and driven away. (This man's name was unknown to us—we had nicknamed him the "Darkman" because we've only ever seen him in the dark.)

The factory worker approached Darkman carefully and spoke timidly, avoiding eye contact. "Sir," the factory worker exclaimed, "we got one . . . but her partner was not onsite."

The man remained in the shadows of the warehouse, obscuring his identity. He crushed his coffee cup, trying to hold back his anger, as he responded sternly through gritted teeth, "Never call me sir . . . do I look like your boss?"

The warehouse worker responded hurriedly, "No, sir . . . I mean, I apologize, si—" He seemed unsure what exactly to say.

I took that opportunity to fly away, and I was not sure, but I thought he spotted me leaving.

As I flew down the back alleys of the city, my eyes glowed red as my robotic brain sent a coded message to my operations centre.

"MISSION FAILED. MOTHER BIRD CAPTURED."

I received a response and my eyes glowed blue.

"FIND THE LAST ONE BEFORE THEY DO!"

I flew up to the very highest building and hid on the roof. I peered down as the Darkman appeared in the streets below, looked around, and then disappeared into the shadows of the night.

I waited about an hour before I started to move, then I flew through the night, across the city, past the bright night lights of Melbourne, and rested on the windowsill of a small townhouse in the Dandenong Ranges.

Exhausted from the flight, I peeped in the window of the townhouse to see (who I believed to be) the Last One—Lila Winters, our last hope.

CHAPTER 2

WHY ME?

Journal entry by Lila Winters

My name is Lila Winters. I'm 25 years old and have the best family ever. Two adorable children—Danny, who is my cheeky little 4-year-old man (who luckily got his father's good looks with his beautiful brown hair and blue eyes), and Ruby, who's 3 years old, but I swear she acts like a 5-year-old bossing her brother about; it's very funny to watch. She was also lucky to get her father's genes, with the same blue eyes and brown hair.

I, on the other hand, had honey blond hair as I was growing up, and as a teen, I hated it! Everyone I met would comment on my hair and how beautiful and sweet it made me look. Yuck! I am anything but sweet!

In the end, I rebelled and dyed my hair purple—not because people thought I looked "sweet," but because my dad ("The General") hated it. He's a military man and wanted so badly for me to join the army and be like him. But you can't have coloured hair in the military, so I've kept my hair purple ever since.

The wonderful man currently sleeping next to me is my husband Matt. He—and I mean this in the nicest way—is my sexy science nerd, with his brown hair and blue eyes, enhanced by his glasses, which he only wears when he's reading, but when he reads, damn, does he look dreamy!

This morning, I woke to the sound of stampeding little footsteps running towards my bedroom. I braced for impact as Danny opened the door, shouting as he jumped on the bed, "Mummy, Mummy, Mummy . . . !"

Matt quickly sat up and grabbed hold of Danny and tickled him, but it wasn't long before Ruby ran into the room, trying to rescue her brother from the tickling hands of their dad, but was soon caught in a trap as I grabbed Ruby and tickled her as well.

Danny and Ruby wriggled all over the bed, laughing. The laughter broke when we were interrupted by the sound of the alarm clock. Sigh!

Matt stopped tickling Danny to turn off the alarm and sighed half-humorously. "You know, just once it would be really nice to be woken by the alarm clock. I just can't seem to remember that feeling of being woken abruptly by the sound of annoying beeps."

I responded with my usual "Yes, dear" look and snickered. "Well, when we're old and grey, maybe it'll happen."

Matt smiled and gave all three of us kisses as he got up to get dressed. My stomach began to grumble, and I grinned at the kids before asking, "So! Who wants pancakes for breakfast?!"

Danny and Ruby both shouted loudly, "Me! Me! Me!" as they ran downstairs to the kitchen.

"Do you reckon they'll ever get sick of pancakes?" Matt asked, as he walked out of the walk-in robe, buttoning up his work shirt. He worked in research at the University of Melbourne. Genetics was his specialty, but I thought if he had the opportunity, he would specialise in all things scientific.

I scoffed at Matt's remark and laughed as I walked out of the room. "No one could get sick of pancakes." Walking downstairs, I yelled back, "Hurry up or you'll hit traffic!"

Matt's phone vibrated on the dresser as it received a text message. He read the message as he tightened his tie, then shouted down the stairwell, "Hey, Lila! Kevin's called in sick—he wants me to teach his class this afternoon . . . that means I'll be late home tonight!"

I yelled back up the stairs from the kitchen, "I'll leave your dinner in the microwave!"

Matt rushed downstairs with his briefcase and hurried into the kitchen to give me a kiss goodbye and to steal some pancakes. "Bye, hon," he mumbled, with his mouth stuffed full.

Ruby sat at the table, waiting as I served up the remaining pancakes and poured her some juice. Danny darted to turn on the television, but I intercepted him before he reached the remote.

"No TV until you've had breakfast!"

He walked back to the table with his head hung and lips pouted. I couldn't help but smile and laugh a little (children and their cuteness—it is their superpower).

Ruby looked out the window and pointed at a bluebird sitting on the windowsill of the dining room. "Birdie!" she said gleefully.

I looked at the bluebird and was very confused—it's not every day you see a bluebird in Melbourne! "Very good, Ruby!" I replied, while taking a seat at the table, "It is a birdy—that one's called a 'bluebird.'"

The bird seemed to watch us as we ate breakfast, then flew away—that wasn't at all weird.

"All right, guys! Time to go. Grab your bags and head out to the car."

Ruby and Danny raced each other upstairs to grab their day-care bags, while I cleared the table and grabbed my keys and handbag. Walking out to the car, I let the kids in and helped buckle their seatbelts, but as I walked to the driver's side, I spotted the same bluebird sitting on my letterbox, staring at me.

"Now it's getting creepy," I muttered, shrugging my shoulders as I got in the car.

I dropped the kids off at day care and went to work for the day. As my car pulled into the driveway that night, the bird was still sitting on my letterbox!

Danny and Ruby ran into the house, dumping their bags at the door and turning on the television. I walked in, picked up their bags, and walked upstairs to put them away.

After getting changed into some gym clothes, I headed out into the backyard to exercise. Today was tai chi and kick-boxing.

I have named my punching bag "Bruce," and I painted an angry face on it to keep me motivated. The entire time I was training, I kept getting distracted. I started to feel like I was being watched by that small bluebird, perched on our back fence. I tried to ignore it by shaking my head and saying, "It's nothing—it's just a bird." But it just sat there on the fence, watching me. I made a menacing move towards it and shouted, "Shoo!" trying to scare it away, but it seemed undeterred—it even watched as I walked back inside to make dinner. It watched from the fence as we ate dinner, as we watched TV, and when we ran to welcome Matt home from work. That bird just sat there . . . watching. This was now more than unusual; it felt creepy.

At the end of the night, after saying good night to Danny and Ruby, I walked around the house turning off all the lights. I took a quick glance outside to check if the bluebird was still there, and sure enough, it was. I was beginning to think he might have been a lost pet. I walked upstairs into my room and got changed into my pyjamas. Matt watched as he lay comfortably in the bed.

"Matt . . . which country are bluebirds native to?" I asked as I started brushing my teeth.

Confused by my seemingly random question, Matt responded in an unsure tone, "Um . . . I don't know. North America, I think." He looked at me quizzically. "Why?" he probed.

With a mouth full of toothpaste, I managed to burble, "'Ust . . . 'ondering." Thankful for no further questions, I spat out the toothpaste and climbed into bed, kissing Matt good night and turning off my bedside light.

Journal entry insert by Agent Bluey

I was still perched on the fence in the backyard as I watched the house go dark, then chirped as my eyes glowed red, sending another message: "TARGET FOUND."

I received an immediate response, reading: "SECURE TARGET."

I acted quickly, flying up and into the house through the young female child's open window. I flew silently through the rooms and down the hall and into my target's bedroom, landing on the edge of the bed. Silently and carefully, I crept up towards her head and ruffled the feathers of my wing, pulling out a small red gem and gently placing it in the curve of the target's neck. I then used the claw of my foot to cut the skin just under the gem.

The target must have felt the pain, as she woke up, holding her neck, unknowingly rubbing the gem into the wound.

Silently, I hopped off the bed onto the floor, making my way behind the dresser to hide. I looked around the room and saw nothing but darkness.

The target sat up and looked around the room, then became disoriented (which was expected) and fell back onto the end of the bed.

I watched from behind the dresser as the wound healed almost instantly, the gem now embedded in her neck, and it began a pulsating red glow, creating a tribal tattoo-like mark.

Original journal entry continued by Lila Winters

The next morning, Matt woke up early and got dressed. When I finally woke, I saw he already had his briefcase ready to go. He brushed the hair from my face and smiled at the odd position I had ended up in the bed.

"Hey," he said, with a gentle whisper.

I yawned and stretched and replied, "Hey." I looked out the bedroom door to see Danny and Ruby running downstairs with their day-care bags. I quickly looked over at the clock to realise I had slept in. "It's 8.30, why didn't you wake me?" I asked Matt as I hurried off the end of the bed.

As soon as I stood up, I began to feel dizzy, and the lights seemed to become very bright. Matt held on to my arms to prevent me from falling, before gently placing me back into the bed and pulled the blanket back over me.

"That's why," he responded. I detected an underlying worried tone in his voice. "You had such a rough night's sleep last night, so I let you sleep in. I've called your work, and they said they can manage without you today. I'm going to take the kids to kinder and day care, and you are going to stay in the bed and get some rest. Okay?" He looked at me sternly, knowing that rest and sick days were something that I wasn't very good at.

I smiled and nodded as I lay back down on the pillow, before suddenly realising I was naked. Matt noticed as my face looked at him, shocked and confused, and explained, "You had a fever during the night. I stripped you off to keep you cool." He kissed my forehead and quietly walked out of the room as I drifted in and out of sleep.

From my bed, I looked out the window, listening as Matt's car pulled out of the driveway. I closed my eyes for what felt like a few moments (but was actually two hours) and woke to a small bluebird sitting on my bedside table, staring at me. I started to scream and moved very quickly to the other side of bed so fast that I actually fell to the floor but kept my eyes on that little bluebird.

I stopped screaming to take a breath and thought I heard the bird speak. It said, "Please remain calm. My name is Bluey."

I screamed again, petrified at the thought of a talking bird, and began to edge slowly back towards my en-suite door, reassuring myself, "This is all a dream—this can't be real. If I just close my eyes, it will—"

Bluey quickly interrupted, as he hopped on to the bed, moving closer towards me. "This is not a dream. Here . . ." He flew and pecked at my shoulder.

"Ouch! That hurt!" I exclaimed as I swatted Bluey away. It landed back down on the end of the bed. I grabbed Matt's pillow to try and hit him, but I missed as he flew out of the way.

I kept trying to swat him again and again, but he kept dodging and flying around the room, shouting intermittently, "If you . . . would please . . . calm down . . . for just . . . one moment! . . . I am not going to hurt you!"

I eventually gave up and threw the pillow in a desperate last attempt to hit him, but I missed again.

Bluey perched on top of the curtain and looked back at me, cautiously waiting.

I began to pace back and forth on Matt's side of the room, occasionally looking up at Bluey.

"Okay, then . . . If I'm not dreaming . . . and I'm not nuts . . . then what is happening? More importantly, what are you?" I stared at him, waiting for an answer.

Bluey flew back down onto the bedside table. "I am a bluebird," he replied, "I will explain everything in time, but first I think you may want to get dressed."

I gasped, quickly grabbing the blanket to cover myself. "Okay, fine, I'll play along, I'll get dressed. But you need to wait in the kitchen."

Bluey looked back at me, as if he were offended. "I assure you, your nudity is of no interest to me—I am a bird after all!"

I shrugged my shoulders, continuing to cover myself. "Look, I don't care what you are or who you are, but I don't feel comfortable right now. So if you want me to stay calm and not start screaming again, I strongly recommend you wait in the kitchen."

Bluey chirped in protest, then flew out of my bedroom.

I stared after him as he flew down the stairs, then I sighed and sat down on the bed, looking dumbfounded and dazed. I shook my head in disbelief, then got dressed.

I went into the bathroom to brush my hair, and as I peered into the mirror, I gasped in panic, staring at the new tribal tattoo on my neck just behind my right ear. Horrified, I tried to rub it off. I used anything I could find in the bathroom— soap, a cloth, even nail polish remover. When I realised the mark was permanent, I just knew this had something to do with that pesky little bird. I stormed out of the bedroom and down the stairs double-time, marching into the kitchen in a huff, and furiously glared at Bluey.

"WHAT THE HELL IS THIS?!" I shrieked, pulling my hair back to show Bluey the newfound tribal tattoo.

Bluey, quite conscious of the rage in my voice, edged back cautiously. "That is your birthmark," he explained.

I looked back at Bluey, still very enraged. "I don't have a birthmark."

Bluey continued to keep his distance. "I assure you that I am not lying. The mark appeared when I inserted a nanochip into your neck."

"YOU DID WHAT TO ME?!" I struggled to get the words out of my mouth as I tried to process my thoughts through the rush of rage and other emotions that I can't possibly accurately describe. All I could do was start pacing the floor again. "All right, bird. Start explaining right now before I crush and cook you in a frying pan! And trust me . . . I will catch you this time." I meant every word as I glanced over at the frying pan drying on the sink.

"I do not doubt your ability to catch me," replied Bluey, searching around to see no open doors or windows. "My name is Bluey . . . the nanochip I inserted into your bloodstream is programmed to monitor your body and track your development. It is designed to give your body a kick-start to activate a dormant gene."

Still enraged, I glanced over at the frying pan again. "Why?" I asked.

Bluey flew over to the table to keep his distance from me—as if I didn't notice!

He continued his explanation. "You are what we call a 'Guardian.' You have abilities other humans do not have."

While Bluey was talking, I started to walk over to the sink to grab the frying pan. Bluey became more and more nervous. "Wait . . . please! If you let me explain . . .," he shouted. "Guardians are able to harness and control the elements. There are Guardians of Fire, Water, Wind, Rocks, and Soil. There are also Guardians of Flora and Fauna. You are a Guardian, and we need your help . . . please! . . . People are dying."

Bluey held his wings up to shield his body. I stopped, standing in front of him still wielding the frying pan, and stared at Bluey for a few seconds as I processed what he had said. Slowly and cautiously, I walked towards the table, placing the frying pan on the bench, before sitting down at the table, still staring at Bluey.

"All right," I said calmly, "I'll make a deal with you."

Still sceptical and still half-thinking I was in a dream, I was willing to hear him out—mainly because my father always told me to hear people out before you punch them in the face (that way you know the reason as to why you punched them!).

"I will listen to what you have to say, and I will do my best to understand. But if in the end I am not convinced, I want you to promise me that you will leave—and not come back. Deal?"

I stared at Bluey, waiting for his response. Bluey took a moment to respond, probably wondering why I became calm all of a sudden. Honestly, at that point I was still analysing the best and fastest way to catch him, while minimising the damage to my kitchen.

But Bluey responded reluctantly, "Deal."

I smiled and grabbed a piece of fruit from the fruit bowl and made myself comfortable at the table.

"Okay, tell me your story."

Bluey hopped to the centre of the table and carefully positioned himself beyond arm's distance as he began to explain. "Do you know the story about Adam and Eve?"

"Everybody knows that story," I remarked, rolling my eyes. "God makes earth . . . God makes Man and Woman . . . man and woman eat the fruit and get kicked out of the garden—"

Bluey interrupted, "Yes, we all know that part of the story, but do you know the finer details of the story? It is believed that the first humans ever created were given the power and the knowledge to work and care for the earth . . . where humans and elements work in harmony together."

Bluey paused for a moment, probably to see if I was following along. I really wasn't, but I continued to listen anyway.

Bluey continued. "It is also believed that this power has been handed down from generation to generation."

Bluey jumped slightly as I stood up to throw my fruit in the bin.

I interrupted to ask, "So this power is passed on through generations, right?" I waited for Bluey to nod in confirmation. "Then, why me? Why not choose the guy next door?"

Bluey looked almost chipper at the fact I was following along with his story.

"The abilities are passed on only to the eldest child. We are unsure why. Throughout history and cultures, it was common for the eldest child in one house to marry the eldest child of another. However, over time that custom was forgotten, leaving most bloodlines impure and eventually completely void of the gene containing these abilities."

I began to walk around the table, fiddling with my hands, taking brief moments to think.

"Okay, let's say I believe you—there still must be thousands of people like me."

"That is true," Bluey replied, "You are not the first Guardian we have recruited."

I stopped and looked cautiously at Bluey. "We?" I became defensive and suspicious. "You said 'we'."

"Mission Control," Bluey replied.

I couldn't help but laugh in disbelief of such a cliché name as Bluey continued to explain.

"We had thousands of recruited Guardians. But they've gone missing—which is why we need you. We believe they've all been taken by the Darkman, and—"

"The Darkman?" I chuckled. I knew this story was far-fetched, but now it was just getting ridiculous. "Who names their bad guy 'Darkman'?"

Bluey became confused as to why I was laughing. "We are not in the habit of nicknaming our bad guys. Unfortunately, that is the only description we have of him. We know that he is male, and because he has always been sighted in dark shadows, we have no further description than that." Bluey attempted to get back on topic. "Nonetheless, we are still in need of your help. So . . . will you help us?" he asked pleadingly.

I stopped chuckling and looked at Bluey as he stared at me waiting for an answer.

"No," I replied, shaking my head.

I opened the back door for Bluey to leave, but he pleaded and begged.

"Thousands of your kind are in danger or possibly dead. We need you, and we can't afford for you to decline. Please."

I continued to hold the door open, and I politely repeated myself, "No. We made a deal—you agreed that if I listened and heard what you had to say, that you would leave." I paused, looking back at Bluey's pleading eyes. "Even if what you say were true, I have a family—I have children—and a job. I can't just 'up and leave' them, endangering my own life, all because someone somewhere needs my help. I'm sorry, but my answer is no."

Bluey took a moment then flew out the back door, perching on the patio steps.

"Please think about it, and not just about the thousands of people who need your help . . . you must realise that you are the last free Guardian left . . . you'd be a fool to think your family is safe from all this. It took me just two hours to track you down—and I'm just a bird."

Bluey flew off and over the fence. I closed the door and stared into the backyard in disbelief, shaking my head as I went back upstairs to rest.

Journal entry insert by Agent Bluey

I was disappointed when Lila declined our request of her assistance. I watched from the backyard fence as she disappeared up the stairs. My eyes glowed red as I sent a text message: "MISSION FAILED. RECRUIT DECLINED."

I received a response that very much agitated me: "UNACCEPTABLE. YOU HAVE 24 HOURS."

Original journal entry continued by Lila Winters

That night, Matt and I tucked Danny and Ruby into their beds. I turned off all the lights, and this time, I made sure all the windows and doors were shut. I didn't tell Matt what had happened, and I wore my hair down so he wouldn't see the tribal mark on my neck. (I also tried covering it with foundation.) I was hoping it had all been a dream and that when I woke up tomorrow, everything would be back to normal, but I was beginning to doubt it.

The next morning, I woke up, and everything seemed normal. I had forgotten about the tattoo and didn't even bother looking in the mirror. Matt kissed me goodbye on his way to work, while I got Danny and Ruby ready for day care. I grabbed the keys to leave, and at that moment, I spotted Bluey sitting on the fence in the backyard. I let out a loud sigh, rolling my eyes as I led the kids out to the car.

After I dropped Danny off at kinder and Ruby off at day care, I sat in the car in the day-care centre car park, trying to think things through. I couldn't go to work because it was my day off, and I couldn't go home because that stupid creepy bird was there. I could have gone to my parents' house, but then I ran the risk of running into Richard (my father), and I certainly didn't want to get into another fight about how I didn't join the army like a good little soldier girl. Richard works in Special Ops. I never knew when he's going to grace us with his presence, or what mood he'll be in when he's home. I sat and tapped my fingers on the steering wheel, thinking about where I could go, then I remembered my old gym down the road. I still had an active membership. So I finally made up my mind and drove down the road to the gym.

As I walked in the door of the gym, I was greeted (a little too excitedly) by my old personal trainer Carmen. She ran to me screaming with excitement. "LILA! LILA! LILA!" She jumped up and down, trying to hug me. My hand got tangled in her extremely long blond hair.

I attempted to untangle my hand, while Carmen was somewhat helping, but more talking really fast.

"OMG, I am so sorry. That is always happening ATM. My boyfriend's always telling me I should go to the hairdresser's and cut my hair, but I so don't want to, 'cause I love it to pieces, you know? I mean WTF? Where have you been these last few months? I totes missed you."

She spoke incredibly fast, it was ridiculous trying to keep up and interpret. I finished freeing my hand, and it suddenly dawned on me why I stopped going to the gym! I could never understand why Carmen always abbreviated half her sentences; it's not like she saves any time or effort saying the letters as opposed to the words.

This was the point where I wanted to leave, but I pulled the best fake smile I could muster and said,

"Hi, Carmen."

Carmen jumped up and down again in excitement as I began to regret not going to my parents' house. Arguments about my life's failures started to sound a lot easier to handle, instead of being stuck with an over-excited 30-year-old personal trainer.

Carmen grabbed two water bottles from the fridge and handed one to me. "So what BYB here after so long?" she asked curiously.

I smiled and hesitated to tell her the real reason I came to the gym. "I, err . . ." I looked around the gym and said the most obvious response ever: "I came to exercise."

I smiled, weakly, hoping she would accept that reason.

Carmen just grinned from ear to ear, then grabbed my hand. "All right then . . . let's take you on the usual rounds."

I sighed in relief; all I had to do now was finish the exercises then leave—easy.

Carmen took me around the gym, spending fifteen minutes on each machine. We started on the bike and then the row machine, before moving on to the squat station and barbells. Eventually I used every piece of equipment she had, until we stopped at the treadmill. Carmen looked at me, confused and almost astonished. I looked back at her, starting to feel nervous.

"What's wrong?" I asked.

Carmen's wide grin narrowed. Still looking at me, she replied, "Nothing . . . nothing's wrong . . . I'm just surprised—I mean, seriously."

I looked at Carmen as I became more and more nervous as she stared back at me. "What?!" I asked again.

Carmen broke her stare by shaking her head in disbelief. "OMG, I've put you through the hardest workout I could think of—you've tried every piece of machinery we have in this joint, and you're not even tired or sweating! I mean, you're not even short of breath! Even my fittest client wouldn't be able to work the whole room and still be standing for the treadmill."

I looked back out to the car park, feeling my nervousness increase.

Carmen scurried to grab a heart rate monitor from the front counter.

"Take off your shirt," she demanded.

I looked at Carmen confused as she waited for me to take my shirt off. I had no intention of taking any of my clothes off, especially not in a gym.

Carmen scoffed. "It's just a heart rate monitor. It works better on your chest, and your shirt is too tight, so . . . quickly before your heart rate goes down."

I think it was because I was also curious, but I ended up taking my shirt off. I stood on the treadmill and allowed Carmen to strap on the heart rate monitor below my bra. I glanced around the room to see a few of the guys staring.

I couldn't help but feel exposed but also a little bit sexy. I smiled as I started running. Carmen increased the speed slowly, until the treadmill was at its maximum speed. She looked amazed and started reading the stats from the heart rate monitor.

"OMG, your heart rate is sitting at 72 BPM . . . it hasn't moved!"

I took another look at my car sitting outside, as that feeling of nervousness increased.

By now, everyone in the gym was watching on in amazement.

Carmen looked at me, excitedly. "This is totes amaze! We have to runs some more tests. You might be the healthiest, fittest person I've ever met—and you don't even look the part!"

I wasn't sure if that was supposed to be an insult, but at that point, I was ready to run out the door.

Carmen grabbed the first printout of my heart rate and was about to walk away, then turned to me (still running on the treadmill) and said, "Keep going. I've got to show this to my boss. He's a fitness scientist, and he would totes love to see this."

Carmen ran into the office, and I took that as my chance. I quickly unhooked the heart rate monitor, grabbed my top and bag, and ran out the door. As I did, I felt like I needed to run faster, and then I don't know how, but as I blinked, I suddenly appeared outside and crashed into the side of my car, leaving a dent in the passenger side door. I looked back at the gym, shocked. It took me less than a second to get across the car park!

"That's impossible," I whispered to myself as I hurriedly got into my car and drove off.

That night, I couldn't sleep. I kept staring at the ceiling, trying to make sense of what happened at the gym. The last things Bluey said to me kept playing in my mind:

"Thousands of people need your help!"

"It took me two hours to track you down, and I'm just a bird!"

Those words, I couldn't ignore them. I got up quietly and tiptoed out of the bedroom so I wouldn't wake Matt. I crept down the stairs and out into the backyard where, of course, Bluey was waiting, as though he knew I would come. I stood in front of him, unsure what I was going to do. I wanted to hurt him, but instead I just asked questions.

"You said before that I had abilities that other humans didn't have."

Bluey stared at me. "Yes," he replied.

I slowly drew nearer to him. I didn't like my next question, but I had to ask it.

"And all of these abilities—I've had them all my life? I was born with them?"

Bluey continued to stare and responded, "Yes, you've just never used them, so they are weaker . . . similar to a muscle."

My curiosity was piqued. "What kind of abilities?" I asked hesitantly, but at that stage,

I wasn't sure if I wanted the answer. Any answer would only increase my curiosity, and I would want to know more. But since all of my "kind" have gone missing, I ran the risk of putting my family in danger if I chose not to know. I had to know.

"I am unsure, exactly," Bluey responded, "but there is a way to find out."

I stared at him, eagerly awaiting an explanation.

"You have to try to use your powers" he said.

I scoffed, still sceptical, and asked, "And how would I do that?"

Bluey continued. "We can start with something basic. Close your eyes and concentrate. Picture yourself being able to see in the dark."

I closed my eyes—I wasn't fully sure why, but I did. I thought about what the world would look like in the dark. As I opened my eyes, they faintly glowed a light-green hue, and the world around me lit up! I could see everything in my garden, the leaves rustling and the birds flying in the night sky. It was as if someone turned up the brightness of the moon.

"It's beautiful," I exclaimed, looking around the garden, amazed, "I can see everything." I turned back to Bluey and asked, "What else can I do?"

Bluey flew down from the fence to the garden table next to "Bruce" (my punching bag).

"A few days ago, I saw you training. Try doing some of your moves—only this time, concentrate on improving your movements . . . putting all your strength into the move", he explained.

I began to punch Bruce. I started off slow, throwing in a few kicks. I could tell that Bruce was copping a beating. My speed and precision was so impressive, even the great General Richard would have approved. I was moving so fast it felt like the rest of the world had slowed down. Before I could throw my last punch, Bruce broke in half, falling to the ground as foam and beads fell out of him. I gasped, "Poor Bruce!"

My next-door neighbour, Mr. Wilson, must have woken from the sound. He walked out into his backyard and yelled over the fence, "Who's there?"

Bluey flew up into the trees to hide.

"It's just me, Mr. Wilson . . . Lila," I yelled back, "I was just admiring the moon. I'm sorry if I woke you."

Mr. Wilson climbed up on a chair to pop his head over to see me. He was rather spritely for a 64-year-old. He looked at my punching bag stand that was now in pieces and rolled his eyes.

"Are you okay, Lila?" he asked.

I smiled back at Mr. Wilson and walked over to the fence. "Yes, Mr. Wilson. I'm sorry, I just had trouble sleeping, that's all."

Mr. Wilson responded, slightly disgruntled. "Well maybe you should go watch TV instead . . . quietly."

"Okay, Mr. Wilson. Have a good night, Mr. Wilson." I replied, returning inside. I waited until Mr. Wilson was gone and looked back outside to find Bluey. My eyes glowed as I used my new cool night-vision ability, but I couldn't see him. I gave up and went upstairs to bed.

But I knew Bluey was still watching, hiding up in the trees.

CHAPTER 3

THE VILLAGE

Journal entry by Adela Eden

I was taken prisoner to what looked like an island village. As I was being dragged from one of the bamboo huts, I had one swollen eye from being beaten, and the other had a few cuts above it. I could open my eyes wide enough to see I was being dragged into a large old-style hospital.

I was dragged down a long hallway by two orderlies (or at least they looked like orderlies), then into a room and placed onto a hospital bed, and handcuffed me to both handrails.

The orderlies walked out of the room, locking the door behind them. I could see them through the window into the hallway; they nodded to some guy standing just outside my room, dressed in a fancy business suit. I couldn't see his face; he kept it covered by a dark baseball hat. I strained to listen for any clues to my whereabouts.

"Agent Toby," the suited man said, as another man walked up to him in the hall.

"Yes, sir" the other answered.

The suited man sounded angry, as he asked for another update.

Toby replied softly, ensuring no one else could hear (or so he thought), "Sir . . . the last of the Guardians have gone underground. All but one."

The man in the suit sounded eager when he asked, "Who?"

Agent Toby nervously ruffled through the paperwork in the portfolio he was carrying. After a moment, he seemed to find a sheet of paper, before responding, "Alex Woods—last seen heading to Melbourne."

The other just grinned and said, "Got him! Increase the patrols out in the field. I want him found by the end of the day."

Agent Toby nodded and said, "Right away, sir!" before walking quickly back down the hall.

The suited fellow started walking away and yelled back, "And find me that bluebird!"

CHAPTER 4

THE SCOUT

Journal entry by Lila Winters

It had been a week since I met Bluey. Every morning he would fly around the town—to scout the area, I guess—but he always landed back on my fence in time to watch me and my family get ready for the day. Nothing had changed, and so far, my family was in no danger.

I started to grow fond of seeing Bluey sitting on the fence as if he was standing guard. I never agreed to help Bluey, and I think he respected that. I won't lie—it made me nervous as hell when he went out to "scout" the town. It always got me thinking, what does he look for, or who does he look for?

I finished eating my breakfast, while my kids sat and watched television. As I grabbed the keys and handbag, I asked Danny and Ruby to head out to the car. I glanced back at Bluey to nod goodbye (as had become our custom), but for some reason, he looked agitated. I was about to go out to see if he was okay, but he flew off in a hurry.

I finished dropping Danny and Ruby off at day care, and as I walked back down the hallway of the day-care centre. I noticed the indoor plants seemed to grow slightly and moved towards me as I passed them. It seemed odd, but I was quickly distracted by my phone buzzing. I had to work the closing shift today, so it gave me enough time to "chill" and do some grocery shopping.

As soon as I walked into the shopping centre, Big Mike, the security guard, walked up to greet me. He's a big fellow from New Zealand, and he suited the role of security guard very well! His demeanour displayed perfectly his "Don't mess with me" look, which deterred those pesky shoplifters, but deep down, he's like a big teddy bear. His frown turned into a huge happy smile as he wrapped his arms around me, giving me a big bear hug. I responded by hugging him back just as tightly.

As Mike let go, he felt the muscles on my arms, and asked, "Have you been hitting Bruce a bit harder lately?"

I didn't know how to respond to that, so I told a half truth. "Bruce . . . had to retire from my training schedule," I replied.

"I can tell," Big Mike replied, "Maybe we need to find you a tougher punching bag."

I eagerly asked, already knowing his answer, "Are you volunteering? I could always use a good sparring partner."

Big Mike chuckled. "Oh, hon, everyone knows I wouldn't last two seconds in the ring with you. But Christmas is just around the corner—maybe you could ask Santa for a new Bruce."

Christmas is always my favourite time of year. My eyes lit up as I glanced inside the shopping centre at the decorations hanging from the roof.

With a sigh, I looked back at Big Mike. "All right, I'll ask Santa. Smooth move trying to distract me with Christmas . . . but that doesn't hide the fact that you're afraid to fight a girl!" I snickered as I started walking down the hall.

Mike chuckled as he walked with me. "Afraid? Ha! I'm just smart enough to pick my battles."

He smiled and patted my back to say goodbye, then walked up into the food court.

As I looked around the shopping centre, I noticed all the stores were being decorated with tinsel. That reminded me that I needed to get a new Christmas tree. Our old tree was looking a bit worse for wear. This year, Danny and Ruby had their hearts set on a big white Christmas tree they had seen in the Target windows.

Luckily for them, I am a big pushover, so I had to buy it. I even bought new tinsel as well.

I quickly popped in to say hello to my work friends. I work at a sports clothing store called Cotton-On Body. It's the absolute best store to work at since it's where I buy all my gym clothes! There was new line coming out today, and I had my eye on one of the T-shirts.

Emma and Ali were working today. Ali was the manager and Emma was her daughter—she's studying at school to be a make-up artist, so it's no surprise that she likes wearing make-up—a lot of it. She asked to give me a makeover once, but she couldn't convince me!

I think I'm happier with my natural beauty—tinted lip balm is about the only make-up I use.

I walked out the store, waving goodbye to the girls, and got this weird vibe that someone was watching me. I looked around but couldn't see anything. I shrugged it off; it was probably just Bluey getting in my head and making me paranoid.

I walked into Woolworths to grab some veggies and milk. As I went through my shopping list, I picked out all the fruits and vegetables I needed. Bananas, I need bananas. There wasn't much to choose from; it was either green bananas that weren't ripe enough, or over-ripe bananas that looked like they'd been kicked around. I picked up a hand of over-ripe bananas and pulled a sour face as I inspected them. I watched in amazement as the brown bruises on the bananas suddenly disappeared, including the others on the stand, and the green bananas started to ripen! Soon the whole crate of bananas was ripe and fresh. I looked on in shock and accidentally dropped the hand of bananas I was holding.

"Weird," I muttered to myself. I looked around to see if anyone saw me (they hadn't), then quickly rushed into the next aisle, forgetting to actually grab some bananas. Good one, Lila!

After I finished the grocery shopping, I stopped at the bakery to grab a snack. I smiled at the baker. "Hi, Sam—can I get my usual please?" I asked nicely.

You know you shop too much at a store when they know your usual order. I always order my favourite: a toasted tomato and cheese sandwich with a bottle of Coca-Cola—best snack ever!

Sam smiled as he prepared my sandwich and grabbed my drink from the fridge, placing it on the bench in front of me. "That'll be $5.50, Lila," said Sam, smiling. "I added extra cheese this time."

I smiled back. "You know me far too well, Sam."

As I reached into my bag to grab my wallet, the man standing behind me offered to pay for me. "Don't worry, I got this," he said smiling smugly. He placed his hand on my shoulder, acting as if he knew me. I glared at him, trying to figure out if I really did know him. He had long dark, shaggy brown hair that you could mistake for a girl. He was tall and roughly my age. Too scruffy to be in the military, and I had never met any of Matt's friends from university or work. Perhaps he mistook me for someone else he knew, so I politely smiled and pulled his hand off my shoulder.

"I'm sorry, you must have the wrong person, and I can pay for my own meal," I explained, handing him back his $5.50.

He looked at me with a friendly smile. "My mistake, I'm Alex," he said, still sounding smug, but I assumed it was his way of flirting with me.

Mustering some further politeness, despite getting a little annoyed, I offered a polite, "Hello, Alex."

I paid Sam with my own money, leaving Alex's money on the bench in front of him, and took my bag of food. Still a bit perturbed, I accidentally left my drink behind. I pushed my trolley of groceries to a nearby table to sit down and eat.

Alex grabbed my drink and followed me, leaving the money on the counter while smiling back at Sam. He sat down at my table and handed me my drink.

I smiled and said, "Thank you," hoping he would leave, but he didn't. At this point, I was beginning to get suspicious of his motives.

He asked cheekily, "Do you mind if I sit here?"

What was wrong with this guy? He clearly wouldn't take the hint.

"I guess I can't stop you," I replied, adding a definite agitated tone.

Alex continued to sit and watch me eat, before interrupting with, "I just need to say I really like your hair, the purple really suits you."

Totally awkward!

I didn't know what to say, so I just kept eating in silence. It became very uncomfortable and very weird—very quickly. He still didn't get the hint!

As I finished my sandwich, I remembered to grab my drink this time, placing it into my trolley.

"Well, it was . . . nice to meet you. Have a good day, Alex."

I walked away quickly, hoping he wouldn't follow.

But he did. Alex raced up and walked next to me.

"So . . . I didn't catch your name."

"Married . . .," I replied and started to walk faster.

This guy was relentless and kept the same pace, continuing to talk.

"That's a very unique name—you must have hated growing up with it. Especially if you had to attend a wedding."

I started to lose my patience at that point.

"That's not my name," I rebuked, "that's my relationship status. It's also why I'm not telling you my real name. Now would you please leave me alone?" I made sure I spoke loud enough for others to hear.

"Well, that's not a very good reason to not tell me your name," Alex persisted.

I was almost at the car park. "Yes, it is," I snapped back it him.

He continued to follow me into the car park. "I just want to know your name. Why is that so bad?"

I stopped the trolley to face Alex and respond, "Hmm . . . let me think . . . A strange man comes up and sits with me while I'm eating . . . then follows me around the shopping centre, wanting to know my name, and clearly does not take the hint when I ask him to leave. And you're still wondering why I won't tell you my name... Think really hard about that, and stop following me."

Alex then grabbed the trolley before I could move away. "I'm sorry... I was only trying to be nice," he stammered apologetically.

Thankfully, Big Mike walked up behind Alex and looked at me.

"Are you all right, Lila?" he asked, concerned for my safety.

I sighed in disappointment at Big Mike revealing my name, but I was grateful he came to my rescue.

Alex looked back at Mike and smiled victoriously.

I nodded my head to Big Mike. "I'm fine, Mike, thanks."

Rounding on Alex, I snapped. "Are you happy you got my name? Now please, let go of my trolley."

I suspect Alex didn't want a confrontation, and I think he could tell that I was now in the mood for a fight as he looked at my clenched fists. He quickly let go of the trolley and stepped back, smiling.

"It was nice to meet you... Lila."

Big Mike watched Alex walk away, then looked at me and said, quite gallantly. "Come on, Lila, I'll help you to your car." He accompanied me to my car and helped load my groceries into the boot.

CHAPTER 5

THE SCOUT'S PITCH

Journal entry by Lila Winters

When I got home from the shopping centre, I walked into the house carrying all fifteen bags of groceries in one hand, as if I was carrying a pillow. I must admit my new abilities did make my day-to-day chores a lot faster (it almost felt like I was cheating!).

I placed the bags on the bench, turning the radio on, and danced a little while I put the shopping away. Sometimes I sang along to the songs I knew. At the end, I gathered up all the empty shopping bags and placed them in the bag box under the sink. You never know when you need spare bags.

I continued dancing out into the backyard to look for Bluey.

"Bluey!" I shouted.

I was oblivious to Alex, sitting on the patio chair, watching me dance. (I guess I was distracted by the music).

"Bluey!" I shouted again.

I gave up and turned to go inside and completely jumped in fright as I spotted Alex. I sprang instantly into action and roundhouse-kicked him to the ground, then straddled his chest, pinning his arms under my legs.

With my arm poised, ready to punch, I asked, "Who the hell are you?"

He sputtered out, "I told you—my name is Alex . . ."

As he freed his hand and pushed me off his chest, I was thrown high into the air like a rag doll. He stood up and caught me, forcing me to the ground, and straddled my hips, pinning my hands under his.

"And I am here to help you," he continued.

After a brief tense silence, he tried to change the subject.

"I liked your singing, you have a beautiful voice."

I wasn't sure what his game was, but I got this mild feeling he was attempting to be friendly. I smiled back at Alex, catching him off guard as I kneed him between the legs (ouch!), pushing him forward. I freed both hands by dragging them on the concrete in a twisting motion.

Alex, shocked at seeing my hands begin to bleed, loosened his grip on my wrists. I took that opportunity to punch him in the face.

Suddenly vines sprung up from the garden behind Alex, wrapped around him, and pulled him off me. I stood up and looked back at the vines, quite frightened, then ran into the house and grabbed the phone. Alex grabbed at the vines and pulled them from their roots, which made them limp. After breaking free, he ran into the house after me.

"Lila, please! I'm not going to hurt you."

Alex grabbed the phone from me and threw it on the couch.

"I'm here to help. That's all . . . We should clean your hands . . ."

I pulled away from Alex as he tried to look at my bloodied hands.

"I don't want your help!"

I ran as fast as I could towards the back door, but Alex ran faster and stood in front of me. I didn't know how, but he seemed to run faster than any normal human could. It didn't take me long to realise he must be another "Guardian".

I weighed my options and remembered Bluey saying that all the Guardians had been taken. "You're one of them," I yelled, punching Alex in the nose and then somersaulted backwards, kicking him in the face. He held his face in pain and stumbled.

I seized the opportunity to sidekick him in the stomach. He crunched over in pain, holding his winded stomach, and screamed, "Argh . . . What are you—some kind of ninja?"

I tried to get past him, but he pushed through his pain and reached out to grab me and pinned me to the wall, wincing in pain as he lifted me off the ground. His body pressed close to mine.

I couldn't move, I looked around to analyse my next move, but I realized I couldn't do anything without damaging the house. I felt the muscles in his stomach tighten as he pinned me against the wall. He held my hands still with his hands, but he watched, careful not to touch the wounds on my hands.

His actions confused me, so I stopped fighting and looked at him. At that moment, Bluey had flown into the house in a hurry, landing on the dining table, shouting, "Stop, Alex! You'll scare her! Or worse—hurt her!"

Bluey looked at my bloodied hands and Alex's bloody face and became agitated.

"Alex, let her go!" he shouted again.

Alex continued to hold me against the wall. "You're late," he remarked, looking back at Bluey.

Bluey spread out his wings and shook his feathers.

"Unfortunately, her neighbour has a cat. And you weren't around to help."

I took the opportunity while Alex was distracted to kick him in his "big boy parts" again harder than before. Alex dropped me to the floor as he doubled over in pain, holding his crotch.

I stood to my feet and furiously glared at Bluey. "Bluey, start explaining now," I demanded, "or you're both going to start feeling pain!"

Bluey hopped nervously backwards to the end of the table, trying to explain. "He's one of ours, his name is Alex. Mission Control thought I could use some backup to help protect you."

"Protect me? Protect me from what? From being stalked in the shopping centre?!" I shouted, getting more upset.

"From being taken like the rest of us," Alex quickly interrupted, trying to talk through the pain while still cupping his crotch.

I smirked at that point and felt a bit proud of myself—he had been annoying me all day.

"Alex is like you—a Guardian," Bluey explained, "I swear he is only here to help you." He moved farther away and perched himself on the chair at the far end of the table, in an obvious attempt to get out of my arm's reach.

I started to calm down and looked back at Alex cautiously. I admit I chuckled a little as I watched him gently rubbing his crotch. "What do you mean by 'being taken'? Have you put me in danger?" I asked, looking at Bluey and waiting for an answer.

Alex slowly stood to his feet to answer my question. "For now, no. Nobody knows you exist, and we want to keep it that way." He began to feel dizzy and stumbled a bit. Putting his hand to his face, he discovered blood dripping from a large cut above his eye. "Wow . . .," he slurred, "you sure know how to fight . . ." He started to lean against the wall.

I felt a bit smug, but I also started to feel sorry for him. He was, after all, just following orders. I rolled my eyes and sighed as I walked towards him. Alex looked at me hesitantly. I gently lifted his arm and led him over to the table, helping him to sit down. I grabbed a bowl of water, a cloth, and the first-aid kit and stood before him. I soaked the cloth in the cold water, wincing slightly in pain as the water ran into the open grazes on my hands.

Alex watched as I pulled my bloody hands from the water and saw how badly my hands and part of my forearm were grazed.

"That looks bad," Alex said, worryingly, "we should get you to the hospital . . ."

I interrupted him with a shush as I moved closer to see his wound, leaning over his knee. Alex looked up at me, still nervous, as I began to clean the cut above his eye. He tried to act manly, but I saw him wince in pain a few times.

"How are you not in pain?" he asked me.

I calmly responded, "I am in pain, I'm just able to control my emotion better than you . . ."

He remained silent in disbelief.

"Besides," I continued, "the damage to my hands is not that bad, the pain will pass in a few minutes, but yours is a head injury, you risk a possible concussion. I need to know how badly I hit you."

Alex didn't know what to say. He was in pain, but he didn't want to seem like a wimp. "I've had worse," he said, almost regretting it as he said it. He began to smile at me and slowly looked over my body, now pressed up close to his.

I suppose that was all he could see at the time, so I didn't argue. He commented, as I placed a large bandage on his wound, "You're a good fighter and quite strong for your size."

I grinned slightly. "My father taught me," I replied, "and that was not me fighting, that was me trying to get away."

Alex nodded. "Understandable." He cleared his throat and chuckled, "I was about to say, I'd like to see what you're like in a real fight. But honestly, I'd rather listen to you sing."

I took the bloody bowl and cloth to the kitchen to clean, and I looked over at Bluey who was staying unusually quiet.

"So, Alex," I said, throwing out the bloody cloth, "you say you are like me . . ."

I stood at the bench waiting for him to complete my thought. Alex nodded his head in agreement but stayed quiet.

I pressed the issue more. "How come I've never heard about Guardians before?" I enquired.

He took a deep breath as if he was ready to unveil some mystical truths, saying, "We tend to keep who we are a secret. So we don't cause unnecessary fear in people."

I sighed, still feeling unconvinced, and glanced at Bluey again. "Great, and I thought it was vampires that hid in the closet!" I joked, trying to ease the tension a bit.

Alex looked at me confused, remaining at the table as I handed him a glass of water and sat next to him, ready to interrogate him.

I asked, "What do you want from me? And why are you really here?"

Alex couldn't answer me. For some reason, he seemed busy staring at my eyes. "Blue . . .," Alex said softly.

I looked at Alex, guarded and confused, when Bluey piped an answer.

"We need you to help us rescue the other Guardians and stop the world from being destroyed."

I stood up, rolled my eyes, and held back a smile. "How cliché of you."

Alex broke his stare and remarked, "It's true." He gently grabbed both my hands, being careful not to touch the wounds, and stood up, looking at me with a seriously stern face. "I know it sounds crazy and you have no reason right now to trust or believe us, but we really need your help."

I pulled my hands away and sat back down at the table, prepared to hear them out.

Alex sat next to me and started to explain. "There is a man we call the 'Darkman.' He uses large companies to control the stock market and influences the politicians of multiple countries. We can't prove it, but we believe that he has manipulated a few warlords into starting civil wars in their own countries. We're not sure why— most likely a cover for what he's really doing."

"Greed, most likely," I scoffed. "Look, this type of thing sounds like a job for the army or a trustworthy politician," I suggested as I stood up to look out the back door.

Alex got up and stood next to me. "If you know of any politicians you trust, I'm all ears."

I tried to think of someone who could be of use. I mean I didn't, not, know anyone of use. For a brief second, the thought of asking General Richard went through my mind, but then I quickly shook that thought away, unwilling to consider it again. I looked at Alex and sighed, shaking my head.

"Tell me the truth. What are you expecting from me? I already told Bluey that I will not fight your war."

Alex walked out into the backyard and held his hand out to me, hoping I would follow.

"If you will not fight . . . then I ask, will you please train with me? I'll teach you how to use your abilities if you teach me how to fight like you can."

I looked at Alex's hand and took a step back.

"Lila," he pleaded with begging eyes, "I can't do this without you."

I didn't know what possessed me, but I remembered again what Bluey said to me:

Thousands of people need your help.

It took me two hours to track you down and I'm just a bird.

I held Alex's hand and followed him out into the backyard. There, looking at the garden, still holding Alex's hand, I started to feel a little bit like an idiot.

"Okay, if this is your version of training, I'm going to get very bored very quickly," I remarked politely.

Alex looked at me and nervously smirked.

"Sorry, I was . . . thinking."

I glanced at Bluey as he flew outside to sit on the fence, then back at Alex. "About what?" I asked.

"Well, from my observation of you today, you're a Nature Guardian—a very rare type of Guardian, which in itself is a worry," he said, observing the flowers in my garden all in full bloom.

"How rare?" I asked nervously, instantly regretting the moment I asked.

"Have you heard the story about the black cats of Salem?" asked Alex. I nodded cautiously as Alex continued to talk. "A few hundred years ago, your kind were considered 'uncontrollable' because none of the other elements were effective in fighting or controlling your kind."

He began to scare me with this story, but I had to ask, "Why would you want to control people like me?"

Alex looked at me as if I should have known. "Since history first recorded our kind, we have been viewed by humans as a collectable or a method for personal gain—or in some cases, weapons. Guardians have been hunted for thousands of years because of what we can do.

And if any of our kind resisted, they died. The Guardians of Nature were always on the side of protecting the earth, so they were a threat, and—" He stopped as he saw the tears rolling down my cheeks.

"Do you think that's what happened to my real parents?" I asked.

Alex looked at me, confused. "Your real parents?"

I began to explain. "My current mother and father are actually my aunt and uncle. My biological parents died when I was a baby. Bluey said that the gene was passed on through the generations. Could my parents have been Guardians?" I asked, somewhat hopefully. I was certain my real parents were dead, but perhaps if they died through some noble cause, standing up for what they believed in, it might bring some comfort to me.

Alex glared at Bluey and looked back at me, not knowing what to say. "I'm not sure about your parents, I didn't know . . . I'm sorry." He didn't know what to say, so he tried to return to the present. "Okay, right . . . now we need you to learn how to control your element so you can use it to protect yourself."

I nodded, pretending I understood what he was talking about. "How do I do that?" I asked.

Alex looked over at the garden, saying, "Well, before, when I was on top of you, you pulled me off using the roots from the ground—"

"Wait . . . I . . . did that?" I asked, interrupting.

Alex nodded and continued to explain. "And if you remember back at the grocery store, you made the bananas ripen in your hand."

Shocked, and a bit creeped out, I yelled, "You stalked me in the grocery store? You are one weird and twisted man!" I paused to think, then added, "Creepy and arrogant as well."

Alex smiled because he knew I was right. "I'm also stronger and a lot better suited to be your sparring partner than your friend Big Mike will ever be."

I gasped at the challenge, as Alex led me to the rose bushes at the back of my garden.

"Now, see this rose bush?" he asked, pointing to a small rosebud that had not yet blossomed. "I want you to make it bloom. Focus on the rose and on the emotions inside you."

I stood and stared at the rosebud for a few seconds and grinned as the bud began to blossom. I was so excited. "I did it!" I shouted, jumping for joy. I turned to look at Alex and was horrified to realise he had been tied up in creeping vines and roots, all weaved around him. He fell to the ground, trapped and struggling to breath as the vines grew tighter and tighter.

"Help!" he gasped. "Lila . . ."

Bluey started pecking at the vines, attempting to free him. I ran into the house and grabbed a steak knife from the drawer. Running back out, I started hacking away at the vines. "I'm so sorry. I don't know what happened."

I got distracted as more roots grew up from the ground, wrapping around Alex and tightening even more. He winced in pain and gasped for air. "Lila," he mustered.

I looked at Alex and began to feel helpless. "I'm sorry," I cried helplessly, "I don't know how to stop them."

Alex, still gasping for air, croaked, "The elements are connected to your emotions. What are you thinking about?"

I looked at him, not knowing what to say. I didn't want to tell him the real answer and hesitated.

Alex screamed my name in panic. "LILA!"

"I was considering whether I should trust you or not," I blurted out nervously. "I'm sorry, Alex, I don't know how to stop this," I said, continuing to cut the vines away.

Alex mustered up all his energy to break one of his hands free and stopped me from slashing the vines. He grabbed my hand, and I winced in pain a little as he pulled me close, then let go and gently held the back of my neck instead, pulling me closer. We were so close I could feel his breath on my lips. He looked into my eyes with such intensity, I could see them filled with fear and pain. But when he spoke, he was soft and calming as he said, "You can trust me, Lila . . . I promise." The vines began to loosen and retract back into the ground as we continued to stare into each other's eyes.

Our stare was broken as we both got distracted by the sound of the garage door closing, and my husband, Matt, stood on the patio with Danny and Ruby behind him. He just stood there, confused, looking at Alex.

Alex let go of me as I stood up and looked at Matt. My first words were, "I can explain!"

Seriously, those were my first words. I sounded like a 16-year-old who had just crashed her daddy's car.

Matt gently asked Danny and Ruby to go inside, all the while continuing to stare at Alex. I glanced up to see Danny and Ruby watching from the window—they knew something was up.

"Okay, Lila," Matt replied, still staring at Alex (the stare seemed to become very territorial), "explain to me why there is a strange man lying down in our backyard, holding your head while you press a knife to his chest?"

Right. I wasn't expecting him to ask such a direct question. It did get me to realise I was still holding the knife and instantly dropped it to the ground. I struggled to get the words out— what I wanted to say made sense in my head, but then didn't make sense when I thought about it logically. Honestly, this whole day didn't make sense to me—how could I ever expect it to make sense to Matt?

"I can't...," I whispered under my breath and sighed, looking back at Alex.

Alex quickly stood up and dusted himself off and smiled at Matt, who was still staring at him.

"Hi, I'm Alex," he said as he offered to shake Matt's hand.

Matt declined and continued to stare. I could tell Matt wanted answers, and I was still trying to think of one—one that made sense anyway.

Alex cleared his throat and glanced over at me, still stunned. He made up a lie, probably in the hopes of protecting me. "I'm an old friend from school. I was in the area and I dropped in to surprise Lila. She was just giving me a tour of this lovely garden, and I got caught up in one of the rose bushes."

I looked at Alex, shocked and surprised that he could so easily lie. Alex looked back at me and smiled, as if he was asking me to just go along with it.

Matt broke his stare at Alex, observing both Alex's cut above his eye and my stained bloody hands, as he turned to me looking for confirmation.

I avoided looking at Matt as I quickly thought through my options. Do I lie to Matt and risk fighting with him later, or do I tell him the truth and risk him either calling the police or trying to beat the crap out of Alex and losing?

I took a deep breath and smiled, looking up at Matt. "It's kind of true," I exclaimed. "Yes, his name is Alex, and yes, he did surprise me today, and yes, he did get tangled up in the rose bushes. But I wasn't giving him a tour . . ."

At that stage, Alex looked at me with pleading eyes when he thought I was going to oust him.

Instead, I told the slightly "bent" truth with one small white lie. I sighed and went on to explain to Matt, "We were sparring, and he lost his footing. He's an old friend from cadet school, he just popped in for a visit."

Matt looked back at Alex suspiciously, then smiled. "I didn't know Lila still had friends from those years. I thought you were all recruited into black ops . . . or dead."

He shook Alex's hand to welcome him. "You're not here to recruit her, are you? 'Cause I'm pretty sure I know what she'll say."

Alex looked at me nervously and smiled back at Matt. "She would make a great asset . . . but I think she might be happier here," he said, almost sounding sincere in his response.

Matt held my hand and pulled me close to greet me with a very passionate "hello" kiss. A little over the top for my liking, but I think he still felt a bit territorial. Matt whispered softly to me so that Alex couldn't hear him, "It's getting late and we need to put dinner on."

"Oh," I replied, then turned to Alex, "would you like to stay for dinner?"

Somehow, I got the feeling that Matt wasn't expecting me to say that, but it was the only thing I could think of to keep Alex around.

Alex looked at me, confused. "Sure," he replied, hesitantly.

"Great," I said excitedly, "and if you like, our guest bed is yours for as long as you need it."

I could feel Matt getting more upset, and he said softly through gritted teeth, "Honey, don't you have work tonight?"

I looked back at him and replied sternly, "I'll call Ali and ask her to cover for me. She could use the extra money. Alex and I will go make up the guest bed—and I think it would be easier to order takeout tonight . . . Chinese and pizza sound good?"

I kissed Matt on the lips as I walked past him and whispered, "Remember that favour you owed me when your brother came to stay? I'm cashing in that IOU."

Alex looked at Matt and was both grateful and nervous as he walked past him to follow me into the house and up the stairs. Matt sighed, still upset because he knew he had no power to say no to this favour.

A month after our marriage, he had told his little brother Shane that he could stay with us, without talking to me first. Shane then stayed in our guest bedroom for two years while he figured out his life.

That night, after we finished tucking Danny and Ruby into bed, Matt restarted our conversation from the garden as we walked into our bedroom.

Alex was downstairs in the lounge room, watching television and pretending he wasn't listening to us.

As Matt and I finished our talk, Alex heard me walking back downstairs and quickly engrossed himself in the television as I walked into the kitchen in a huff and began to clean. He followed shortly after and started to help by clearing away the empty Chinese containers. He spoke in a gentle voice, "Are you okay?"

It was nice that he cared. "Yeah," I replied through sniffles and wiped a tear from my eye. "I told him you worked for my father in Special Ops and that Richard's cover had been compromised. You were sent to protect me."

Alex looked at me, slightly amazed at the cover story. I continued to talk through the sniffles as he started drying the dishes. "He didn't take it well, because he knows how dangerous Richard's work can get . . . and our conversation didn't go as well as I'd hoped."

Alex stopped cleaning and stood next to me. "I know, I heard everything." He sounded as if he regretted ever showing up unexpectedly on my patio.

As I wiped away another tear, I asked, frustrated, "Were we really that loud?"

Alex chuckled. "No . . . Guardians have incredibly good hearing. I mean, I can hear your heart beating right now."

I looked at Alex in disbelief yet was slightly impressed at his abilities. I couldn't help but feel that nagging sensation in your gut when know something bad was about to happen. "I really hope I'm right about you," I said, putting the last dish away. "I mean, I've put a lot of trust in someone I just met. Please, don't let me down."

Alex nodded and gently held my arms and whispered, "I promise you, I will never hurt you, and I will never lie to you. All I need you to do is to trust me. Can you do that?" he pleaded.

I nodded my head as Alex hugged me excitedly, picking me off the floor and briefly saying, "Thank you."

As my feet landed firmly, I awkwardly smiled. "So what's your plans now?"

Alex replied, "My plan is to stay here and protect you."

I scoffed. "I can clearly protect myself," I rebuffed, hinting to the cut on his eye. "How about you stay here, and we protect each other . . . deal?"

I held my hand out for Alex to agree.

"Deal," he said, confidently shaking my hand.

CHAPTER 6

WHAT'S LEFT OF ME

Journal entry by Adela Eden

I was still at the village, pretending to be asleep, still handcuffed to the hospital bed. They were feeding me some sort of purple fluid via an intravenous drip. It was starting to make me feel a bit funny. I could still hear the footsteps in the corridor and could hear every time the suit guy came around to check on me. I even heard one of the nurses call him "Mr. Connors."

I was learning.

Mr. Connors, still obscuring his face, watched from the door window as he listened to what looked like a doctor explain my current condition.

"The patient is responding well to the treatment. The process should be fully completed by the end of the night."

Mr. Connors stood silently and continued to watch me as the doctor walked away. Agent Toby ran up the hallway, wheezing and out of breath. "Sir," he puffed, "we've found another lead. Alex's car was found abandoned in a town east of Melbourne at a local shopping centre. We have agents searching the area as we speak." He handed a mobile phone to Mr. Connors, suggesting, "Sir, Agent Katie has also found something and is waiting for your orders."

Journal entry insert by Agent Bluey

I was ordered that night to investigate a small log cabin in the parklands of New South Wales. The cabin was being raided by a swarm of agents, looking for something. One of the agents had knocked a photo frame from the wall, portraying Alex and his parents. He also glanced at a picture of Alex and Adela.

I recognised Agent Katie from the missing Guardians list—she was probably no more than 18 years old and sat on the car outside the log cabin, playing with a fireball. She was throwing it from one hand to the other, watching the agents exiting the house with a few stacks of old books.

Katie's mobile rang as she answered, "Yeah? Nobody's home, but we got the books, and we found his father— he claims he doesn't know where he is."

Katie listened as she received instruction via the phone. It was a male voice saying, "You know what to do," and the call was disconnected. She signalled to the agents as they all got into the back of two black vans, while she walked towards the house still playing with her fireball. She tossed the fireball into the door of the cabin, watching as the cabin was engulfed by flames. Katie smiled getting into the white van, seeming to not care that in the cabin's kitchen lay Alex's unconscious father.

CHAPTER 7

TRAINING DAY

Journal entry by Alex Woods

I was absolutely amazed at the trust Lila had given me. We had made it to the weekend without any incidents. Sparring with her was epic and difficult.

Today, Lila's mother invited the family to have a beach BBQ on Phillip Island. Lila suggested on the drive here that her mother's farm was in the middle of nowhere, but it's really just a twenty-minute drive from the small town called San Remo.

When you look around the farm, all you can see are fields, and trees, and more fields. At the back of the farm, there stood a very old, very large willow tree. Lila said she was constantly reminded by her father growing up that it was over a thousand years old, which is what made the land incredibly valuable. And because it was a willow tree, it suited them perfectly, considering their last name was Willows.

I waited in the sheep paddock and watched as Lila waved goodbye to her family and mother driving away. I ran at full speed towards Lila and suddenly appeared, standing right next to her, smiling as she jumped in fright and held her chest.

"Don't do that!" she shouted.

I couldn't help but chuckle. "But it's fun," I replied.

She tried to hide it, but I could tell she was smiling a bit. She walked back towards the house. "All right, it's time to get to work."

I walked along with her and agreed. "All right . . . But I want to know one thing . . ." I said it as if I was making a demand.

Lila looked at me and smiled (I won't lie—her smile looked amazing).

"And what is that?" she enquired.

"I know you're wanting to get more answers out of me today—and I can't argue, this does seem like a pretty secure location . . . but why were you so quick to say no to going to the beach?" I asked and waited intensely for her answer.

She was stunned that I asked such a serious question, but she also didn't look too keen to answer it and avoided looking directly at me.

"I . . .," she started, struggling to answer. It was clear she didn't want to tell me, so she answered, "I just don't like the beach . . . there's too much sand."

"Too much sand?" I scoffed in disbelief.

She quickly changed the subject and walked into the house. "I'm hungry. Do you want something for lunch?"

she shouted back at me, "I make a pretty awesome tomato and cheese!"

I quickly followed her into the house, eager for something to eat.

As she prepared lunch, she watched me looking around the house at all the photos displayed on the walls. I stopped to look closely at the picture of Lila and Richard, both dressed in army uniforms—she in what looked like a cadet's, and him as a sergeant.

"Is that your dad?" I asked.

"Yep!" she shouted from the kitchen. "He's a General now."

I was impressed. "So . . . you're an army brat?" I queried as I walked back to the kitchen. "Is that where you learned your cool ninja moves?"

She stared out the window and responded, seemingly lost in thought, "Yeah, something like that."

She started telling me the stories of her training days.

"I remember my teenage years—something I would much rather forget. As a teen, I spent my years training morning and night. Every day I would spar with my dad in hand-to-hand combat. It got pretty intense. I don't think I ever walked away without a bruise. At one stage, I was thrown to the ground as Richard kicked me in the stomach. He stood over me as I writhed in pain and interrogated, 'Now tell me, what rule did you break?'"

Lila looked upset at the story she was retelling. I began to see why she didn't speak fondly of her stepfather.

She continued the story as we sat down at the table, handing me a cheese toastie to eat.

"I slowly stood up and responded to Richard: 'Rule two, never let down your defences.' Richard yelled back at me, 'And how did you break that rule?' Getting ready to fight again, I responded, 'I was distracted by pain.' Richard continued to berate me, yelling and demanding that I never let it happen again. It wasn't until Hanna walked out of the house to see me standing in the rain, all bloodied and bruised, before Richard dismissed me for the night. Back to fight again the next morning."

Wow, Lila really wasn't kidding when she said she didn't feel pain. We sat in silence and ate our sandwiches. Unsure how to break the tension, I chuckled and said with a mouth half-full, "Well, this is ironic. Our first meeting was me rudely sitting at your table watching you eat a sandwich . . . and now I get to join you! We've come a long way in just a few days," I remarked, swallowing the last bite.

Lila smiled and added, "It's not my fault that you were creepy. I mean, who sits there and watches someone eat a sandwich?"

I rebutted, trying to defend my actions, "Hey! I paid for that sandwich. I wanted to make sure you enjoyed it."

She stood up to clear the dirty plates and said smugly, "I paid you back—it's not my fault you left it at the bakery."

"I was happy to pay," I replied, "it was my way of thanking you."

She looked at me confused as I continued to explain. "I was relieved to see you. It's not every day I find a Guardian like you. So . . . attractive and young, and you come 'fully packaged' with ninja skills too. I mean you're . . . perfect!" I suddenly realised I was rambling and tried to awkwardly smile at her.

She clearly heard me when I had called her attractive. What was I thinking?

She just smiled and quickly changed the subject back to me—very clever of her.

"So you said I can get more answers from you," she asked.

I thought this would be a good time to tell her the truth that I was new at this whole thing as well and that I only had a year's worth of experience. She didn't look like she was taking it too well, but she calmed down when I said, "I can still teach you what I've learnt, and you can teach me your ninja skills like we agreed?"

She took a few seconds to think about it, but eventually agreed. Phew, I really thought that would be a lot worse than it was.

We walked out into the paddock towards the old willow tree. I rubbed my hands together excitedly and asked "So what do you want to learn first?"

Lila looked around the farm, thinking, then shrugged her shoulders. "I don't know. Why don't you show me what your teacher—"

I interrupted to correct her. "My elder."

I could tell she thought it was funny as she bit her lip, holding back a laugh.

Putting thought into it, I realised from her perspective it was kind of a cliché. But she apologised, saying,

"Sorry. Why don't you show me what your elder taught you and I'll see if I can copy?"

Excited, I turned around in circles, looking for something, then raced around the paddock collecting a large stack of thick fire logs. I held in one hand a large stack and placed it down in front of her, separating them into two piles.

"Okay," I said, looking up at Lila, "every Guardian has different abilities according to their elements. I am an Animal Guardian. I can communicate with animals, and I can track them."

I piqued her interest at that point, because I had not yet revealed much about me and my abilities. We were too busy sparring.

Lila interrupted, "Can you control them as well?"

I shrugged my shoulders. "I don't know—I didn't get that far into the elements lessons. But I do know that I have a special bond with the animals—they can sense if I need their help, and if they can help, they do." I explained, "But since you are a rare Nature Guardian, little is known about your kind and their abilities. So we'll have to learn as we go with you. We do have some similar abilities—strength and speed being two of them. So let's start with speed. I'm going to start running, and I want you to try and keep up."

I started running at a normal steady pace, and she ran alongside me, keeping the same speed. I increased my speed, and Lila kept the same speed. Looking around, we were going ridiculously fast, running roughly 150 km per hour. We ran out the driveway and onto the road.

Lila looked at me and yelled, "This is awesome!"

I smiled and shouted to Lila, "This is half speed!"

We then ran faster and faster until we were running so fast that the world around us seemed to slow down. Lila looked around in awe and amazement as she ran next to me at the same speed. I shouted again, saying, "This is full speed, the fastest we can go!"

At full speed, the world often looked amazing, but it felt different now that I was running with Lila. She looked at the world differently.

We kept running and stopped suddenly just before the bridge leading to Phillip Island in the town of San Remo. Lila couldn't believe we had cut a twenty-minute drive into a thirty-second run. It was incredible, but her joy was quickly overshadowed by fear. I could hear her heart begin to beat faster and faster. I looked at her, worried as I listened to her erratic heartbeat.

"Lila, what's wrong?"

She struggled to breathe. "No . . .," she mumbled and ran at full speed back to the farm, leaving me at the bridge confused and worried.

I ran at full speed back to the farm and found her huddled in a ball in the far paddock, sitting against the fence, playing with the grass. I didn't know what to do, so I stood at the fence staring at the grass. She looked up at me with tears streaming down her face and said, "Don't ever do that again."

I sat down next to her and hugged her, trying to comfort her and nodded apologetically.

"I'm sorry," I whispered, "I didn't know."

She hugged me back, taking deep calming breaths until her heartbeat eventually returned to normal.

She let go of me and cleared her throat as we walked back over to the two stacks of firewood.

"So what's next?" she asked, waiting for me to catch up.

I leaned down to pick two large logs, handing one of them to Lila. Then with one easy pull, I broke the log in two like a twig. I looked over to Lila, indicating for her to do the same.

She picked up a log and hesitated for a second, then took a breath and snapped the log in two. She smiled in disbelief, glancing at me then down at the remaining stack of logs.

She threw the broken log to the ground and walked towards the stack of logs. With one swift stomp of her foot, she crushed the log stack, smashing all the logs into little pieces.

I watched as her sad face disappeared, and she looked at me rather competitively as she walked over to my stack of fire logs and crushed it as well.

I applauded and cheered. "Nice, very nice . . . now let me show you another neat trick."

I ran at full speed towards the tall pine trees at the edge of the paddock and jumped from the ground to the highest branch of a very tall pine tree in a single bound. I perched on the top branch and smirked, looking back at Lila.

Lila didn't look too confident with this challenge as I heard her whisper to herself, "You can do this, Lila. It's just one big jump." She ran at full speed towards the pine tree and jumped up as high as she could, but as she was about to reach the branch I was sitting on, she stopped mid-air and began to fall back down to the ground.

My heart stopped in sheer terror as I watched her plummet to the ground, screaming my name. Before she hit the ground, I was jolted sideways as the tree shook. I held the trunk of the tree as the branch I was sitting on suddenly grew, reaching down to catch her. That tree had the best timing—it caught Lila just before she hit the ground.

I watched, still terrified, as the branch retracted back to its original position. Lila was holding on to the branch, tightly hugging it and trying not to throw up. I held on to her as she slowly inched backwards towards me. She was definitely scared as she clutched onto my shirt.

All sorts of questions raced through my head.

What the hell just happened? Did she do that? Or did the tree do it on its own? And how did the tree do that?

I reminded myself that she's a rare Guardian, with no idea what she's doing. Great.

I looked at her and asked if she was okay, but all she could respond with was, "High . . ." I think she was still in shock. She just kept repeating the words, "High, high, high."

All I could think to do was laugh. "That's cheating," I chuckled.

Lila shook her head and looked at me confused; somehow my comment managed to break her from her shock as she began to laugh as well.

"Clearly, we'll need to practice that trick a few more times," I said, putting my arm in front of her and slowly de-clawing her hand from my chest. I wrapped her arms around mine, pulling her closer to me so that she felt safe. "So I guess you're not a fan of heights either?" I asked jokingly.

"Not anymore, no," she replied sarcastically, clutching my arm for support. "That is an experience I will struggle to forget," she added, attempting to laugh it off.

We sat up in the tree and watched the world go by for a while. Lila caught me getting a bit distracted and looking at her chest—Whoops.

"It's not what you think, Lila. I can hear your heart racing," I tried to explain softly. "It sounds so beautiful."

But Lila didn't believe me. "How can you possibly hear my heart?" she asked.

I broke my stare and cleared my throat, explaining, "We also have good hearing, remember? I told you the night we met. You could hear mine if you listened hard enough."

I slowly pulled Lila's hand from my arm and pressed it onto my chest, speaking softly, "Try and feel my heart beating."

Lila started relaxing her hand and rested it on my chest, trying to feel for my heartbeat.

I watched as she smiled. "I found it . . .," she whispered and started sounding out my heartbeat. "Ba . . . bom . . . ba . . . bom."

"Good," I replied quietly. "Now try to listen to the beat. Close your eyes and block out all other sounds but my heartbeat."

She took a deep breath and closed her eyes, clutching my arm tightly so she wouldn't fall, still feeling for my heart beating through her hand.

I watched her focus as she explained to me what she heard. "I can hear the birds chirping . . . the wind rustling . . . the leaves and animals running through the branches . . . Oh wait! I can hear it—ba . . . bom . . . ba . . . bom . . . It's so slow and calm," she said, looking at me in amazement. All she could say, excitedly was, "Wow."

We sat in the tree for a while looking out at the view, watching the animals graze in the paddock below.

Lila broke the silence. "Alex, what happened to your Guardian friends?" she asked in a worried voice.

I sighed, not wanting to answer, but did anyway. "I don't know. I only heard the stories, and they're not very kind." I sat in silence thinking about a friend I had lost, then she asked me again, "What about your elder? What happened to him?"

I looked away, trying to hide my sorrow as I began to explain.

"His name was Henry. The night before he disappeared, we were training at his house. He got a phone call from some guy—I didn't know who it was, but they argued. I couldn't understand what they were saying. All I heard was, 'You can't do this,' and, 'The others will find you.' He got so angry, he smashed his phone against the wall! He managed to calm down long enough to send me home, but I could tell something had got to him. I came back the next morning to check on him, but he was gone. The house was destroyed by fire."

As I finished telling Lila the story, I felt distraught and angry. I clenched my fists and said, "I couldn't help him. I couldn't protect him." The anger rose in me so much I vented by punching the trunk of the tree with a lot of force, such that the wood in the tree trunk cracked as the bark fell away.

At that same time, Lila clutched the side of her ribs as she felt a sharp pain shooting into the side of her chest. Yelping in pain, she let go of my arm and fell backwards off the branch, screaming, "Alex!"

Instantly I moved at full speed, pushing myself off the top branch to gain more speed and landed on the ground, just in time to brace and catch her As Lila landed in my arms, she screamed in agony.

I placed her gently down at the base of the tree, lifting her shirt to inspect the damage. I recoiled with a sharp intake of breath, knowing that this was my fault, looking at the sight of a large purple bruise spreading from her hip bone up and under her bra. I didn't dare to look that far up, but I knew it was bad.

"I think something's broken," I tried to explain, "I need to get you to a doctor."

Lila nodded, trying to breathe through the pain as I slowly lifted her up and cradled her in my arms, whispering, "There's a clinic not far. Go right at the driveway, and at the end of this road, turn right. Follow it two streets down and it's on your left." She gasped for air and held me tightly as I ran at full speed down the driveway.

CHAPTER 8

NOTHING BUT A MEMORY

Journal entry by Alex Woods

When we arrived at the clinic, the nurse opened the door of the surgical room and directed me to gently place her on the bed. She cut what was left of her shirt open to assess the bruise, then looked at Lila as she struggled to breathe, exclaiming, "Lila, I think we need to call you an ambulance."

Lila shook her head profusely, still writhing in pain. "No! . . . No hospitals," she demanded through a wheezing voice.

The nurse brushed the hair from Lila's face and placed a cold cloth on her sweaty forehead before looking at her sternly. "Lila, I've known you since you were a little girl, and I know you don't like hospitals, but I need to call an ambulance."

But Lila remained firm in her decision and continued to shake her head.

The nurse threatened, "Do I need to call your father to tell you to cooperate?"

Lila gave the nurse an angry look and spoke through gritted teeth, "My father would tell you to just get the doctor, then he would command me to suck it up and quit whining." She gasped for another breathe of air and reiterated, "No hospitals."

The nurse gave up and nodded, "Okay, I'll get the doctor and bring you back some morphine." She walked to the door then looked back at me. "Matt, is it?" she asked, but before I could correct her, the nurse continued, "Try to keep her still and don't let her move. She needs to slow her breathing before she breaks any more ribs."

The nurse rushed out of the room, closing the door. I quickly rushed to sit next to Lila holding her hand, trying to comfort her and apologising.

"Lila, I'm so sorry. I forgot that you were still bonded with the tree," I said, trying to explain.

Lila looked at me and tried to speak, saying, "No . . .? You . . . ?"

But I couldn't understand her, so I continued to explain what had happened. "When the tree saved you from falling, you formed a connection with it—a bond. The tree must have sensed you were still afraid and stayed bonded with you. I'm sorry . . . I really am sorry."

Lila just looked at me, confused. She still didn't fully understand how this was my fault, but she just nodded, trying to follow along. She winced and squeezed my hand; the pain had become unbearable for her. Every movement she made caused more pain. She screamed, and I could hear another rib start to break.

Just then, I remembered something I learnt in my training that would possibly help. "Lila, I'm going to try and help you relax, okay?" I didn't sound too confident—because I really wasn't. I grabbed her hand and placed it on my chest and held it there. "Listen to my heartbeat," I said. I took a few breaths in and out, then placed my free hand on her chest gently.

It was a bit awkward, seeing as all she was wearing was a bra.

All I could think about was not causing more pain. I looked into her eyes and she looked into mine as I said again, "Listen to my heart beating."

I repeated it over and over, almost pleadingly, until Lila started to listen to me. "Remember what I taught you. Ignore everything and listen to my heartbeat."

She stared into my eyes, scared of what was happening, as my eyes focused on hers. I could feel her heartbeat slowing as she watched my eyes. "Feel my heartbeat through your hands," I whispered softly.

I started breathing slowly in and out, hinting for Lila to copy. As she did, it felt as if both of our hearts were beating as one. Ba . . . bom . . . ba . . . bom . . . ba . . . bom.

Lila started to relax and rested her head against the pillow. She fell asleep looking into my eyes.

As Lila slept, I called Matt and told him where we were and that Lila had fallen from a tree.

Well, I told him some of the truth.

Journal entry insert by Lila Winters

While I was at the doctor's surgery, I started to dream and remember my teenage years. I was 16 years old, standing on a wooden raft with my friend Brody—he was the same age as me. We were partnered in the training exercise, and Richard was standing on a nearby boat with the other cadets, watching and observing.

"Begin!" Richard shouted.

Brody was nervous. He didn't want to fight me (and he knew he would lose), but he didn't want to look weak in front of the other cadets. Luckily, it began to rain. The raindrops masked the beads of sweat on Brody's forehead.

I didn't want to fight either. I knew what would happen to the loser of the match, but then Brody threw the first punch, so I thought it was fair to fight back. I stayed in defence mode for most of the fight, always blocking or deflecting, but there was only so much time a fight could go on before Richard lost his patience.

I finally took the opportunity to knock Brody onto his back and I stopped, hesitating to throw the final hit.

I couldn't; he was my friend.

Richard shouted from the boat, "STOP! Lila, I thought you said you were ready for this?"

I looked back at Richard as I breathed in the rain, shouting, "I am! I just—"

He interrupted impatiently, shouting, "You just what? In order to graduate, you need to display your skills and not hold back. You know this, Lila, so quit dancing with the boy and complete your training."

I looked at Brody, lying on his back panting and afraid.

"But he's my friend!" I shouted, begging Richard not to make me go through with it.

Richard shook his head, disappointed. "There are no friends here—only enemies."

Brody stood to his feet and spoke quietly, "It's all right, Lila, I can take it."

Richard shouted, "Start again!"

Again, I let Brody throw the first punch. I quickly dodged his fist and grabbed his arm, twisting it back as he screamed in pain. I spun him around to face the other cadets and kicked the back of Brody's knees. With Brody falling onto his hands and knees, I could tell he was struggling to cope with the pain. He tried to kick back and hit my legs, but I cartwheeled over him, landing at the edge of the raft, and with a final punch, he fell face-forward onto the raft, unconscious.

I turned to look at Richard as I tried to catch my breath, but Richard just stared at me, waiting.

"The loser must be in the water in order for the match to end!" he shouted.

I looked at Brody still unconscious, struggling to breathe. "But he'll drown!" I screamed back at Richard.

I just couldn't do it. I couldn't push my unconscious friend into the water. I didn't have the stomach for it, and I knew Richard knew that about me.

He sighed, shouting, "We'll be out here all night if you don't end the match."

The other cadets started grumbling. I had to do something. I knelt down to try and wake Brody but failed—he was out cold. I stood up and looked back at Richard with a defiant glance, then jumped into the water.

Original journal entry continued by Alex Woods.

Matt met me at the doctor's surgery, and we waited together as they X-rayed and bandaged Lila's ribs. Because Lila refused to go to the hospital, there was not a lot the doctors could do there. Matt already knew to respect Lila's wishes about the hospital but wouldn't tell me why.

We took Lila back home, and I carried her carefully up the stairs as Matt cleared the children's toys out of the way.

I sat with Lila as she slept, while Matt fed the children dinner and put them off to bed.

I don't know what she was dreaming about, but she seemed distressed and woke up in panic, screaming. I tried to calm her down, saying it was okay and telling her where she was, but she was really disoriented with the morphine still in her system. She seemed to calm down pretty quickly when she realised where she was.

I called for Matt, and he came rushing in to sit with her. I thought I would take that as my cue to leave, going downstairs into the lounge room. I couldn't help myself as I listened into Matt and Lila's conversation. I was genuinely concerned for Lila's well-being, but I also wanted to know if my cover had been blown.

Matt talked with Lila, explaining what had happened and how she broke her ribs falling out of a tree. He went on to explain how impressed he was of me and how I carried her to the doctor's, saying, "That was pretty impressive, considering how far away the doctor's clinic was—I mean, I know you're not a fan of your dad, but I have to say, he sure knows how to pick his soldiers."

It started to sound like a sales pitch. Obviously I did something to get in Matt's good books, and I smirked just a little.

My smirk disappeared, however, when I heard Lila's voice for the first time as she wheezed, "I thought you didn't like Alex."

"I don't," Matt remarked, "but I know you, and I know you don't trust others easily. So whatever he's done, that somehow managed to earn your trust, in doing so he has earned my respect."

That's when the guilt hit me. I sat down on the couch, and I remembered that this was all my fault. How could Lila ever trust me again? And if she doesn't trust me, then Matt won't, and I'll be . . .

"Alex," Matt said, standing right in front of me, breaking me out of my mild panic attack, "Lila's asking for you." He handed me a toasted cheese sandwich and whispered, "I get the slight suspicion from the look on your face that this injury was somehow your fault. So give this to her as a peace offering, and whatever you did, don't ever do it again."

I nodded and held on to the plate. "Oh god," I mumbled under my breath (praying for a miracle, I guess) as I walked towards the stairs.

I slowly made my way up the stairs to see Lila smile at me as I handed her a cheese toastie. I avoided looking at her because I didn't want her to notice my guilty look.

"Alex," she said quietly (I still wouldn't look at her), "Alex, thank you," she said, reaching over to hold my hand.

I was a bit befuddled, not knowing what to do. She started to move and wince in pain as she squeezed my hand. I looked at her, hoping she would tell me what to do.

"Ha!" she said victoriously, "I got you to look at me."

I smiled with a little sneer, knowing I had been tricked, and graciously admitted my defeat. Lila got serious as she said, "Alex, this wasn't your fault. You didn't know."

I sighed and shook my head. "It's my job to protect you, and I made you fall out of a tree . . ."

Lila quickly interrupted, saying, "But you caught me—and that's what I choose to remember about the day . . . you didn't mean to hurt me and I'm still alive. So stop beating yourself up about it. Besides, it's not the first time I've broken my ribs—at least this time it was an accident," she offered, "I'm stronger than I look," as she handed me half of her cheese toastie.

"You should get some more sleep," I whispered.

Lila consented but asked me to do one favour. "That thing you did at the doctor's . . . can you do it again, please?"

I was reluctant, but honestly couldn't say no to her at that point. She held her hand up against my chest, but she struggled to hold it there. I helped her by holding her hand and placed my hand on her chest. She looked into my eyes and we listened to each other's hearts beating. She smiled as she drifted back off to sleep.

Perfect timing, as Matt walked into the bedroom and cleared his throat as he saw me with my hand on his wife's chest while she slept. Not at all awkward.

"Sorry," I said to Matt apologetically, trying to explain. "It's little trick I learnt to help people sleep."

Matt held back his comments as he glanced over to see Lila sound asleep and smiling.

He wasn't happy, but he mustered up a smile and quietly said, "Looks like it worked."

We stood in awkward silence before I broke and said, "I'm going to grab some air . . . your turn."

Matt then said my name in a stern voice, saying, "Alex . . . I am telling you now, if you ever touch her again, I will hurt you. Your job is to protect her, and you can't even do that right."

I sighed looking back at Matt and nodded in agreement to his threat as I walked down the stairs.

Journal entry insert by Lila Winters

I began to dream of my teenage years again. I was back at the boat, floating in the water, breathing in the rain, watching them drag Brody's unconscious body from the raft.

Richard looked in the water watching me float there, waiting and tsk-ing. "Now, sweetie," Richard mocked with a smug tone of anger, "can you tell me what rule you just broke?" he asked.

I floated in the water staring at Richard in rebellious silence. I wasn't planning on giving him the satisfaction of me admitting my weakness.

Richard turned to the other cadets. "Anyone?" he shouted.

One of the cadets stood to attention and shouted, "Rule 8—never let your feelings affect your actions."

Richard looked back at me, but before he could start speaking, I cut him off and shouted, "And I would do it again!" I looked at all the other cadets and shouted, "For anyone of you!"

I watched as the cadets all gave a subtle nod of appreciation. They all knew I was the sergeant's daughter; they knew if I wanted to, I could win every match, but I always took it easy on them. I glared at Richard and bellowed, "I thought you were training me to be a soldier." I cried out defiantly, "Soldiers look out for their brothers."

Richard groaned. "And that is why you will always lose," he barked back at me as the boat began to drive away, leaving me behind.

I floated in the ocean and watched the boat disappear into the distance as the sun began to set. Then started to swim in the boat's wake left behind in the water; at least that way I knew the general direction of land.

I swam for an hour. Exhausted, I stumbled on to the shore, crawling further up onto the beach. I saw flashing red and blue lights surrounding the docks.

"Brody," I gasped. I mustered up all the energy I had left and ran up to the docks as fast as my legs could take me. I stopped when I saw an ambulance van and two police squad cars standing at the docks; there was even a media crew there filming a report. It was then I knew something had gone wrong; my gut felt like it was twisting in knots. I knew what had happened.

"Brody!" I shouted through my tears running to the ambulance, but I was stopped by four of my fellow cadets, who tried to pull me away from the ambulance. I knew their intentions were good and they were just trying to protect me, but I didn't care. I wanted to see what I had done. I shouted louder as I tried to look past the cadets.

"Brody!" I shouted, punching one of the cadets and kicking and pushing the other three to the ground. "I'm sorry," I spluttered to the cadets through the tears. I ran to the back of the ambulance to see the paramedic pulling the body bag zip up over Brody's dead body. I screamed and whaled in shock and disbelief; all I could say was, "No," shaking my head, I pushed the paramedic aside and pulled back the zip to see Brody's face.

I felt his cold hardened cheek and watched my tears drip onto the body bag. "I'm sorry," I whispered, "I'm so . . . so sorry!"

Richard gestured to the other cadets to pull me away. But none of them moved; they wouldn't even try to pull me away.

But Ben did. He had already graduated from cadet school and became my father's favourite soldier, following him everywhere, doing whatever Richard asked of him. He gently rubbed my shoulder then tightly held my hands as he pulled me close to him and attempted to comfort me. I tried to pull away, but he was too strong. He whispered in my ear, "Lila . . . not in front of the media. Please. Sergeant Willows will handle this, but for your safety, I need you to come with me."

He hugged me tightly and started walking with me back down towards the beach. I didn't argue with him; I just kept crying as I walked.

Original journal entry continued by Alex Woods

I walked back up the stairs on my way to the guest bedroom when I heard Lila crying in her sleep, saying, "Brody . . . I'm sorry." Matt tried to comfort her as he pulled the covers up over her.

But I had to ask, "Is she okay?"

Matt nodded his head and stroked Lila's hair and began to explain, "Yeah, she's just remembering a few bad memories. The farm does that to her."

"Who's Brody?" I asked, "I heard her say his name at the doctor's."

Matt sighed. "It's odd she usually only remembers Brody after she'd been to the beach," he answered.

Damn yet another thing that was my fault.

Matt continued to explain that Lila blamed herself for what happened to Brody, which began to explain why she freaked out at the beach.

I was distraught as I processed the story, unsure how to react. I mean I had always had a mother and a father who loved me, and my childhood was pretty normal, where playing x-box was the afternoon pastime.

I interrupted Matt to ask, "And her parents, her dad . . . what did he do about it?"

It was then Matt stopped stroking Lila's hair and stared at me suspiciously.

"It's interesting . . .," Matt said, "Richard's soldiers always referred to him as the General, even when they were off duty."

Damn, I honestly believed my cover had been blown, but Matt said nothing and snickered, "Looks like the General's getting sloppy," then answered the original question. "The General did what he always did. He swept it under the rug . . . He lied to the police and told them that he got seasick and fell . . . Lila wanted to confess, but the General told her to stop wasting her tears and that everyone was going to die one day, and Brody's day was that day."

I was appalled and blurted, "That's horrible."

Matt smiled down, so proud at Lila, saying, "I know." He smirked as he continued his story. "That was the day Lila rebelled against the General . . . she quit being his little soldier and never spoke to him again unless it was absolutely necessary . . . she only visits the farm for Hanna's sake."

Matt started to yawn, and I took that as sign to finally go to bed. I wished Matt a good night and walked into the guest bedroom, but as I turned off the light, I heard Matt whisper to Lila, "I don't get it, why would you lie?"

Damn, busted.

CHAPTER 9

IT BEATS THE TRUTH

Journal entry by Lila Winters

As the sun was rising the next morning, Alex woke in panic as he heard the sound of me panting and grunting and my heart racing. It sounded like I was in a fight, and I was. He ran at full speed frantically looking all over the house and found me in the backyard kick-boxing with a brand-new punching bag stand.

I was so excited, and I had a really big smile on my face. Matt had found an equipment store across from the beach yesterday and wanted to surprise me with it. It was perfect; Matt knew me too well. Whenever we visited the farm, I would always wake up the next morning needing to work it out, so he had set it up while I was asleep. He probably wasn't expecting me to use it, given my injuries. But he knew me too well.

Alex watched me fighting aggressively. He could tell I was ignoring the pain of my broken ribs; he noticed I favoured my left side when I kicked and didn't swing as hard when I punched with my right arm.

"Do you like him?" I asked as I turned to show Alex the happy face I drew on the punching bag stand. "I was going to name him Hector."

Alex grumbled and stood beside me, lifting my shirt to look at my firmly bandaged ribs. "Are you sure you should be up at the moment?" He looked at me as if I was a fragile doll, one tap and I'd break. It infuriated me.

I wiped the sweat from my brow and glared at Alex. "I told you. You're not the first person to cause me pain. The training helps me focus the pain. Plus, I think it's starting to get better."

Alex thought for a second and commented, "Our recovery time is faster than the humans, but you broke your rib cage and hip and severely bruised your abdomen. It will take more than one night to heal. You should be in bed asleep."

I glared at him again. I was not in the mood to be babied; I knew his mission was to protect me, but this is my thing. So I challenged him to a little competition. "All right, I'll make a deal with you . . . if you manage to tap my left shoulder, I'll go back to bed and get some rest. However, if I tap your shoulder, you answer one of my questions. Deal?"

Alex shrugged his shoulders and smiled. "Counter-offer: you go and sit down, and I answer your questions while I make you breakfast?" he waited for my response. And it sounded like a fair deal, but I was in the mood for a fight and he interrupted my session with Hector.

I casually turned to Alex and grinned, taking him up on part of his deal and asked my first question, "How did you find out about me?"

Alex pulled a sour face; he didn't want to answer that question. He quickly moved left to try and tap my left shoulder, but I dodged under his hand and spun around to stand behind him and tapped his left shoulder.

I sternly suggested to Alex, "If you want to continue this new friendship we have going, I suggest you be honest while we play this game . . . How did you find out about me?" I asked again.

Alex turned to face me. "Mission Control had you on their database," he answered.

"Why?" I replied back. My trust in Alex slowly started to disappear as I thought to myself, why didn't he tell me about this database before, why did he want to hide it from me, and how did I get on the database?

"Answer the question," I demanded.

Alex positioned his feet ready to fight. "I thought we were playing your game," he replied.

I tried to tap his left shoulder again, but this time he caught my hand instead. I quickly broke away by spinning and elbowing him in the jaw.

Alex rubbed his jaw and glanced at me and saw a glimpse of me wincing in pain. I tried to hide it with a smile of determination, but every now and then, the pain did get to me.

Alex was now determined to get me to stop and rest, but that morning, he learnt very quickly, I wasn't going to go down without a fight, and I certainly didn't like being told what to do.

Alex and I started fighting both trying to tap each other on the shoulder. As he moved, I dodged. As I moved, he dodged. It almost looked like a dance.

"You're holding back," I commented to Alex as I smiled.

I did kind of get excited, and he was right, I had finally found a good sparring partner. And I know Alex would never admit it, but I think he was having fun too.

Alex replied, frustrated, "I don't want to hurt you again," still trying to tap my shoulder.

I moved around Alex excitedly, because I knew then how to win. "If you hold back, I'll win, so you may as well answer my questions," I contended. "Why am I in your agency's database?" I asked as I elbowed Alex in the chest then tapped his shoulder again.

Alex sighed as he reluctantly answered, "From what I've read in your file, you were flagged at a young age after your blood was tested."

Alex tried again to tap my left shoulder and missed, again and again he tried and failed. I winced as Alex accidently knocked my right side. He apologised as I fell to the ground holding my lower ribs. Alex hesitated but apologised again as he seized the opportunity to tap my shoulder. But before he could reach me, I grabbed his hand

and kicked him in the stomach, causing him to flip over me onto his back. He writhed in pain as his back tightened from the shock.

I moved to kneel at his head and pinned him to the ground using my right foot to hold his right hand to the ground and my left hand to hold his left arm. I then reached with my free hand for the letter opener that I had decoratively hidden in the ponytail of my hair. I pressed the letter opener to the side of his neck next to the corroded artery.

Alex looked up at me and stopped moving. "I was wondering what that was for," he noted.

I pressed the letter opener harder against his neck. "How did you get my blood?" I asked angrily.

I didn't let it show, but I was in agony from the pain; my chest felt like it was on fire. But I wanted to know the truth without him distracting me with new Guardian tricks, like jumping up trees.

Alex tried to move until I whispered to him, "I warn you now, I am in agonising pain, if you try to fight me, you _will_ make my injury worse. Now answer the question."

I held Alex down and glared into his eyes, pressing the letter opener against his neck.

Alex stopped struggling to avoid injuring me. "Lila," he said softly, "please . . . you can trust me, I swear. I only want—"

I interrupted his speech in anger and barked, "To protect me! . . . Bullshit . . . if your agency knew about me since I was a child, they would have known the history and training I have and that I need no man's protection . . . You're here because you want my help . . . And if that's the case, I suggest you start telling the truth and start telling it fast. How did they get my blood?"

Alex took a breath; he knew at that point that if he wanted my trust that he would have to earn it.

"Mission Control is a government organisation. There is a test that is done on all blood samples that are given to any hospitals, doctor surgeries, or medical laboratory in that particular country. If you have ever given blood or had blood taken from you, then that blood has been tested. If the test comes back positive of a particular protein, then you are placed on Mission Control's list," he answered regretfully.

"And then what?" I asked firmly.

Alex hesitated in answering, which agitated me, and my emotions began to distract me from controlling the pain. At that stage, Alex could tell. I began to feel dizzy and started to fall sideways. Alex freed his hands, moving at full speed, pulling the letter opener away from him, then got to his knees just in time to catch my head before it hit the pavement. He then pulled my head up and cradled me in his arm and said in panic, "I don't know, I swear. Now please stop hurting yourself and let me help you."

I ignored him. I was filled with rage and anger. As the dizziness wore off, I stood up frustrated and placed the letter opener back into my ponytail. I was so angry and confused and I ignored the pain in my chest.

Alex stood up and watched as I paced the garden. "Lila, I really think you should rest now," he said hesitantly.

I shouted back at him, "Don't tell me what to do! You said I could trust you . . . and right now, I don't trust you."

He looked at the ground and nodded, saying, "You're right, I'm sorry."

"Why?" I asked. "Why pick my file?"

"I don't know," he replied. "All I know is that I was sent to you. I don't know why. Maybe because of your history and your training. They thought you would be willing to help them."

I glared at Alex. "Help them! I don't even know them!" I shouted, gasping for air.

Alex tried to walk closer to me, and I stepped backwards. "Stay away from me," I said fearfully.

I could hear Alex's heart beat faster as if he had felt some kind of pain. He pleaded with me, "Lila, I'm sorry. I didn't tell you the truth. I promised when we first met that I wouldn't hurt you and I failed. I told you could trust me, and I lied, and I know it's hard to earn your trust. But I promise you now I will never lie to you again, please . . . please trust me."

At that moment, I couldn't take the pain of my injuries anymore, it overwhelmed me, and I collapsed from exhaustion. Alex moved at full speed and caught me again.

I looked at him in fear and started breathing slowly in and out to try and cope with the pain. With tear-filled eyes, I stared at Alex and gasped for air, saying, "I'm sorry, but I don't know if I can."

Alex pleaded with me, gently wiping a tear from my cheek, and said with a soft voice, "Yes, you do . . ."

I didn't understand what he was saying as he tried to explain.

"You're a Nature Guardian, you have the ability to sense a person's nature—what they feel, what they desire. You could feel it when we first met, and you can feel it now."

Alex held my hand gently and said, "Trust your instincts . . . focus and tell me what I desire most."

I took some slow deep breaths and tried to ignore the burning pain of my ribs to focus. I placed my free hand on his cheek and suddenly felt a wave of emotions that weren't my own, all his desires.

"Fear . . .," I said softly. I looked at Alex as he hesitated. He knew it was true.

I continued to decipher the emotions that Alex was feeling "Regret . . . sadness and longing . . ." I stopped to gasp for air, then continued, "You lost someone . . . and you're scared you're going to lose me like you did her."

Alex looked away and sighed as he remembered the last conversation he had with his partner.

"Adela," he said, holding back tears.

I was impressed. I knew it wasn't easy for him to actually show his emotions.

"She was my partner. We had a fight before our last mission. I had just found out my mother had died." He sniffled and wiped the tears from his eyes. "Adela was upset because I was acting as if my mother's death meant nothing to me. But really it did . . . I just didn't want her to know. Adela went on to complete the mission without me and . . ."

Alex clenched his fist in frustration and through gritted teeth said, "It was a trap . . . I couldn't save her." He slammed his fist on the concrete in a burst of rage. "I lost her, and I lost Henry, and I lost my mother."

Alex looked at me with tear-filled eyes and begged, "Please . . . I can't lose you . . . I can't fail again."

I was speechless as he held me in his arms. I didn't know what to do or what to say. How do you console a man who's lost everything?

Bluey flew down, landing on my knee in a flurry. He chirped, "Alex! I have an urgent report. Agent Kelly has been taken. And Mission Control has gone dark for their protection and yours."

I looked at Alex as he helped me stand and held Bluey in my hands. "What does that mean for you guys?" I asked.

Alex looked at me very protectively and said, "It means we're on our own."

Nervously I looked at Bluey, and confused, I asked, "Bluey, your heart feels like it's filled with sadness. What's wrong?"

Bluey looked at the ground, not wanting to say anything. "It's your dad . . . Alex. Two days ago, your safe house was . . . burned to the ground, your father was still inside. He . . . he didn't survive."

Alex became engulfed with rage as he screamed. I could feel his heart breaking; it felt like it was being torn out of his chest. Alex had to vent his anger somehow; he let go of me and ran at full speed towards my new punching bag stand and punched it so hard that the bag was shattered tearing into pieces and thrown across the backyard. He then fell to the ground and began to sob.

The noise was so loud it had woken Matt and the kids. Matt ran to the back door to see what the commotion was. He looked at Alex holding torn pieces of the punching bag and crying, then Matt looked at me confused, wanting an explanation.

I delicately sidestepped around Alex and limped my way to Matt and whispered in his ear softly, "He's just found out his father died."

Matt nodded in an understanding way, but he was clearly worried about my safety as he looked around at the mess in the backyard.

I casually smiled a Matt and said, "I'll be fine."

Matt sighed and reluctantly walked back inside but watched from the dining room window.

I stood next to Alex and grabbed his hand from the ground, pulling him up to stand with me.

He avoided looking at me, so I held both of his hands.

"I'm sorry," I said softly, trying to console him, "I know what it's like to lose people you love, and I know how it feels when you know you could have done something . . . I've thought of a million things I could have done or not done to save them. But after I had thought of all the possibilities, it still never changed the fact that they were gone. But . . . it did change the way I treated the people I still had in my life . . . I protect them, and I make every moment with them count."

Alex looked at the ground trying to hide his rage and miserably failing and said through his sniffles and tears, "I have no one . . . They're all gone."

I held his face and made him look at me. "You have me . . . you also have Adela and Henry, who both need your help. You'll find them, I know you will . . . until then, you'll stay here, and you will do your best to protect me . . . remember what you promised me," I said.

Alex took a deep breath in and out, trying to compose himself. "I promised to protect and promised I wouldn't lie to you."

"And I'm going to hold you to that promise," I said, holding my hand out to agree on the deal again, and as we shook hands, I looked at Alex and said, "Alex, this morning you didn't earn my trust . . ." He began to look dismal again as I hugged him tightly and whispered, "You earned my friendship . . . Thank you for looking out for me today. Even though I kicked your ass and threatened you with a knife . . . you still protected me and cared for me. You're definitely one of the good ones."

Alex smiled as he hugged me back; he hugged a bit too hard as I winced in pain. He quickly let go and said apologetically, "Sorry."

He was then finally able to help me into the house and sat me down at the table to have breakfast. Alex stayed home while Matt went to work, dropping the kids off at day care.

The day ended up being great. Alex looked after me, and I, reluctantly but graciously, accepted.

We sat on the couch as he talked about his parents and his childhood memories. It was an amazing feeling for him, being able to just sit and talk and not worry about the world.

CHAPTER 10

REGRET

Journal entry by Alex Woods

It had been a few weeks since Lila's accident and all had been quiet. I even got to share Christmas with her family. It was an amazing feeling as things started to get back to normal. Lila was healing really fast, so fast that she had to start pretending to feel pain so that Matt wouldn't get suspicious. I was still staying in the guest room, and Bluey popped in to check up on us every night.

Until one morning I had fallen asleep on the couch listening to music from my headphones and woke up to find the house empty. I looked around the house and found a small Post-it note on the kitchen bench. Lila's handwriting was so messy, and the paper had some milk spilt on it from breakfast. But somehow, I managed to read it: "Alex gone to work back at 3. Any probs call. P.S. I saved you some pancakes in the microwave . . . enjoy." She even signed her note with a smiley face at the end.

I grinned grabbing the stack of pancakes from the microwave. But just as I was about to sit down at the table, Bluey flew into to the backyard and landed on the garden table and chirped furiously in panic.

Something was wrong. I ran out into the backyard at full speed to talk to him.

"Alex, it's Lila, I followed her to work to make sure she got there safely. But when I was in the car park, I spotted two agents watching the centre. And they're not ours."

I became overwhelmed with fear thinking the worst.

"Lila," I said, leaving the plate of pancakes on the table and running at full speed through the house and out the front door. As soon as I reached the shopping centre, I didn't slow down as I ran through the open doors brushing past customers as they looked around confused at the odd breeze rushing past them.

I stopped and sat at the coffee shop just across the hall from Lila's work, casually reading a paper, and watched as Lila walked around the store, talking to a customer, showing her the new clothing range, and helping her with the sizing.

I sighed with relief knowing she was okay.

Emma, Lila's other co-worker, was taking down Christmas decorations and waited until the store was empty before she started asking Lila questions. "So who's the guy?" she whispered. Lila jumped in fright, puzzled as to what Emma was talking about, then started neatening up the store as a distraction.

But Emma followed Lila around the store pestering her and she was extremely persistent. She started to gossip, and I couldn't help but listen in. "So, Bec, saw you a few weeks ago at the bakery . . . with another man. And now we found out he's staying at your house," Emma said almost accusingly.

At that point, I became a little uneasy shuffling in my chair as I pretended to read the paper listening in. I watched intently when I saw two agents dressed in classy business suits walk down the corridor. I didn't think they noticed, because they were still looking around dumbfounded, all I could think to do was slouch a little further down and hope they didn't notice me as they passed through.

When the coast was clear, I continued to listen to Lila still trying to hide the presence of another man in her life. Emma just kept talking about what she heard. "I heard that he pushed you out of a tree and broke your ribs . . . but clearly that can't be possible, 'coz you're standing here . . . clearly not in pain. Or . . ."

Lila interrupted Emma's rant as she turned back to her, asking, "How could you possibly know all this? Where are you getting this information?"

Emma just looked at Lila as if she was expected to know that answer. "Um, hello, my aunt works at Ruby's day-care centre. You honestly think Ruby's not going to talk about the strange new man staying at her house?" Emma said, rolling her eyes as if it was a no-brainer.

Damn, we really should have thought about that potential information leak.

Lila just deflected and asked Emma to get back to her work. But instead Lila just kept smiling and folding clothes, while her co-worker continued her interrogation, asking the weirdest of questions.

"Argh! Why are you keeping this so secret?" Emma gasped with a sudden realisation. "Oh my god . . . is he your lover? . . . No, it can't be. Matt would have beat the crap out of him by now . . . oh . . . no . . . is he Matt's lover?" she asked and waited in shock for Lila to answer.

I watched in awe at Lila's ability to keep a straight face and not crack under this weird interrogation method—that was a really good game face.

I do admit it was interesting to know what kind of illogical conclusion people could come up with in such a short span of time. I mean I've only known Lila a few weeks, but I'm pretty sure, if she had found out her husband was gay, she wouldn't be okay with them living under the same roof.

I watched as Lila snickered and pulled a sour face, saying, "Emma, you really need to stop watching those stupid reality TV shows. They're clearly not good for you or anyone else for that matter."

Emma looked around the store and started randomly folding clothes to look busy, as she quietly whispers, "Psst," trying to get Lila's attention.

Lila walked casually towards her, nervously grinning, "What" she asked, probably starting to get frustrated at Emma's lack of work ethics.

She whispered quietly as she quickly looked outside the store, pointing to the coffee shop where I was sitting. "Isn't that your new bakery friend?"

"Damn," I whispered as Lila looked at me watching her and rolled her eyes.

Emma got excited with a huge and obvious smirk on her face looking at me and said, "If he's not yours and he's not Matt's, can I have him?" she whispered to Lila.

I glanced over the newspaper looking into the store to see Emma licking her lips and most likely thinking a lot of dirty and inappropriate thoughts. She quickly stopped as she realised I could see her and pretended to fold clothes.

Lila was about to walk out of the store until I signalled to her to stop.

I stayed quiet as she whispered, "Alex, what the hell are you doing here?" She knew I could hear her, yet I didn't respond. All I did was get up and walk away, handing a scrunched-up paper to a nearby cleaning lady and asking her to deliver it to Lila.

I didn't look back as I disappeared down the corridor hearing Lila say, "I'm going on break."

The scrunched-up paper had a note that asked Lila to meet me in the food court. I thought that would be the best place given there was so many people. I had thought about it, and I didn't want to put Lila in any more danger, so it was time I said goodbye.

I picked up a cheap phone from Big W and called Lila from the opposite end of the food court, staying where I couldn't be seen. Given that Lila's friend Mike was on duty, I thought it was best to give Lila her space.

"Hello?" Lila said, answering her phone. She sounded worried.

I began to explain to her that they had found me and that I was sorry I dragged her into this.

"I'm going to fix this, I just wanted to know you were safe before I said goodbye," I said, trying to explain.

"Alex, what are you going to do?" she asked fearfully.

I couldn't see her, but I could tell she was scared. At that moment, I closed my eyes to focus and listened for Lila's heartbeat. It took me a moment to sift through the surrounding noise and chatter, but I found it. She was just as scared as I was, and her heart was racing. I mustered up the words to say, "I'm sorry," before I hung up and disappeared out of the food court.

I had managed to make it to the escalators before I was cornered by two agents—the same ones who passed me in the coffee shop. Guess they were just waiting for me to make a stupid move.

One of the agents stood confidently and said, "Alex, there's nowhere to run, we have the place surrounded . . . come with us quietly and no one else will get hurt."

I took a moment to contemplate my options. I didn't want to cause a scene, and I also didn't want to run the risk of them finding Lila.

So I gave up.

I walked with the agents back down the corridor past the food court and past Lila's work.

I tried not to draw attention to me, and to the untrained eye, I just looked like another rich guy with bodyguards to protect me.

But Lila knew better as she watched them parade me past her work.

I glanced over to her just briefly as I heard her whisper, "I'm going to regret this . . ."

Before I knew it, she was chasing after me and the two agents shouting, "Excuse me . . .," standing in front of them.

She smiled at me then said, "Hi, I'm sorry but . . . where are you taking this man?" she asked.

The two agents were not impressed and were clearly not in the mood to deal with her. One of the guys who Lila had named Bill for the purpose of this story turned to her with a snide and brief remark, demanding, "Go back to your shopping, ma'am."

Bill then turned and continued to walk, holding my arm tightly so I would cooperate.

But Lila didn't listen and stood in front of me again to stop the agent from walking and instead addressed the other agent who Lila had named Jack.

"I'm sorry but who the hell are you two? I mean, this really doesn't look normal. Three guys walking through a shopping centre, two in really nice but creepy suits, next to one scruffy possibly homeless man. It kind of looks suss, and honestly, I'm tempted to alert security . . .," she said, looking around the corridor for her friend Mike.

Jack quickly interrupted her, saying in a huff, "We are security! Now if you please go back to your shopping, ma'am," he said one final time, leading me by the arm to walk around her, but instead Lila blocked them again and again, pretending it was accidental and apologising each time.

Wow, she really couldn't take the hint as she said smugly, "See now I know that's a lie . . . you're not security. Because I know Big Mike and he's a lot bigger than you and a lot nicer than you. Plus, myself being on the staff speed dial, I've already alerted the real security to your presence."

She held her phone out to show Jack and Bill. I guess it was to try and scare them away.

She hadn't really alerted security, and it was a total bluff, but it had them freaking out.

Bill grabbed Lila's phone and threw it to the ground, breaking the screen, then pushed her aside in a hurry and said very rudely, "Move!"

Jack and Bill began to quickly lead me towards the exit, when I heard Lila whisper, "God, I hope this works."

Before I knew it, Jack and Bill were tied up in roots from a nearby indoor pot plants.

I looked back at Lila scared at what she had done, then ran back to her at full speed. But instead of freaking out, she told me off for using my full speed and quietly said, "I still hopefully have to work here tomorrow, and I'd like them to think I'm normal . . . okay?"

But I definitely wasn't concerned about that as I whispered to her, "What are you doing? You need to run," pushing her into the side of the corridor to hide.

Lila stared back at me sternly and replied, "Not without you . . . You came to me for protection remember? I protect you and you protect me. That was our deal."

I looked down the corridor to see Jack and Bill still trying to break free of the tree roots when they were greeted by six more of their friends. Jack freed himself and shouted to the other agents, "There's two of them, the target plus a female, mid twenties, purple hair!"

Lila swore as she heard that last part and said, "Okay . . . I think I have a plan." On a whim, she grabbed my hand and ran towards Cotton-on Body. As we ran, she asked, "Can you tell if they're Guardians?"

I shook my head and shouted no.

We hid behind the counter of the Cotton-on Body store.

"What are we doing? What's the plan?" I asked, looking up to see Emma who was just staring at me.

I waved, awkwardly saying hi.

Emma looked down at us and asked, "Why are you hiding?"

Lila was still thinking of a plan and said, "My main concern at that point is the safety of the other people in the shopping centre."

God, I love that about her; she always cared for the people first.

It was the summer holidays, which meant there was more people out shopping and more kids here to entertain themselves.

We both knew we had to evacuate the centre without causing a mass panic. Then it hit me. "Bomb," I said under my breath. Lila heard me and smiled at the idea.

She looked up at Emma and said very clearly to her, "There's a bomb in the store, do you remember the procedure for that?"

Emma nodded her head, trying not to freak out, then walked quickly and calmly into the back storage room to make a phone call.

Emma wasted no time walking back out of the storage room trying not to cry and looked back at me and Lila still hiding behind the counter. "Okay . . . that was the security centre, they are calmly evacuating the centre now," she said and quickly hinted for us to leave. Emma looked out to see a large crowd of people walking past the store and decided to quickly run out to join them.

I looked up to see if the coast was clear and noticed a few of the agents looking around at the sea of people leaving the centre.

"There's no way we can leave without being noticed," I said doubtfully.

Lila then grabbed a hoodie vest from off a coat hanger and put it on to cover her hair then grabbed a hat for me and whispered to me as she put it on my head, "Whatever we do, we do together. Got it?"

I nodded in agreement, holding on to Lila's hand.

"Don't lose me," I said confidently.

We briskly walked out of the store and joined the crowd to evacuate. We carefully avoided a few of the agents and thankfully didn't draw any attention to us as they looked through the crowd.

But a few seconds later, I bumped into Mike who was looking for Lila and accidently knocked the hoodie off her head.

"Lila?" he said. "The team is looking for you, Emma said you were the one who called in the bomb. I need you to come with me to meet the police, give them more information."

Mike looked over to see Lila holding my hand and quickly grew suspicious. "Hey, I recognise you," he shouted.

Mike didn't realise it, but he had gained the attention of our unwanted friends who had started walking towards us.

I glanced around to see the agents getting closer, then in a hurry pushed Mike to the ground and said, "I'm sorry, Mike, but she has to run."

I held on to Lila's hand and ran down a corridor that was almost empty. Mike screamed back at us, "Hey . . . that's the wrong way!"

As he screamed those deafening words, all six of the agents as well as Jack and Bill ran past Mike chasing after us.

Mike quickly realised that Lila was in danger and grabbed his radio to call in the report.

"We got a situation. Lila's in trouble. If anyone's available, send help," he said as he began to chase after us and the agents with determination. But we were too fast for him as he slowed, trying to catch his breath.

Lila and I ran through the food court towards another exit, when we were cut off by two more agents just as big and just as scary as the other eight that were chasing us.

Great. We were surrounded as all ten agents closed in on us. Jack smiled at me and looked across at Lila, saying arrogantly, "Couldn't leave without your girlfriend, huh?"

I tried to ease the situation and stall as we tried to come up with a plan.

"Guys, come on now . . . this hardly seems fair . . . ten of you against two of us," I said jokingly.

The agents laughed, smiling at each other, as I whispered to Lila, "Take who you can, and I'll get the rest!"

Lila screamed in disbelief, "What!" as she watched me charge at Bill.

Jack tried to grab hold of Lila's arms, but she ducked to the ground and kicked his legs, causing him to fall. As she quickly stood back up, she apologised kicking Jack in the face, knocking him out cold.

Awesome move.

Lila then saw a gap in the circle and took a run for it, running to the other end of the corridor, leading four of the agents away from the pack.

It took two seconds for me to knock Bill to the ground. But the other four were a bit harder. I suspected they were actually Guardians given their strength; they were almost an even match for me.

It made me wonder why none of them were using their abilities. Was it because they didn't want to expose themselves, or was it because they needed us alive? Or at least me alive, while I was throwing one of the agents into a stack of tables, I glanced across to see Lila being attacked by two Fire Guardians, with glowing red hands, they threw fireballs at her as she ran. I was distracted, and the other agent took advantage of that as he tackled me to the ground.

As I fought to get them off me, I kept looking back at Lila. She had managed to get a hold of some plant seeds and made exploding pollen bombs, causing the Fire Guardians to be incapacitated. As they coughed and spluttered, Lila ran through the pollen cloud and kicked all four agents to the ground using her sweet ninja skills.

I, on the other hand, was not as lucky as the three agents left piled on me to hold me down; there was no way I was getting out of this one.

But Lila was determined as she ran towards them screaming and with both arms out. She summersaulted over the agents piled on me and at full speed, grabbing the backs of two of the agents' jacket and pulling them into the air with her and sending them flying into a wall as she landed.

The last agent was taken by surprise, and she sidekicked him in the face.

Damn! Do not tick this ninja girl off!

Lila helped me to my feet as I whispered to her sarcastically, "What happened to not using superpowers?"

Lila grabbed my hand again and started running and said, "You and I both know if I'm not fired, we've either been arrested or we're dead," as she pointed to six more agents running into the corridor, rudely pushing past the store patron.

"How many of these guys are there?" Lila shouted sarcastically as we ran into a pet shop to hide.

We hid behind the counter of the pet shop trying to catch our breath and think.

Lila peeked over the countertop to keep watch.

"I don't think they saw us." She sighed in relief. Every now and then the actual shopping centre security would walk through the corridor helping store patrons to the exit and the agents would get distracted. That bought us more time to think of a plan.

"We can't keep hiding here. We need a plan," Lila said softly.

I looked around at the store pets and sparked an idea as I asked, "Where's the closest exit?"

Lila thought for a quick moment. "Probably Big W at the loading docks, it's just across from the food court," she said, confused and eager to hear my idea.

I looked at Lila and smiled. "That's perfect, they probably don't have enough agents to cover the loading docks."

I cautiously looked up over the counter to see four agents in the corridor looking in each of the shops. "Do you have any ID?" I asked Lila.

She nodded and handed me her wallet. I quickly grabbed the wallet and slid under one of the display cabinets, saying, "I don't think they know who you are yet, so if we get caught, let's not make it easy for them."

Lila nodded in agreement as she watched me looking around at the animal cages. I whispered to Lila the plan to make sure she was in agreement. And on three, we ran at full speed to open all of the bird cages.

I looked at the birds and pointed to the four agents in the corridor and pleaded with the birds, "Please help us. We're in danger!" I shouted. "There's men in suits wanting to kill us!"

At that moment, all the birds flew out of their cages and started to attack the agents. That was our moment to run.

We ran back into the food court, where Bill and Jack had recovered, along with their friends. They rushed to intercept us, and by this stage, Bill looked really ticked off. They tried to block the corridor spreading out ready to attack.

I let go of Lila's hand ready to attack, when she said, "Wait, I have a plan." She caught the attention of some of the birds and gave them some open seed packets pointing to the food court. As the birds flew around the food court, the seeds dropped from the torn open packet. I looked back to see Lila's eyes glowing green and watched as the seeds sprouted, growing quickly into shrubs and flowers and trees. It was amazing. There were vines growing from the rafters grabbing hold of the agents as they tried to escape.

The plants made a clear path and a big-enough distraction for Lila and I to run into Big W, but we were intercepted by Jack and Bill. Jack ran at full speed tackling Lila to the ground as Bill ran up and kicked the back of my legs as I fell to the ground and watched Lila writhe in pain holding her ribs. The tackle must have broken her rib again.

I kicked Bill backwards into a clothing rack, knocking him out cold. Which just left Jack standing over Lila. Jack looked back at me and snickered, "Looks like you got yourself a little nature freak," he chuckled, "the bosses are going to just love you . . . but just to make sure you stay distracted . . . I'm going to give you something else to focus on . . ."

I watched as he moved at full speed with his hands glowing a fiery red and pressing down onto Lila's stomach and arms burning through her clothes and leaving blistering burns in the shape of his hand on her skin.

As I heard Lila scream, I was filled with rage as I ran at full speed, grabbing Jack's arm and spinning him around in the air and back out of the store. By the time he landed, I had moved at full speed picking Lila up and running out of the store's back loading dock. I kept running away from the shopping centre down the street and into one of the housing estate alleys. I placed Lila down carefully and lifted what was left of her shirt to see the large bruise on her rib cage again and two blistering burns on her arm and stomach. I looked at the wound not knowing how to respond.

"Lila, I'm so sorry . . .," I said but was quickly stopped by Lila pressing her hand on my mouth.

"Alex . . .," she gasped, "we made a deal . . . to both protect each other . . . It was my choice to help you . . . so stop blaming yourself," she said demandingly.

I didn't want to argue with her given her condition, so I just nodded even though I knew this was all my fault.

She then smiled at me and pointed out that I also didn't look too crash hot. Pointing at my bruised eye and cut lip, grazed arm, and I didn't want to mention the giant pulsating bruise I could feel on my shoulder blade.

I guess all I could do was thank her for saving my life, but before I got the opportunity, a white sedan pulled up onto the nature strip stopping behind me, the driver quickly shot both of us with tranquilizer darts. Because we were both too weak to fight, we fell to the ground and watched disoriented as a group of men dressed all in black picked us up and locked us in the boot with handcuffs on.

It was pitch-black as I held Lila's hand and said, "I'm sorry, Lila."

CHAPTER 11

THE DEAL OF YOUR LIFE

Journal entry by Lila Winters

Alex and I were out cold for a long time. They'd dragged us into a big office, gently placing me on the couch, still pretending to be asleep. Alex was thrown on the floor next to the desk then handcuffed to a chair.

As if for some reason they thought a chair would stop a Guardian.

The office door slammed open as a woman storms in. She looked like she was barely 22 years old and dressed as if she owned the place, with her long wavy blond hair tied up in a bun. She glared at Alex and, in a furious huff, demanded to the security guards to "Get out!"

Her security guards scampered out of the room, closing the door behind them.

Alex awoke to see the woman in front of him. He took a moment, then quickly looked around the room in panic to see me still unconscious—or so he thought—and handcuffed on the couch.

He could see I wasn't in good shape, my broken ribs had worsened and bruised, and the burns had started to blister and weep.

The woman stood over Alex to sit at her desk and watched Alex pull himself up to sit on the chair he was handcuffed to.

"You're quite a difficult man to get a hold of, Mr. Woods," she said, tapping her long fingernails on the desk. "I noticed you 'redecorated' the Hills shopping centre," she said sarcastically, turning on the television to the news report of the shopping centre bomb threat.

"The police were baffled at the sight of it, they didn't even hear an explosion, worried it could be a new type of weapon. But what's more interesting is that the police can't seem to find any evidence of explosive devices, or even the persons responsible . . . isn't that interesting?" the woman said, looking back at Alex sarcastically.

Alex didn't flinch, didn't even look at the news report, he just stared at the woman and spoke quietly asking, "What do you want from me?"

The woman stopped tapping her nails on the desk and introduced herself. "Alex . . . my name is Jessica . . . tell me if that rings any bells for you . . ." She paused and waited for Alex to respond, but then continued, "No? Okay . . . Alex, I want information from you . . . and I'm willing to do just about anything to get it," she said, placing a Glock 36 on the desk in front of her.

Alex rebutted, claiming, "I don't know anything."

But Jessica got up and stood next to Alex to whisper in his ear, "You're lying."

She walked over to the couch to get a better look at me, then said, "First question . . . who is this?" she asked, pointing to me.

Alex didn't look back and casually responded, "She's no one."

Again, Jessica didn't believe him. "Then why is she helping you?" she asked.

Alex sighed. "She's a friend. I was having lunch with her at the food court when we were told to calmly leave the building. Like I told you, I don't know anything. We were just in the wrong place at the wrong time."

Jessica smiled, completely disregarding what Alex said. She knew it was a lie. "So you do know her . . . well, that changes things . . . if you're not going to give me the answers I want, then I'm sure I'll get all I need from your—what was it you called her?—friend" she said smugly.

She then smirked back at Alex and indicated to the guards waiting outside. The guards walked into the room and injected Alex with a needle, causing him to be very relaxed and calm. He tried to protest, mumbling, "No!" and, "She doesn't know anything," as he was dragged out of the room. "Please," Alex mumbled, "please . . . let her go."

Jessica grabbed a small vial of smelling salts from her desk and waved it under my nose. I opened my eyes and stared at her as she smiled back and chuckled, "I knew you weren't sleeping," then knelt down to inspect my wound, sarcastically saying, "That looks bad . . . you should see a doctor."

She continued to play the nice act, sitting down on the couch next to me and offering me a glass of water.

"Alex is fine," she said, "I just wanted to talk."

I denied the drink and continued to stare at her in silence.

She eventually gave up and walked back to her desk.

I stood up and followed her, knowing I was still handcuffed. I sat down in the chair Alex was sitting in.

I looked around the office and saw the news clipping of the shopping centre incident on replay, showing the interior of the shopping centre covered in trees and flowers and shrubs.

"What do you want from us?" I asked, almost scared of the answer. Deep down I was hoping this whole thing was just a test orchestrated by Bluey or someone in a police station and they just want to ask some questions.

But my optimism had a few flaws to it.

Jessica looked back at the news and commented, "It looks like a jungle in there . . . I was wondering if you could tell me what really happened at the shopping centre?" She grinned back at me, waiting for the truth.

I glanced outside to see the guards step out of the elevator down the hall and my optimism disappeared. "Why don't you ask one of your henchmen? They should know first-hand!"

Jessica stood up and disappointedly sighed. "Unfortunately, the men in the shopping centre weren't mine," she remarked, "And if we knew where those men were, you wouldn't be here."

"So you weren't there to capture Alex?" I asked.

Jessica quickly interrupted, "Oh yes, we were there for Alex. We've been watching Alex for some time now, but my men lost track of him for a while—until they spotted him at a bakery store in your shopping centre. But by the time my men arrived at the shopping centre, the place was swarming with police. One of my men spotted Alex holding hands with you in the shopping centre, so we know you're involved with him."

I lied. "I don't know anything," I said timidly.

Jessica walked to the office window and stared at her pale reflection in the glass, sighing again. "I don't have time for this," she huffed then said, "Okay . . . I'll tell you what I know then . . . I know that Alex doesn't possess the type of power to cause something like this," Jessica said, pointing to the news report. "And I know you are not one of his usual friends."

I stood up and rebutted, glaring at her, "And what . . . you are his friend?"

Jessica walked back over and stood in front of me, glancing down at my handcuffs, probably in the attempt to intimidate and remind me of where I am, as she answered, "No, I am most certainly not his friend, however, I do know one of his friends . . . and she's now missing . . . Her name is Adela . . ."

I took a step back in surprise. Jessica could tell I knew something. "You know her, don't you?" she questioned.

I shook my head and said nothing.

"That's why you're here," she explained, "I believe Alex knows where she is . . . I was hoping he would lead me to her, but instead he led me to you. So I'm asking you nicely. Where is she?"

I looked out at the guards waiting at the door and then looked at my handcuffs. "If this is your version of nicely, I'm curious what your 'not nice' version would be," I commented and asked, "Why are so desperate to know?"

Jessica hesitated to answer and stared back out the window teary-eyed as she replied, "She's my sister . . . my father has trusted me to find her . . . And I will do anything to get her back."

Gotcha!

At that moment, I had to come up with a plan. But I had to stall; I glanced at a family photo on the desk and then knew what I had to do.

I stood behind Jessica and said in an apologetic yet defiant voice, "I'm sorry . . . but I can't and won't help you."

Jessica snapped turning to me and slapped me so hard I fell to the ground. She yelled to the guards as she opened the office door, "Do what you have to, if she still doesn't cooperate, throw her back in the holding room!"

That's the last thing I remember of that incident, then next thing I knew, I was lying on the floor of the holding room, with Alex gently cleaning the blood off my face. I was sore all over and I struggled to talk with a swollen bloodied lip looking up at Alex. I had clearly taken a beating, but I wasn't confident I had said nothing, seeing how I ended up here.

Alex brushed the hair off my face, whispering, "It's okay, Lila, I got you."

I smiled up at Alex as he wiped the blood from my lips.

This day was not going so well for me, but seeing Alex safe, for some reason, made me feel happy.

"Alex," I said with a feeble raspy voice.

He interrupted me, saying, "Lila, I am so sorry. This is all my fault." He looked as if he had been crying. "If I weren't there at the shopping centre, you wouldn't be here. I was st—"

I stopped him talking by putting my hand over his mouth again. "Alex," I whispered, "shut up . . . I have a plan."

Alex was shocked. "You have a plan. You look like crap, yet you have a plan."

I slowly stood to my feet and adjusted what's left of my burnt shirt. "I know it may not look good, but getting beaten was part of the plan."

Alex started to get angry. "Are you out of your mind? You have three broken ribs and yet you wanted to get beat up."

I snapped at Alex, "Alex, you were the one who broke into my house a few weeks ago, asking for my help. And today I took a risk trying to help you. So if you don't like my plan and you don't want my—"

Alex stopped me from talking by putting his hand over my mouth. He totally stole my move. He said, "I'm sorry . . . and thank you . . . I'm just freaking out a little bit. This is my first time being kidnapped."

He hesitantly pulled his hand away and stepped back and sighed.

I was still upset, and I admit I was freaking out as well, but I was definitely not going to let Alex know that. I took a look around the room and realised we were in an empty hotel room. I peered out a small window in the bathroom to get a look at where we were and that's when I started to freak out.

Shocked, I looked back at Alex and blurted, "Holy mother . . . That's the Sydney Harbour Bridge . . . We're not in Melbourne anymore . . . We are nowhere near home . . . we are . . ."

I took a moment to compose myself with some calming breaths.

Realising we weren't in Melbourne hindered my backup plan, which was to run, but it didn't interfere with my original plan, and that was to negotiate. The one good lesson I learnt from the General was that the enemy will only keep you alive if you have something they want. And I am very confident I have something they want.

I smiled at Alex and reassured him, saying, "We can do this, just do not leave my side. And no matter what, just trust me . . . okay?"

He nodded his head, and I took that as cue to knock on the door loudly and repeatedly.

I eventually got the attention of the guards and Jessica, who walked in and ushered me back away from the door.

Jessica then asked, "I'm going to assume you've finally come to your senses and tell me where my sister is."

"Actually no, I have no plans to help you at all," I replied, grinning.

I was hoping to piss her off and it worked. She looked at the guards and nodded her head. The guards began to beat the crap out of me again. This time I fought back. Alex took one guard, and I took the other. I pinned my guard to the wall and held him there with one hand as I looked back at Jessica and smiled, saying, "I will however negotiate with your father, Maxwell Eden, in the release of me . . . and my friend."

Jessica stammered as she asked, "How did you—"

She clearly was not fully aware of what Alex and I were, so I interrupted before she could finish her question. "I recognised your father from one of the photos in your office, and since I woke up in a hotel room, it's kind of a dead giveaway. And because you were just so rude to me and my friend Alex . . . we have decided that we will only talk to Mr. Eden himself about the information we have on your sister."

Jessica started to get angry, pulling out her gun and threatening to shoot me.

"You could do that . . .," I said smugly, "But I guarantee you will miss. At which point I would just beat the crap out of you and walk out of this hotel with no remorse." I grinned and continued my threat. "I'm sure you'd rather your other hotel guest not ask questions about a bruised and bloodied female leaving your five-star hotel in panic after hearing gunshots as well . . . But this is totally your choice," I said confidently, waiting for her answer.

Alex looked at me confused while he was pinning the other guard on the floor.

While Jessica took a moment and responded, "You wouldn't make it to the lobby," trying to call my bluff.

I smiled and said sternly as I squeezed the guard's throat, "Try me."

Jessica looked at her two guards struggling to break free and conceded, putting her gun back in her holster.

"All right," she said, "I'll take you to see my father. Just put them down."

I looked back at Alex and nodded. We both let go of the guards and took a step back as they tried to compose themselves.

Jessica rolled her eyes then snidely demanded we follow her down the hall and into the elevator.

The guards hesitantly followed us, staying a good kicking distance away.

We walked into a ridiculously oversized office at what looked to be the very top floor of the hotel that overlooked the city of Sydney.

And yes, seeing the Sydney Opera House made me panic a little. We were a long way from home.

Maxwell Eden was standing on the balcony talking on the phone when he saw Jessica waiting in his office with Alex and I standing behind her. The smile on his face disappeared as he hung up from his phone call and walked back into the office, closing the balcony door. Maxwell looked past me and glared. It almost looked like the death stare at the guards as they very quickly hustled back out of the office, closing the door behind them. Again.

Jessica then walked around the desk to kiss her father on the cheek. "Hi, Daddy . . .," she said as she began to explain the situation to Maxwell in a whispered voice.

Alex and I could hear all of it, but we stayed quiet. I looked over to Alex and smiled. I could tell he was nervous and freaking out on the inside.

"Alex," Maxwell spoke, breaking the tension, "Jessica tells me you know where my daughter is."

Alex remained quiet and shook his head. I stepped in front of Alex to get Maxwell's attention. "We don't know where your daughter is, which is exactly what we told your other daughter." I casually smiled back at Jessica.

Maxwell didn't seem happy, looking more confused as he questioned, "So instead you beat my staff—"

I interrupted defensively, "They started it."

Jessica was about to rebuke my statement, but Maxwell stopped her by continuing his question. "You beat up my staff . . . by retaliation. But you clearly had the upper hand, otherwise you wouldn't be in my office. . . So if you don't have any information about the location of my daughter, then what the hell are you doing in my office? And why didn't you take the opportunity to leave when you had the chance?"

I stood tall and confident even though it hurt to speak as I said, "I'm here to offer our assistance in finding your daughter."

Jessica burst out laughing as both Maxwell and Alex stared at me gobsmacked at my offer.

But I stood firm and waited for Maxwell's response.

He was intrigued when he realised my offer was sincere. "My dear . . . what makes you think you have the skills to find my daughter?" he asked.

I was reluctant at first, but I was confident that if I confirmed what I was, then Mr. Eden would be more inclined to take my deal.

So I smirked and took a quick breath, saying, "For starters . . . growing up, my father taught me to be a damn good tracker when we went hunting . . . so there's that skill. And I also have other skills similar to Alex."

Maxwell was shocked by my comment and looked back at Jessica as if to get confirmation from her, but Jessica looked up at me in disbelief and shrugged her shoulders in ignorance.

I continued to talk through all of it as I confessed, "I was the one responsible for the shopping centre mishap."

Alex quickly grabbed my arm and pulled me to the back of the office. "Lila, what are you doing?" he said sternly.

I responded in a calm tone, "I am telling them what we know."

Alex sighed, fearing what would happen next. I held Alex's hand and asked, "You still trust me, right?"

Alex took a moment and nodded, still unconvinced; he allowed me to walk back to the desk to continue the conversation, but he stayed very closely behind me. Just in case.

I explained to Maxwell what had happened in the shopping centre and how I suspected the men who attempted to take Alex were the same men who took Adela. And if those men didn't belong to Maxwell, then that was our first clue.

I ended the conversation with a proposal to Maxwell. "So here's my deal . . . You are going to fly us back home to Melbourne and preferably give us a change of clothes and medical attention. This should give you enough time to think about my offer and maybe do a little research as well. And hopefully we can come to some sort of arrangement."

Maxwell was cautious as he asked, "How do we know we can trust you?"

I casually reminded him, "First off . . . you were the ones who abducted us. And second . . . I'm pretty sure the trust needs to go both ways for this to work. So I guess we'll need to work on that."

I held out my hand to Maxwell ready to make a deal, saying, "I'm willing if you are."

Maxwell took a moment and I watched as Jessica shook her head in disapproval as Maxwell shook my hand, agreeing to the deal.

A sigh of relief was hidden beneath my overconfident composure.

CHAPTER 12

WHAT HAPPENS
WHEN YOU FAIL?

Journal entry by Adela Eden

I was starting to feel much better, and I was released from the hospital after my horrible accident. They even let me have my old job back working for Mr. Connors.

I was excited to go on my first mission back in the field, but they didn't want to push my recovery, so they put me on bodyguard duties.

I was to accompany and observe Agent Blair as she interrogated two of the agents who had failed their previous mission to acquire a new target suspected of being a terrorist.

We had flown to Melbourne to an old shipping warehouse near the docks on the Yarra River. Agent Blair walked into the warehouse and into one of the storage containers, and as she did, she created a fireball in her hand and sighing in disappointment as she walked up to the first agent. He was a Fire Guardian as well.

According to the reports, he and his partner were the first to apprehend the target but instead lost him and created a media frenzy instead.

Mr. Connors was definitely not happy to hear those results. Both agents were covered in bruises; they had been beaten as punishment for failing.

"I'm disappointed, boys," Agent Blair snarled as she played with the fireball in her hand. "I gave you one simple assignment—and you failed!" she shouted, and as she lost her temper, she threw the fireball at the feet of the first agents. "And to make things real good . . .," she said sarcastically, "the whole world knows you failed." Agent Blair held her phone up showing the media spread of the shopping centre.

The first agent tried to stand and bear his pain as he attempted to explain. Speaking through his bloodied lips, he exclaimed, "We were taken by surprise. He was with another Guardian."

Agent Blair looked at the other agents in shock and disbelief. "That's impossible . . .," she said, "All of the other Guardians are in our . . . control, working for us."

She created another fireball in her hands and prepared to throw the fireball at the agents. "You must be mistaken," she said.

The second agent screamed out in panic, "It's not a mistake! She was a Nature Guardian, and worse, she's a trained fighter. She clearly knew what she was doing. That's why we lost them."

Agent Blair took a moment and quenched the fireball in her hand as she stormed out of the storage container. She stopped outside the door of the storage container as she received a text message reading, "Return."

Agent Blair lost her temper as a blazing fireball appeared in her hand. She screamed in rage, throwing the fireball back into the storage container, engulfing the container in flames. She then stormed off commanding me and her other bodyguards to follow as she left the warehouse and got into a waiting car.

CHAPTER 13

HONEY, I CAN EXPLAIN!

Journal entry by Lila Winters

With Mr. Eden in an agreeable mood, he had organised his private plane to take us back home to Melbourne.

Alex and I sat on the plane and looked out the window as the wings of the plane brushed over the clouds. We were both struggling to fully come to terms with what had just happened.

Shocked and covered in bruises, I glanced at Alex and concluded there was no hiding the fact that he had been in a fight. And there was no doubt I looked worse as we used their first-aid kit to clean ourselves up.

We had a team of Mr. Eden's security guards accompanying us back to the house. Probably to ensure I don't back out of our deal or tell the authorities of Mr. Eden's questionable activities. I stared back out the window nervously, tapping my foot on the ground.

"Lila, are you okay?" Alex whispered, placing his hand on my knee to stop my foot tapping after he finished applying the burn cream on me.

I was completely oblivious to his question still staring out the window. He snapped his fingers in front of my face and called my name again. Finally getting my attention, he asked again, "Are you okay? You look like you're miles away."

I sighed and nursed some of the bruises as I replied, "Thousands actually, I was thinking about Matt. And how I'm going to explain why I didn't come home last night."

Alex didn't know how to help with my conundrum and shrugged his shoulders.

"Are you sure you know what you're doing?" Alex asked quietly, glancing subtly back to the team of security guards, babysitting us.

"Honestly, I'm making this up as I go. But at least I got us on a plane home," I responded, awkwardly smiling at Alex, hoping he would be satisfied with the answer.

I got the feeling he wasn't, as he slouched back in his chair and stared out the window in silence.

One of the security guards walked out of the cockpit and stood next to my chair. "Hello, Miss Winters," he croaked, clearing his throat. "I just wanted to introduce myself. My name is Chase, head of Maxwell's personal security."

But we had already met before. I recognised his beach blond hair and surfer tan from the interrogation room. He was pretty strong for a human, probably no older than me, and for him to be head of security in his mid-twenties was a remarkable achievement.

I stood up to greet him properly, shook his hand, and said, "Nice to meet you properly . . . if I'm not mistaken, I believe we've already met."

He looked uncomfortable as he confessed, "Yes, I was the one who, err—"

I interrupted to finish his sentence, "Shoved me in the back of a car." I could tell by his cringing reaction that I was right.

But I had to know. "Were you the one who knocked me out in the interrogation?" I asked, pointing to a large and very obvious bruise above my eye.

Chase didn't know what to say as he looked at Alex and back at me apologetically. Before Chase could say anything, I interrupted and stood closer to him. The other security guards became tense as they all stood ready to defend Chase.

I glanced and hesitantly said, "Before this gets too awkward, I just wanted to say, I understand . . . you were just doing your job."

Chase and Alex looked at me shocked and confused as I continued to explain, "I understand and I'm happy to put this behind us if you are . . . I also get this nagging feeling we're going to be working very closely together for a while. So it's probably better that we all start off with a clean slate . . . So let's start over." I reached out my hand to reintroduce myself. "Hi, I'm Lila . . . I'm a military brat who apparently has sweet ninja skills."

Chase nodded in agreement and chuckled a bit as he shook my hand. "It's nice to meet you, Lila," he responded with a smile. "Unfortunately I do not have sweet ninja skills, but I'm pretty talented with my fist."

I could see Alex in the corner of my eye. I could tell he wasn't happy and didn't believe I knew what I was doing.

Chase glanced at his security guards and gave the signal to stand down as he walked me to the back of the cabin to formally introduce the rest of the team.

Alex watched me and noticed I lingered holding the security guards' hands, and quickly realised that I was taking the opportunity to sense the nature of all the security guards, test if they were actually going to stick to their agreement. Sneaky, huh?

Chase interrupted before I could get to the last two security guards, saying, "Anyway, I originally just came out to tell you we will be landing soon. We have a car waiting for us at the airport. The plan is to drop you off at your car and then follow you to your home in a surveillance van. We'll keep our distance. If there is any trouble, you'll call us with this phone." He held up a new Samsung phone and handed it to me. "We are number 1 on speed dial. Are you okay with the plan so far?"

I nodded in agreement. "Great, just in time to face the music," I said not very confidently.

It wasn't too long after that before we were back at my car outside the shopping centre where I worked.

It was very late at night and the shopping centre had been closed for inspection and investigations, and there was a team of people in the shopping centre attempting to clean the mess of broken glass and overgrown plants. By that point, it looked like an indoor jungle.

Alex and I looked at each other as we quickly and quietly drove my car out of the parking lot and back home. As I pulled my car into the driveway, I noticed the three very obvious police cars sitting outside my house. I looked at Alex and asked sarcastically, "Well, how do I look?"

He laughed as he replied, "Terrible."

We both laughed as we got out of the car and walked through the door to be greeted by six police officers sitting in the lounge room with Matt.

Matt looked at me with teary eyes and hugged me so tightly. It was painful, and I had to pull away nursing the bruises.

"Honey, what happened to you? Where have you been?"

I saw the police sitting in the lounge room all looking at me and Alex waiting for the answer.

I felt terrible that I lied to Matt, but I knew I had to. The last thing I needed was the police getting involved, or Matt freaking out.

"We were trapped . . . in the shopping centre. I met Alex at the food court on my break. On our way back to work, we got caught in the commotion. Everything happened so fast and people were running, we hid in one of the food storage cupboards . . . of that, um . . . Chinese restaurant. And then we were trapped by some plants and a fallen stack of chairs," I said calmly.

"So you've been trapped this whole time?" Matt asked.

I nodded. "Yeah . . . we only just got out when they were cleaning."

One of the police officers, Dave, interrupted my story and asked, "We searched the whole shopping centre looking for anyone trapped, why couldn't we find you, were you calling out for help?"

Alex chimed in to answer that question, but he answered faking a raspy voice as if he had a sore throat. "I was, but I don't think I was much help."

Dave wasn't convinced. "What about Lila?"

"She got hit by the falling stack of chairs, she was out of it for a while," Alex indicated to the large bruise on my head.

Dave grunted as if that was an acceptable answer and continued his questions towards me. "Is there anything or anyone you saw that was out of the ordinary?"

I shook my head. "I'm sorry. I didn't see anything like that." I yawned and sighed. "I'm really sorry, Officer, but right now all I want to do is take a shower and go to bed. Is this all the questions you needed answered?"

Dave grunted again. "For now, but we should really take you to the hospital, you may have a concussion."

I quickly shook my head and said, "No!" louder than I expected. "I really don't like hospitals . . . if I need to, I'll see my doctor later today."

Looking at the lounge-room clock, I smiled at Dave, hinting to the ridiculous hour of the morning it was.

Dave and the other police officers began heading out the door to their cars, but Dave turned back and asked, "If you're feeling better later today, can you come down to the station? We will need you to make an official statement."

I sighed, reluctantly saying, "Sure, no worries."

Dave closed his notebook and smiled. "In the meantime, we'll pull the security footage from the centre. We struggled to get to the security room because of all the plants blocking the door. But it should be cleared up by now. Maybe you could look through it with us and see if you remember anything."

I smiled and said again reluctantly, "Sure, no worries." I closed the door as the officers drove away and took some deep breath in and out, trying not to panic.

I looked back at Alex and Matt both staring at me. "Um," I said to break the silence, "we should all try and get some rest before the kids wake up in a few hours."

I took that as my cue to walk up the stairs and into the bathroom. I closed the door and turned on the shower to use as cover as I made a phone call with the new phone.

I whispered as I spoke into the phone, "Chase, we have a problem. I need you to get all the security tapes from the shopping centre. You need to go now. The longer you wait, the more danger Alex and I will be in."

I quickly hung up the phone as I heard Matt walking up the stairs. I moved at full speed to shower and dress before Matt had entered the room. I opened the bathroom door just as he was about to knock.

"Matt," I said, pretending to be surprised. "Is everything okay?" I asked, heading over to the bed.

Matt turned and looked at me unconvinced of my calm demeanour. "I was just about to ask you that same question," he commented, helping me pull back the bed covers. "Are you sure you're okay?" he asked.

Yep, here comes the tricky part, I thought to myself, if I can't convince Matt that I'm okay, it's game over, he won't leave me alone for days. He'll take time off work and probably tell Alex to leave. Come on, Lila, put on your brave face and smile.

"I told you, I'm fine. I'm better than fine—I'm peachy," I said in a high-pitched slightly squeaky voice. Perhaps a little too perky.

Matt still wasn't convinced and continued his interrogation. "Did you want to tell me what really happened at the shopping centre? What was Alex doing there? And why were you with him at the food court?" he asked, sounding slightly territorial.

I walked to the other side of the bed to stand in front of Matt and held his hands. "Sweetie," I said in my cute voice, "I don't even know what happened at the shopping centre. Everything still seems like a blur. And as for Alex, you're going to have to ask him. I ran into him at the food court when I was on my break," I explained.

Matt gently ran his fingers around a large bruise on the back of my neck. I guess I didn't realise how bad the bruises were. "You should put some ice on that," Matt suggested as he kissed my cheek. I nodded in agreement as Matt climbed onto the bed.

As I walked downstairs, I did my best to remain smiling. I knew Matt wasn't convinced. But I wasn't going to rock the boat.

I walked into the kitchen where Alex greeted me with an icepack. We both glanced at the back door as we heard Bluey pecking at the window. He looked flustered and upset.

As Alex opened the door for him, Bluey shouted, "Where have you been? I've been looking all over Melbourne for you."

Alex snickered as he closed the back door. "It would help if we were actually in Melbourne," he replied.

Bluey looked at Alex and me, confused.

I shrugged my shoulder and smiled as I iced my bruises. I really wasn't in the mood to explain myself again.

Alex sat down at the table next to me. "Bluey, I need you to get me any info you have on Maxwell Eden," Alex asked.

Bluey became even more confused and asked, "Maxwell Eden? For what reason?"

Alex glanced at me as he answered, "He's a . . . new friend. And I want to know if we can trust him or not."

I interrupted to add my own request. "I also need you to get the dirt on his daughters as well."

As Alex and I continued to talk, we both heard the footsteps of Matt as he crept down onto the stairs to listen in. He couldn't hear much, but I was pretty sure he heard Alex when he asked about Matt and if he believed my story. After that, we reduced our speaking to a low whisper so all he would have heard was mumbling, except for me saying, "If he asks me, I'll tell him the truth, I'm done hiding this from him."

I glanced back inside to see Matt's shadow disappear from the stairwell. Looked like he didn't want to know after all.

Journal entry insert by Matt Winters

I woke up to an empty bed the next morning. I got up and readied for work and sighed as I walked past the guest bedroom to see Alex asleep on the bed.

I think I'm still trying to figure out how I feel knowing that Lila would lie to me, but I'm slowly convincing myself that whatever it is, it's for a good reason. I think.

I went in to wake Danny and Ruby and heard Lila training in the backyard with the new . . . new Hector I bought after the last one was destroyed by Alex.

I raced downstairs and quickly grabbed my breakfast and sat outside to watch her. She was amazing in the way she moved, precise and controlled. I applauded as she high-kicked Hector in the head as she cartwheeled through the garden towards me. She clearly had no intention of feeling the pain of her injuries today.

She kissed me good morning as she took a bite of my toast. "I take it you couldn't sleep," I said as I brushed the hair from her sweaty forehead. I glanced up at the almost-healed cut above her eye and a burn mark on her arm healing in the shape of a hand—that's not at all suspicious.

I just smiled and played ignorant, asking, "Should you be exercising . . . in your condition?" gesturing to her recently broken ribs.

Lila just started punching new Hector gently and answered, trying to be cute, "You know me—rain, hail, or shine—ever since I was little."

I sighed and rolled my eyes. "Lila, the General's not going to know if you take a few days off from training. I mean, for all we know, he's not even in the country," I said defensively.

For some reason, something I said got to her. She agreed to stop training for a few days, and here's the kicker: she told me I was right.

Yep, she definitely felt guilty about something. I was just waiting for the right time to ask her—if I really did want to ask her. She did have me wondering—what if the truth was worse than the lie?

Original journal entry continued by Lila Winters

Matt had left for work, already taking Danny and Ruby to day care and kindly agreeing to pick them up this afternoon. I told him I would be busy at the police station, but that was a complete lie.

The front doorbell rang as I walked through the house, but before I could open the door, Alex stopped me and opened it instead, looking around the front yard. You could tell he was nervous.

He saw a small envelope sitting on the welcome mat with my last name on it, quickly grabbing it and closing the door.

"Would you relax," I said, slightly disgruntled, "It was just Chase and his men. I asked him to drop off the security footage from yesterday . . . I thought while I'm out, you can stay home, out of trouble, and look for anything that might help us to figure out who else tried to abduct us."

Alex opened the envelope to find a USB and a note, saying, "The only copy," then had that moment of realisation and asked, "Wait, where are you going?"

By that stage, I had already moved at full speed upstairs, gotten dressed, and grabbed my keys and handbag, and I mumbled as I walked out the door, answering, "To lie our way out of trouble."

I didn't feel too good about lying to the police and my family and especially my husband, but I didn't know if they'd even believe the truth if I told them.

CHAPTER 14

PLANS CHANGED

Journal entry by Terrence Connors

My name is Terrence Connors. I have been placed in charge of hunting down every last Guardian. I had almost finished my mission until this little hiccup happened. I was meditating on the sandbank of a tropical island (in a classified location) listening to the water when one of my agents—Blair—walked up and stood behind me, nervous to deliver more bad news.

I spoke softly while still meditating, "I can hear your heart beating, Blair. It's racing as if you were scared," I said, standing to address her properly. "What reason do you have to be scared?" I asked.

Blair couldn't find the words. She was so scared. "The agents I sent failed to get the target," she said, looking down at the ground as she started inching away from me.

"Hmm." I nodded, pretending to be understanding. "I can see now why you're scared," I said calmingly.

Blair tried to regain her confidence and rebutted, "My men did report back some news you might be interested in. The reason why they failed was because of another Guardian protecting him . . . a Nature Guardian," she said confidently.

I was stunned as Blair shared her news but then looked out at the ocean as I received the text message I always dreaded, then spoke firmly to her, "Unfortunately, Blair, you still failed . . . and the board doesn't like failures," I whispered.

I sighed and shook my head as I walked off the beach and didn't look back as a spiral of tree roots rose up from the ground wrapping around Blair. She screamed in fear as the tree roots encased her in a cocoon and disappeared back into the ground.

CHAPTER 15

THE HUNT

Journal entry by Lila Winters

Alex and I were on our way to the Eden Hotel.

I had become very distracted as I drove there, glancing in the rear-view mirror at the van following us. I knew it was Chase and our new "friends," but I just couldn't shake that gut-churning frustration.

Alex snapped his fingers in front of my face to try and get my attention. He was attempting to tell me what he had found in the security footage before I zoned out.

"Hey," he snapped, concerned, and asked, "Are you okay?"

Again, that irritating question that people kept asking me. It was starting to get to me. And honestly, I was getting tired of lying to people. What I wanted to say was no, I was not okay. In the past thirty-six hours, I had been abducted and beaten, destroyed the place I work in, was flown to Sydney and back, interrogated by some crazy chick, her father, my husband, and the police. And now I think that the police suspect me for the shopping centre disaster. Which was completely true. And did I mention I've only had six hours' sleep—and that was in Sydney. But I didn't say that—any of that. Instead I just smiled and mumbled, "I'm fine."

As we pulled into the Melbourne's Eden Hotel's car park, Alex's mood quickly changed and his heart started beating faster. He was scared, and to be honest, so was I.

What if I had made too bold of a promise and can't find Mr. Eden's daughter? What if he actually does kill us?

Alex stayed close as we entered Mr. Eden's office. He was waiting for us, sitting at his gigantically oversized desk staring out the window at the city as he said, "Ms Winters, I hope your flight home went well."

I nodded and said thank you. He then turned and began walking closer to me, eagerly hoping for some news. "So do you have anything for me?" he asked.

Alex clenched his fist and stood protectively next to me, causing Mr Eden to stop and look at Alex cautiously.

I glanced back to see Chase and his men step closer as well.

The room began to feel very tense.

"Yes, Mr. Eden," I said, trying to avoid an incident, "and I even have a plan."

I sat down at the desk and pulled out my laptop, inviting Chase to come sit with me (as a show of good faith). Chase respected my attempts to work as a team. As I explained what we had found in the security footage from the shopping centre, I showed Chase a picture of the van the men in suits had arrived in, saying, "I called in a favour with a one of my old army cadets and he found out that the car was owned by a delivery company that had gone out of business a few months ago. They operated out of a warehouse near the docks called Pack 'n' Send."

Mr. Eden got excited and interrupted me before I could tell him my plan and said, "This is great, I'll have my men check it out." He nodded at Chase, giving him the signal to leave when I intercepted and stood in front of Chase, stopping him.

"Now just wait," I snapped, "Mr Eden, if you want my help, you get all of my help, not part of it. I told you I had a plan, that plan includes both of us . . . or I could just not tell you that the last person who was sent to investigate this delivery company was Adela Eden."

That piece of information got both Chase's and Mr. Eden's attention. I looked over at Alex briefly and then back to Mr. Eden. "As I said, we work together on this . . . I'm not interested in losing any more valuable men on this . . ." I looked back addressing Chase and asked, "Are you?"

Chase sat back down at the desk and looked back at Mr. Eden. Mr. Eden then sighed and nodded his head reluctantly. "Okay, Lila, what's your plan?"

We spent an hour working with Chase and his men explaining our plan. By the end, we were all confident, including Alex, about the plan. But there were a few minor details that needed to be addressed. "Mr. Eden . . .," I said a little too excitedly.

He interrupted me, insisting that from now on I call him Max. It felt weird, but I agreed and said, "Okay . . . Max."

This was beginning to remind me of the war games I played with my cadet mates as a teenager.

"Before we go, we're going to need some gear—" I paused and looked at Alex and his long hair, then looked at my reflection at my very bright purple hair and said reluctantly— "and a hairdresser."

Max agreed and walked us down into the shopping complex on the ground floor of his hotel. He led us in to the hairdresser's and said, "Anything you need, Chase will organise. Just say the word and it will be done."

I nodded looking back at Alex who was walking into the hairdresser behind me. I got the feeling as we walked closer to the hairdresser that Alex wasn't too keen on getting a haircut.

While Alex got his hair cut, I changed my hair colour and sent Chase to get a list of clothing items we needed.

It took Chase a bit of time, but he somehow managed to find every item on the list.

As I walked out of the change room, Alex and I both looked shocked at the sight of each other. We almost didn't recognise ourselves. I now had long brown hair, and Alex, wow, he had the prince charming haircut and it looked amazing.

"Wow," he said, staring at my hair. "You look completely different."

I smiled and responded, "So do you . . . hopefully this change will help us not to stand out as much," I said, checking out my new hair colour in the mirror thinking to myself I could make this work.

Alex just chuckled, saying, "It's impossible for you not to stand out . . . you'll always look amazing." When Alex realised what he said, he started to blush and looked around to find a distraction. "Chase, what do you think?" he asked.

Chase looked at me and smiled, saying, "He's right . . . you look really hot. And if you weren't married, I'd be asking you to dinner by now."

Smooth line. I thanked them both for their compliments, but I was quickly distracted. Across the hall in a jewellery store display case, I saw a small dagger in the shape of a medieval sword.

The detailing of the handle with the embossed leaves and vines had me entranced. It was beautiful. Chase saw my amazement and awe of the blade and grinned as he went in and bought it for me.

As he handed it to me, he said, "Never pictured you for the gun type."

I was so speechless and happy that I hugged him, a little too tightly as he gasped, wheezing, "Breakable . . . I'm breakable."

I quickly let go hearing Alex chuckle to himself.

Looked like Matt wasn't the only territorial man in my life. To be fair, it hadn't been that long since Chase had been my interrogator and was beating the crap out of me.

Anyway, back to the dagger.

I went outside and stood in the garden. "One final touch," I said smirking, looking back at Alex and Chase. I placed my hand on the ground as my eyes glowed green. And I watched green vines slowly grow up from the garden bed and wrap around my new boots; the vine wove itself through the leather creating a beautiful pattern and a hidden holster for my new dagger.

"Now they're perfect," I said, walking back into the hotel.

Chase was in shock at what he just watched, stuttering, "Did . . . did you just do that?"

Alex and I smiled and said, "Wait 'til you see what else we can do."

He looked up at Alex fearfully. "You can do that too?" he asked.

Alex chuckled. "No . . . I can just talk to animals and mimic their abilities."

Chase started to look a bit nauseous as he walked with us and uttered the words, "Oh . . . just," before he fainted, falling to the ground. But before he hit the floor, both Alex and I caught him and laughed as we carried Chase back into the elevator.

As we walked back up into Max's office still carrying Chase between us, Jessica Eden was waiting for us with her team of security guards. We clearly gave them the wrong impression as we held up their unconscious head of security.

"What did you do to him!" Jessica shouted. The rest of the security guards looked like they were ready to pounce on us.

"Hold up, guys . . . Chill, he just fainted," Alex said, trying to ease the tension.

While Alex had them distracted, I grabbed out a seed from my new belt and grew a flower behind my back. I pulled the flower out in front of Chase and waved it under his nose. My eyes glowed as a little bit of pollen was sprayed up Chase's nose.

He quickly woke and started shouting, "God, that stinks . . . what is that!" He then sneezed and sneezed and sneezed some more.

I laughed and answered, "That is a Lysichiton . . . also known as a skunk cabbage."

Chase looked up at the flower and then at me, still in shock from what he saw. "That smells horrible," he said, still sneezing and wiping his nose.

Alex jokingly laughed, patting Chase on the back, and asked, "You all right, mate?"

Alex then looked back at me and whispered, "Little overboard with the pollen maybe."

I snapped back in a whisper, "Hey, I'm new at this . . . possibly a bit of revenge too."

Chase took a moment to compose himself then stood in the middle of the room and explained our plan with the rest of his security team. Jessica looked like she wasn't overly happy with the plan, as she glared at me and Alex from across the room.

While Chase's team was prepping to leave, I took the opportunity to call Matt and let him know I would be late home. The phone conversation went surprisingly well, and Matt didn't ask any questions. He just said, "Okay," and, "Stay safe." I was left confused and suspicious. He definitely knew something was up, but why was he staying so calm?

That thought got stuck with me as we made our way to the warehouse.

We got to a side alley and all waited in the van until the sun set. Alex couldn't help noticing that I was distracted. "You all right?" he asked.

"Yeah," I replied, "I just can't shake the feeling that this seems all too easy. I mean . . . if I'm able to track down this kind of information in less than twenty-four hours, why couldn't you guys do it?"

Jessica interrupted our conversation and handed us some Bluetooth communication pieces that were so discreet you couldn't tell you were wearing them.

"These are linked into all our earpieces, let us know the second anything goes wrong."

Alex and I nodded as we slipped out the back of the van quietly with Chase following behind. It was dark in the alley, but we were using our night-vision abilities, except Chase who had goggles.

I still couldn't get over how beautiful the world looked at night as I looked around at the moon's rays reflecting off everything. We snuck up to the back of the warehouse near the back door, and I placed a small seed on the top of the locked electricity box. My eyes glowed as I focused on the seed, watching the vines grow in and around the electrical box, gently turning off the main power switch.

Chase just stood and stared at the vines as they retracted back into the seed and grinned. "Still can't get over the fact that you're a Nature—"

I stopped Chase from saying anything else by putting my hand over his mouth, then silently hinted to the earpieces, saying, "You never know who's really listening."

Chase nodded as he followed Alex and me into the warehouse via the backdoor using a bit of Alex's animal strength.

Alex could hear my heart pounding faster as he looked back at me. I was trying to ignore the fact that we were entering a dark warehouse that was right next to the Yarra River.

(I and water don't mix well together.)

"Lila," Alex whispered. He waited. I looked around the warehouse still suspicious of it being too easy.

I signalled to Alex to go on ahead with Chase and check out the main office.

I looked around to see an overhead beam that ran across the warehouse. With a grin on my face, I climbed to the top of the warehouse using the supporting side beam and crawled along the overhead beam scanning the entire warehouse.

I saw in the distance Alex breaking into the administration's office with Chase. But while they were busy searching through a stack of papers, the back warehouse door opened again and twelve men dressed in all black military gear quietly walked through the warehouse following a woman.

"Damn," I muttered, pressing the earpiece. "It's a trap," I said, trying to warn Alex and Chase.

Alex and Chase started to run out of the admin office but was stopped by the woman standing at the door, smiling as she called to Alex by name. Alex looked up and realised who the woman was.

"Adela," he said, shocked and confused as he looked around at her new team.

"Hello, Alex," she said smugly.

Alex couldn't hide his excitement. "Adela, what are you doing here? Are you okay?" he asked, walking towards her.

Adela replied unkindly, "Oh, I'm fine. Just came back to pick up an old friend."

Chase kept his distance, suspecting something was off, and said quietly, "Alex . . . step back."

Alex looked back at Chase confused and distracted until he realised that Chase was staring at the gun Adela had pointed towards him. They slowly put their hands up, realising they were outnumbered.

"Don't worry, it's just a tranquiliser. It won't hurt a bit," Adela said as she shot at Alex.

Alex moved at full speed, ducking behind the desktop to hide. But Chase wasn't so lucky as he got hit and fell to the floor.

Adela smirked, saying, "Come on, Alex, don't make this harder than it has to be."

Just then someone had fixed the electrical box and turned on the lights, temporarily blinding Alex and me as we both shielded our eyes.

Adela waited outside the administration office looking overconfident and boasting, "I heard you found yourself a new partner . . . I'm hurt that you moved on so fast, I thought we had something special."

Alex yelled back, still hiding behind the desk, "That's a first, I thought you hated working with a partner . . . but I see you've bought a dozen of them."

Adela laughed at his comment, but grew impatient. "Come out, Alex, I'll even let you introduce me to your new friend. I'm sure she's *just dying to meet me . . . Why don't you tell me where she is?"*

As I watched them bicker from my perch on the beam above them, I quietly stood up. My eyes glowed as the vines wrapped around my boots quickly grew tendrils and wrapped themselves around the beam creating a long rope. I took a deep breath regretting what I was about to do and jumped off the beam and swung across the warehouse towards the admin office. I swung in from the side directly towards Adela, kicking her into the wall.

"Heard you were looking for me, so I thought I'd swing in!" I said confidently as I stood in front of the admin door ready to defend Alex against the rest of Adela's team.

I pulled out a handful of seed from my pocket and threw them at the feet of the agents.

Instantly, creeping vines quickly grew from the seeds, wrapping around the legs and waist of the agents.

I was getting good at this.

Some of the agents tried to escape from the vines, but failed, falling to the ground.

But one of the agents managed to cut himself loose from the vines and grabbed hold of my wrist, so I grabbed his wrist and threw him into a stack of storage boxes.

I called to Alex to see if he was all right, but while I was distracted, another of the agents broke free of their vines and moved faster than I expected. I'm guessing she was a Guardian. She moved at full speed and used the butt of her gun hitting my shoulder and dislocating it.

The pain was excruciating but became worse as she used that same arm, swinging me like a doll, throwing me through the admin window, smashing the glass. I landed on the desk where Alex was hiding, writhing in pain and covered in cuts from the glass.

The agent then helped Adela to her feet.

Adela looked at me as I tried to keep a composed face and grinned, impressed at the agent's work.

Just in the nick of time, Jessica burst through the door with her team and shouted to Adela.

Adela became distressed when she saw her sister and the security guards storming into the warehouse, surrounding her agents.

Adela and the other agents who were Guardians ran at full speed, disappearing out of the warehouse, leaving the rest of the "human agents" to fend for themselves, still tied up in vines.

Alex moved at full speed, pulling me off the desk, and whispered, "Something isn't right."

He picked me up in his arms and ran at full speed out of the warehouse. He ran along the Yarra River and stopped in an empty car park, gently laying me on the ground. I tried not to scream as he pulled the small glass shards out my arm.

"Sorry," he said apologetically, "just give me a second to stop the bleeding, then I'm taking you to the hospital."

I shook my head and tried to get up and run, but Alex held me down. "Lila, no . . . you're going to the hospital."

He didn't realise that I was trying to run away from Adela and the five Guardian agents who had escaped with her. By the time Alex realised, the agents had already surrounded us.

"Hello again, Alex," Adela said in a scary controlled voice. "Why don't we try this again . . . care to introduce me to your new friend?"

Alex helped me to my feet and stood protectively in front of me.

Adela scoffed. "Oh . . . looks like Alex wants to try and protect you," she said, leaning sideways to talk to me, "he must really like you . . . must be because you're one of the rare ones."

"You leave her out of this," Alex said as he held my hand tightly, ensuring I was behind him.

Adela laughed sarcastically and sighed smiling at Alex. "Let's see . . . um . . . no!"

One of the other agents tried to pull me away from Alex, but Alex held on to my hand and pulled me back towards him, punching the agent in the process. I then punched another agent using my good arm. But Adela stopped the fighting quickly as she grabbed Alex by the arm and shouted, "Enough!"

Alex stopped and started screaming in pain as steam evaporated off his body and his skin became dry and cracked. He fell to the ground struggling to stay conscious. I didn't know what was going on, so I screamed in shock as she let go of him. "What have you done to him?" I yelled in panic. I tried to get to him, but the other agents held me back.

"Relax . . . ," Adela said, stepping over his body, "he's fine . . . just a little dehydrated . . . now it's your turn." She walked towards me with her hand out, and just as she was about to touch my cheek, the tree roots burst out of a nearby garden and wrapped around Adela's arms and the waist of the other agents, pulling them towards the garden and holding them all tightly to the ground. Every time one of the agents broke free, more roots grew to replace the broken ones.

I was stunned and grateful for what was happening as I helped Alex to his feet.

"Come on, Alex! Work with me," I asked him as he groggily leaned on me.

He struggled to run, but he tried. We made it to the side of the river.

Adela was still struggling to break free but saw us running near the river and smashed her hand on the ground as her eyes glowed blue. A massive wave rose up from the river and landed on us, knocking Alex and me into the river.

At that moment, the tree roots loosened around Adela and the agent, retracting back into the ground. Adela then ran to the river and stared at the water, waiting for us to resurface.

But we didn't, instead I swam deeper, pulling Alex with me, to the point where I could just barely see the shadow of Adela. As I held my breath waiting for Adela to leave, I could tell Alex was struggling for air. He became panicked as he looked at me realising where we were. I pulled him close to me and kissed him, locking my lips around his, as I shared what little air I had left in me. I watched as Adela's shadow disappeared then swam as fast as I could towards the surface, struggling as I pulled Alex with me. As our heads finally made it out of the water, we both gasped, breathing in the cold night air.

Alex kept slipping in and out of a conscious state and I knew I wouldn't be strong enough to swim him to shore with my dislocated shoulder.

So I had one last idea, and I was praying it would work as I pulled the last two seeds I had left hidden in my bracelet locket. I held them tightly in my hand as my eyes glowed green. The seeds grew into a large lily pad big enough for Alex and me to rest on. I used what little strength I had left to paddle our way to the other side of the river.

I was terrified looking around at the water. I tried so hard to hold back my panic attack. I had to focus on saving Alex. I wasn't going to lose another friend. Not again.

"Stay with me, Alex!" I shouted, "Just stay with me, okay! . . . We're almost there."

We had almost made it to the other side of the river, near a football stadium, before the lily pad began to fall apart and sink.

Holding on to Alex, I kicked my legs, pulling Alex towards the pier and started screaming, "HELP! HELP!"

A group of people were on a docked boat having a party when they heard me screaming, "Help me! Please, somebody help!"

Two of the men on the boat saw me struggling to hold on to Alex and dove into the water to help me. They pulled us onto the boat and tried to do first aid on Alex. He had stopped breathing and was fully unconscious.

The group of people from the boat crowded around us to see the commotion and called an ambulance. One of the girls kneeled down to see if I was okay.

"Hey, are you okay? Your nose is bleeding," she said.

I was too worried about Alex to even think about me, but the world started spinning and I fell to the ground struggling to stay awake. And the last thing I remember of that night was loud sirens and flashing red and blue lights.

Journal entry insert by Adela Eden.

I failed, and it was all because of that damn wench who stole my partner from me.

I was so angry as I ran at full speed in to the Essendon airport where a private jet was parked in a hangar.

Daniel, my handler and Mr. Connors's personal assistant, was waiting at the door of the jet. He called out to me as I walked towards him. "Hey, we were starting to worry. Did you get the package?" he asked sarcastically, looking at my empty hand and lack of entourage.

I just grunted walking past him and into the plane cabin where a doctor was waiting for me with my medicine. A blue syringe of pain that helps me to focus apparently.

"Ow," I sighed, rubbing my arm, saying, "No, I didn't get the package, some nature chick ambushed me. And threw me against a wall."

Daniel worryingly looked at the doctor and hurried out of the plane to make a phone call.

I just shrugged my shoulders frustrated and yelled, "Yeah, I'm fine too. Thanks for asking," sarcastically out the plane door.

CHAPTER 16

THE TRUTH WILL
SET YOU . . .

Journal entry by Matt Winters

It had been three days since I got that dreaded phone call saying, "Your wife is in the hospital."

Alex was also in the hospital, still in a coma, and the doctors said they had never seen anyone so dehydrated before.

I thought it would be nice to bring Lila some dinner from the cafeteria since she was stuck in the hospital room.

She also hadn't left Alex's bedside since they were brought to the hospital; she had even demanded they be in the same hospital room together.

Which I didn't think would be that easy, but apparently some rich guy has taken a vested interest in the so far unexplained accident that left my wife swimming in Yarra River. He has covered all of the medical expenses for Alex and Lila, including my parking.

I know Lila hasn't been completely honest with me lately, but I am getting this nagging feeling that whatever Lila's hiding is more dangerous than she thought. But I'm hoping, with me being so patient with . . . this . . . it will make Lila feel comfortable to tell me the truth.

When I walked into Alex and Lila's hospital room, I admit I felt a wave of jealousy rush through me as I saw Lila asleep on the chair next to Alex's bed holding his hand while he slept. I murmured under my breath as I clenched the cafeteria tray, "Great . . . holding hands isn't really helping your case, Lila." I don't know how she heard me, but she woke up when I said her name.

"Hi, sweetie, how's the kids?" she asked as she slowly walked over to kiss me hello. She was clearly trying to hide the pain she was still feeling from her dislocated shoulder, along with the older three broken ribs and the more recent burns and bruises.

As she walked back to her bed, I saw the enormous bruise predominantly spread across her back. To my surprise, it looked like it was healing at a remarkable rate.

"The kids are fine, they're having a sleepover at my sister's house for the weekend," I answered as I started dividing up the food on the nearby table. Lila saw that I had brought up a tomato and cheese toasty and smiled as I handed it to her. I was smart and remembered from her last visit to the hospital she constantly complained about the sucky vegetarian menu the hospital had.

She sighed as she jokingly said, "You know I'm only supposed to eat the disgusting hospital food."

I nodded and replied, "Yes . . . but given the fact that you're actually staying at the hospital and knowing you hate hospitals made me want to reward you a little . . . plus, I didn't want your feelings of hospitals to get worse because of the food. So eat up and think happy thoughts."

Lila laughed as we ate dinner together on her hospital bed. "Don't get your hopes up . . . I still hate hospitals. I'm only staying to keep him safe," she said, pointing over to Alex.

I took this as an opportunity to ask her about what happened, but before I could ask, Alex started to stir.

Lila dropped her sandwich and suddenly just appeared next to Alex.

Which was not creepy or unusual at all, as I whispered to myself, "How?"

"Alex . . . Alex?" Lila said, holding Alex's hand—again.

Alex opened his eyes to see both Lila and me staring at him. Lila then hugged him excitedly, saying, "Alex, thank God . . . you had me so scared."

I at that point was undecided on my thankfulness. Being a good person, I don't wish anyone to meet an untimely demise; however, I felt a great deal of frustration knowing I had been lied to. And also watching my beautiful wife hugging another man, who I suspect is the reason why she is in the hospital, did make me feel slightly bitter in my feelings.

Luckily the doctor walked in to check on Alex now that he was awake. He checked Alex's vitals and asked, "Now that you're awake, did you want to tell me what happened?"

Alex looked at Lila slightly panicked. I don't know if it was the food, I hadn't eaten yet or the lack of sleep, but I swear I saw my wife disappear and reappear a second later. I shook my head in disbelief, then Alex started telling the story of what happened.

"We were exploring an old warehouse, climbing some old shelves when we both fell . . . I must have hit my head pretty hard to end up here," Alex said to the doctor with a cautious smile.

The doctor was writing the story down in his notebook then looked at Alex and Lila confused. "That doesn't explain why you were dangerously dehydrated."

Lila interrupted, saying, "We were on a run before we found the warehouse . . ." She smiled at Alex and said, "Next time we go exploring the world, I'll make sure we pack some water bottles."

The doctor just smiled and closed his notebook. I got the feeling he didn't fully believe the story either, but he wasn't planning on pushing the issue, so he smiled and left, saying, "As long as you can keep your fluids up, I'll check on a few tests and we can look at discharging you in a couple of days."

As the door closed, I stood at the end of the hospital bed, with a disbelieving smirk on my face, and said, "So are you planning on telling me the truth, or are we going to keep on lying to each other . . . because if so . . . Alex, I'm really happy you're alive. And you are doing a great job protecting my wife. I mean so far, she has been at a doctor's surgery with broken ribs, been questioned by police after a terrorist attack at her work, and has now been hospitalised with a dislocated shoulder and don't get me started about the burned hand marks on her body. If you honestly expect me to believe you were just out for a run on the other side of the city, exploring abandoned warehouses, you're going to have to start lying a lot better than that—"

Alex interrupted my rant as he tried to sit himself up to talk to me. "You're right . . .," he said, "you deserve the truth . . . I'm not here to protect Lila."

I sighed as my frustration found some relief. I was finally going to get the truth. I leaned in as Alex admitted, "Lila's protecting me."

I sighed again trying to hold in my anger as he explained.

"My kind are being hunted and I came to Lila because I knew she could help," he explained.

"Your kind?" I asked sceptical, "What are you, an alien?"

Alex smiled and said, "Not exactly . . .," looking at Lila who was petrified and lost for words as he held Lila's hand again, saying, "You said you didn't want to lie to him anymore. Here's your chance."

I looked at Lila waiting for her to tell me her big truth as she walked over to her side of the room and picked up the bouquet of flower left by the rich old man paying for this visit and put them on the bed in front of me. I was still sceptical, but confused when she looked at me nervously, almost as if I was going to react badly.

Lila picked out one of the roses that had not yet blossomed and held it in front on me. Her eyes glowed green as she looked at the flower.

I gasped and stepped backwards to the other side of the room as the flower blossomed in seconds before my eyes.

I stuttered not knowing what to say, "Did . . . did you . . . ?"

Lila nodded as she looked at me with fear and hope in her eyes.

I didn't know what to do or say, so I ran out of the room. I probably looked like the worst husband in the world, right? I got in my car and drove and drove for hours and I stopped at a nearby park to figure things out.

Honestly, I didn't know how to feel. I wouldn't have believed it if I didn't see it with my own eyes. I mean, I'm a scientist, things like this are just not possible. But I couldn't help but think about Lila, that look on her face when she was telling me the truth. I could understand then why she lied, she was so scared telling me the truth. Probably feared I'd react badly—like I just did.

I then realised how much of a terrible husband I had been. I had to go back. I had to fix it.

By the time I got back to the hospital, Alex and Lila had already been discharged against doctor's advice. So I drove home, hoping they would be there.

When I entered the house, some guy named Chase was sitting in the front room watching TV and the rich guy was in the dining room talking on the phone.

I heard Lila crying upstairs, and as I walked up the stairs, the bedroom door was ajar and I could see Lila lying on our bed crying on Alex's shoulder as he comforted her. I stopped and hesitated on the stairs and listened to Lila sobbing, "He hates me . . . he's never coming home," she said.

Alex hugged her and said, "That's crazy talk, you know Matt loves you, he probably just needed some time to think things through . . . It took me a few days to work through how I felt about being a Guardian . . . and if you remember, you needed some time to figure things out as well. It's only fair you give him that opportunity."

Lila wiped her tears away and sniffled. "What if he doesn't come back . . ." She sniffled again. "I can't lose him."

Alex looked out through the jar of the door and it felt like he was looking right at me, but I was sure he couldn't see me as I stood in the dark stairwell.

I decided not to risk the awkwardness and silently crept back down the stairs.

A few minutes later, Alex found me sitting in the backyard looking up at the stars. He sat down next to me and handed me a glass of water. I looked at him confused as he explained, "That glass is for your wife when you go up to see her."

I sighed and looked at the water.

Alex then looked up at the stars and said, "You know your wife is one in a million. She has a big heart."

He continued to stare up at the stars, and I stared up at the stars with him and asked the question I dreaded saying, "Alex . . . you said at the hospital your kind were being hunted."

He nodded in confirmation.

"Is Lila one of your kind?" I asked, dreading but already suspecting the answer.

Again, Alex nodded, and I sighed feeling both fear and sadness. "But you're going to protect her, right?" I asked him, not confident of that answer either.

Alex stopped staring at the stars and shook his head, saying, "I don't know . . . but every time we've been in trouble, it was Lila who was there trying to save me . . . Everything she does is to protect others . . . So before you go and get mad at her, put yourself in her position . . . if you recently found out you had an unusual superpower and what you were put you and your family in danger, how confident would you be in breaking this news to someone you loved . . . one of the people you've now just put in danger?"

I looked down at the glass of water and, shaking my head, then walked back through the house and up the stairs.

When I walked into the bedroom, Lila was so happy to see me. She smiled as she wiped the tears off her face. She started to apologise, but I stopped her, then hugged her, saying, "Sweetie, I love you, and I know it probably wasn't easy telling me this. So I'm not mad . . . freaked out, but not mad. And Alex has explained a few things . . . but I'm hoping you could fill in the rest."

I sat down on the bed next to her and smiled as I waited for her to respond. Lila's smile beamed across her face as she started telling me the whole story.

We talked all night until she had explained absolutely everything.

CHAPTER 17

ONE BIG HAPPY FAMILY

Journal entry by Lila Winters

It had been two weeks since Alex and I got out of the hospital. And Matt was having a blast testing our abilities with all of his science gadgets and monitors that he "borrowed" from the university. He became especially fascinated when he noticed our bodies were healing at a faster rate than the average human. Which explained why the broken ribs, bruised eye, and burns were almost healed. The only one that looked the worst was the bruise from my dislocated shoulder.

Alex and I were sparring in the backyard with Matt's wireless monitors strapped to our chest and one on the temple of our heads. Danny and Ruby were watching from the dining room window cheering us on as Alex and I were throwing each other across the yard. Matt was keeping an eye on us and the computer readings while he was making us pancakes for breakfast. He finished serving up the breakfast and decided to test our hearing, and while staring at the computer readings, he whispered softly under his breath, "Lila, breakfast is ready."

Both Alex and I heard Matt and smiled as we glanced over to see him still engrossed in the computer screen. We both ran at full speed into the house and stood on either side of Matt, with both of us eating a pancake and giggling.

Matt jumped with fright but was impressed with our abilities and commented as we all sat down to the table for breakfast, "I am gobsmacked, you two have been sparring for two hours now and your heart rates only spiked when Alex was thrown over the fence," he commented.

Alex replied, "I'm really excited about finally having a good sparring partner . . . I mean, Lila puts up an excellent fight for a newbie," he said, trying to stir the pot.

I laughed so hard at Alex while I was drinking orange juice that it snorted out my nose, causing Danny and Ruby to start laughing as well.

Alex's face beamed with a cheeky smile. "What . . . I'd say it was a pretty even fight . . .," he said, watching me as I laughed and cleaned up my mess.

Matt smiled at Alex and said quietly, "You know she was going easy on you, right?" He then turned his laptop around and showed Alex the data he collected.

Alex looked at the screen, shaking his head, confused.

Matt explained, pointing to the screen, "Compared to your results, Lila's data shows that she was calm and in control the whole time."

Alex grunted but stayed quiet and started buttering his pancakes.

Matt kept looking at the data on his computer getting more excited and commented, "I really wish I could run some more test in the university lab, I have much better monitors at work that can give a more accurate reading . . . the downside is my lab has more breakables than my backyard does."

Our breakfast was interrupted by a knock at the door. Alex cautiously walked to the door to answer it and greeted Max and Chase standing at the door.

"Good morning, Mr. Woods, I was hoping Lila was home," Max asked politely.

I quickly ran at half speed to stand next to Alex. "Hey, Mr. Eden, how's it goin'?" I asked excitedly. Chase smiled a little when he saw me appear next to Alex.

"Good morning, Lila, we have a proposition for you. And I was hoping I could talk to you in private," Max asked.

Alex looked at me and tried to discreetly shake his head to say no, but it was clearly obvious to everyone.

I sarcastically grinned, saying, "Okay, Alex . . . Danny and Ruby just asked if they could go to the zoo today, so why don't you go and work out safety logistics with Matt and I'll have a quick chat with Max." I nodded to Alex insistently, who then upsettingly stormed back into the dining room as I walked outside to talk with Max and Chase.

Max and Chase spoke with me for a while, and in that time, Matt and Alex had already organised the family outing to the zoo. While the kids were upstairs getting dressed, Matt was standing at the lounge room window "discreetly" watching me talking with Max. Matt must have forgotten that I had really good hearing.

Chase had just handed me a manila folder, which piqued Matt's interest more. Alex snuck up behind Matt and startled him. "You know Lila would be pissed if she found out you were spying on her," Alex whispered.

Nice to know someone's got my back.

Matt, still a bit startled, was more preoccupied with what I was doing and shrugged it off, saying, "So we won't tell her, okay?"

Then both of them watched from the window as I waved goodbye to Max and Chase who were driving away. As I turned to walk inside, I saw Matt and Alex quickly disappear from the window. I walked in to find them sitting at the table eating pancakes.

Yeah, because that's not at all suspicious behaviour.

I decided not to comment on their totally obvious display of guilt, as I was more worried they might want to ask about the conversation I had.

So I just sat down and ate pancakes with them.

We got to the Melbourne Zoo just before it opened. And as we walked up to the entrance, Danny saw my mother, Hanna, waiting and shouted, "Nanna!" as he ran up to hug her. Ruby followed shouting, "Nan, Nan, Nan!"

While Matt and Alex went to get entry passes, Hanna pulled me to the back of the group. "So I thought this was a family outing?" she whispered, asking in a slightly condescending way.

I acted ignorant and said, "What do you mean?"

"Does your friend not have a family of his own?" she asked, slightly annoyed.

I smirked and glanced over to Alex and Matt, finally getting along with each other as they looked at zoo maps with Danny and Ruby. "Mum, you should try to be a little nicer. Alex is going through a rough patch at the moment."

Hanna looked befuddled. "Why? What rough patch?" she asked.

I didn't know what to say. I mean, we purposely didn't tell her about the recent hospital visit to keep her from worrying. It took a few seconds to come up with a response, then I said, "He just lost a very close friend and he's still struggling to grieve."

Hanna started to tear up, and before I realised, she had walked over to Alex and hugged him tightly. Alex didn't know what to do and looked at me confused, and not surprisingly, Matt was just as confused.

Hanna stopped hugging Alex to wipe the tears away from her eyes. "I'm sorry, Alex. I recently lost a close friend too. If you need anything today—anything at all—I can help. Even if it's just for a hug," she said through her sniffles.

Alex didn't know what to say and looked at me as I shrugged with the expression on my face of "Just play along."

"Thank you . . .," Alex said slightly optimistic—that was the correct response.

Seems it was the right move because he got another hug from her, this time Danny and Ruby hugged Alex as well.

To break the tension and just for my own internal laugh, I joined in on the hug and tried so incredibly hard not to make my internal laugh an external laugh.

I suspect Matt may have gotten jealous because he quickly broke up the hilariously tender moment, saying enthusiastically, "Okay, who wants to go see the lions?"

Hanna walked into the park with Danny and Ruby, screaming, "Hooray," really loudly.

Matt had a cheeky smile and grabbed my hand, pulling me close to him, holding me in his arms, and said, "Have I told you today how sexy you look in those pants?"

Matt then kissed me and glanced over to see Alex, who was looking at the ground awkwardly.

Matt and I walked into the park holding hands while Alex followed behind checking out my sexy pants. I caught him as he shook his head and looked back down at the ground.

We were having a great time at the zoo, and we finally made it to the lion enclosure after first visiting the giraffes, penguins, and seals. We did fine when we visited the giraffes, but when we were watching the seals frolic behind a large glass window in all that water, my fear of water started to stir.

Alex noticed my heart rate increase and stayed close to me from then on.

When we got to the lion enclosure, Matt and Hanna were busy trying to help Danny and Ruby get a good view.

I stood at the side window watching a few of the female lions that were asleep on a landing next to the window in front of us.

Alex leaned in close to warn me, "You might want to look away. This next part is a bit . . . awkward."

The next thing we saw was the lion showing his dominance to the rest of the lionesses. I gasped then laughed as we watched this intimate display.

I covered Alex's eyes turning him away, still laughing, saying, "Don't look. Give the guy some privacy."

Alex joked, saying, "What, you can look but I can't?" as he tried to cover my eyes as well.

Hanna and Matt had a similar thought for Danny and Ruby and quickly shuffled them onto the next enclosure. Matt looked back at us to ensure we would follow but sighed and looked away when he saw how much fun we were having.

We all started getting hungry and decided we would have a picnic near the tortoise enclosure.

We sent Alex to the café to get some meals for us while Hanna and I were setting out a blanket. Danny and Ruby ran off to see the tortoises, so Matt had to follow. When I stretched out my arms to set the picnic blanket out, I felt a bit of pain from bruise where my shoulder had dislocated. I cringed in pain slightly but tried to hide it from Hanna, but she saw the expression on my face and asked, "What's wrong with your shoulder?"

You can't hide anything from your mother.

I tried to play it cool and brush it off, saying, "Nothing . . . it's just a knot . . . I must have slept on it wrong or something."

Hanna just smiled and rubbed her hands together to warm them. "This sounds like a good time to put my old massage skills to the test. Sit down and take off your jacket," she demanded.

I quickly moved away but tried to make it look casual. I knew I hadn't completely healed from the dislocation and that the area still had some pretty bad bruising. "Um, no, Mum . . . that's okay. I think it's all better now—thanks," I said, rotating my shoulders as if it was all okay.

Hanna didn't believe me and persisted as she said, "Nonsense! I've heard that line from you before. You know this massage always helped you after your training session. And don't tell me you didn't train this morning because the kids have been telling me all about your wrestling match with Alex."

Hanna stood behind me and started to pull my jacket off and wouldn't take the hint as I tried to keep the jacket on.

She lost her patience and grew suspicious then in a stern voice demanded I take my jacket off. "Lila Willows . . . now!"

I started to feel like a rebellious teenager again, rolling my eyes as I took my jacket off.

Hanna saw the very large, old, but still prominent bruise on my back and gasped in horror as she just stared at it.

I tried to continue the charade of ignorance, saying, "It's just a bruise, Mum, try not to get worked up."

But Hanna wouldn't have a bar of it. She started her usual interrogation questions. "Who did this to you?"

I lied, replying, "No one. I got it while I was training the other day."

She didn't believe me and threatened, "Lila Willows, if you don't tell me the truth right now, so help me I will call your father."

Unfortunately, at that moment, Alex walked up and placed the tray of food down on the blanket and asked, "Hey . . . is everything okay here?" looking at me slightly worried, knowing that we had all agreed before we left the house for me to keep my jacket on. And I was guessing he already heard what the argument was about.

But Hanna quickly drew her own conclusion and started accusing Alex. "You! I know it was you. Don't you dare touch her again!" she shouted and swung her handbag up to hit Alex. But instead I moved at full speed to stand in front of Alex to protect him. Alex watched my face as I felt the full force of the handbag strike my shoulder and scrape along my back. The pain was too much, and I lost my balance, pushing Alex to the ground along with me. He tried to soften my fall as he moved at full speed, pulling me closer to him so I would land on him instead of the ground. I yelped in agonising pain as we landed, getting the attention of Matt, Danny, and Ruby as they ran to help us. Alex helped me to stand, asking if I was okay. I nodded my head hesitantly, but I suspect Alex didn't fully believe me.

Hanna dropped her bag and started to feel guilty as she apologised again and again and asked, "Why-why did you do that?"

I turned to Hanna and tried to hold back my anger and said frustratingly, "To save you from making a scene . . ." I exclaimed, "Alex was not the one who hurt me . . . It was me . . . I got into a fight and I lost—end of story."

I dusted myself off and continued my rant of frustration. "And my last name is Winters . . . not Willows. I haven't been a Willows in a long time."

Matt grinned slightly as he helped me put my jacket on. I guess he felt happier when I reminded everyone of our marriage. It was understandable how he felt. Getting a bit territorial was part of the husband's job.

"Now, can we please all get back to having a nice family day at the zoo?" I asked, sitting down on the blanket next to the tray of food.

Hanna took a moment then apologised to Alex as he helped her to sit down on the ground.

Alex sat next to her as she explained, "I sometimes get a little too overprotective when it comes to my daughter. She's all I got . . . now that her father has this new job. He's rarely ever home. But whenever he's home, he always talks about how important Lila is to him . . . the last thing I want is for him to hear about this and come rushing home for no reason . . . I guess I just panicked a little . . . I'm so sorry."

Alex then started asking some very curious and intentional questions to get Hanna talking about something else. "Your husband seems like an important man," he commented, handing Hanna her food.

"Oh, he is . . . he's a General now and he loves it . . . all that hush-hush business is right up his alley."

Alex continued to listen to Hanna talk about her husband and glanced over to see me smiling at him while I was helping my kids open their drinks.

He held his soft drink can in front of his mouth, pretending to drink, and whispered quietly, so only I could hear him, "Are you sure you're okay?" he asked. I nodded as he continued to say, "I could have taken the hit, you know."

I sighed and turned away from the group pretending to look in Matt's backpack for a water bottle and whispered softly, "I know, but I can take a blow to the back if it gets my mother to like you . . . She knows I'd do anything to protect my family. Now, no matter what you do, she will just shrug it off and be a bit grumpy instead."

Alex smiled still pretending to listen to Hanna talk about her husband and she even showed him some pictures of Richard and me when I was younger. "Awe," he whispered into his can, saying, "You consider me family now."

I looked at him and sighed as I whispered softly, "Dude, we nearly died trying to save each other's lives . . . more than once. You're stuck with me now . . . for the rest of your life."

We both smiled at each other as we ate our lunch.

After we finished lunch, we headed up to the butterfly house.

Alex was still stuck with Hanna as she told him all the stories about her family and how stubborn I was as a child. Matt and Danny weren't so interested in the butterflies and went straight to the cocoon displays. So I stayed back and watched as Ruby jumped around trying to catch the butterflies. She became agitated and started crying when she failed to catch one.

I looked around and had an idea. As I knelt down next to Ruby, I made sure no one could see us and whispered, "Let me show you a special trick I learned." While Ruby stood still watching the butterflies fly past, I picked a flower bud from a nearby plant, and discreetly, my eyes glowed green as the bud grew into a large beautiful brightly coloured orange flower. I handed the flower to Ruby and started to film Ruby with my phone as all the butterflies around her began to land on the flower and on her hair and arms. Ruby tried not to giggle as the butterflies tickled her skin then walked very slowly towards the rest of the family to show everyone all the butterflies.

After we finished looking at the butterflies, I got Ruby to gently place the flower back in the garden, and we rushed out to make it to the elephant show in time.

I looked back as I did my headcount to see some old guy who looked like a tourist with a bumbag and notebook and camera around his neck, holding the orange flower and writing in his notebook as butterflies stopped to land on it.

Guess Ruby wasn't the only one who liked butterflies.

While the group was watching the elephant performance, I took the opportunity to go to the café and grab some ice creams for everyone. That's when I ran in to the tourist guy again. He introduced himself as Sabastian Weller, a university professor from America, who was over to do a lecture at the Melbourne University down the road. I tried to be nice and said hello and smiled, but I was conscious that I didn't want the ice creams to melt, so I tried to excuse myself apologetically. He walked with me, talking to me about his work and how he was studying butterflies and their behavioural patterns.

When we got to the path where we were alone and shaded by trees, Sabastian quickly pulled a syringe from his pocket and injected it into my leg. I became so weak and dizzy that I dropped the ice creams and began to fall. Sabastian caught me and gently sat me down on a nearby bench.

A zoo staff member drove past in a buggy cart and stopped to offer assistance. "Is she okay?" the staff member asked.

Sabastian then pretended to act like he was my father and placed his hand on my cheek. "Sweetie . . . are you okay?" he said, then turned to the staff and explained, "She's my daughter, I think she's overheated and became dehydrated."

The staff member became concerned and offered to call an ambulance, but Sabastian interrupted, saying, "No, no . . . I'm a doctor, if you help me get her to my car, I can take her back to my clinic and hook her up to a saline drip."

The staff member was a bit hesitant but began to help him after he said, "Trust me, that's exactly what the hospital will do after they ask me how much she had to drink last night and then probably make her wait four hours before she gets the drip . . . If you help me, I can get it done faster."

The staff member then drove us through the staff-only section and out into the car park, helping Sabastian carry me into car and drive off. That's right, I was abducted. Again.

Journal entry insert by Alex Woods

I was watching the elephant show with Lila's family and realised she had been gone for long time.

Maybe it was the past few weeks playing in my mind, but I started to get suspicious that Lila had taken so long to get ice cream and began looking around to find her. I tried listening for her heartbeat and could not find it and became slightly panicked and discreetly grabbed Matt's attention to get him to help me look.

We left Hanna with the kids as I started to track Lila's movement.

As soon as Matt and I had stepped away from the crowd, I ran off at full speed running around the entire zoo and reappeared next to Matt slightly out of breath.

Matt jumped in fright. "Don't do that, I haven't gotten used to it yet," he said as he waited for me to catch my breath.

Matt was actually surprised that I was out of breath and commented, "Wow . . . how fast were you running?"

I stood up to compose myself and answered, "Fast enough so that no one could see me, not even the cameras."

Matt nodded, impressed, thinking mathematically just how fast it would have had to be, then asked, "So I'm guessing you didn't find her."

"No, but I did find something," I said, grabbing hold of Matt's arm and ran at full speed to the secluded footpath where the ice cream was left melting.

When I stopped and let go of Matt, he quickly moved to throw up in the nearby bushes and yelled, "Okay, I'm not used to that either."

I tried really hard not to laugh and focus on the ice creams. Sniffing the cone and the air around them, I said, "These were the ice creams that she bought us, I can smell her on them. I can also smell some sort of chemical . . . I recognise it from the hospital. Some guy had just come back from surgery and reeked of it."

Matt was fascinated that my sense of smell was so strong but freaked out when he realised the possibility that the chemical I was smelling was an anaesthesia.

"We have to call the police, Lila's been kidnapped," Matt said as he rushed towards the front entrance to talk to the staff at the gate.

The staff then scrambled to call the police and organised search parties as they began searching the zoo. It had only been an hour, but the sun was setting and the gates had closed for the night. Matt and I were still waiting for the police, zoo staff, and security to finish walking the park, looking for Lila.

Matt had just finished putting Danny and Ruby in the car and sent Hanna home to look after them. Hanna was beside herself with worry and was not helping the situation, which was probably why she was sent home.

I sat in the office scanning the security camera footage with a police officer and one of the zoo staff members.

"There she is . . .," I said, pointing to the footage of Lila and an old man talking on the footpath.

Matt rushed over to look at the computer screen as well and watched as Lila was injected with something in the leg. The staff member paused to zoom in on the footage, when she recognised the guy, "Hey, I know that guy . . . yeah, he's Professor Weller, the butterfly guy."

Matt and I looked at the staff member, confused, wanting more information than just "the butterfly guy." So the staff member continued to explain. "He's an ex-field scientist who was a professor at a university in America. He comes in every couple of days to watch the butterflies. He should have a membership . . ." The staff member pulled up Professor Weller's membership form on the computer.

The policer officer pulled out his phone and started to make a call. "I'll send a police car over to his house, see if she's there," he said hurriedly.

Original journal entry continued by Lila Winters

When I woke up, I still felt groggy and a bit panicky, realising I was tied to a chair in some sort of laboratory with duct tape on my mouth. I was still woozy from the drugs he had given me, and he had hooked me up to a saline bag as well; no doubt he was still drugging me with that. I was sure my metabolism was fast enough to flush the drugs through my system by now.

My vision was blurry, and I kept drifting in and out of consciousness. But I knew we were at least on the second floor, because I could see the tops of the tree branches from the window. Sabastian was kneeling next to me drawing blood from my arm. I looked over to a bench where all the other blood vials were. I counted at least ten full blood vials and started to get scared. I tried to move away but failed as I squirmed in the chair.

Sabastian tried to comfort me by stroking my cheek. "Shush . . . shush," he said almost as if he was infatuated by me. "I just needed a bit of blood . . . to run a few tests."

I tried to respond looking down at the tape on my mouth. "Mmm," I mumbled softly.

"You want me to take the duct tape off?" he asked and waited for me to slowly nod. "Okay, I'll take off the duct tape as long as you promise to stay quiet . . . Deal?" He waited again for me to slowly nod before he gently removed the duct tape.

For a crazy scientist, he was surprisingly considerate.

It took a lot of effort, but I was able to ask a few questions to him. "What . . . what tests?" I asked.

Sabastian got excited about it as he explained the type of test he would be running and what he was looking for. I was still discreetly trying to break out of my binds and had to keep him talking, so I asked, "Why?"

And he responded with a condescending tone, "To find out what you are. Obviously."

That was the part where I got a little more squeamish but continued the charade and replied slowly and slightly out of breath, struggling to stay awake, "What do you mean, what I am? . . . I'm human," I whispered.

Sabastian's grin got bigger. He knew I was lying. "Nice try, but no human I know can grow picked flowers with the touch of her hand," he said, kneeling back down to look into my eyes.

I began to tear up as I realised this was my fault. I could have just told Ruby to be patient and let the butterflies come to her. But no, I just had to show off. I wanted so badly to make her happy.

Sabastian wiped the tears off my cheek and leaned in close to me, whispering in my ear excitedly, "I know what you are . . ."

My fear increased, and I began to cry more as he whispered what I was.

"You're a garden nymph," he said crazy excitedly.

I sighed with relief and glad I was too weak to laugh. It surprised me that a grown man who claimed to be a scientist still believed in fairy tales.

"A what?" I asked, confused yet happy he was wrong.

"I have always known that they existed. And now, I will have proof of you as well," Sabastian said as he started to draw more blood from me.

By then I had become so tired I fell back to sleep.

Journal entry insert by Alex Woods

Matt was literally pushing me out the door of the zoo in what seemed like a panic.

"Matt, what are doing?" I asked, frustrated.

Matt then looked around the car park to ensure no one could hear him and quietly whispered, "I know where Lila might be."

I was still confused as to why he was being so secretive and waited for Matt to explain.

"That guy is an American professor on loan to the Melbourne University where I work . . . I recognised him from the staff function I went to last month . . . He is a super crazy scientist who will stop at nothing to prove his theories."

I still had trouble following what Matt was trying to say until he said, "Think about it, if I were a super crazy scientist who might have possibly seen Lila do something odd, where would I take her?"

I interrupted Matt, realising the answer, and shouted, "You'd take her to your lab!"

Matt hinted to me to stay quiet as he agreed with the answer and continued to explain his theory. "I suspect he may have taken her to Melbourne University, which is just around the block."

I was just about to run at full speed before Matt stopped me and said, "But . . . there's a problem. The university is really big and has a lot of off-campus building that has locked doors. The best thing we can do for Lila, if she's in trouble, and I think she is, is to find her discreetly . . . Which means you can't go breaking down every locked door to find her," he said damningly.

I suddenly remembered a cool trick I saw on a TV show and turned to Matt, asking, "Matt, did Lila have her phone on her today?"

Matt realised what I was thinking and loudly and frustratingly said, "Why didn't we think of this before?" as he pulled his phone out of his pocket.

"I'll just go and find a police officer," he said excitedly.

But instead I grabbed the phone and stopped Matt. "Hang on . . . I need to make a phone call."

I regretted making this phone call, but I knew if anyone was able to help Lila, it would be them.

I had called the Eden Hotel and asked for Maxwell. After explaining the situation to him, he hung up on me, and a few seconds later, Chase had texted me back with Lila's exact address and location, with an additional message saying, "Already en route."

I handed Matt back his phone and rolled my eyes, listening to him say, "Wow, this guy's amazing . . ."

He was too distracted to notice when I grabbed hold of his arm and said jokingly, "This time, try not to vomit."

I started running at full speed holding Matt next to me and stopped just outside the new science building that had apparently just opened a few weeks ago.

Matt recognised the building instantly and quickly explained to me, "Okay, they haven't finished installing all the equipment for this building yet and the first and second floor are lecture halls and meeting rooms . . . you should check the third and fourth floors."

Matt then handed me his entry key card and pulled out his phone to make a phone call, saying, "You go ahead, I'll give the cops the heads-up and call an ambulance."

I was impressed. Matt was actually handling this really well. I wasted no time and ran at full speed searching the third floor. I tried to be quiet, but one of the doors had slammed shut and echoed throughout the building.

I then heard a male voice coming from the fourth floor saying, "Damn . . . this place isn't as secure as I thought."

I ran at full speed up the stairs and snuck into the hallway leading into a laboratory filled with boxes and fancy new equipment.

I peeked around the corner to see Professor Weller filling the last empty vial with Lila's blood and hurriedly packed at least sixteen of the large vials into an esky of ice. He must have heard me sneaking into the lab because he grabbed a gun from the desk drawer and started randomly shooting.

I ducked for cover behind one of the lab benches and waited for the gunfire to stop.

I could hear Professor Weller starting to get agitated, looking around the room, shouting, "You can't have her! I found her! She's mine!"

I looked back at the hallway door to see Matt waving to get my attention, then whispered softly, hoping I could hear it, "If you draw his fire, I'll tackle him," he said.

It was a terrible plan, considering I wasn't bulletproof, but I guess Matt was hoping I'd be smart enough not to get shot. So I nodded and counted to three before I got up and ran the long way around the room.

The professor then started shooting randomly towards me and didn't notice as Matt tackled him to the ground and punched him in the face.

Matt stood up and kicked the gun away from the professor and excitedly and territorially said, "No . . . she's mine!"

Matt then ran to untie Lila as he called out to see if I was okay.

I appeared at full speed next to Matt to help untie Lila as Matt checked her pulse and looked at the colour of her skin. "She's lost a lot of blood. I can't feel her pulse," he mumbled in panic and turned away from her, not knowing what to do and was beginning to freak out.

I placed my hand on him to pull him back into reality and shouted, "Hey . . . I can still hear her heart beating . . . That means we can still save her."

I got Matt to pull out the saline drip in Lila's arm, and I scooped her up out of the chair and started walking to the door. Matt saw the ambulance light from the window and followed me to the stair, shouting, "The ambulance is here, can't you run at full speed down there?"

I shook my head and shouted back as I hurried down the stairs, "Her body's too fragile. If I run, I might kill her."

Matt stopped in shock, properly realising the morbidity of the situation and the danger Lila and I both faced being a Guardian, as he looked back at the laboratory and the chair Lila was tied to.

"Right. . . . don't run!" he muttered to himself.

We passed the police as they ran up the stairs. Matt shouted to the police, explaining where to find Professor Weller and what he had done.

The ambulance drivers wasted no time loading Lila into the back of the van and driving off to the nearest hospital.

Matt and I watched as Professor Weller was being walked to a police van. The professor looked over at Matt and me and became agitated again, shouting, "You can't hide her forever! I know what she is! The world will know about her. Everyone will know about her!"

But I saw something else that made my stomach churn and my hairs stand on end. As I watched a police officer walk past me carrying the esky of blood vials in his hand, I could have sworn I recognised him from the missing Guardian's files we had back at Mission Control.

"Daniel . . . ," I whispered, but as I turned to take another look at the officer, he was gone.

CHAPTER 18

THE BIG MOVE

Journal entry by Alex Woods

It was starting to feel like a déjà vu. Lila had slipped into a coma from losing too much blood. The hospital doctors said that her body had essentially shut down, and that the best they could do was monitor her and hope she wakes up.

So that's what we did—we waited.

Matt waited for a while and we took turns to sit with her; but after a few days had passed, he had to go back and calm the children and Lila's mother down.

Lila lay so still in the hospital bed, with a blood bag attached to one arm, a saline drip in the other, and tube in her mouth to help her breath. It was heart-wrenching to look at her.

I had eventually fallen asleep on the couch next to Lila's bed watching TV. All the news channels were covering "The Zoo kidnapping" and a few of the reporters had even parked outside the hospital, waiting for an exclusive interview.

Lila's room was overwhelmed with flowers from the Zoo's staff members. My guess is they were feeling kind of guilty, that one of their own accidently helped in the abduction.

It was dinner time and I could hear the food trolley coming around as I drifted in and out of sleep.

I opened my eyes to see the food tray had arrived. Knowing that Lila wasn't going to eat it anyway, I quickly wolfed down her dinner and sat back into the chair to watch TV again. It wasn't long before I drifted off to sleep, thinking the hospital food here tasted awful, thinking nothing of it as I closed my eyes again... then opened them to see a male nurse checking Lila's chart. He had a mask covering his face.

I tried to wake up properly so I could talk to him, but I felt overwhelmingly tired, so I closed my eyes again.

I woke in panic to the sound of Lila's food tray being thrown to the floor. The room was filled with plant pollen that had been sprayed from the many flowers in the room. As the pollen settled, I looked over to see Lila still unconscious but with plant vines and giant flowers defensively suspended above her and threatening the male nurse, whose mask had been pulled off amongst the scuffle.

I looked at him, still half asleep, slowly beginning to realise who he was . . . It was Daniel, so I tried to stand to confront him, but he disappeared running out of the room at full speed. I quickly rushed to see if Lila was okay and watched as all the flowers around the room returned to normal.

As I began to investigate what had happened, I found the broken syringe on the nightstand and could smell the anaesthesia on the bed. I traced the smell and the trail of broken glass and green leaves back to where I was sleeping, and realised Lila had again saved my life, all while she slept.

I was gobsmacked.

I quickly disposed of the syringe and broken glass and pulled the couch closer to the bed to hold Lila's hand as I heard the footstep of the head nurse walking into the room. I casually smiled as I helped her clean up the mess made by the food tray and take it away.

I sat back down next to Lila and held her hand, excitedly whispering, "I don't know how you did that, but you just gained a whole new level of respect from me."

I was seriously impressed as I looked around the room at all the flowers. I then sighed and began to tear up a little as I listened to Lila's heart beating slowly.

"You really gave me a scare the other day . . . that moment when I was watching the elephants and couldn't hear your heart beating in the crowd, I felt a sharp pain in my chest as if someone had ripped out my heart . . . . And then . . . when we finally found you, and you were barely breathing, the fear of losing you was too much . . . Just hearing your heart still beating has been all that's kept me going . . . I know you took a big risk when you took me in, and when we first met you were just another asset, needed to complete my mission. But you're so much more than that," I said, confiding in her as she slept. Becoming sentimental, I teared up some more as I leaned over to kiss Lila's cheek and whispered, "I promised I would be there to protect you, and I know I haven't been too good at that lately. But if you wake up, I promise to work harder and always be there for you . . . But I'll also understand if you wake up and ask me to leave and never see you again. I won't be happy about it . . . but I'll respect it. I'll do anything you ask of me. All you have to do is wake up . . . please."

I stared at Lila's eyes praying that they would open and whimpered as I let out my tears, feeling like a failure.

I didn't even notice that my tears were falling onto Lila cold, pale cheeks and became startled as Lila began to stir and opened her eyes to see me leaning over her crying and smiling at her.

She began to smile back at me, then she realised she had a tube down her throat.

She started to panic and cry not knowing what to do and tried to reach up to take the tube out and saw the tubes from the blood bags and saline drip in her arms. Her heartbeat increased as fear overwhelmed her body; she was trying to remove the drips. I quickly grabbed hold of her arms and held them down trying to calm her, "Lila, stop!" I shouted, "Please . . . stop. I promise you're okay, you're safe . . . just try to breathe. Okay, can you do that for me? Just . . . breathe."

I stared into Lila's eyes and held her hands against my chest. "Listen to my heart, remember?" I said as I placed my hand on her chest and took some slow deep breaths, encouraging her to copy.

"Listen," I whispered. "Listen."

Lila stared back into my eyes and began to relax and mimic my breathing and listening to our hearts beating as one.

I was filled with joy and smiled, listening to her heartbeat and staring into her eyes.

We were both distracted when we heard the door open to see Matt, Danny, and Ruby standing by the door, staring at us. Danny and Ruby were excited to see their mother awake and ran to the bed excited to greet her.

I stepped back clearing my throat and wiping the tears off my face as Matt stood next to me and asked, "Please, tell me that was some weird animal trick that you can do . . . because that's the second time I've caught you feeling up my wife."

I nodded trying to explain that she woke up in panic, and I was just trying to calm her down.

Matt just looked at me curious, angry and fascinated, and unsure what to say all at the same time.

"Well then . . . thank you . . . ," he said relieved, I think, but added a final word, "Just try to watch where those hands go. Okay? That is my wife."

Matt yet again delivered his not so subtle marital reminder with what looked like a smile as he walked over to greet Lila.

As I watched the family reunion, I thought it best not to cause any panic by letting Matt know about the recent intruder.

I slowly backed out of the room saying, "I'm going to let the nurse know she's awake."

As I walked out of the room, I quickly grabbed the bin that had the broken glass and syringes in it and disposed of it in the larger bin in the hallway.

Then I let out the biggest sigh of relief looking up and saying, "Thank you."

The doctor decided to keep Lila in for a few more days to monitor her recovery. And each day, they asked Lila to complete some puzzles and name pictures from flash cards. I guess they were checking for brain damage. They also got her to complete basic exercises like walking and lifting a water bottle. It was agonising to watch Lila struggle to pick up a water bottle, and Lila hated being in the hospital. She also hated that the doctor refused to take out the blood drip and saline bag.

When the doctors finally did give her the green light to go home, she was over the moon with joy.

The sad thing was when she got home, Matt put her on bed rest, and she was still too weak to argue.

While Matt was cooking that night, we got a visit from Chase, the security guard from Eden Hotel.

I answered the door and had mixed emotions about seeing him standing there, holding a large bouquet of roses and a box of chocolates.

I stared at Chase blankly then shouted, "Matt! It's for you."

Matt came to the door and greeted Chase with a happy hello and an excited handshake as he thanked Chase for helping us to find Lila.

I rolled my eyes and turned away, sighing sarcastically, and as I did, I saw Lila running at full speed down the stairs. But when she got to the bottom step, she lost her footing. Luckily, I was fast enough to catch her; I moved at full speed quickly carrying her into the lounge room and onto the couch, while Matt was distracted with Chase.

Lila smiled at me and whispered, "Thank you" as I placed a blanket over her.

I then ran at full speed into the kitchen and came back with two hot chocolates one for me and one for her and sat down next to her whispering "You are so welcome."

Matt then walked into the lounge room with Chase, "Lila . . .," he said startled to see her, "you're supposed to be in bed."

Lila put on her pouty face and replied, "But . . . hot chocolate . . . so tasty. Bed . . . so . . . boring," all the while smiling innocently at Matt.

When she realised the pout wasn't working, she quickly changed the subject in a not so subtle form.

"Hello, Chase . . . It's good to see you again . . . What brings you here?" she asked, looking at the many roses in his hand.

I joked just to annoy Matt and said, "Lila . . . can't you see? He's here to woo you with flowers and chocolates."

Lila laughed along with me, but Matt didn't seem too impressed. And Chase awkwardly cleared his throat and explained, "Not quite. I'm just the delivery boy . . . not that I'm not interested in your well-being. I am . . . it's Maxwell who's trying to woo you."

Matt and I both stopped laughing and glared at Chase wanting to hear more information as he handed Lila the roses and chocolates.

"Max hopes that you are feeling better and wanted to assure you that his job offer still stands if you want it. And he's even happy to wait until you're back on your feet," Chase said, sitting down on the couch opposite me.

I watched as Lila's smile disappeared, and Matt, still very confused, asked, "What job offer?"

Chase held his breath looking at Lila apologetically, saying, "I'm sorry I thought you would have discussed this with them by now."

Lila sighed, looking back at Chase and replied, "Yeah . . . I've been little busy for that."

Chase nodded realising what he had done. "Right, I am so sorry . . . I swear, I wasn't trying to rush things. I was just really eager and excited to have you partner with me as head of security."

Lila looked back at Chase hinting for him to stop talking as she sunk deeper into the couch knowing that she was so totally busted.

I began feeling sorry for her and jumped in to save her, interrupting Chase saying, "You know, I think Lila's starting to get a bit tired. Maybe you should come back in a few days, once she's had a bit more time to rest and think."

Chase took the hint and excused himself saying goodbye to Lila as I walked him to the door myself.

Matt stood staring at Lila, waiting for an explanation, and I decided to join him staring at Lila, waiting for any kind of response.

Lila looked back at Matt with an innocent pout. "I don't know why you're both angry at me. It's not like I said yes," she explained.

Matt responded in a scary, angry yet calm tone. "But you didn't say no either," then walked into the kitchen to finish cooking dinner.

Lila slowly followed Matt into the kitchen and explained that Maxwell offered her a job in hotel security partnering with Chase to find his daughter. She listed the perks of the job—that it's high-paying with a company car, as well as health insurance and living expenses covered.

"Matt this is a job offer that I wanted to give serious thought to, and thought it would be fair to talk to you before I made any decisions," she said as Matt placed dinner on the table.

"Lila, you can't trust him," I interrupted, trying to convince her to say no. "He abducted us and flew us halfway across the country," I said furiously.

Matt interrupted, shocked at hearing this new information. "He what!" he shouted.

Lila and I continued to argue while Matt listened trying to follow along, as he helped Ruby and Danny get up to the table to eat their dinner.

Lila finished arguing, saying, "Alex, enough . . . Max is trying to work with us . . . and may I remind you that the last person who dropped in and asked for help was you.

Lila stopped, realising she had little ears listening to her, glancing at Danny and Ruby, and calmed down saying, "All he wants is his daughter back. He wants the same thing as you. And he has the means and the resources to do it. So if Matt's okay with it, I'm taking the job . . ."

I turned to Matt, hoping he was going to say no, but instead he took a moment to think and answered, "Sorry, Alex . . . I got to take Lila's side on this."

I was torn inside remembering the promise I made to Lila in the hospital, and I was beginning to think the worst. If Lila takes this job, I'll be back to square one, on my own with no home and no family.

I didn't want to make matters worse and speed up the eviction time. So I conceded, walking out into the backyard to cool off.

Lila waited until Matt was putting Danny and Ruby to bed before she started to slowly stumble her way out onto the patio, holding my dinner as a piece offering. I got up to slowly help her walk to the outdoor table, saying, "You shouldn't be out here," but I knew she wasn't going to listen to me.

She sat in silence with me as I ate my slightly cold dinner. After a while, she eventually spoke, to break the ice, I guess.

"So I don't know what to do here . . . I thought we made a pretty good team. You know, working towards saving your friends."

Lila choked back some tears, a little lost for words while shrugging her shoulders. "If you don't want to do this . . . if this is getting to dangerous for you . . . I will understand if you don't want to stay. I can make some calls . . . find a place for you—"

I interrupted her before she said the things I was dreading to hear and said, "Lila, I care for you . . . a lot. You are the most amazing friend I could ever have . . . you're currently the only friend I have, and seeing you almost die . . . it scared me . . ."

Lila sat and listened as I poured my heart out to her, and this time, she was actually conscious to hear it. "I can't lose you . . . you're all I have," I said pleadingly. "I know I agreed in the hospital to respect your decision to send me away, but I am begging you please."

Before I could say anymore, Lila stopped me and held my hands kneeling down in front of me to look me in the eyes, placing my hand on her chest, so I could feel her heart beating, and she held hers against mine and said, "Listen . . ."

I took a breath and did as Lila asked, listening to her heart beating. I could feel all my fears and worries drifting into the background, as she whispered, "Alex, I don't know what you said to me in the hospital. But I promise you now I will never send you away . . . I promised to help you and protect you. And I don't break my promises, especially to family. All I ask is that you trust me."

The next day Lila had made arrangement to meet with Maxwell and discuss the offer.

As soon as we walked in the door, Danny and Ruby gasped seeing how big the hotel was. And Lila, Matt, and I were greeted by an overly excited Chase and Maxwell, who were very eager to give us a tour around the hotel showing us all the facilities—indoor pool, sauna, games room, ballroom, and function rooms, the lower ground promenade with all the boutiques and shops.

Lila was especially excited when she saw the training room and gym, with a sparring mat and a lot of cool new toys to train with. Let's just say Lila's new punching bag—Hector—would fit in very nicely.

With each room that Matt and Lila saw, they got more and more excited. I, on the other hand, wasn't sold on the idea yet, but I just kept reminding myself of the promise I made to Lila.

Even if she was unconscious when I said it.

Max stopped on the rooftop garden to allow everyone to take in the city views. And he said to Lila, "There is one more thing I wanted to put on the table."

Lila looked shocked at Maxwell. "There's more to this?" she said pointing to the rooftop garden. Maxwell then led everyone down the stairs to Apartment 147 and opened the door showing Matt and Lila the empty apartment. "This is what I want to put on the table. Your own apartment, with round-the-clock access to all the facilities, including security. You know . . . so we don't have any more disappearances," he said, with a subtle guilty look on his face. "I think this will be the safest place in Melbourne for you."

Matt grew suspicious (FINALLY) as he watched Maxwell hand the apartment keys to Lila. "And what exactly do you want from us in return?" Matt asked.

Maxwell looked back at Chase with a confirmatory nod and replied, "Lila will be given the job of head of security alongside Chase, but her main objective is to find my daughter . . . You found her once, so I am confident you can do it again."

Maxwell smiled as he saw Danny and Ruby running around the apartment looking out all the windows to check out the views.

He then looked back at me, who had been very well behaved (upon Lila's request), and said, "And I didn't forget about you, Alex. I was told you were going to continue working with Lila as well . . . That's fantastic news. I have arranged for an apartment just across the hall from this one. It's slightly smaller, but I'm sure it will be adequate for you."

Maxwell then smiled at Matt and Lila. As he was beginning to leave, he said on his way out of the apartment, "Take your time, have a good think about it. I'll be downstairs when you've made up your mind."

It didn't take Matt and Lila long to make up their minds, considering Danny and Ruby had already picked out their rooms. But before Lila made the final decision, she turned to me and asked for my opinion. And honestly, I couldn't find any fault with the offer other than the fact that I think Maxwell was a jerk.

So I told her to take the offer.

CHAPTER 19

ALWAYS BAD NEWS

Journal entry by Terrence Connors

I have spent far too long and far too many of my recourses on capturing this pesky Animal Guardian.

I sat in my greenhouse near the coy pond, looking at the blood reports of the samples Daniel had brought back.

It infuriated me knowing that there was another Nature Guardian out there. I scrunched up the blood report and threw it in anger.

Daniel walked cautiously into the warehouse, looking almost as if he had worse news and was afraid to share it.

"Sir," he said tentatively, "we seem to be having more trouble than we expected acquiring the targets."

I was trying my best not to lose my temper, but it was a struggle. "You have hundreds of men and Guardians at your disposal, and yet you still fail to capture one little Guardian!" I yelled.

Daniel tried to explain himself with little success. "This new Guardian he's working with . . . she's strong . . . stronger than any Guardian I know of . . . even you," he said as he closed his eyes and braced himself expecting something horrible to happen to him.

His statement intrigued me; he must have genuinely believed this new Guardian was stronger than me, if he was willing to risk his own life to tell me so.

Daniel opened his eyes relieved he wasn't dead yet, then suggested, "Maybe it would be safer if we just left these ones. I mean we have enough Guardians now to complete all our objectives—" Daniel got interrupted as he saw the rose bush next to him, grew sharp thorny vines that began to wrap tightly around his arms and legs. He winced his face trying to be brave as he felt the thorns pierce his skin.

I was clearly growing impatient. "Be careful . . .," I warned him, "if you start thinking too much, you might end up back at the Village."

I walked closer to him to see the blood dripping from his arms as the thorns dug into his skin and his heart started to race in fear.

"Although, you have made me curious. Why would a Guardian such as yourself, with all your training and expertise, be more scared of one little girl than of me," I remarked as my eyes glowed green and the rose vines retreated back into the ground.

Daniel dropped to the ground and struggled to bear the pain as he asked, "Are you going to kill me?"

"I wouldn't have let you go, if I was planning on killing you," I snapped. I was then interrupted by a text message from my phone. As I paused to read it, I noticed two doctors from the village walking into the greenhouse towards Daniel.

I sighed, feeling a little sorry for him. "Unfortunately, your fate is out my hands. I'm sorry, Daniel. I hope to see you around," I said patting his shoulder, walking past him to exit the greenhouse.

As I was leaving, I glared at the security cameras and shook my head in disappointment. I knew "they" were watching. I looked back to see Daniel fall to the ground unconscious and rolled on a stretcher.

At that moment I knew it was my turn to get the job done or this time it would be me on that stretcher.

CHAPTER 20

I'M SO POPULAR

Journal entry by Lila Winters

Matt and I were unpacking all the moving boxes into the new apartment while we were listening to music. Danny and Ruby were busy setting up their new rooms and arranging their toys and teddies in all the right spots.

Matt took a quick break, checking out the city views from the balcony as Alex walked in carrying three more large boxes and placed them down next to the table, sighing in relief. "That's the last of them," he said, boasting proudly, smiling at me.

I opened the boxes and started to unpack and glanced out to the balcony to make sure Matt was distracted. Then at full speed, I unpacked all the boxes, roaming around the apartment, placing everything perfectly.

Alex watched me zoom around the apartment and poured out two glasses of water. He placed one of them on the bench in front of an empty bar stool. I then appeared at the bench, sitting on the barstool, drinking the glass of water.

Matt walked back into the apartment looking around the room shocked, "Wow . . . I can't believe we're finished already," he said impressed with the look of the place. "I don't know about you, but I am absolutely exhausted. Moving really takes it out of you," he mumbled, slouching down on to the couch.

Alex and I smiled at each other and said nothing as we drank our waters.

Matt then asked, "Alex, did you need any help getting settled?"

Alex pointed over at the small bag of clothes next to the door. "I think I'll be right, but thanks for the offer," he replied.

Our quiet relaxation time was then interrupted by the apartment phone ringing. Matt walked excitedly to answer it. "Our first phone call. I wonder who it could be," he said.

I used my super hearing to listen in on the conversation. It was Maxwell's voice on the other end. "Good afternoon, Mr. Winters, I have a guest in my office claiming to be from Mission Control and is requesting an audience with Lila."

I looked at Alex with a sad face then sighed looking at the ground. Matt turned around to see Alex and I walking out the door.

"I take it you heard?" he said sarcastically as he hung up the phone.

As I walked in to Maxwell's office, I saw Maxwell sitting at his desk with Chase standing next to him, looking concerned at the man standing opposite him waiting for us to arrive. His name was John, he was a 'human' agent that worked for Mission Control, who claimed all he wanted was to talk.

But that's not what I had planned for him. As soon as I saw him, I ran at full speed and punched him in the face.

I know I shouldn't have, but it felt really good, watching John fall to the ground, holding his bloody nose.

Alex rushed to pull me back screaming, "Lila! What are you doing?" furious at what I had done.

Mission Control was after all who Alex was really working for. I broke free of Alex's hold and frustratingly explained, "I'm giving this man the welcome he deserves, and then throwing him out."

Max got up and stood between me and John, trying to ease the situation. "All right, let's just all calm down now," he said in a stern negotiating voice. "All he asked for was an opportunity to talk to you. Just talk . . . So why don't we all just sit down, hear him out, then I will gladly have Chase kick him to the curb for you. Deal?"

But before I could agree to the deal, John stood to his feet and interrupted, "Actually . . . I need to speak to Lila and Alex alone."

Max turned to him shocked. "Are you sure you want to be left alone with her?" he asked.

John looked at Alex and nodded, then Alex hesitantly nodded back, knowing it would just infuriate me more.

Alex looked at me and held my hand and said only the word "please."

Damn. He used the word please. I then caved in asking Maxwell and Chase to leave promising I wouldn't destroy his office while we "talked".

As soon as the office door had closed, John started demanding answers from Alex and giving him a dressing down, like some kind of soldier.

"Explain to me what the hell you're doing here? Your orders were to remain hidden and protect her from danger," he barked. The yelling drudged up some old memories of my father yelling at his cadets like they were nothing but broken tools.

Alex tried to defend his actions and shouted, "I am protecting her!"

John pointed to me with his bloodied fingers and asked Alex sarcastically, "Then what is she doing here?"

At that point I'd had enough and stood protectively between Alex and John and shouted, "Hey!" to get both their attention.

I think Alex suspected I was going to punch John again because he held my arm cautiously.

But I ignored him and continued to yell back at John. "This "she" you're talking about is right here and _she_ would like to be spoken about and to properly. Before _she_ loses her temper again!"

John then stopped looking at Alex and glared at me instead, most likely contemplating how possible it was for me to follow through on my threat, then broke the tension by speaking in a more civilised voice, "Fine . . . Why are you here?" he asked.

I answered sarcastically seeing how the answer was obvious, saying, "I work here."

John replied, starting to get angry again, "No—you work for Mission Control."

I snickered amused at his ignorance and replied, "I will never work for you or your Mission Control."

The conversation started to get more intense as Alex stood watching, not entirely sure what to do.

"We recruited you to help us." John snarled.

I interrupted, responding in the same tone, saying, "And I chose not to help you."

John scoffed at my perceived ignorance and asked, "What makes you think you get to choose?"

"Because you need me, and I don't need you. I'm not stupid. I know how to play this game. And I know when I'm holding all the right cards, I get to make the choices . . . and I choose not to work for people who spy on me, invade my home, and implant tiny things in my head all to better serve their own agenda. Whatever that may be . . ."

My eyes began to glow green as I glared at John. He glanced around the room at all the potted plants beginning to grow bigger and taller, as if they were taking an interest in the conversation.

Alex took this opportunity to step in and try and ease the tension and asked pleadingly, "Lila, Lila, please look at me."

I took a deep breath to calm myself, turning to look at Alex. He cleared his throat, preparing to deliver his opening argument, hoping I would be willing to see his reasoning as he said "I know that you don't trust Mission Control . . ."

I sighed wondering where he was going with this.

"But you trust me, right?" he asked unsure of his current status of friendship.

I tentatively answered, "Right," looking confused at Alex, expecting a little more information.

"I still work for Mission Control, and I still need your help," he pleaded.

I smiled at Alex as I began to explain. "Alex, I told you I'd help you. But I will never work for him." I glared back at John as he rolled his eyes at me.

I then said calmly, "Now I am still happy for you to stay here with me, and we'll keep looking for your friends . . . here. But unless John has come with some new information on where to find the missing Guardians, I'm not leaving. Right here is where we have the best chance of keeping my family safe."

John interrupted with a loud and sarcastic sigh saying, "You cannot stay here. We do not let other humans know about your existence. That rule is there for a reason."

I turned and snapped, "I don't care about your rules. I care about my family. Now you have said your piece, it's time for you to go."

I opened the office door and looked back at Alex, who was looking down on the ground nervously and watched as John wiped the dried blood off his face. He walked out, saying his final words to me, "You have no idea who you're messing with," he whispered, he then walked out of the office to be greeted by Chase and two other security guards waiting to escort him from the building.

I looked back at Alex and commented, "You are welcome to leave with him, if you want. It won't affect our deal."

Alex looked up at me with puppy dog eyes like I had broken his heart as he said, "Lila—" but before he could finish his answer, Jessica walked in carrying a stack of paperwork for Maxwell to sign, completely oblivious of our presence as she listened to music though her headphones.

Alex held my hand protectively as we tried to quietly walk out of the office.

Unfortunately, Jessica heard us and demanded we explain why we were there. After she accepted our explanation of what just happened, she kindly offered us to arrange a driver to drive us home.

It then became clear to all of us that Maxwell had not been completely honest with his daughter as Jessica stormed out of the office, shouting angrily, "Father!"

I tried to muffle my laughter as I walked into the elevator. Alex followed me into the elevator but didn't seem as amused as I was.

He began to pace back and forth in the elevator. I watched and waited for him to let out his feelings, but I wasn't in a particularly patient mood.

So I asked, "Is there anything you want to . . ." but before I could finish the question, Alex began to unload.

"How could you think I would do that to you?" he asked.

He was vague with the question, so I just gave him a blank look and shrugged my shoulders.

"How could you think I would ever leave you? We made a promise. How, Lila?"

Not sure what to say, I stated the obvious, "Well, you do work for him, don't you?"

Unsure, Alex tossed between answers saying yes, no, maybe, and I don't know. And with me still not in a patient mood, I needed an answer.

"Alex it is a yes or a no. So you're going to need to choose one," I replied.

Alex stopped pacing and stood looking at me with the puppy dog eyes again and said, "Lila, you know I'll always choose you. You're my family . . . I just don't want to lose you like everyone else."

I put my hands on his shoulder trying to comfort him, "Alex, we've been through this. I'll be fine, you're not going to lose me."

Alex began to calm down as the elevator doors opened on the ground floor where my father, General Richard Willows, was waiting in his shiny, very intimidating uniform in the lobby.

I quickly let go of Alex and stepped out of the elevator asking, "Richard . . . what is he doing here?"

Richard answered as if it were obvious.

"Your mother," he said as he walked over to greet Alex and shake his hand. "Matt, good to see you again. How are the kids going?" he asked.

Alex cleared his throat, feeling very uncomfortable, and I quickly stepped into correct him, "That's not my husband," I said trying not to be snarky and added, "but that's okay . . . you've only met him once."

Then came that awkward and tense silence before I inquired, "No offence, Richard, if I'm skipping over the social niceties, but you've only ever visited me when you want something. So can we skip to that part, and say our goodbye."

Richard sighed. "Lila, your mother called me. We need to talk."

This next part got really boring and I kind of tuned out, so I'm not entirely sure what he said. But I'm sure it was something about all the trouble I had been getting into, the unexplained hospital visits, the bruises, and the recent kidnapping at the zoo . . . Yadda yadda yadda.

I tried to shrug it off as just a bit of harmless fun, gone terribly wrong. But he didn't believe me.

"So tell me, how did you really get the bruise on your back? And don't give me that crap about losing a fight because I know I trained you to be better than that," he snapped, demanding answers.

I shook my head in anger. "You trained me to be a killer," I replied.

Alex looked at the ground, trying to remain ignorant of the statement.

And Richard, insulted by the insinuation, defended his parenting skills. "I taught you how to survive. And now you've let your guard down, finding trouble everywhere you go!" he shouted.

The argument got more intense, and Alex thought to quickly and calmly push us all back into the elevator, where we wouldn't make a scene.

Which thinking back on it now was a very good idea.

Because I then yelled at Richard, "Then what would you have me do, kill everyone who pisses me off?"

It probably wouldn't have been the best thing to say in a hotel lobby—where I had just gotten a new job.

But my comment seemed to get us closer to Richard's true agenda as he proposed that I come back and work with him again.

"You'll have a nice home, a good steady income, and most of all, you'll be safe on the base."

"You know it's surprising. Not long ago I lost my job due to a major stuff up that I was responsible for and now out of the blue, I get three new job offers all in the same week. That's not suspicious at all," I commented sarcastically.

But before Richard could respond with another half truth, the elevator door opened back onto the lobby where Chase and the two security guards were waiting. Chase looked at Alex who was just as confused and then looked at me asking if everything was okay.

I grinned grateful for Chase's timely arrival and said, "It is now. The General was just leaving." I glared back at Richard sternly until he reluctantly got the hint to leave.

Alex and Chase both looked at me confused as I excused myself, running off at full speed.

Chase then looked back at Alex and said softly, "We're going to need to set some ground rules . . . about using your super powers in the hotel."

But Alex was distracted as he ran off at full speed after me.

Journal entry insert by Jessica Eden

I was so mad at my father, after we finished arguing about his new employees, and I stormed out of his office and into the elevator.

How could he do this? He put me in charge of finding my sister. And for what? to be replaced by two freaks with super powers.

You know what . . . I don't care what my father says, I am going to find my sister.

When the elevator doors opened, I became enraged as I saw Lila and her happy little family walking through the lobby, with Alex, following her around like a little lost puppy.

Lila shouted across the lobby to get Chase's attention as she said, "Hey, Chase, we're going out for dinner. Do you want to come?"

To my shock and horror, Chase just followed them excitedly, obviously another lost puppy.

"Seriously," I whispered frustrated as I stormed out through the side exit to my car mumbling to myself.

When I got in my car, Adela was sitting in the back seat, smiling at me from the rear-view mirror and said in a really creepy voice, "Hello sister."

I jumped in fright and must have blacked out because it was the last thing I remember until I woke up in my apartment the next morning.

CHAPTER 21

CAT AND MOUSE

Journal entry by Alex Woods

We had survived the weekend in our new home at the Eden Hotel. Lila even took me shopping to get some "homey" things for my apartment, to help me feel more comfortable, I guess.

It was Monday morning and Lila had been in the gym since sunrise, trying out all of the fancy new equipment.

When I finally arrived, she wasted no time rushing onto the sparring mat. She almost looked like she was itching for a fight.

I hesitated but asked the question anyway. "Is everything okay?"

Lila's nose scrunched up as she pulled a sour face. "I got a phone call from my mother last night," she replied. "It didn't go well."

We spent an hour sparring on the mat, each taking turns to be thrown to the ground.

Chase and a few of the other security guys came in to train before they flew back to Sydney with Mr Eden, but instead of training, they decided to watch and take bets.

That just made it more interesting for Lila. As she innocently smiled at me before grabbing my arm and twirling around, twisting my arm back along with her. If it wasn't for feeling the pain in my arms, I would have almost mistaken this for dancing.

As she locked my arms behind my back, I grinned back at Lila and accused her of being a show-off. She didn't take it well because before I knew it, I was in the air being sidekicked across the sparring mat.

She called for a time out when she spotted Matt standing at the door, grinning from ear to ear, watching me lose to his wife.

He walked over to give Lila a goodbye kiss and whispered in her ear, fully knowing that I could hear him as he said, "Kick his butt, hun," and walked out with an evil grin on his face.

I stood to my feet and grabbed a quick drink before we started the next round.

"You know I'm starting to get this not so subtle feeling that Matt doesn't like me very much," I commented.

Lila just laughed it off as she got back on the mat, ready to fight. I got a bit more competitive when Chase cheered, yelling, "Wooo! Go, Lila!" from the sidelines.

I took that as a challenge and formulated a plan to win.

As Lila went in for the first punch, I moved at full speed, diving out of the way and grabbing her by the waist, tackling her to the ground with me. As she landed on the ground, I moved at half speed straddling Lila's waist and pinning her hands down. "Hah! I win!" I exclaimed excitedly.

Lila squirmed, trying to escape gritting her teeth, "You cheated!" she said.

I leaned down and whispered, "Prove it" with the cheekiest smile. She kept trying to wriggle out of my hold on her as I snickered saying, "Give up, Lila . . . I've won."

She stopped squirming and glared up at me with a smirk and glowing green eyes. I soon realised her struggles were just a distraction while the nearby pot plant had grown large enough to wrap around my leg and throw me across the sparring mat. Lila stood to her feet, then looked back at me saying, "If that's the game we're playing . . . catch me if you can." She then ran at full speed out of the gym.

I quickly broke free of the plant and took off at full speed after her, leaving Chase and his team stunned, scratching their heads.

I chased Lila through the city through backstreet and alleyways, passing people and cars as they moved at a snail's pace.

I almost caught up with Lila a few times, but as she ran into Queen Victoria Gardens, I knew I had her. I pulled back to make her think she had lost me, then made a quick turn, cutting through the park and caught up with her, running alongside her. I quickly tackled her onto the grassy field, rolling to a very quick stop and laughing at each other as we tried to catch our breaths.

I was impressed and complimented Lila, "I see you mastered your running ability," I said, still gasping for air.

Lila smiled and confidently boasted, "I could totally run faster, if I didn't have to dodge all these people."

I laughed, agreeing with her statement, as we were rudely interrupted by the sound of my stomach growling.

Lila looked at me with a grin and said, "I guess all that running made you hungry. Come on . . . I'm buying."

We walked out of the park arguing about what we should eat for breakfast. I wanted a bacon and egg burger, but because Lila was vegetarian, we quickly scrapped that idea and settled on pancakes—her favourite.

We caught the tram to Melbourne central and had breakfast at the Pancake Parlour.

Lila must have been hungry because she wolfed down three stacks by herself, and I lost count of how many I had.

I thought this would be a good opportunity to talk, given that we were alone with no other particular people around.

"So what's our next step?" I asked, "in finding Adela."

Lila wiped the maple syrup off her chin and answered cautiously, almost as if she knew I wouldn't like the answer, "I was thinking . . . maybe we go back to the warehouse."

She was right, I didn't like the answer.

"The warehouse? The one where we were both ambushed and nearly died. Are you nuts?" I asked slightly sarcastic.

Lila tried to downplay the severity of the plan with a joke and said, "I'm not sure. I really don't like nuts," but then became serious and explained.

"Look, I know that last time we went there, things didn't go so well—"

I interrupted to state the obvious in a sarcastic tone, "So well, we walked blindly into their trap."

"A trap set for you," Lila rebutted "But I still think we could find information there that can help us. At the very least, we can find out who worked there or who owns it, and if they own other buildings in the area."

Her argument began to make sense, and I groaned saying, "So you're thinking that whoever owned the building might be in contact with Darkman?"

Lila rolled her eyes annoyed. "You know, we really need to come up with a better name for this guy," she said, walking to the counter to pay.

I snickered and finished off the last of the pancakes before we left and quickly caught up with her as she waited at the door for me and excitedly asked "So when do we leave?"

We ran back to the hotel at full speed, but before we could make it to Lila's apartment, we were greeted by Jessica Eden and her loyal gang of security guards.

Lila looked at the group and casually said hello and asked if Chase was still here. But Jessica didn't look like she was in a chatty mood and answered, "On his way to Sydney. And where have you two been?"

Lila and I both looked at Jessica and just shrugged our shoulders.

"I've got security footage of you running out of the hotel at a ridiculous speed . . . Care to explain?" she huffed.

Lila then sighed in relief thinking it was just a misunderstanding. "Oh, yeah, no . . . we were training."

But Jessica didn't believe her and kept up the interrogation. "For two hours?" she asked.

I tried to ease the tension by explaining that we went for a run then got hungry and stopped for breakfast. But as I explained, it became very clear to Lila that Jessica didn't care about where we were. Lila stopped me from talking and began her own interrogation, asking Jessica, "Why do you need to know?"

Jessica glared at Lila probably trying to intimidate her, which didn't seem to be working.

"It's my job to ensure the safety of everyone in this hotel. So from now on, you are to inform me of when and where you are. Is that understood?" she asked still glaring at Lila.

Lila took a slow breath. "Are we your prisoners again?" she asked.

Jessica glanced at the security guards and answered a reluctant no. This gave Lila the perfect opportunity to remind Jessica of a few things, saying "If that's the case, then let me remind you that we do not work for you. We work for your father. And he has told me, we can come and go from this hotel as we please. And until that changes, I suggest you let us do our job. Is that understood?"

The other security guards were shocked, staring at Lila, almost as if they had never seen anyone speak to

Jessica in such a way. And what confused them further was Jessica conceding and saying "Fine" as she walked away.

But because Jessica had to have the last say, she yelled back angrily, "No running in the hotel. Got it?"

Lila happily shouted, "Got it!" as she watched Jessica and her team walk into the elevator.

I stood in front of Lila, so proud of the moment and whispered, "I really don't trust that woman."

Lila shuddered in disgust, pinching her nose as she said jokingly, "And I really don't trust that smell. One of us really stinks. You should go get cleaned up and meet me in my apartment in twenty."

Lila took way longer than twenty minutes to shower because I was cleaned up and ready to go, waiting on her couch forty minutes later.

I'm guessing she still hadn't realised I was there, because when her mobile phone rang on the kitchen bench, she had walked out of the main bedroom wearing only a towel, completely oblivious to me lying on the couch, playing with one of Danny's bouncy balls. I didn't want to startle her, so I stayed quiet as she answered the phone.

"Hello?" she answered, then became really agitated. I could tell it wasn't someone good because her heart began to race nervously as she clenched her fist on the kitchen counter. "No, today's not good—I'm working . . .," she responded. It was a female voice on the phone, it sounded like Hanna; she was inviting Lila to the farm for dinner.

Lila responded getting angrier at the phone call. "Well, he'll just have to pick another day. Mum! I'm not the one who called him—you did. So if you want a family dinner, you're going to have to pick another day."

She didn't sound very happy when she hung up the phone and threw it down on the bench, still clenching her other fist.

I took this opportunity to announce my presence and stated, "So you're avoiding your mother now?"

Lila jumped in fright and threw a vase of flowers at me at full speed.

I moved at full speed to stand in front of her, with my hand up as a sign of surrender. "Whoa, it's just me. I'm sorry," I said, trying to calm her.

As Lila began to calm, she adjusted her towel attempting to cover more of herself. "Alex I said twenty minutes," she snarked.

I took the hint and turned away from her as she walked back to her room. But who am I kidding? I looked, and damn, it was good . . . But still trying to defend myself, I casually mentioned that it had actually been forty minutes.

Lila opened the door, so she could yell at me, "You could have waited in your apartment a little longer," she remarked.

"I did knock, but when you didn't answer the door, I got worried something had happened to you," I cautiously said, hoping she would buy it.

Lila came out of her room this time fully dressed and sighed, looking at me suspiciously.

She could definitely tell I was hiding a smile as we walked out onto the balcony.

Before we went any farther, I asked Lila, what she was planning on doing about the "Queen of Security".

Lila cleared her throat and responded, "Yeah, that's actually why I was taking so long in the shower. Other than enjoying the peace. I was thinking we'd play a game first."

A game . . . yeah, I wasn't sold on that idea and asked, "Why don't you just tell Max what's going on?"

Lila just shrugged her shoulders saying, "Oh, don't worry. Max already knows." She rolled her eyes and began to explain the full plan telling me that this game was going to test a theory Lila had about Jessica and the security as well as testing their abilities to track and capture a Guardian.

"Now, no more questions," she said, "let's go have some fun!" She climbed down to the ground using a vine she had created from the outdoor pot plant.

I couldn't fault her on the plan. It did give us the opportunity to weed out the bad eggs in the hotel's security. So I followed her down the vine saying, "Let the games begin . . ."

It didn't take Jessica long to realise we had gone, mostly likely alerted by one of the floor security guards.

We looked back at the hotel to see a group of security guards running out of the lobby, watching us board a tram and began to run after us, but the tram had already taken off.

I snickered a little, watching them running so "slowly".

The tram travelled around the city and up Swanston Street. There were a lot people on the tram, which made it easier for Lila and me to blend in as we stood in front of the tram, with Lila watching one door and I watching the other. When the tram pulled off from yet another stop, Lila leaned in close to whisper, "Two at the back of the tram, one sitting in the middle."

I discreetly nodded as she signalled to the tram driver to stop at the next stop. The tram stopped at Bourke Street Mall, and just as we suspected, as we got off the tram, so did the three obvious security guards.

Lila would definitely want to address that issue.

Lila grabbed my hand and quickly pulled me into a restaurant, packed with people out for lunch. She waved at the chef in the kitchen as she hurried me through the kitchen and out the back door. Lila looked up and smiled looking at the barred windows on the second level of the building, then jumped up to one of them and signalled me to do the same.

As we perched up on the windows the three security guys were shoved out of the back door of the restaurants kitchen as the chef started yelling at them to get out in what I think was Vietnamese.

The guys looked around the alley then started running back towards Swanston Street. We watched one of them touch his earpiece saying, "Lost them, they wouldn't be able to get far with this many people in the streets. Fan out and sweep up towards La Trobe."

Lila looked at me and nodded impressed at their knowledge and skills.

As they disappeared out of the alley, we both jumped down to the ground, but Lila must have lost her footing and grabbed my arm to regain her balance. I grabbed her other hand and looked at her "Are you okay?" I asked.

Lila smiled and tried to shake it off as she replied, "Yeah, I'm just not so great at the landing part of this yet. But I'll get there."

As I let go of her hand, I commented, "I'll give them credit, they know their stuff. We wouldn't be able to run fast enough with all these people in the streets. We would struggle to even get to half speed without being noticed by someone."

That didn't do anything to faze Lila as she walked down the alleyway in the opposite direction of the security guards.

"We're not planning on using our speed—that would ruin the fun. We're going to elude them the old fashion way. Besides, we want to give them some chance in finding us," she said as I followed her across the pedestrian crossing into Chinatown.

We were followed up to the Bourke Street's Target, so we hid amongst the clothing racks and moved around them as if we were in a maze.

When we left Target, we ran at a normal speed up Tattersalls lane towards the QV shopping complex. Running through the parking garage up into the main shopping area, Lila grabbed my hand again and pulled me into a coffee shop and stood at the counter looking at a store menu book. I looked at her confused as she still held my hand and asked, "Do you want one, babe?"

I played along leaning in to have a look and spotted in the corner of my eye one of the first security guards running past the store window, saying into his radio "They're not here, is someone still covering the trams? What about the train station?"

I was taken by surprise as the barista greeted Lila by her first name and handed her two cups of hot white chocolates saying, "No marshmallows, just the way you like it."

I looked up at the barista and then at Lila as she lets go of my hand to pass me a hot chocolate. She sat down at a table and looked at me as if she was waiting for me to say something. I just sat down at the table and sipped my hot chocolate, still looking at the barista.

Lila chuckled and said "To answer your question, that was Arthur and he's a friend from high school . . . Okay, we should have enough time now to compare notes. From what I've seen so far, they kind of know their stuff, and they use their tech and their team work efficiently, but they stand out really bad. What about you, any thoughts?"

She looked at me waiting for an answer, but I was drawing a blank. Damn. I didn't know what to say, so I just nodded and agreed with everything she said.

"Okay, we should probably head down to the Myer Complex next, it will be easy to dodge them through there, then we'll head up towards the warehouse. You ready?" she asked.

It was right about now, when I realised that Lila had way more training than just her sweet ninja skills.

All four of them coughed and spluttered until they fell to the ground asleep. All the other security guards just watched in shock, watching the pollen settle to the ground. Lila then carried Jessica to the van and gently placed her at the back. She signalled to the other security guards to help out their sleeping friends.

Maxwell pushed the hair back from Jessica's face saying, "I don't understand. Adela would never do this to her sister or the hotel staff. It's just not like her."

Lila took a moment to think and said, "Max, I need you to take Jessica to a doctor, one you can trust. Ask the doctors to do a full blood test and a pharmaceutical screen as well . . . Then bring me back a copy. And you should also keep them all in custody until we can figure this out."

She walked back towards the warehouse, still determined to get what we came here for.

As Lila opened the warehouse door, a burst of flames which filled the warehouse greeted her. The force of the sudden explosion sent Lila flying to the back of one of the white vans, and she fell to the ground, unconscious.

I ran to see if she was okay, but as I knelt down to help her, I saw across the street a woman watching with an outstretched arm as the building went up in flames. I looked down at Lila briefly then looked back up to see that the woman was gone.

I picked up Lila and looked back at Maxwell and the security guards, as they helped me load Lila into a van and drive away.

CHAPTER 22

PLAN B RUINED

Journal entry by Adela

I was enraged and threw my phone and earpiece against a tree as I listened to the sound of Alex's annoying voice through the earpiece, talking about his new girlfriend and how hurt she is by the explosion.

Argh! He makes me so mad . . . And she—what does anyone even see in her, she's just some newbie wannabe.

She's reckless that's what she is. "Why, why, why!" I screamed, chucking a minor tantrum and kicking the water of a small nearby pond.

I held my hand over the pond, creating a whirl pool in the middle, just to vent.

I turned around to see Mr Connors watching me and grinning, "I take it you failed," he sarcastically stated.

"No," I told him, "I just under estimated the targets, and I certainly wasn't expecting my father to interfere."

Mr Connors just continued to smile as he played with the branch of a nearby tree then walked towards the exit.

"I will give you one more chance to get the targets away from your family, or you know what will happen," he said in a seriously threatening tone.

I watched in fury as he left the greenhouse. Then looked over at the case file of Alex and Lila, and smiled as I came up with a brilliant plan C.

CHAPTER 23

FAMILY TIME

Journal entry by Lila Winters

Matt, Danny, and Ruby were sitting at the table having dinner when Alex and I walked through the door.

Alex was standing very close to me and looked very nervous, and it was obvious to Matt.

Danny and Ruby ran over to give me a hug, but as they wrapped their arms around me, they hit a very large bruise on my lower back, from being flung backwards into a van. I tried to hide my pain as I hugged them back. They were really excited telling me all about their first day at the new kinder and day care.

"All right, all right, it's my turn for a hug," Matt said, standing behind the children. "Now you two go eat your dinner. Then get ready for bed."

Danny and Ruby ran back to the table to eat their dinner as Matt gave me what felt like an over-the-top romantic kiss, but I got the feeling the kiss was for Alex's sake, not mine.

As Matt's hand slowly ran down my back, he could feel me moving away. He looked at Alex then back at me and asked, "How bad is it?"

I shrugged my shoulder and said, "It's not that bad."

But Alex didn't agree as he interrupted loudly, "Not that bad," he said. "There's a building on fire and a giant bruise on your ass, not to mention the two hours we just spent in the Emergency Room waiting for you to wake up. And it's not that bad."

Matt became agitated and questioned Alex, "Emergency room! Why didn't you call me? And why are you looking at her ass?"

It was then I got to realise that Matt wasn't overly concerned about the bruise or my hospital visit, as he glared at Alex.

"Anyway," I said trying to break the tension, "it's been a long day and I am starved. Are there any leftovers, honey?"

Matt responded through gritted teeth, "There're two dinners in the microwave for you."

I smiled and kissed Matt on the cheek saying, "Aww, two dinners . . . Either you think I'm not eating enough or you actually do care about Alex."

That comment was bound to stir up tension.

I grinned at Alex and chuckled, as they huffed at the very thought of them liking each other. Scandalous.

I got the dinners out and sat down and asked Matt if he was available to help in translating Jessica's lab results when they came in. I could tell Matt was excited, being able to help with the search.

So after dinner, Matt and I finished tucking the kids into bed, while Alex was in the study researching previous suspicious warehouse fires and discovered a pattern occurring. I popped my head in to check on him, "Hey, any luck?" I asked.

Alex turned to me excited. "Actually yes, I'm beginning to think that the warehouse fire was caused by Fire Guardian, not an explosion . . . and I think I know where their next target will be."

"That's great, I'll just go and finish fighting the dragon, and I'll bring out some chocolates as your reward," I mentioned, disappearing back into Danny's bedroom.

Alex must have tweaked when I said dragon because he followed me and watched from the door to see Danny, Ruby, and myself hiding under the bed, looking at a large dragon teddy sitting in the corner of the room hidden by some plants and a large box of Cadbury's Favourites being held captive by the dragon.

Danny and Ruby were wearing crowns and holding pretend swords.

"There he is . . .," I whispered to Danny, "the ferocious dragon that has stolen the towns chocolates, will now face his doom by the hands of the mighty knight Danny and fierce princess

Ruby. What are your orders, Sir Danny?" I asked waiting eagerly to attack the dragon. Danny held his sword towards the dragon and shouted, "Get him!"

He started crawling out of the bed and charged towards the dragon with Ruby and I right behind him. I used my powers to grow the plant leaves around the arms and head of the dragon to give it some life, as it starts moving around to protect the chocolates. The dragon moved to pounce on Danny, but I dramatically grabbed Danny and rolled him out of the way, and instead the dragon had me pinned. I looked back at Danny and Ruby and yelled, "Ruby, SAVE ME!"

Ruby charged with a fierce screech and pounced on the dragon teddy bear while I was still pinned underneath. I again dramatically yelled, "HELP!" Danny saw Alex standing by the door and ran to him pleading, "Alex, save my mummy . . . please."

Alex joined in with a beaming smile, "Don't worry, fair maiden, Sir Alex is here to rescue you!" he shouted in a husky deep voice. Alex grabbed hold of my foot and pulled me from underneath the dragon and held on, hanging me upside by my foot as Danny grabbed the dragon and threw it across the room yelling, "Ruby grab the treasure."

Ruby grabbed the chocolates and crawled up on the bed with Danny, eating the chocolate and laughing at the sight of mummy hanging upside down in Alex's hand.

I continued the act and looked up at Alex and in a maiden voice said, "Oh, Sir Alex, thank you for rescuing me . . ."

But Alex's face became serious when he saw Max and Matt standing at the bedroom door, looking amused and confused at the scene we had created.

"Sir Matthew and Sir Maxwell," I said, still hanging upside down, "to what do we owe the pleasure of your company? Hath thou brought more treasure to share?"

Maxwell stopped giggling for a second and said in a knightly voice, "No, my lady, but thy hath brought papers with strange writings for us to uncover."

Matt looked at Max shocked, that he was playing along.

Then he looked at Alex still holding me upside down and took a moment to come up with, "Well, if Sir Alex would put my fair maiden down, we shall share in the treasures together," he said hesitantly.

Alex quickly grabbed my hands and let go of my foot pulling me the right way up.

Danny and Ruby tapped on Alex's leg to get his attention and gave him a chocolate. Ruby had the giggles as she hugged Alex and said, "Thank you for saving my mummy, Uncle Alex."

Alex glanced up at me then back at Ruby and said softly, "Any time, Princess." He picked Ruby up and tucked her into bed saying, "You have sweet dreams, okay?"

After the kids were asleep, we all stood around the island bench sharing the last of the Cadbury Favourites, looking at the lab results that Max had brought and the news articles and police reports that Alex had found.

We looked at Matt, eagerly awaiting is findings as he looked over the lab results of Jess and the three security guards.

"Here's something," he said, quickly googling something on his phone. "At a glance I can tell, this isn't a full workup of bloods. Probably because it was a rush job. But there are a few chemical compounds that stand out and are present in all four blood tests. If I am right, they've been dosed with a drug called Neuritamine."

Max became anxious. "Jessica doesn't do drugs," he said defensively.

"No, it's not that kind of drug," Matt replied. "To my knowledge, this drug hasn't even been FDA approved."

"So how do you know about it?" Alex asked suspiciously.

Matt responded in a snarky tone, "I read a journal article about this drug years ago when I first went to university. There was an argument in the science industry of the drug to be destroyed and banned from ever being created again."

Confused, I was the first to ask, "Why?"

Matt looked at me scared and said "It's a neurosuppressor. It causes users to be highly susceptible to hypnotic suggestion."

Max sat down on one of the bench stools trying to absorb all of the information, muttering, "That explains Jessie's sudden change in behaviour."

"And it might explain your other daughter's behaviour, if she's been drugged as well," I added and turned to Matt asking the dreaded question, "Is there any way to reverse the effects?"

Matt shook his head as he looked at the search results from his phone. "There's one theory that if you flush the drug out of the patient's system, they may come out of the hypnosis . . . but it's just a theory."

Max stood up excited, saying, "I'm willing to test that theory," and he picked up the phone to call his doctor.

I turned to Alex and waited for him to share his results.

He laid out a large map of Australia with little red X's marked in most of the major cities and a few small towns. "I found out that the warehouse was owned by a delivery company that's part of a chain, but when I googled them, they all seem to have gone up in flames," he said pointing at the X's. "Each X mark shows where there's been a warehouse owned by this company, which had been burned down."

Alex then pointed to a little blue X and said, "This one hasn't burnt down yet."

I looked closely to read the town's name. "Bendigo," I said confused. I looked at the map again and all the red X's and took some time to think as Max hung up the phone from the doctors.

Still studying the map and looking at the news articles, I mumbled, "It almost looks like they're cleaning house or trying to get rid of the evidence."

Alex nodded in agreement. "That's what I thought. I was also thinking that if we hurried and got there first, we'd find the evidence we needed. Nobody knows that we know about this, so we wouldn't be walking into a trap this time."

I grinned as I came up with a brilliant idea and said, "No, but we can set a trap" and started pacing the kitchen floor deep in thought. "You said you suspected it might be a Fire Guardian setting all these fires, right? So he or she might be working with Adela . . . If we drive to Bendigo tonight and visit the warehouse early morning. We could set out traps surrounding the building . . . thus, protecting us, and if we catch something, it's just an added bonus to help lead us to the other Guardians."

I looked at Alex and Matt to get their opinions.

Alex seemed sceptical but up for the road trip. But Matt wasn't too impressed, at the thought of me going so far away, especially after being in the hospital for two hours.

Max jumped at the idea. "I will call and organise a hotel for you to stay in tonight and arrange Chase and a team of my security guards to follow you up—"

"No," I blurted, interrupting Max.

Both Matt and Max looked back at me, wanting an explanation and said in unison, "Why?"

I sighed and started to explain that a smaller team of two is less likely to be noticed.

Matt and Max both responded in unison, saying, "You can't go with just Alex, it's too dangerous."

I looked at Matt and Max and then at Alex who seemed just as surprised.

I stopped pacing and exclaimed, "Okay . . . first of all, that's weird. Second of all this is a long shot at best, we may just be on a wild goose chase here. And third of all, Max your team has been compromised, and there's no way I'd feel safe working with them until they've all done a full blood test. Which is why Matt has to stay back and help you. Once a few of your security guards have been cleared, then you can send them up to Bendigo to meet us."

Max and Matt both nodded in agreement with a sad face, and the whole unison thing they were doing was still weirding me out.

Alex walked towards the door and said, "I'll grab my gear and meet back in five."

I grabbed the keys and packed a bag, kissing the kids goodbye before I left. Matt walked us down to the basement carrying my bag to the car. But before I could get in the car, Matt pulls me back to give me, yet another over-the-top romantic kiss.

I could hear Alex huff as he got into the driver's side and waited.

As we drove off and out of the city, I spent the better part of the drive drawing out my plan on a town map of Bendigo.

CHAPTER 24

ROAD TRIP

Journal entry by Lila Winters

It was just before midnight when we arrived at the hotel; but by that stage, I had fallen asleep.

Alex quietly got out of the car to collect the room keys, then gently pulled me out of the car and carried me into the room, carefully placing me on the bed. He was even nice enough to avoid touching the bruise on my back by placing me on my side. He then began set up a makeshift bed on the floor. But as he went to get a spare pillow, he stubbed his toe on the end of the bed.

I sat up to see him silently screaming in pain and asked, "Are you okay?"

Alex tried to put on a brave face and lay down on the floor and said apologetically, "Sorry, I was trying not to wake you."

I popped my head over the side of the bed to look at Alex strangely. "What are you doing?" I asked again.

Alex sat up and explained that the hotel only had one room available and wrongly assumed that because we were male and female that we were a couple or at a least family.

"Okay, so we'll just have to share the bed . . .," I stated demandingly, "it's better for us to both have a good night's sleep. So climb in . . . I promise I don't bite."

Alex hesitantly climbed into the bed and got comfortable, trying to keep some distance between us. Which I thought was very gentlemanly of him.

"Good night, Lila," he whispered as he turned off the light.

Journal entry insert by Matt Winters

It was early morning, and Max and I had already arranged a nurse to draw blood from all the staff members, claiming there may have been a possible drug ring running in the hotel.

I sat at the dining table and asked, "Is what we're doing legal?"

Max just smirked and said, "Technically, yes, it's in the employment contract, stating that we can request a blood sample if we suspect they are under the influence of drugs or has a contagious disease that may put other staff or guests at risk," he explained.

I was impressed at his legal knowledge and asked, "So what do we do now?"

Max sat down at the table and said, "We wait."

He looked over at me and saw the worry on my face.

"I wouldn't object to you going after her," he said glancing at my keys on the bench.

I just shook my head. "I want to . . . but I can't. I don't want her to think I don't trust her," I replied.

Max looked at me and questioned "Do you?"

I nodded with absolute certainty. "Yeah I trust her with my life," I said. "It's Alex I don't trust . . . I mean, he's a guy, isn't he?"

Max shrugged his shoulders and said, "Perhaps he's just not interested in her that way."

Original journal entry continued by Lila Winters

Alex woke up to the sun peering through the window and onto his face and grimaced, trying to move, when he realised that I was asleep with my head resting on his chest and my arms wrapped around him. He brushed the hair from my face to see me smiling as I slept, he placed his hand on my cheek, smiling as I opened my eyes looking up at him. I then quickly realised what I was doing and pulled away, hastily getting out of the bed. "Sorry . . . um . . . Force of habit," I mumbled nervously.

"It's okay, Lila, I didn't mind," he replied, he then laughed as he heard the sound of my stomach rumbling. "I take it's time to hunt for breakfast," he asserted as he got up to stretch.

We both became startled when my phone started ringing on the dresser I looked at Alex suspiciously as I went to check caller ID, I sighed in relief. "It's the General," I explained.

Alex grabbed the keys and opened the room door for me and questioned, "Remind me again why you're avoiding him?"

I dodged the question and began to explain to Alex the plan that I had drawn up on a local map as we walked to the car.

We stopped at McDonald's to pick up some breakfast on the way to the warehouse and stopped a few blocks away to stake out the place while we ate.

As we finished eating, I commented, "It looks abandoned."

Alex looked at me worried. "And does that affect our plan?" he asked.

I shook my head, stepping out of the car and looking back at Alex I said, "Meet me back here in an hour," and ran at full speed into the nearby nature reserve that was surrounding the outside of the industrial park.

Journal entry insert by Matt Winters

I walked out of my room after having a shower, still drying my hair and glanced over to see Danny and Ruby watching cartoons on TV. When I walked over to the kitchen to prepare breakfast, I noticed a large yellow envelope poking under the front door of the apartment.

"Curious," I mumbled, picking it up to investigate. It had no marking and wasn't addressed to anyone.

I carefully opened it and became fuelled with rage when I saw a photo of Alex lying on top of my wife, at what looked like a city park.

My jealousy must have overtaken me because I was out that door with the kids in under five minutes.

Original journal entry continued by Lila Winters

I was almost finished setting my last trap standing in the nature reserve with my hands resting on two trees, concentrating as I watched the small branches from the trees grow and weave a large net, and resting it down on the ground. The tree rustled, shaking off some of its leaves over the net to disguise it.

Suddenly a parrot flew and landed on my shoulder, holding a flower. Squawk, it said dropping a flower into my hand and then flew away.

At that moment, Alex jumped down from the trees behind me, almost as if he was trying to startle me.

I pulled a sour face pointing down to the net he had almost landed on. "Alex, this is no time to play games. You nearly got caught by my net!"

Alex huffed saying, "But without games, it's just no fun. Besides, it's always good to keep you on your toes."

My phone started ringing again, I checked the caller ID—it was the General again, So I turned the phone to silent mode.

We cautiously crept into the warehouse, through the now broken back window. And as we looked around, we saw old food left on the table in the lunch room, boxes half packed, and safety vests just thrown on the floor.

Alex picked up a vest and studied it for any name tags and smelled a strong chemical odour soaked into the material. "Eerk, whoever they were and whatever they were doing, they certainly left in a hurry," he whispered.

I walked over to inspect the half-packed shipping box to see hundreds of small vials labelled Neuritamine. "Wow," I commented, "now that's a lot of drugs!"

I pulled out my phone to take a photo of the vials, but before I could take a photo of the shipping label, we were startled by a loud crackling noise coming from outside in the trees, followed by dozens of birds squawking very loudly.

"And that would be our guest . . .," Alex boasted. "Race you there?"

I accepted his challenge as we raced at full speed out of the warehouse, into the trees following the sound of the squawks, and stopped to stare at the sight of an elderly lady, probably in her seventies trapped in one of my nets. I looked at her, shocked at her age, and turned to Alex and asked in panicked whisper, "What do we do if it's not a bad guy, and we've just trapped an old lady."

Alex looked inside the net then began to carefully approach her, "Wait, I know her . . . I think she's a Guardian."

I held up my fist ready to fight and asked, "Good or bad?"

The old lady didn't take my question too well as she yelled, "What do you mean, good or bad? Who the hell are you?"

I shouted back in defence, "Hey, that's my question—"

But Alex interrupted me and answered, "We're Guardians."

The old lady called him a liar as she claimed all the Guardians had been taken.

I rebutted her claim. "Well, are you a Guardian?" I asked.

She looked at me with a dumbfounded look and answered sarcastically, "Well of course I am—"

I cut her off before she could say anything else and asked, "Have you been taken?"

That seemed to shut her up pretty quickly as she turned to properly look at us.

"I wouldn't bother burning through the net. It's made out of wet branches . . . It will take you hours to get out," I said smugly.

She looked at me with a cocky smile. "A Nature Guardian . . . aren't you a rare one."

I grinned back and replied, "And a Fire Guardian. Just a plain old common one. So glad we've worked that out."

She rolled her eyes and sighed. "So are you going to let me down or am I just going to hang here all day?"

Alex leaned over and whispered to me asking, "Can't you just sense what her nature is?"

I glared back at Alex then whispered, "Not unless I am touching her. And since she's a Fire Guardian, I'm not going anywhere near her."

The old lady just yelled, "I'm waiting," as the net began to swing.

I looked at Alex who clearly had no idea what to do and eventually, I put my hand on the tree to lower the net.

But as the old lady stood up from the nets, she turned quickly to throw a fireball towards me.

"Look out!" Alex yelled, tackling me to the ground. At that moment tree roots sprung up from the ground, creating a shield protecting us from the fireball and another set of roots reached up from under the old lady, wrapping around her before she could run away.

Alex looked up at the shield in awe, as he held me in his arms "I didn't know you could do that," he whispered back to me.

"Neither did I," I said quietly as Alex helped me to my feet.

We walked out from behind the shield to see the old lady tied up in the root, struggling to escape its tightening grasp.

She furiously glared over at me and snickered. "Well played, Nature girl. You have more experience then I gave you credit."

I brushed off the leaves and dirt from my pants and walked over to put my hand on the old lady's face, trying to concentrate.

Alex hovered closer to me, staring at the old lady nervously.

I shook my head in confusion. "All I sense is anger," I mumbled.

The old lady snickered and pulled her face away, snarling "Well, of course, I'm angry! Wouldn't you be, if your family was taken from you, while you had gone out for simple a walk . . . If I had gotten home sooner, I would have saved my dear Henry—"

Alex interrupted her rant to confirm, "Henry? Henry Hooper?" he asked.

The old lady scowled at Alex with suspicion with the "I'm going to kill you when I get out of this" look on her face.

But as Alex began to explain, she began to calm down, slowly. "Henry Hooper was my elder, before he went missing. That's how I know you. Your name is Jennifer, right?"

The old lady then confirmed her name "Yes, my name is Jennifer Hooper, but if your name is really Alex. Then you're in a lot more danger then I am, along with your girlfriend over there. I've heard rumours that the Darkman himself has been sent to obtain you, and the woman you travel with . . . What on earth are you doing out here?" she asked in sheer confusion.

"We're trying to find them," Alex replied, "your husband and the others."

I butted into their conversation and frustratingly commented "But we don't seem to be having much luck. When all of our leads keep going up in flames."

I then reached my hand out towards the roots wrapped around Jennifer as I ordered the roots to retreat back into the ground.

Jennifer regained her bearing as she stood dusting herself off and admitted to starting the fires. Alex became enraged and accused her of nearly killing me.

She stood back, creating a fireball in her hand saying apologetically, "Look, I'm sorry about what happened yesterday. I didn't know you were trying to help find them. I was just trying to send a message to whoever took him."

I scoffed in disbelief and asked, "What was it . . . 'Here I am, capture me now!'"

Jennifer explained, "They'd never take me— I'm too old. And as you said before, I'm common."

"No, but they might just kill you instead," I replied.

I turned to Alex and asked, "So what do we do with her now?"

He took a moment to think. "She is one of us," he mumbled. "And she may be able to help."

Jennifer interrupted his thought saying, "I don't know how much help I can be . . . "

"I'm kind of agreeing with the old lady here," I snickered. Jennifer looked back and scoffed at my old lady comment.

Alex pulled me aside and began to justify his thoughts. "Lila, we're both learning this stuff as we go—and it would be a lot easier if we had someone who knew what they were doing," he pleaded with me, and when he looked at me with his puppy dog eyes, I had no choice but to cave in.

"Fine," I answered with a condition, "as long as she agrees not to torch every lead we find. That includes people."

I stared at Jennifer, waiting for her to agree to the terms.

She took a moment to think, then looked down at the fireball she still held in her hand and at full speed tossed it towards the warehouse, watching it go up in flames.

She turned to me and said, "I'm assuming you already got what you were looking for . . . and I did come all this way . . . but yes, I will join your team and help you find my family."

I scowled at Alex and huffed, "She's your recruit . . . you handle her," and ran at full speed back to the car.

Alex and Jennifer followed me to the car, and we drove quickly away from the burning building, listening to the sound of sirens in the distance. We pulled down a few side streets and stopped at Lake Weeroona Park to check in with Max and Matt.

But when I phoned Matt's mobile, no one answered.

Jennifer began to walk alongside the lake, and Alex followed her to ask questions.

And since I didn't fully trust Jennifer, I followed as well. She turned around to face me and asked, "Forgive me, but I'm assuming that because you're a Nature Guardian and that your kind disappeared centuries ago, that you did not have an elder to guide you, correct?"

I tentatively nodded, as Jennifer began searching the park for a particular tree and muttered to herself.

"I'm sorry, Mrs Hooper, but what are we doing here?" I asked, "It's getting dark, we should start heading back to Melbourne."

She gasped excitedly when she finally found the tree she was looking for, replying, "Don't be ridiculous. The last thing we want is to be caught in the centre of Melbourne while you're mid-bonding, by a human or worse one them."

Bewildered by her statement, Alex and I just silently stared at her waiting for her to explain.

Jennifer rolled her eyes and sighed. "You're new at this, right? When you begin training, you must first go through a meditation phase to better understand your element."

I turned to Alex and pulled a sour face and barked, "I take it you forgot about that?"

He shook his head explaining, "I tried to do the meditation, but Mr Hooper told me that my mind was racing too fast for me to concentrate long enough. Plus, I didn't think it was that important."

Jennifer continued her explanation, saying, "It is difficult, but I think you will be successful—especially considering how much control you already have with your element."

I looked at Jennifer in disbelief—there was no way I had as much control as she thought.

Jennifer watched me and grinned shaking her head. "Look, I know it wasn't you who created the shield back at the warehouse . . . Something in nature wants to help you, and you need to let it," she said as she hinted for me to sit at the base of the large old pine tree.

Still sceptical, I huffed then stood amongst the group of trees, scowling back at Alex.

Jennifer just accepted it, then took a few steps back as she instructed me to relax, close my eyes, and open my mind.

How cliché . . .

"Try to sense nature, its feeling, its movement, its life . . .," she said softly, "and once you have done that, try to call to it."

I did as she instructed and began to feel my heartbeat slowing, and hear the trees as they swayed. I smiled as I felt the warmth of the moon on the flowers. Everything began to slow down and settle.

I could sense Alex was nervous as he looked around at the trees, but before he could say anything, he watched in horror as the roots from the old pine tree sprung up from the ground and pulled me down to the base of the tree. The roots then wrapped tightly around my body, binding me to the tree.

Alex shouted my name again and again, but I remained in a half-meditative state, still aware of my surroundings but only barely. He turned back to Jennifer and yelled in panic. "What have you done to her?" as he began to pull at the roots that were binding me.

Jennifer gasped uncertain as to what was happening. "Alex . . . I'm not sure. I've never seen this before. I'm not a Nature Guardian. I can't tell you if this is normal."

Alex then spotted the dagger that I kept tucked in my boot and started slashing away at the vines, but as he pulled the vines away, more of them sprung up to take their place.

Alex kept slashing until he watched as two of the vines pierced into my body, one in my stomach and one in my shoulder. I screamed in agonising pain as they entered my body but still stayed in a trance, unable to move. He tried to pull the vines out, but the more he pulled the more they grew in to my body.

Jennifer stopped him, pulling him away, as I screamed trying to bear the pain. He gently held my face up trying to wake me, screaming my name, but then gave up kneeling down next to me and wiping the tears from my cheek.

He became enraged, turning back to Jennifer and shouting, "This was your idea—now fix it!"

But Jennifer didn't know how to fix it. "Alex, as gruesome as I think this is . . . part of this was supposed to happen. From what I understand, the tree is simply trying to protect the host as it tries to bond with her. I think you need to just give her time . . . and pray she wakes up," she suggested, nervously looking at all the vines wrapped around me and in me.

Alex just looked at me and teared up saying, "You're not allowed to die, you hear me . . . You have to wake up."

He sat down next to me and held my hand as he tried to hold back his tears.

CHAPTER 25

IT WAS ALL A DREAM

Journal entry by Lila Winters

The meditation I was in felt like a dream but then it also felt real. I was standing alone in a rainforest surrounded by tall trees that almost blocked out the sun. I opened my eyes as I heard Alex's voice screaming my name. I looked around and called to him, "Alex? Where are you? Alex!" Looking around again, I asked myself, "Where am I? . . . Hello . . . Can anybody hear me?!"

Journal entry insert by Alex Woods

I sat next to Lila holding her hand as the night grew colder. Jennifer had gone back to the car to get some blankets from the boot and had grabbed a few packets of chips from the petrol station down the street. She draped the blanket over me and handing me a packet of chips, suggested I eat something.

"Are you kidding me? How can I eat something when my best friend is being eaten by a tree?"

I stared at Lila, holding back tears and feeling her cold hands and cheeks and in panic said, "I think she's getting worse."

Jennifer shone a torch to inspect the vines digging into Lila's body and shook her head. "As long as her heart's still beating, I have hope," she remarked, sitting down and making herself comfortable with the blankets.

I stood to my feet and towered over Jennifer shouting. "Her heart may be beating but that tree is killing her!"

But I was quickly interrupted by Matt as he barrelled up from the footpath and tackled me to the ground punching me and screaming, "You bastard! How could you do this to my family!"

I didn't even try to protect myself. I knew that this was my responsibility. I vouched for Jennifer, and Lila trusted me. All I could say was "I'm sorry . . . I'm trying . . ."

Matt continued to punch me until Jennifer pulled him off and threw a fireball at his feet to get his attention, standing between me and Matt.

"Young man, explain yourself and do it fast," Jennifer demanded as she created another fireball in her hand.

I moved at half speed to stand in front of Matt to protect him and explain, "Wait, he's Lila's husband," begging her to refrain.

Jennifer quenched the fireball and apologised as she sat back down.

I attempted to explain to Matt what was going on, but Matt was still angry as he punched me again then started asking questions. "What did you do with my wife?!" he shouted, as he punched me again. "Where is she?!" he shouted again as he continued to punch me.

I then realised Matt didn't know what was going on and stopped Matt mid swing and calmly suggested "I don't know why you're currently angry with me, and whatever it is I'm truly sorry. But you need to calm down, if you ever want to help her."

Matt pulled back his fist as I shone the torch up to the tree where Lila's unconscious body was being held.

"Oh god . . .," Matt gasped as he ran to try and help her and did exactly what I did trying to pull the vines away and shouting, "What have you done to her?"

I rushed to stop him, pulling him away, as Lila yelped in pain and more of the vines pierced into her leg and arm in reaction to Matt's actions.

He tried again, but I grabbed his hands snapping, "Stop! You'll only make it worse."

Matt looked at Lila and agreed with me as he relaxed his hands and gently held her ice-cold hands. "Lila," he whispered. "Lila . . . come on, honey, wake up."

Original journal entry continued by Lila Winters

I could hear Matt's voice as I walked through the rainforest, still stuck in the meditation, I think. I was scared and confused as I looked around for him, "Matt!" I yelled, but I saw nothing.

I walked through the rainforest which felt never ending and shouted, "Hello! Can anyone hear me? At least tell me what I'm looking for!"

Suddenly I heard a raspy voice say, "You're looking for me."

I turned around, looking for whoever spoke and saw a large figure climb down from the trees and stand before me. It looked like an old man, but his skin looked like wood, covered in bark with leaves and moss growing from his limbs. Completely stunned at the sight, all I could say was, "Whoa! What in God's name are you?" I asked.

The tree man looked at me curiously and answered, "We are nature . . . You have summoned us . . . why?" he asked as he walked around me in a circle as if he were inspecting me.

"Um . . . I'm here to better understand nature, right?" I asked.

I wasn't sure if that was what I was supposed to say, but I said it anyway.

The "tree man" stopped and looked at me saying, "If that is your wish . . ." and began to walk away.

I followed, still unclear what to do, asking, "Okay, so how do I do that?"

The tree man stopped and glanced back at me, answering, "You must stop fighting us," and continued to walk away.

I was beginning to get very annoyed at this whole mindful spirit mumbo jumbo. I just wanted an answer that would get me out of this weird place.

"What do you mean fighting you? I'm not fighting you," I replied, but as I spoke, the tree man was absorbed into a tree and disappeared. I just stood in shock and knocked on the tree saying, "Hello . . . Mr Tree man."

Journal entry insert by Matt Winters

I was starting to lose hope as Lila remained unresponsive. I struggled to believe that after all Lila's been through this past week, that she would meet her end by a tree. I thought nature was supposed to be her element.

I turned to Alex and his new friend Jennifer. "We should call an ambulance," I said, turning to Alex.

Alex quickly shot my idea down saying, "And what are we going to say? Please help . . . our friend is being attacked by a tree."

I wasn't overly fond of the sarcasm but before I could respond, his friend Jennifer ran up and shushed both of us, whispering, "Someone is coming."

She quickly grabbed Alex's blanket and covered Lila to hide her, then quickly hid with us amongst the trees.

A small group of teenagers walked by on the footpath, but noticed nothing out of the ordinary distracted by their own tomfoolery.

We all looked nervously at Lila as she winced in pain, making the slightest noise, mumbling Alex's name. But the teenagers continued on, walking farther around the lake.

As soon as the teenagers were out of sight, both Alex and I rushed to see if she was okay, but she was still unconscious. I felt her cheek and forehead and discovered she was getting colder. "Alex, I need you to find some more blankets. We have to try and keep her warm, or she risks hypothermia," I said to Alex.

Alex ran at full speed back towards the car as I took the blanket off Jennifer and placed the second blanket over her.

Jennifer stepped in closer to offer assistance, and I watched cautiously as she placed her hand on Lila's chest and arm, creating a warming red glow around Jennifer's hands.

"This should keep her warm for a while," Jennifer said trying to reassure me.

Original journal entry continued by Lila Winters

Still stuck in the rainforest, I had given up and decided to sit down on a fallen tree log, when I felt this warm feeling surge through my body.

I could even feel Matt's hand holding mine and hear is whispers in the wind saying, "Stay with us."

I closed my eyes and whispered back, "I'm coming back . . . I promise."

I stood up again and started running through the rainforest, trying to find a way out or a way home.

I kept running until I was stopped by another tree creature, this time a woman. She looked very similar to the man, except she had a gold necklace around her neck with the name Agatha engraved on it.

"Agatha," I questioned as she stared back at me and nodded once. I assumed it was to confirm her name, but then she spoke accusing me of fighting them still and questioned why.

"I don't know what you mean. How am I fighting you?" I asked again, as I watched her disappear back into the trees.

"No, wait, please. I need your help," I pleaded. "Please, help me get back."

I looked around in panic, worried I may never return home.

Journal entry insert by Alex Woods

Something definitely started to go wrong, when I heard Lila's heart rate increase. Even Jennifer started to get anxious as she watched Lila trying to wriggle and squirm around, trying to free herself. But every time she moved, the vines grew tighter and deeper, still keeping her in a deep meditative state.

I felt helpless when she called out my name and a tear rolled down her cheek; Matt didn't seem to be taking this too well, probably didn't help that she kept calling my name and not his.

But he kept a brave face and just kept saying, "Hold on Lila . . . just stay with us, okay?"

Jennifer must have heard something because she quickly pulled her hand away from Lila and signalled Matt and me to hide.

We hid back in the same spots as last time and watched as a local police man patrolling the area walked past following the footpath. Unfortunately, at that exact moment, Lila whimpered and let out a small yelp. The police man heard it and shone his torch towards her, and asked, "Hey, buddy, you okay?"

He then pulled the blanket away from Lila to see if she was okay but stumbled backwards when he saw the state of her body and what the vines had done to her. He rushed over to a nearby bush to vomit and scrambled to grab his radio to report the scene and probably call an ambulance.

That was when Matt and I ran out to plead with him and ask him to stop.

"Wait . . . Please!" I begged.

Matt quickly grabbed hold of the policeman's radio to stop him, but the policeman was still in a state of panic as he pulled out his gun towards Matt.

Matt stepped back and put his hands up and said, "It's okay, we can explain . . . Please . . . we're not here to hurt anyone."

Suddenly a large wave came up from the lake and crashed down on the policeman, knocking him to the ground, but not before he let off a gunshot, hitting the tree Lila was trapped in.

She screamed in agony as the tree reacted and wrapped more vines around Lila, piercing further into her skin.

The policeman watched and fainted at the sight of what was left of her.

Adela appeared in front of us, standing over the policeman's unconscious body. "I despise men with weak stomachs," she sighed as she glanced at the vomit stains on the man's uniform.

I stood protectively between Matt and Adela and demanded Matt to stay behind me.

Matt hurried back to Lila in panic, trying to wake her up. I guessed at that point, Matt knew who Adela was and that we were in a lot of trouble if Lila didn't wake up.

I had to think on my feet, looking around the park for something to use as a weapon and tore a large branch off the tree. But again, I forgot that Lila had bonded with the trees and screamed in pain.

Matt looked at me angrily as I shouted, "Sorry!" then stood ready to fight Adela.

She laughed and confidently boasted, "Give it up, Alex. You'll never beat me."

I held up the large branch as if it were a baseball bat and replied, "Then I'll die trying!"

I swung the branch at Adela, sending her flying into the lake. But before she hit the water, she held her hands out and froze part of the lake as she landed on it, then ran at full speed back towards me.

Matt looked back to see Adela and I fighting at a ridiculous speed then looked across to see a group of Adela's agents trying to apprehend Jennifer and failing miserably. Jennifer stood in front of Matt and Lila trying to protect them by throwing fireballs at the agents, but instead of hitting the agents, most of the time she ended up singeing the nearby trees, each time she hit a tree, Lila screamed in pain.

Matt watched as burn marks appeared on Lila's abdomen, hands, and legs, and quickly realised that Jennifer was causing more damage and rushed to stop her. But in the process the agents got the jump on them, knocking Jennifer unconscious.

Matt, however, put up more of a fight before Adela lost her patience and at full speed sidekicked me backwards, landing on Matt, and causing us both to become dazed and confused.

The agents then hurried to handcuff us and dragged us all back towards the parked van on the other side of the lake.

Matt screamed back at the tree where Lila was still trapped, shouting "Lila! Lila! If you can hear me, I really need you to wake up. Lila! Wake up!"

Adela took one look at the state of Lila's body and scoffed as she left her there.

I guess she thought Lila wouldn't make it through the night.

Original journal entry continued by Lila Winters

Something was wrong. I could hear and feel Matt's panic and frustration as he screamed my name.

I got so angry, feeling helpless, and I kept running trying to find an escape, shouting Matt and Alex's name hoping they could hear me. I looked around at the trees and begged, "Help me!" I pleaded, "Whoever you are, help me . . . I'll stop fighting, just help me!"

I felt like an idiot looking around at the trees and seeing nothing and shouted again, "Please! Help me!"

All at once the forest leaves started to spin around until I was surrounded then suddenly sucked down into the ground.

I woke up from the meditation back at Lake Weeroona Park but still in a trance with my eyes white and hazy.

The tree vines and roots retracted out of my body and as I stood to my feet my wounds healed instantly, even the bruise on my back.

I looked across to see Matt, Alex, and Jennifer being dragged into a van on the other side of the lake.

The tree vines began to spiral around me, creating a flexible armoured body suit. I looked down to inspect and admire the suit and felt empowered, ready to take down some bad guys.

I held my hands out and called for the fallen leaves. They then spiralled beneath my feet, creating a vortex of air pushing me up off the ground. I didn't know how I was doing it and was amazed and stunned at the new abilities, but somehow, I knew exactly what to do next, like I was on semi-autopilot.

By the time I had crossed the lake, the van that Matt, Alex, and Jennifer were travelling in was already on the move and about to leave the parking lot.

I reached my hand out aiming at the tires of the van and was amazed watching as the sleeve of my armoured suit created arrows shooting the tyres and causing the vans to come to a screeching halt.

Alex, Matt, and Jennifer were handcuffed and had inched themselves to the front of the van and perched themselves up to peer out the window.

Adela was sitting in the front passenger seat and was not amused at what she saw.

"What the hell is that?" she questioned as she rushed to get out of the van.

I could see Matt and Alex watching from the back of the van as I landed in front of Adela with eyes white and ready for a fight.

Adela angrily yelled, "How did you do that? Nature Guardians can't fly."

I grinned and answered smugly with an echoing voice, "We do not fly . . . we ride the winds."

Yeah, that was the time I realised I was not alone in my body, and I was definitely getting help from something else. But I didn't care. All I was focused on was saving my family . . . and Jennifer.

Adela didn't take too kind to my answer and almost sounded jealous as she looked at her fellow agents and said, "Well aren't we the clever one then." She raised her hand towards the lake and arrogantly watched as a wave of water rose up and raced towards me. All I did was glance at the water, and the leaves that had fallen at my feet rose up again creating another vortex surrounding the wave and morphing it into a twister moving it towards Adela and her agents.

Adela struggled as she was bombard by the water again and again, but managed to raise her hand up and slice into the water of the tornado, causing the water to fall to the ground, bringing the leaves down with it.

Adela looked at her now unconscious team of agents and glared back at me, furiously determined to kick my awesomely armoured butt.

She didn't stand a chance; she ran towards me and tried to punch and kick and throw spikey balls of ice at me.

I had to admit the spikey ice balls were a pretty cool move. But every move she made, I dodged—it was just like playing shoulder tag with Alex . . . only with an angrier and more determined opponent. And every time she missed, she became even more frustrated and enraged.

Matt and Alex watched the battle between me and Adela in confusion and amazement. Matt was baffled, and I heard him say to Alex, "That's Lila . . . but she looks—"

Alex still in awe, he interrupted and finished Matt sentence saying, "Absolutely amazing."

I'm not sure what happened next, but for some reason, Alex ended up on the floor of the van again. Must have lost his balance.

I, on the other hand, was still dodging punches with a now pissed off Water Guardian who was starting to get tired.

She stopped and stared at me trying to subtly regain her strength, "What's with you. Why won't you fight me?" she yelled.

I just stood still and waited for her next move as she screamed, "Fight me!"

I held out my hand and called from the trees a long branch that looked like a much cooler version of my sparring sticks from home. As I caught the sparring stick, I nodded to Adela and said with an echoing voice, "Very well."

I fought without mercy and so fast that Adela struggled to keep up as she tried to fight back, inevitably failing as she was sent flying across the car park and landing unconscious on the hood of the van Alex and Matt were in.

I rushed at full speed to check if she was still alive then glanced at Matt and Alex as they celebrated the victory. I rummaged through one of Adela's unconscious agents for handcuffs to bind Adela's hands and drag her with me to the back of the van to free my family. As I opened the van door, Alex and Matt jumped out still handcuffed attempting to give me a celebratory hug.

Matt stood back looking at my armoured body tree suit and white glassy eyes. "Honey, you have no idea how happy I am to see you alive and not eaten by a tree. You really had me scared back there with the—"

I interrupted Matt's rambling and must have scared both Matt and Alex as my voice echoed, emotionless saying, "This area has been compromised, we must leave."

Matt studied my glassy eyes and doubted for a moment, "Lila?" he questioned.

I nodded and echoed, "She is here," as I snapped their handcuffs apart, freeing their hands to find the key amongst the agents. It was then that I sensed an unsettling disturbance amongst the trees, as if something even more dangerous was watching us . . . even the trees were scared.

Once Alex and Matt had properly freed themselves and Jennifer, they helped load Adela into the back of Matt's car.

I sat in the back with Alex as Matt drove back to Melbourne with Jennifer following in my car. We sat in silence the entire drive.

I suspected they might have been a bit intimidated and possibly processing what had just happened.

Max was nervously waiting for us in the basement car park of his hotel, along with Chase and the rest of his security team. He anxiously watched as Alex opened the back of the car to reveal his daughter, still unconscious and bound. He burst into tears and hugged Alex, thanking him over and over again. I was quick to interrupt his emotional outburst as I stepped out of the car. Chase and the other security were unsure how to react as they looked at the armoured suit and eyes.

But I was quick to remind them all that Adela was not yet out of the woods and was still possibly under the influence of the Neuritamine drug.

Max, Chase, and his team didn't respond well and looked like they were in shock. They stood in fear, pointing their guns at me.

Matt and Alex rushed to protect me yelling to Chase and Max to put their weapons down.

But amongst all the commotion no one noticed that I became overwhelmed and dizzy, my armoured tree suit began to shed away, as I collapsed to the ground wearing what was left of my torn, shredded clothes.

Alex picked me up and followed Matt into the elevator.

I could barely hear Alex as he whispered, "I'm so sorry Lila," while the world around me became dark.

❦❧

CHAPTER 26

❦❧

SLEEP IS SO OVERRATED . . .

Journal entry by Alex Woods

I was trying so very desperately to hide my fear and panic as I held Lila's comatose body in my arms and carried her into her bedroom, placing her onto the bed.

Matt rushed to her side and tried to wake her, looking back at me in desperation and begged, "Please just tell me she's still alive."

At that moment, Maxwell, Jennifer, and Chase came rushing into the room to check on Lila.

I held her hand and closed my eyes to concentrate. I had to shush Chase when he asked what I was doing.

While I tried to concentrate, Jennifer quietly explained, "Alex is an Animal Guardian. He has the ability to sense the life of an animal, when they are nearby, their mood, if they're in danger or if they're dying."

Matt became anxious as he stared at me, probably worried why I was taking so long, but it was difficult given so many people were in the room.

"I can feel her heart beating," I explained, "but she's scared. I don't think she knows what's happening to her."

Maxwell pulled out his phone and exclaimed "I'm calling my doctor in. I'll get him to do a house call," and walked out of the room.

It was a long wait but three hours later as the sun began to rise, Maxwell's doctor had arrived to examine Lila. We all watched anxiously at the end of the bed.

The doctor's name was James Ellis, and damn he knew his stuff. He examined Lila's body looking for any signs of injury or internal bleeding. He checked along Lila's abdomen and asked, "Has she experienced trauma in the last twenty-four hours?"

Matt glared at me, expecting me to answer. I took a moment to think and decided to just answer honestly. "She may have gotten one or two bruises yesterday. There was an incident at the park, and she had gotten into a fight with a crazy woman."

The doctor nodded asking "Any injuries to the head?" I shook my head and smiled remembering how Lila kicked some Eden butt, in epic style.

The doctor stood back from the bed, addressing Maxwell to give his conclusions. "As far as I can tell, she's just sleeping. I can't find anything abnormal that would be keeping her from waking up naturally. However," he paused almost looking baffled, glancing back at Lila, "most people who are just sleeping will show some sort of awareness and rouse from their sleep during an examination as thorough as mine. I would strongly recommend you take her to the hospital for further examination."

It was uncanny but immediately Matt and I shouted in unison "No . . ."

The doctor suspiciously stared at us then said to Maxwell, "Okay, how about I come back tomorrow morning before I start work. If she hasn't woken by that stage, I will have to insist she goes to the hospital, at least for a nutrient drip," then he looked at Matt pleadingly, hoping he would agree.

Matt reluctantly nodded in agreement.

The doctor then packed up his things and walked out of the room with Maxwell.

But before Matt got the chance to turn and yell at me, as I knew he desperately wanted to, Maxwell popped his head back into the room to let me know I had a guest waiting in the living room.

So instead, Matt just followed me out into the living room, to greet Agent John from Mission Control talking with Jennifer and Bluey sitting on a large stack of boxes.

John stood to greet me and formally introduced himself to Matt, but Matt didn't seem to be interested on who he was, but more on why he was here.

He got straight down to business and explained that Bluey had been monitoring from a distance the incident at Weeroona Lake, when Lila had begun the bonding meditation up to and including the fight between Adela and Lila.

"What you didn't realise is that there was another person watching the incident. Bluey had spotted him hiding amongst the trees across the lake. He suspects that it might have been him—the Darkman."

Matt looked at me for an explanation, but I quickly glanced over to him and shook my head, indicating for him to ask me later.

Instead Matt pushed again for an answer as to why John was here. John sighed in disappointment and placed his hand down on a stack of boxes.

"This is all the information we have on the previous Earth Guardians in our agency and database. I thought there may be some information in here that could shed some light on the current condition of your wife, given that she is a Nature Guardian and rare. We do not have a lot of information regarding her bonding experience and how it was supposed to go, but I am guessing this was not what anyone was expecting. Hopefully, they will be of use to you," he replied.

It was surprising but Matt actually liked the offer and agreed with John.

I, however, was not impressed. "That could take us forever to get through!" I snapped.

John apologized and explained, "There are only two other Nature Guardians who may know what she is going through, but they will more likely kill you than help you."

Matt thanked John as he began to scan through the books excitedly.

Before John left with Bluey, he added one final word saying, "Matt, your wife has a very unique talent, and it's not one we want lose. If there is anything else you need, please just ask."

Matt looked up at Jennifer, and I and said "We only have until morning. So I suggest you pick up a book."

We sat at that the table all day reading. Chase had joined us for part of the day, but gave up, struggling to understand the documents and journals. Instead he just brought us up some food from the ground-floor restaurants.

Before we knew it, the day was gone, and tomorrow morning had arrived. Matt had fallen asleep on the couch, and Jennifer and I were asleep hunched over the table, halfway through some mission briefings.

Mrs Willows, Lila's mother, had arrived at the apartment to drop off Danny and Ruby, who had been staying at her house for the night while Matt drove up to Bendigo in a jealous rage.

The children let themselves in and had helped themselves to a snack while Mrs Willows put the bags away. I woke as I heard the sound of cartoons playing on TV. I then nervously woke Matt as I watched Mrs Willows disappear into Lila's bedroom. Matt looked at me in panic as we both rushed into the bedroom after her. We tried to act casual as we watched her pull the blankets up over Lila to tuck her in, acting all motherly. She then looked up at us and whispered, "Let me guess . . . rough night."

I knew Matt wouldn't want to alarm Lila's mother, so he just awkwardly grinned and nodded.

Mrs Willows then quietly walked back out into the living room with Matt to say goodbye to Danny and Ruby then headed off to work.

By that stage, Maxwell had arrived with Chase and room service. Pancakes and maple syrup, I could smell it from the bedroom. And then my heart almost skipped a beat when I heard Jennifer shout, "Hey, I think I've got something!"

I ran at full speed out to the living room to stand with Maxwell, Chase and Matt, all eagerly waiting, as Jennifer explained what she found, holding up a Fire Guardian's journal. "Here. This is a diary entry of a Fire Guardian who went into a bonding meditation and struggled to come out."

She began to read aloud, "It was so beautiful being in the dreamland. The sight of everything made me feel in a state of pure happiness. Every time I had the urge to leave, something more beautiful drew me into a deeper state of meditation. Everything made me feel happy and safe—I was almost afraid to leave."

Matt looked around the room to see all our faces still puzzled at what Jennifer had found, and he asked, "What has this got to do with Lila?"

Jennifer pointed to the book and questioned, "What if she is still in the bonding meditation . . . in the dreamland . . . and doesn't want to leave . . . or she's afraid to leave?"

I started to panic, thinking back on all the time Lila and I have been in a dangerous and deadly situation, and thought for a second, she may be right in her theory.

Matt interrupted, disagreeing with Jennifer's theory. "No no, that doesn't sound like Lila. I know Lila she would break every bone in her body to get back to her family."

Jennifer asked Matt, "But what if there is something else keeping her from waking up, from leaving the dreamland?"

Matt pondered the thought for a while, until his mobile alarm buzzed, reminding him to take the kids to day care. I could tell he didn't want to leave, but he knew it would be better to keep the kids away from the situation.

He grabbed Danny and Ruby's backpacks saying, "I will drop Danny and Ruby at day care, while you two will keep working on another theory. Because if you knew Lila, you would know she's only afraid of one thing . . . and this is not it."

We continued to look for other answers, and we all argued possible theories while Matt was away, but ended up with nothing.

While Max and Jennifer continued to debate theories, I went in to check on Lila. She looked so peaceful, as if she really was sleeping.

I sat down on the bed next to her and brushed the hair off her face, saying, "I'm so sorry, Lila . . . I'll fix this, I promise."

I thought I was imagining things when I heard her whisper my name ever so softly. I leaned in closer to try and hear her as she whispered in panic, "Help me . . . Help me, Alex . . ."

All of a sudden Lila reached up and kissed me.

I didn't know what to do, I think I was in shock, but I was so happy as I kissed her back. I had wanted to do this since the day we met. I was so distracted by the kiss, I hadn't realised that she was still in the meditation. And then it happened.

Somehow Lila had managed to pull me into her meditation, into the dreamland.

I couldn't believe my eyes as I stood in the middle of what looked like a rainforest, and Lila standing in front of me, holding my hands and trying to say something to me. It looked like she was shouting, but I couldn't hear anything. I shook my head in confusion, and she sighed and hugged me tightly. As I held her in my arms, I heard her whisper fearfully, "Alex, help me! Please!"

I could feel her being pulled away from me. I watched helplessly as the leaves flew up from the ground, circling around Lila like a gust of wind trying to pull her away from me, and the moment Lila let go of my hand, everything went dark.

I was then pushed out of the dreamland by something, and woke up back in Lila's bedroom still kissing her as she slowly let me go and became once again comatose on the bed.

It was all so freaky, and I was still unsure what had just happened as I pulled away from Lila and fell off the bed.

I stood and stared at Lila, hoping she had woken up, but she had no movement, so I called for Maxell and Jennifer.

They both came rushing in as I paced the room still in shock, trying to process things and attempted to explain, "You were right. She's trapped . . . something's keeping her in there . . ."

Jennifer looked at Lila, still unconscious, then back at me, puzzled and shaking her head, trying to understand.

"She showed me," I said still a bit befuddled, "She pulled me into her dream . . . How? How did she do that?"

Jennifer shook her head again stating, "She couldn't... It takes years of practice to enter another person's meditation. Let alone pull someone into yours . . ."

I pointed back at Lila and exclaimed, "Well somehow, she did it... And she needs my help."

Maxwell stopped me from pacing and tried to get me to explain as he asked, "What did you see?"

"She was scared—and she was running from something," I explained. "I have to go back . . . How do I go back in?"

Jennifer was baffled at the thought and shrugged her shoulders, "Um . . . Just do what you did before, I guess . . ."

I looked back at Lila, unsettled at what I was about to do, again. "I'm gonna need you to leave," I said, hurrying both Maxwell and Jennifer back out the room and closing the door.

I then sat down on the bed next to Lila and whispered, "Lila... if you can hear me, whatever you did before, I need you to do it again."

I then closed my eyes and kissed her in the hopes that something would happen.

Before I knew it, I was standing back in the rainforest, holding Lila's hand. She quickly pulled me out of the clearing to hide behind some large trees, then hugged me so tightly and gasped, "Alex . . . you found me!"

I sighed in relief, hugging her back, saying, "You have no idea how happy I am to see you."

Lila quickly looked around as she heard the trees rustling. "She's here . . .," she said quietly. She grabbed my hand and started running at full speed away from the area.

We ran into a clearing when she stopped and looked around frantically.

"Lila, what's going on? Who's here?" I asked, slightly out of breath.

Still frantically looking around, she explained, "Adela's here . . . I don't know how she did it. But last night, she showed up and started destroying the forest," she stopped and held her breath trying to stay quiet as she listened to the rustling of the trees. "And there's something else . . . something a lot stronger . . . something dark . . ."

Lila looked into the distance with sheer terror on her face as she saw a large dark shadow moving towards us.

I shouted at Lila to run, but she was frozen staring into the shadow.

Journal entry insert by Matt Winters

I had just arrived back at the apartment to see Max and Jennifer waiting in the living room. I grew anxious and asked, "Where's Alex?"

I wasn't overly happy when Jennifer explained where he was.

I ran into the bedroom to see Alex lying on my bed, hugging my wife and holding her hand, in a deep meditative sleep.

I was so angry, I yelled loudly, so loud even the neighbours would here, "Son of a #***#!!"

(We won't include that word in the journal, seeing how I am a father who should live up to certain standards, and never wants his children repeating it.)

Besides, I was glad that I had walked in on them just hugging. Honestly, I was thinking the worst.

Journal entry continued by Alex Woods

We had managed to find a good hiding place up high amongst the trees. I held on to Lila tightly as we perched on the highest branch, watching the ground below for signs of movement. I looked at Lila, worried. "We can't keep running," I said. "We need to find a way to get you out of here."

Lila shook her head saying, "I can't. The spirits are gone. I can't find them anywhere."

Confused I just looked at her hoping she would explain more.

"They're the ones who helped me to save you at the lake. The last thing I remember was sitting in the car, driving to Melbourne. Then the spirits disappeared, and everything went dark and I ended up back here."

I then had an epiphany and realised what we had done, "I know what's wrong . . . it's the elements. We took you away from your element when you hadn't finished the bonding meditation. You were in the basement when you fainted, and we took you upstairs to your room, away from nature."

Lila began to understand my thoughts and queried, "So if you take me to a park, I can wake up?"

It was worth a try, so I nodded and said, "Hang on. I just need to wake up first."

I closed my eyes to concentrate on the apartment. I could feel my physical body lying on the bed holding Lila's hand. I could even sense Matt's rage as he yelled at me to wake up. But I couldn't get back there. I opened my eyes and whispered, "Damn" when I realised, I was stuck here as well.

Lila began to freak out as she asked me what was wrong.

"I can't get out," I answered.

She screeched in panic. "What do you mean you can't get out? You left before . . . try harder."

I heard some rustling in the ground below and quickly covered Lila's mouth to stop her from talking as we both watched Adela walking though the rainforest, looking around.

"Lila!" she called, "Come out, come out—wherever you are." She looked around and tried to listen for Lila's movement then ran off at full speed to continue her search.

Lila pushed my hand away and asked, "How did she get into this world? Last thing I remember she was unconscious in the back of the van. How is she connecting with her element?"

I took a moment and answered regretfully, "Because it's raining outside, in the real world. There's a thunderstorm forecast the rest of the week."

Lila became distressed at the thought of being stuck here for another week, then smiled with a beaming idea in her head. "Alex, nobody knows you're here, right?" she asked.

I nodded hesitantly, afraid of what idea she might have come up with.

I was right to be afraid . . . because she asked me if I could ask my element for help; she wanted me to meditate.

"Okay, so first of all . . . that's a terrible idea, because, second, I have never been able to do this before and I don't know how. You're the one who's gotten me this far," I said in a snarky whisper.

She just looked at me with those cute pleading eyes, saying, "I know you can do it if you just try. I'll walk you through it—"

I interrupted that sentence, highlighting the fact that her current circumstance indicates her lack of success with meditations as well, and that it wasn't filling me with a lot of confidence.

She rolled her eyes and snapped "Just try . . . Please . . . Close your eyes and concentrate. Try to sense the animals around you in the hotel. I know there are a few animals in the apartment next door to us."

I let out a sigh of annoyance and doubt. And reluctantly I closed my eye, trying to concentrate on the apartment again. I could sense my physical body and Lila's, and I could still hear Matt yelling at me trying to wake me up and starting to panic, thinking both of us were stuck.

He was totally right to panic.

But as I began to relax, I could hear Lila's voice guiding me, saying, "Focus on finding the animals . . . ask them for help."

In an instant, I could feel myself being pulled out of the rainforest and into the real world again.

I found myself crouching on the bed next to Lila, looking up at Matt who was staring at me flabbergasted. I didn't understand at first until I looked in the bedroom mirror to see me as a large black cat, in panic I screamed but instead it came out as a growl. That then caught the attention of Jennifer and Max, who came running into the room and began to freak out.

I don't think this is what Lila had planned. I know I asked for help from the animals, but I struggled to see how turning into an animal myself was helpful. I mean how am I supposed to help Lila like this?

It took me a few seconds, but then I started pawing at her blanket and looking back up at Matt trying to give him the hint.

Once he had calmed down, he watched my movement, and he finally figured it out. He picked Lila up and walked out of the apartment, following me.

Max and Jennifer followed behind curious as to what we were doing.

We rode in the elevator down to the recreational floor where the rooftop garden was, but we unfortunately stopped at a few floors along the way. Matt wasn't too confident about what was going on, turning to me and saying, "Are you crazy? You can't just walk around the hotel like that! You're a large black cat. You'll scare anyone who sees you—"

Just then, the elevator doors opened to a couple who, in their shock, just stared at the scene—a large black cat and a man holding an unconscious woman.

Matt glanced at me and said condescendingly, "Like that."

Max just apologised and smiled as he closed the door on them. When we finally got to the recreations floor, we were met by Chase, who was getting some very odd security calls and was being asked to investigate. He stopped us in the corridor and asked, "What the hell is going on? And what . . . is that?" pointing down at me.

Matt just calmly responded "That . . . is Alex . . . and to be honest, I don't know what's going on, but we're following him."

Chase then began to follow us as well, as I led them out on to the rooftop garden that was now saturated by the rain.

Max and Chase then called up extra security to section off the area.

As I walked over to the small tree at the centre of the garden and stomped my foot on the ground beneath it, Matt took that as clue to place Lila down next to me. It was very quick as we watched the tree's branches and roots wrap around Lila's body again, digging into Lila's chest. I watched Matt turn away as I fell back asleep, again being pulled back into the dreamland.

I opened my eyes to find me back in the rainforest, sitting next to Lila who was struggling to cope with the pain. She could feel her physical body being pierced by the vines, and she began to scream. It became so painful that she fell off the branch.

I moved at full speed to catch her and pull her back up, holding her close to me as she tried to cope with the pain. She tried to stay quiet as we watched the dark shadow circling the trees beneath us, then disappeared into the trunk of the tree. I then wiped the tears from Lila's eyes and asked, "Now what?"

Lila sat up and stretched out as she began to feel rejuvenated and smiled. "I think I'm starting to feel better . . . I'm starting to feel stronger."

She looked at the ground and confidently jumped, scaring me to no end. But before she hit the ground, the lower branches of the trees began to break her fall and create a slide for her down to the ground.

I watched in awe then made my own way down to the ground. The moment I landed on the ground and had asked, "So which way?" The spirits, which for the purpose of my journal I will call the tree man and tree woman, because that's the best description I got, appeared behind me.

The tree man startled me as he complimented me, saying, "You have done well, for a beginner. Your fellow animals must be proud."

I didn't know what to do or say, so I just nodded and thanked them.

The tree woman then looked at Lila and said, "We know . . . it is not safe for you here. It has been an honour to meet you and to fight with you. You are a true Guardian . . . both of you."

She then placed her hand on my shoulder and pushed me into the trunk of a tree.

I could feel myself returning to my physical body on the rooftop garden in the real world; it was now back to its human form and unfortunately fully naked.

Maxwell kindly took off his jacket and covered me when I woke. I stared back up at Lila to see the vines and branches retracting back into the ground. I held her hand and looked at Matt apologetically. I didn't know what had happened, and I was just hoping whatever I did, worked.

There was a moment of silent and tense suspense as we all watched and waited for some sign of life from Lila.

And finally, she gasped and woke in panic, looking around to see me and Matt next to her.

Matt was so relieved that he lunged over Lila to hug her tightly saying, "Don't ever scare me like that again. Please, please, please."

Lila was still in panic looking around, and it got me concerned, as I wondered why she took longer to come out of the dream world. So I asked if she was all right, and she shook her head, trying to mask her fear. "He was there . . . the shadow, it was him," she said in a shaky voice.

"He was waiting . . . without you . . . we were vulnerable. We fought and . . ."

Her hands started to tremble as she looked at me with fear in her eyes. I could feel it overwhelming her as she said, "Alex, the Darkman . . . he's like me . . . he's a Nature Guardian," she explained.

Jennifer interrupted to try and get clarification asking, "Who was it? Did you see his face?"

"No," Lila answered as she started to regain her confidence and stood to her feet. "But I know his weakness now . . . I know how to stop him."

CHAPTER 27

THE MISSION BRIEF

Journal entry by Terrence Connors

I've been staying at the Eden Hotel for weeks now, monitoring our new objectives. While analysing their movement and behaviours, I thought I had found the perfect opportunity to make my move when the targets had separated and left for a small town called Bendigo.

But instead they have procured one of our assets and has her in their custody.

When the female Nature Guardian, Lila, had entered the dreamland, I attempted to weaken her, and keep her in the spirit realm. But my plans were thwarted. I underestimated her abilities and her connection with the elements.

I have now three broken ribs and a large cut on my upper lip, and I am awaiting for the medical team to meet me in my hotel room as I contemplate my next move.

I am however, finding it difficult. There is something about her that caused me to hesitate. I somehow got this feeling that I know her, that we've met before.

Nonetheless, next time, I will not fail.

CHAPTER 28

THE LAST-MINUTE BIRTHDAY SAGA

Journal entry by Lila Winters

We had finally made it to the weekend after a week of absolute chaos. Max was over the moon that we had found his little girl, and his doctors were confident in their ability of finding a cure.

But <u>that</u> was not my problem . . . Today was going to be <u>my</u> Saturday.

I woke up to the sound of our very annoying alarm clock and had a very big over-the-top stretch, turning over to see Matt grinning as he said, "Good morning, sexy."

I however was not convinced on the good part of his good morning comment and grumbled, "Debatable . . ."

He chuckled and asked jokingly, "Which part? The morning or the sexy?"

Naturally offended, I responded by throwing a pillow at him while he got dressed and opened the blinds to let the far-too-bright sunlight in.

"Why are you so cheery?" I asked pulling the covers over my head to shield my eyes from the blinding sunlight.

He sat back on the bed, pulling back the covers to kiss me and answered, "Because I have an extremely sexy wife . . . and it's Saturday."

Exactly it's Saturday, the day where most sane people who have had a rough week would take the opportunity to sleep in and chill for the day. But not my husband, certainly not. As I continued to grumble, I reluctantly and very slowly started to get up, watching Matt energetically skip out into the kitchen. I then yelled loudly, "Fine, but I want pancakes, and lots of them!" as I walked into the bathroom still grumbling to have a shower.

By the time I had come out into the kitchen Matt, Ruby, and Danny were sitting at the table, eating away at the pancakes. Matt had set a large stack of pancakes aside for me . . . he's so nice like that.

When I sat down at the table, Ruby handed me a large shiny, pearl-coloured envelope, saying, "This was left at the door for you, Mummy."

I looked at her and said, "But it's Saturday."

I opened the envelope to find an invitation addressed to all of us to Max's fiftieth birthday ball being held tonight at the hotel.

Matt huffed, "Well this is a bit last minute. What are you supposed to wear to a billionaire's birthday ball?" he asked, frustrated and confused.

Just as he finished his sentence, the apartment phone rang. It was Max's assistant, and she was requesting that I come up to Max's office as soon as possible.

I quickly grabbed my plate of pancakes and headed to the door.

Matt watched and grumbled using the same tone of voice I had used back in the bedroom, saying with his pouty lips, "But it's Saturday."

Sarcastically, I grinned back and said, "And it's his birthday."

Danny grabbed one last pancake and followed me up to Max's office, just to tag along.

Danny and Ruby have really grown to like Max. He acts like a grandfather around them, giving them big hugs and spoiling them with lollies and treats.

I suspect Max will be over the moon when he finally has grandkids of his own.

When we arrived up at Max's office, Danny couldn't wait, bursting through the door, shouting, "Happy birthday, Max!" and giving Max a huge hug.

Max, happy to see Danny, naturally gave him a handful of lollies that he had stashed away in his draw.

I then wished Max a happy birthday as I rolled my eyes at the sight of the lolly stash.

"So what's with the last-minute birthday party?" I asked.

His answer really surprised me,

"Actually, it's not. My wife has been planning this for months, up in Sydney. She flew in this morning to make the final preparations."

I was lost for words, who knew he had a wife? At least a current one, anyway. I mean, he hadn't even mentioned her up until now, and there's not even a single picture of her in his office. I played it cool and pretended I knew who she was and casually said, "So the bigger boss is responsible for this one . . ."

He nodded and rolled his eyes. I got the suspicion he was not overly keen for an extravagant birthday party either.

"That's why I called you here. I need your help with my daughters," he pleaded.

I then became very unnerved as I watched both Jessica and Adela walk into the room unaccompanied by Chase or his security team.

I casually stood in front of Danny protectively, who seemed too busy scoffing down the bag of lollies to notice.

Max tried to ease the tension and explained that they were both cured now, and that the doctors discovered the drug starts to break down after a certain period.

Jennifer had suggested a forty-eight-hour detox program; it should have done the trick. Max was convinced that they were all better, but

I suspected that this was the original reason why he called me up to his office.

"If anyone can determine whether the detox worked, it would be you," he said pleadingly again. He was really starting to push his luck, but I understood, it was his birthday, and his wife's coming into town. The last thing he would want is both his daughter either not present or going bonkers at the party, trying to kill everyone.

I tentatively walked over and held Adela's arm. I could sense she was trying to hide something, and I got a really bad vibe from both of them.

When I looked at Adela's and Jessica's face, I could tell they had something planned. I know it was probably a bad idea, but I decided to go along with their charade.

I wanted to see what they had planned, and I was definitely not going to allow them to ruin their father's birthday.

I turned to Max and smiled. "They seem fine to me."

Adela and Jessica rejoiced as they hugged their father and asked, "Now can we go?"

Max hadn't quite gotten to that part of his request, as he then asked if I would escort Adela and Jessica to the shopping centre as their bodyguard while they picked out dresses for the birthday party.

Max tried to explain. "Given that the girls had been a bit cooped up, they asked if they could treat themselves to a pamper day. And I only agreed as long as they went with some security—"

Adela then interrupted saying, "But the last thing we want is to have Chase and his men following us around all day. That would draw way too much attention to us."

I took the opportunity to finish her thought and said sarcastically, "And let me guess, that's where I come in?"

Adela and Jessica both nodded and explained, "Well of course, aren't you on Daddy's payroll as head of security? And this way, we can buy you a party dress as well, you know . . . as a thank you for saving us?"

I think I was beginning to see their plan, and I reluctantly nodded. The girls had clearly planned this out, and I could smell a trap.

But instead of outing them then and there, I played it cool and agreed to the shopping spree.

"Sure, let me just drop Danny back downstairs, and I'll meet you in the lobby in twenty minutes," I said casually, walking Danny out of the office, sporting a fake smile.

I let Matt know where I was going as I got changed. I decided to dress up a bit hoping to blend in with Jessica and Adela's high-profile style. So I pulled out from the back of my cupboard a stunning baby-blue sundress that I hadn't worn in a long time, and to top off the outfit, I didn't forget my new favourite bracelet with all the secret compartments filled with plant seeds. I created a leg holster from the leaves of the apartment pot plant for my dagger, hiding it under my dress. Luckily for me, the dress was flowy, and you wouldn't notice the holster unless you were feeling me up.

Adela and Jessica were in the lobby eagerly waiting for me. When arrived, they looked at me and nodded. It was evident by their expression they were impressed at how I presented, given that twenty minutes ago I was in torn jeans and a tank top.

"Wow, Lila, you look really good," Jessica said as she handed me the keys and sat in the passenger side of a yellow Lamborghini. I got the subtle hint they were expecting me to drive as Adela got comfortable in the back seat.

"Okay," I said, not at all confident in driving a three-million-dollar car.

Journal entry insert by Matt Winters

While Lila had gone out shopping, Alex and Jennifer had made a horrible discovery and came up to my apartment to warn her. Instead they were stuck with me.

Alex almost hit the roof when I told him Lila had gone out shopping with the Eden sisters.

But that wasn't what got him so worked up, as he tried to explain to me what they had found.

It was a YouTube video of the incident in Bendigo. Alex pulled it up on my laptop to show me.

It was a video shot from a smartphone, probably by the group of teens that were hanging around at the time. They had recorded the whole thing—the flying leaves, Lila flying across the lake, and the fight between Lila and Adela. The video had been viewed over 9000 times and still rising.

Jennifer commented, "Matt, I've been an elder for a long time and I have never seen anyone more powerful then Lila. It's amazing to see how much control she has over her element."

I then very quickly realised the possibility of the Darkman seeing this.

"If that's true, and your Darkman guy gets a hold of this video, they're going to see Lila as either a threat or their next collectable."

Original journal entry continued by Lila Winters

I was in hell. This was absolutely the worst possible way I could ever spend my Saturday. I was being "pampered" with nail polish, hairdo, and make-up. Eeerk. It gave me the chills just looking at me, looking so . . . not myself. I looked . . . pretty . . . and I just don't do pretty in this any way.

I do badass, I do sexy, and I do fierce and strong, but not pretty. The worst part was they were buying me a ball gown for tonight. I mean I hardly ever wear this sundress, and now they're putting me in a ball gown.

Hell... sheer hell.

The only bright side to this was it wasn't pink.

But enough about my feelings and back to what I was really doing here. I had managed to scope out the shopping centre, while Adela and Jessica were busy getting their hair washed running at full speed.

The last thing I wanted was a repeat of the shopping centre incident from a few months ago.

I got back just before they sat back down in the salon chair to get their make-up done. While I waited, I asked "Correct me if I'm wrong but if this is your father's birthday shouldn't he be the one getting the pampering and the new outfits?"

Adela just sighed rolling her eyes as she answered, "Yes, but we're really doing this for our mother."

I was baffled at the statement as Jessica then explained, "When we make the effort to look presentable at our mother's social events, she's happy. And when our mother's happy, our father's happy. So we all win."

Their argument began to make sense, but I began to feel a little bit of pity for Max for having such a high-maintenance family.

But if Max was happy, who was I to question it.

Once we had finished at the hairdressers, Adela and Jessica decided on having a late lunch at one of the restaurants.

I followed behind them counting the minutes 'til the end of the day, as they chose their dining venue.

At that stage I was starving and would have settled for pastry from the bakery, but they were shopping on their daddy's expense, so only the finest would do. When they finally chose a restaurant, I was overjoyed but was distracted by the flower store two doors down. I rummaged through my handbag and pulled out one of the old journals that Agent John had left in our care.

This book in particular had some old herbal remedies that supposedly cured people of certain ailments like common colds and hangovers. It also listed a number of plants and herbs and what affect they had on people.

I quickly popped into the flower shop to buy a few seeds and flowers. As I walked around the flower shop, I heard what sounded like Agatha's voice whispering, "This one . . . over here." The voice led me to a bouquet of white lilies. I picked out three of the lilies and walked over to the counter to buy them. I was fairly confident I knew exactly what to do with them.

I walked out to see Jessica and Adela waiting for me.

"Ooh! What are they for?" Adela asked.

"I'll show you over lunch," I replied following them into the restaurant.

Journal entry insert by Matt Winters

Alex had run with me at full speed, which I am still not quite used to as I struggled to keep the pancakes from breakfast down. We ran into the underground parking structure of Chadstone shopping centre, when Alex abruptly stopped, staring at two black vans parked in adjacent car parks.

We both recognised the vans. They looked like the same vans from Bendigo.

We cautiously walked over to inspect the vans, as Alex opened one, I opened the other.

My van was empty, but Alex's van had four men in black suits, unconscious, tied up in vines and covered in flowers.

"Wow, she's good," Alex commented as he closed the van door again.

I was pessimistic as I highlighted that there's still one empty van.

"Let's move and be careful not to let the girls know we're here, or it might get messy. We don't want a repeat of last time," Alex said as we hurried into the shopping centre.

Original journal entry continued by Lila Winters

We had just finished ordering our lunch and were sitting at the table, trying to make small talk not to feel awkward.

They commented on the fact that I was a vegetarian, but the conversation started and ended quickly.

There's really not a lot to talk about with those sorts of ethical choices in life, without it getting awkward, especially if the others don't feel the same.

Adela kept staring at the three white lilies resting on the table. "So spill. What's with the lilies?" she asked.

I grinned and handed one lily to Jess and one to Adela and told them to place it on their forehead and close their eyes.

"Why?" Adela asked defensively.

"It's a day of pampering right," I asked casually then explained, "This is a remedy to help us relax. Lilies can have a calming effect, if you know how to use them properly."

Adela looked at me suspiciously and asked, "How do you know this?"

"I'm a Guardian of Nature," I replied.

Adela looked at me, then looked at the flower and Jessica. I guess she had no choice at this stage but to play along. Considering I was "supposedly" falling into whatever trap they had planned for me.

Jess and Adela placed the lilies on their foreheads and closed their eyes. My eyes quickly glowed green and the petals of the lilies gave off a faint glow of light, then turned a brown colour and started to die.

Adela and Jess looked at the flower confused and started to feel dizzy and a bit woozy.

Adela looked at me and gasped, "What have you done?"

I leaned over and whispered, "Your heads will clear up in a few seconds—but until then, stay very quiet. I have some business I need to take care of."

I looked over to see a man walk into the restaurant. It must have been him who Adela was waiting for because he walked directly to our table and sat down grinning, "Hello, ladies. Sorry I'm late. I hope I haven't missed the main course."

He looked across the table at me and for a brief moment looked surprised when he saw my face.

Adela looked at the guy still dizzy and confused and mumbled, "Terrence?"

I tried to stay calm and act like nothing had changed and asked, "Terrence . . . is that your name?"

He smirked and nodded his head, replying, "Yes, my name is Terrence. And it's nice to finally meet, isn't it, Lila?"

Not sure if he was trying to be creepy there, but I just played it cool and replied jokingly, "It's better than 'Darkman', I suppose."

Terrence just looked at me unsure how to react, as the lunch was served, and three plates had arrived.

I looked over at Terrence and gasped at the fact that they hadn't served him anything. "I'm so sorry. I don't think the girls were expecting you for lunch. I'm happy to share mine if you don't mind vegetarian," I offered as I moved closer to him and placed my bowl between us. "It's spinach fettucine, with mushroom in creamy sauce," I stated handing him a spare fork.

Terrence took the fork from me hesitantly and commented, "You're a difficult woman to get a hold of."

I started eating my lunch and mumbled between mouthfuls, "As are you."

Adela and Jess started to rouse with clearer heads but remained quiet as they looked at Terrence.

He looked back at Adela and complemented her saying, "You've done well, Adela. Excellent plan."

I added to his complement and said, "Yes, excellent plan. It's such a shame it didn't work."

Terrence just looked at me and smirked, "You underestimate us. I have several of my best men waiting outside, to ensure you come quietly this time. Best not to make a scene, if you know what's good for you . . ."

I slowly finished the last of my lunch and innocently grinned back at Terrence and said, "Terrence, you insult me. When will you learn? Four of your best men have already been detained. And as we speak, two of my best men are handling the others."

Journal entry insert continued by Matt Winters

We had finally found Lila in a restaurant having lunch with Adela and Jessica and for some reason, she was talking to another man. Alex freaked out as he saw him and recognised him instantly. When he pushed me into one of the service corridors, we accidently found the other men in black suits from the empty van, waiting.

In a fright, I tackled one of the men to the ground as Alex punched two of them in the face, knocking them backwards. Honestly, I should have thought of that.

But before Alex could get to the fourth man, a large tree vine started to grow from the homemade rose bracelet Lila had given me as a gift.

The vines grew large enough to wrap around all four of the men, pinning them up against the wall.

Alex looked at me gobsmacked, saying "Wait, what just happened?" as he inspected my bracelet and realised Lila knew it was a trap this whole time.

I scrunched my nose up and shook my head, saying, "She could have told us."

Alex just looked back at me and asked sarcastically, "Would you have honestly let her walk into a trap, by herself if you had known?"

I pondered for a few seconds then shook my head, "Probably not," I replied.

I wasn't surprised when Chase and his team walked into the corridor to greet us.

Chase looked at us funny and asked, "What are you doing here? We were told you two weren't going to be involved in this one."

Alex looked at me and replied, "Um . . . we weren't . . . we were just, um . . ."

I could tell he was struggling with this lie, which surprised me given how well he lied to me when we met. Maybe he's getting rusty.

But I also didn't want to get busted this time, so I interrupted Alex's fumbling and answered, "We were just passing through on our way to pick up dress suits for tonight, when we ran into these guys."

Chase nodded and continued to handcuff the guys.

Alex then added before Chase left, "Hey, do us a favour and not mention this to Lila. We don't want her to know that we're actually getting along."

Chase just smiled and said, "Sure", as he led his team and the suited men down through the service corridor and out the exit.

Original journal entry continued by Lila Winters

Terrence looked at me confused and waited for his team to respond as he tapped his earpiece, with no success.

He then became frustrated, glaring at me as if I'd ruined his plans. Which I totally did.

"I still have Adela," he added.

I just shook my head and smiled. "I wouldn't be so sure about that," as I placed two brown lilies in front of Terrence.

He just looked at me and then up at Adela and Jessica who were staying uncharacteristically quiet.

"You have no idea what you've just done," he snapped as he stood up to tower over me.

I stood to my feet, so we were face to face and replied, "I think I've just cured your mindless drones. And now, it's down to just you . . . and me."

He chuckled. "So what are you going to do? Fight me?"

I looked at him then around at the wait staff in the restaurant and other patrons there having lunch and replied, "I'm going . . . to let you go."

He looked at me suspiciously and took my offer to leave but before he left, I grabbed his hand and placed the last lily in his hand and said, "Terrence, it was very nice to finally meet. I just wish it were under different circumstances . . ."

I glanced around the room, to see the other patrons looking at us. So to keep up an unsuspecting act, I walked Terrence to the door of the restaurant and kissed him on the cheek goodbye.

He looked at me puzzled as I explained, "It's like you said, I wouldn't want to make a scene." Glancing up at the cameras, then added, "But the next time I see you, rest assured I will not be so . . . kind."

Terrence nodded his head and glanced down at my hand that he was still holding and fiddled with my wedding band asking, "Your maiden name was Willows, wasn't it?"

I just looked at him defensively, but before I could ask him how he knew that, he disappeared at full speed.

I sat back down at the table with Adela and Jess both still looking at me confused, as Adela said, "I'm sorry—but do we know you?"

I sat back in my chair as my dessert was served to me and replied, "I'm a friend of your father's, his security team should be here soon to pick us up, so I suggest you eat something."

The rest of the day went quite smoothly after that.

Chase escorted the Eden sisters home, and we all got ready for the big birthday ball.

Chase and I escorted Adela and Jess into the ballroom to ensure they had made it to the event. Chase was still on duty for the night, so I offered to assist him since I was there.

We both agreed that night that it would be better if we waited until after their mother had left to tell the Eden sisters what had happened.

We were all dressed in fancy ballroom attire including me, and I swear I felt extremely uncomfortable as I fidgeted with the dress to make it sit right. Chase giggled as he watched me and commented, "I'm guessing you're not a ball-gown person either."

I shook my head with a pouty face, as he laughed harder.

We waited at the door, greeting the guest as they arrived. And when my family finally arrived, it was just Danny and Ruby. I suspect they ran ahead, all excited for the party. It wasn't long before Matt and Alex came rushing in to the ballroom to catch up with them.

They both looked up at me as I smiled back at them, holding the kid's hands.

"Lost something, boys," Chase said still laughing.

Alex and Matt were too busy staring at me to answer as Matt said, "You look—"

And Alex finished his sentence saying, "Amazing."

That didn't go down too well with Matt as he elbowed Alex in the ribs.

Max and his wife Sarah Eden came up to greet us all and hugged Danny and Ruby as he introduced them to Sarah.

Alex and Matt were still elbowing each other in the ribs, and I am assuming Alex only did this next move to really annoy Matt. But as the next song started to play, Alex grabbed hold of my hand and said, "Would you honour me with a dance?"

I humbly agreed as he led me out onto the dance floor. I could just hear Chase holding back the laughs as he tried to act serious. Matt just watched and walked with Max and the others to their table.

I was surprised. Alex was actually a really good dancer, as we danced to an orchestral classic. (Oh . . . the classic irony.)

I beamed with a smile as Alex twirled me around. And I whispered to Alex, "Thank you for your help today."

Alex glanced over at Chase and then back at me, a bit perplexed as we danced, so I explained and whispered, "The plants told me everything."

Alex started to laugh as he realised, I had known him and Matt far too well, to not expect them to help.

We both smiled as we continued the dance, until Alex led me over to Matt and suggested he dance with me instead.

See, their friendship is already starting to blossom.

CHAPTER 29

MISSION CLARIFICATION

Journal entry by Terrence Connors

I waited on a park bench in the Melbourne botanical gardens, staring at the white lily the target had given me, when Odele Connors, my adoptive mother, walked up to sit next to me, all rugged up and shaded by an umbrella as the rain gently fell.

"Beautiful night," I said, trying to create small talk.

My mother and I do not have the best of family relationships; it's more like a business relationship.

Odele just shrugged her shoulder and mumbled, "Yes, if you say so."

We both sat and watched the waters of the Yarra when I broke the tension. "I was told the Willows family were off limits. What changed your mind?" I asked.

Odele huffed and sneered. "That girl has disrupted our plans too many times. And it's time we ended it."

She stood up about to walk away then glared back at me, trying to calm herself and said, "You're a Nature Guardian as well, so you have an advantage with her. Either convince her to work for us or kill her. At least that way, you will make yourself an extremely rare collectable for me."

I stood and followed Odele as she began to walk away and shouted, "And what if I don't want to do either . . . Mother? What if we just leave this one and move on?"

Odele just glared at me curiously and asked "Why are you so eager to save her life, all of a sudden?"

I didn't know how to explain it without risking my life.

Odele may have adopted me, but I knew what really happened. I was seven when I was taken from my real father and kept in a hospital at the village where they ran all sorts of tests on me. After a few months had passed, I was brought into Odele's home to join her family—I was collected like all the others. I had an entire life ripped from me, but there was one thing I never forgot . . . the day I was taken. I was at the park with my best friend. She had a fall and they blamed me for it.

I couldn't remember her name or even what she looked like . . . until today. When I saw Lila's eyes, and when she was holding my hand, I knew.

Odele continued to glare at me, waiting for an answer, trying to keep her rage in check and replied, "If you cannot acquire this target, then I will simply put you back in your box and arrange someone else to do it instead." She turned to face me to ensure I understood when she said, "I strongly recommend you do as you mother asks and try not to fail this time."

I nodded and tried to hide my sadness as Odele stepped into a waiting car and drove away.

I sat down on the park bench, and the white lily began to wilt in my hand.

Now what?

CHAPTER 30

THERE'S SOMETHING FISHY

Journal entry by Alex Woods

It had been a few weeks since we had any incidents or visits to the hospital. And things were starting to feel a bit normal. Adela and I had a lot of catching up to do, and she was so grateful to Lila and me for not giving up on her.

She says she doesn't remember anything that's happened and when she was examined by the doctors, the head scan came back with tissue damage in the brain that may not ever recover. But if I were in her position, I wouldn't want to remember either.

Today Lila had organised a family outing to the aquarium, out of request from one of the kids. And she decided to make it a big outing, inviting Chase and Maxwell as well.

But I wanted to see her before we left. I had found something really important I wanted to share with her.

When I knocked on the apartment, Lila answered the door with loud music blaring from the radio, and Lila, Matt, Danny, and Ruby were all dancing away to the music.

Lila shouted, "Hey! What's up?"

I shouted back and asked if she could come out into the hall to talk—away from the children.

As we walked back into the hallway, she confirmed if I was still coming to the aquarium. Maybe she was worried I'd found something that changed her plans.

I nodded my head struggling to hold back the excitement as I blurted out "I've been reading some of the diaries and notes that John left—"

Lila interrupted me quickly saying, "Alex, no . . . I promised the kids I would take them to the aquarium today. You can't ask me to work, not today."

I tried to ease her scepticism and assure her that it wasn't work, it was more like helping out a friend.

She was still sceptic, but was willing to hear me out and said, "You have fifteen minutes."

I went back into my apartment and showed Lila a journal entry, excitedly explaining, "So this is one of the diaries I was reading, and it was written by an Animal Guardian. It claims that he was able to bond with his animal friends."

Lila nodded her headed to show she was following along as she looked through the book

So I continued to explain, "So, I don't know how, but once he bonded with the animal, he was able to take the form of that animal at any time."

"Well that explains why you turned into a panther a few weeks back," Lila commented. "But what do you need me for?"

I took a deep breath still nervously excited and said, "I searched the hotel for the cat that I bonded with, and I couldn't find it. I was hoping, since you're head of security, you might be able to track it down for me."

Lila just looked at me and I could tell she was trying not to laugh. "You want me to track a cat?" she asked.

I nodded and looked at her with my pleading eyes and could tell she was about to cave.

She sighed, saying "Well you still have ten more minutes . . .so let's go."

We walked down into the lobby and sat at the concierge desk to look up the room details for the hotel.

And we were greeted by Adela who had just come back from a walk and asked, "Hey, Lila. What ya doing?"

Stupid me stood up defensively, staring at Adela then fumbled the paperwork off the desk.

Lila asked as she helped me pick up the papers if I was okay, and I sighed looking back at Adela to apologise and said, "Sorry—force of habit."

She just smiled saying, "It's okay, Alex, I get it . . . kind of," and she turned to Lila and said, "Lila I don't think I've properly had the chance to say how sorry I am for the things I was responsible for. I truly am thankful for what you've done for me and my family."

Lila held Adela's hand and said, "No sweat. Just do me a favour and never ever take me on one of your pamper days again." They both smiled at each other in agreement as Lila sat back down looking at the computer and said to me, "So there was an old lady staying in the apartment beneath us, but it was a short-term lease, which ended a few days ago. But according to these records, there are four other permanent tenants who have pets. And we're in the presence of one of them now."

I looked at Adela shocked. "You have a pet? How did I not know about this?"

Adela just shrugged her shoulders and stated, "Actually it's my father's."

Lila added, "Max got it for his birthday from his wife . . . and on that note your fifteen minutes are up. I will leave you to do your thing with . . . Prince," she said as she got up to walk to the elevator and then asked to confirm that both Adela and Jess were coming to the aquarium with Maxwell. Wow, Lila sure has put a lot of effort in to the aquarium visit.

Adela nodded then looked back at me asking what the hell I was planning to do with her dad's dog, and that was an awkward thing to explain.

But Adela eventually agreed as she walked me up to her dad's office.

I sat on the floor trying to meditate as I sat in front of Maxwell's new dog, Prince.

It didn't help that Adela and Max both stood behind me, whispering to each about how weird this looked, and Prince just sat there looking at me.

I really had to focus, and I thought back to what and how I felt when I was pulled into Lila's meditation. It helped, at the fact that every time I remember that kiss, I felt warm and fuzzy inside, filled with happiness.

It was that feeling that caused me to morph into a golden retriever, that looked exactly like Prince, only a little bit bigger.

Max looked at me and jumped screaming, "Whoa! Now that is cool and creepy at the same time."

I barked and suddenly had this overwhelming urge to find Lila and show her the good news. I ran to the office door and jumped onto the handle to get out.

Max said as I left, "Smart dog."

But Adela rushed to try and catch me yelling, "Wait! Stop that dog." She then grabbed my clothes from the office floor and chased after me. But I had already made it to the elevator.

By the time I got to Lila's apartment, I was being chased by Chase and two of his security guys. I scratched at the apartment door, and as Lila opened it, I jumped up on her excitedly, knocking her to the ground and licking her face.

She shouted as she tried to pull away, "Okay, okay, Prince, stop . . . get off." She pushed me off her and commanded me to sit, but I was so excited I couldn't keep still. This was such an amazing feeling that I so badly wanted to share with Lila. But the party soon got crashed as Adela and Chase both ran into the apartment behind me.

Hello . . . Trying to have my moment here . . . but no one was listening to the dog, as they stood and chatted with each other.

Adela explained to Lila what had happened and looked down at me angrily asking, "Why are you still a dog? We have to go in like ten minutes."

I don't know what came over me but my excitement was too much and jumped up on Lila barking to get her attention.

Lila sighed grabbing my clothes off Adela and called me out of the apartment and into mine, saying to the group to just give us a minute.

I was excited to see my apartment in a whole new way, as I jumped on the couch and the bed, barking and howling. Lila shouted to get my attention and sat down on the couch to call me over and gave me a good scratch on the back of my neck, which felt amazing. She said sternly, "Alex, you're supposed to be calming down. Now, sit!"

I rested my head down on her lap as she tried to calm me down. She then closed her eyes and began to meditate, pulling herself into my meditation. She looked around at the dreamland and how different it was compared to hers. We were both sitting on a large boulder in the middle of a floral garden surrounded by forest animals. Frolicking and playing around.

Lila nodded and said, "Wow, this is a lot calmer than the last dream we had together."

But I was still hyped on the bonding experience and still bursting with excitement, I said, "That was amazing! Why did we stop?"

Lila stood up and replied, "Because you can't stay a dog forever, and it's nearly time to go to the aquarium. So can we please go back to the real world?"

I began to think about my physical body back in the real world and smirked and cheekily asked, "I don't know I kind of liked sitting on your lap . . . I'm getting a good neck rub at the moment."

When we woke up back in the real world, Lila was sitting on the couch. And I had turned back into a human self fully naked lying on the couch with my head resting on Lila's lap.

"We're back," I said excitedly, hoping Lila would be just as excited, but she had kept her eyes closed and said, "Please tell me you're getting dressed now!"

Oh, right that . . . I quickly grabbed my clothes and got dressed at full speed, then said, "It's safe now."

Lila got up and smiled congratulating me on my success in meditation, as we walked down to the lobby to meet up with the rest of the group.

When we finally arrived at the aquarium, we had a large group consisting of Matt, Lila, Danny and Ruby, myself, Chase, Maxwell, Jessica, and Adela. As well as Matt's sister Jane and her teenage boy Jake and little sister Chloe, and we were apparently going to meet Mrs. Willows inside.

As we walked through the aquarium into the 360-fish bowl, Lila and I watched and laughed at the fish that began to follow Adela as she walked. Lila jumped as she saw her mother walk into the aquarium fish bowl with her husband, General Richard Willows, the person Lila has been avoiding for at least two maybe three months now.

Danny and Ruby both rushed to greet them as Matt chased after them.

Now that we were all present and accounted for, Lila took the opportunity to introduce everyone to everyone else while we waited for a special tour guide kindly arranged by Maxwell.

As we were led through the tour, I held on to Ruby's hand and Danny had Lila's hand, and for some reason, Matt was roped into walking with his sister and her two children. Lila and I were both listening and overheard Matt's sister whispering to Matt saying, "I know that he's your wife's friend but seriously he's hot."

Adela must have heard it as well because she glanced over at me and Lila, struggling to hold back our laughs and as we all listened, we all burst into a hysterical laugh. It was clearly an in joke as the rest of the group looked at us baffled.

But Lila's laugh quickly stopped when she saw her old friend from Myer walk in and stand with General Willows.

Lila pulled the General into the next room and questioned him. "Richard, what is he doing here?" she asked. Richard huffed and said casually "Well, I figured since you've been dodging my calls, you already knew why he's here."

Lila sneered through gritted teeth, "I don't need a bodyguard!"

Richard popped his head back in to look at the group and then whispered to Lila. "By the looks of the company you keep, I think you do."

"Richard, I've told you before—you don't get to choose my friends. Plus, I already have my own team of security, trained by me. You can't get any better than that," she replied.

Richard's voice started getting louder and more stern, as he tried to play the dad card. But since he hadn't acted like a father in years, it didn't get received well, and he commanded Lila, saying, "You will follow my orders and work with Ben and his team. End of discussion."

That's when Maxwell tried to intervene and asked, "Is everything all right here?"

Richard barked back, "Everything's fine, thank you."

But Maxwell wasn't convinced and turned to Lila for confirmation. Both Adela and I were listening in closely, both unsure if we should act as Lila's heart rate increased. Lila just nodded her head and said, "I'm okay, Max," as she walked off into the women's toilet.

Adela and I sat down and watched, listening to Lila crying in the toilet. She was soon joined by Jane as she walked into the toilet to wash her hands. Jane asked if she was okay and then asked, "So what's with the entourage? You have such a large crowd with you today."

Lila chuckled and sniffled as Jane continued to ask her more and more questions. "Oh, and what about the hottie with the yummy muscles? Oh, he looks tasty."

I cleared my throat feeling uncomfortable as Adela elbowed me and laughed again. I shushed her so we could keep listening as Lila answered, "I'm assuming you mean Alex. He's a-a friend from work. And the others are also friends from work—"

Jane interrupted saying, "That's right, you live where you work now. What exactly do you do at the hotel?"

I could hear Lila fumbling to answer the question until Adela came into rescue her, saying, "Hey Lila, we're all waiting for you outside, are you coming."

But Jane stopped and asked Lila one last question, very seriously she said, "Look I'm sorry for asking you all these questions. I just wanted to ask one more if that's okay . . . Is your friend Alex single?"

I couldn't bear to listen any further as I got up to look at the fish with the rest of the group. Then I watched as Lila and Adela hurriedly walked out of the women's toilets, looking at each other and laughing.

Oh, no . . . what had just happened?

We all went up to the cafeteria for lunch and I sat down at the end of the table with my tray and was quickly joined by Jane, who seemed very interested in me.

Unfortunately, I was too distracted as I heard Lila's heart rate increase again and felt her fear rise. I glanced over to see her looking out the window into the water of the Yarra River. I wanted to go and talk to her, but I seemed a bit stuck as Jane started telling me how she's just recently divorced. Because that's what a guy wants to hear, apparently.

I started to understand how Matt felt around me, when I watched Ben walk up to Lila and break her out of the trance she was in. She jumped in fright as Ben tried to reassure her and asked if she was okay. Lila nodded saying yes. But it seemed Ben knew her well enough to know she was lying and hugged her tightly.

She was willing to jump down a six-story building a few months ago to get away from this guy . . . and now they're hugging.

I was clearly distracted as I got up to talk to Matt who was still buying lunch for him and the family.

"Hey, what's the story with them?" I asked.

Matt glanced over and answered, "That's Ben. He's Lila's old training buddy."

I hated to ask but I did anyway, "Why are they hugging?"

Matt just laughed and jokingly accused me of being jealous before he answered my question. "Lila has thalassophobia remember, and he knows why."

I looked at Matt still waiting to hear for more information.

And Matt replied in a whisper, "He was there when it happened," as he walked away with his tray of food.

Yep, I was jealous. Lila and I had shared a lot together, but that story was one I found out by accident and not from Lila—and I had been waiting for Lila to tell me the story herself.

That was Ben, the guy who dragged her from the beach and sat with her for days as she grieved the death of her friend. But that wasn't the worst part of the story, Matt had also told me, that when Richard found out that Lila had fear of water, he arranged a training day for Lila, to help her get over her fear. He left Lila and her fellow cadets on an island off the coast of Queensland and ordered them to swim back to the mainland. Ben was the one who stayed with Lila and helped her to swim all the way back to shore.

I watched Lila and Ben talking as I sat and ate my lunch in a kind of jealous rage . . . friendship jealousy, of course.

There was no way I could top that in the friend's department. The only thing I had going for me is that I was a Guardian like her, that's gotten her abducted and hospitalised several times.

When we had finished our tour, we were left at the gift shop. I admit I was a bit pouty-faced for the rest of the tour, but I had Ruby there to distract me as she was determined to stay with me for the entire tour.

Lila was saying goodbye to Max and the Eden sisters as they left, and Ben stood a few steps behind her just watching.

Mrs Willows and the General wanted to buy something special for all of the kids in the group, so they stayed in the gift shop with Matt, Danny, Ruby, and Chloe. But Jake wasn't interested and followed me out of the store to see Lila.

Ben and I both got very protective standing close to Lila as a group of young teenage girls ran up and took selfie pictures with Lila, screaming "OMG! I can't believe it! Guys, I am so positive it's her," as they crowded around her.

Ben and I both worked to pull the girls away and stand protectively in front of Lila, as Lila replied "I'm sorry, I think you have me confused with—"

But one of the teens interrupted, saying, "Oh my gosh, I watched your stunt videos, like so many times, and it still looks amazing!"

And another teen looked at me and Ben and screeched, "Unbelievable! She has her own bodyguards. This is so cool! You have to tell us what the movie's called or is it a TV show?"

"I'm sorry, what are you talking about?" Lila asked.

One of the teens pulled out her phone to show Lila the YouTube videos: one of Lila jumping down six floors in Myer and another of Lila flying across the lake in Bendigo.

Crap. I thought Max was arranging for them to be removed.

Ben started to lose his patience and demanded the teens to "Please step away," and hurried Lila into the car park, leaving me waiting for the rest of the family, along with the many questions that followed. I even had to listen to the General boast to Mrs Willows, saying, "And that's why I insisted on Lila having one of my men as her bodyguard."

OH, THE AGONY . . .

That night when we arrived safely back to the hotel, I decided to wallow in my own self-pity down in the hotel bar, only to be greeted by the man I was feeling petty about.

Ben sat down next to me and ordered me and him the same drink and said grinning "I know that look."

"What look?" I barked back.

"It's the same look I have when I'm with her," he replied. I think he was trying to be nice when he handed me a business card of a local strip club, saying, "Here . . . it's a distraction that will take your mind off her."

I handed the card back to him and said, "Thanks, but I don't need a distraction."

Ben handed me the drink and chuckled. "Correct me if I'm wrong, but I'm guessing your friendship with Lila means everything to you. You'd do anything to keep her happy—even if it makes you miserable," he said. He placed the card down on the counter next to me and whispered, "This might just be a safer alternative to her sister-in-law."

Ben finished his drink and walked out of the bar as I looked down at the business card.

CHAPTER 31

THE NIGHTMARE

Journal entry by Lila Winters

That night Ben had managed to convince Matt for him to stay on our couch for a few days; and to be honest, I didn't mind the company. It was nice to remember old horror stories of our training days and finally laugh about it.

The family was sleeping soundly except for me. I was having yet another nightmare. They were the same every night of me being stuck in the rainforest and running continuously.

But this night was different. Tonight while I was running through the forest, I was stopped by Terrence who grabbed hold of my hand and said, "I know who you are now, Lila . . ."

But before he said anything further, a burst of fire surrounded me, and I woke up in panic with Ben sitting next to me trying to calm me down. I looked around the room as I tried to calm myself and watched as the plant on my bedside table finished retracting one of its plant leaves, that on closer observation looked singed on the side.

I looked at Ben in panic, who seemed to be completely oblivious to the plant with all of his focus on me. He picked me up out of the bed and walked me out on to the balcony, so I could cool down and get some fresh air.

I asked Ben to promise to keep the nightmares a secret, just between us, and he agreed.

Then he sat up with me all night and stared up at the night sky in silence until we fell asleep out on the balcony.

CHAPTER 32

THE REUNION

Journal entry by Lila Winters

Alex and I had been working really hard for weeks, looking for any clues that would lead us to the other missing Guardians. If you remember, we also promised Jennifer that we would help find her family.

Now that we had more Guardians on our team, we were able to divide our efforts.

The only problem was Ben. He was following me everywhere, so to avoid my cover being blown, I stayed back at the hotel and did research instead.

I guess Alex was feeling a little territorial with another protector around because he offered to stay back and help.

We were coming up with a lot of dead-ends looking in Victoria. It was either a recently abandoned warehouse or was a pharmaceutical retail outlet selling only beauty products. It was starting to feel like we were always one step behind. So we widened our search. And as you can guess, it was taking a long time and we almost stayed up all night.

Ben had fallen asleep on the couch, and Alex and I were sitting in the study. Alex was looking at the computer, and I was falling asleep on his shoulder.

Until Alex had found something and tapped my hand to wake me up.

"Lila, I found something," he whispered.

I woke up and rubbed my eyes to get a clearer picture. It was a large industrial park located in Sydney.

"That's it," I whispered. "Print that map, then delete the browsing history. I don't want anyone accidently finding out where we're going," indicating back to where Ben was asleep on the couch.

We both realised it was 6.30 a.m. and that people would be waking up soon. So we both snuck down to the training room. And while we were down there, we brainstormed through the plans as we trained at full speed.

"So what are we looking for exactly," Alex asked in between punches.

I replied as I tried to kick him in the head and missed, "We need to find more information on the Neuritamine drug—where it's being made, who it's been shipped to, or better yet who's funding this whole thing—anything that may lead us to where Terrence is hiding."

Alex interrupted saying, "You know I'm really not too fond of us calling him Terrence."

I kicked the back of Alex's legs, causing him to fall and then kneed him in the face, pushing him backwards on to the mat, then straddled his torso and snickered, "And you think Darkman is any better . . ."

But before we could continue our sparring session, Ben walked into the gym to see me with a bloodied and bruised eye and grazed fist, sitting on Alex who now had a bloody nose dripping onto the mat.

I sighed knowing that our super-powered sparring session was over.

Ben said nothing as he smiled, walking over to help me up and inspected my injuries, saying, "Now what am I supposed to tell your father, when he finds out about these injuries."

I pulled away from Ben in frustration and snapped back, "Tell him he can go to hell."

I pulled Alex to his feet as we made our way back up to the apartment . . . along with my babysitter.

As we walked into the apartment, I was greeted by my mother, who wasn't at all that impressed at the sight of me and looked back at Ben with a furious scowl.

"Mother, what are you doing here?" I asked.

Matt walked out of his bedroom, holding his dress suit to show Hanna what he was planning to wear.

It was a sudden realisation as I smiled and whispered to myself, knowing Alex would hear me, "Crap. I forgot about Matt's reunion party."

Matt stood looking at me oddly and could definitely tell what I was doing and glared back at Alex.

Alex just smiled back, doing the manly thing and bailed out, saying, "Well . . . I have a field trip to plan with Chase, so I'm gonna go . . ."

Coward . . .

Matt pulled me into the bedroom to talk while Hanna and Ben waited outside. It was no surprise that my mother was telling on me to the General and Ben was getting an earful from him.

Matt sat on the bed and asked, "I thought you weren't working today."

I didn't want to disappoint him, so I lied, a little. "I was only coordinating the mission. But now, I'm all yours," I said with an "it's all-good" smile.

Matt seemed to be too preoccupied about tonight to pick up on the lie as he nodded and inspected my injuries, saying, "I'm assuming these will be healed by tonight."

I explained that they were only superficial, so it would only take an hour at the most.

Matt smiled either nervously or excitedly. "Good. You should get some rest," he said, and as he walked out of the room, he looked back and pleaded, "I was hoping you could wear the dress you wore on your birthday, with your hair up . . . Is that okay?"

I was tired, so I just smiled and nodded as I lay down to get some rest on the bed. Matt left the room giddy and excited.

Journal entry insert by Matt Winters

I left Lila to get some sleep and helped Hanna to get settled in the guest room. I had asked her to stay the night and watch the kids while Lila and I went to the reunion.

I was nervous about seeing my old classmates again. I may have been school captain, but I was also a science geek, which meant I had my fair share of bullies, especially one in particular. But I was confident knowing that Lila was going to be with me tonight, and I can show my old classmates that being a science geek does lead to a really good life. I have an amazingly sexy wife, beautiful kids, and a cool job. Tonight, was going to be a good night.

But first I had to deal with something or to better clarify someone. I grabbed the envelope from my hiding place behind my astronomy books and headed down to Alex's apartment to finally confront him. He kept Lila up all night last night, and now I've had enough.

Alex invited me in and immediately I started my interrogation, throwing the envelope on the table. As it landed, the photos of Lila and Alex slid out, and I asked, "I need you to tell me what's going on between you and Lila?"

Alex just shook his head and replied, "What do you mean?"

"Look, I know we're not the best of friends, but we are trying to be nice to each other, right?" I said, trying to remain calm. "So please explain these photos to me . . . and this time, don't lie."

Alex looked through the photos of him and Lila hugging and eating breakfast together, looking a little bit too cosy, then he looked back at me and accused me of spying on him.

The nerve of him. I controlled my temper (reasonably) and explained, "I haven't, but someone else has. I don't know who or why, but they are sending a pretty clear message."

Alex responded saying, "Matt, it's not what you think . . . These photos don't show the whole picture. They were taken when we were training and working. I'm sorry—I don't know what to say here."

"Alex . . . I know you're in love with my wife. That much is obvious. But let's make this clear. The only reason why you're still here is because you're useful to her . . . you protect her," I explained, trying to maintain my cool. "But Lila is my wife. So do us all a favour and keep your damn hands off her."

I stormed out of the room in a huff and took a breath of relief, trying to compose myself before I walked back into my apartment to get ready to go.

Original journal entry continued by Lila Winters

By the time I had caught up on enough sleep, the day had flown by and it was 4.40 p.m. We had to be out the door in twenty minutes.

I raced out of bed and moved at half speed to get dressed and brushed my hair up, just like Matt asked, and I know I wasn't a fan of make-up, but I thought because it was a special event for Matt, I'd put a bit more effort into it.

Matt was pacing in the lounge room, all dressed up in his evening wear, and I must have startled him when I appeared standing at the front door of the apartment, ready to go with one minute to spare.

I was wearing the blue party dress I wore on my birthday, just like Matt asked, and I was really hoping he'd be happy with the way I looked. "Is this okay?" I asked.

Matt opened the door for me and smiled, saying, "It's perfect."

Matt and I walked through the hotel lobby when Matt stopped to go and talk to Max . . . for some reason.

I ran into Ben who seemed to be in a hurry and very distracted as he dropped his computer tablet. I moved my hand at full speed to catch it, hoping he wouldn't notice. "Is everything okay?" I asked.

Ben nodded then looked up realising who he had bumped into and said, "Wow." Then looked over at Max handing a set of keys to Matt, smiling and muttered, "I take it Matt organised a different set of wheels for tonight. He's really going all out for this reunion thing, isn't he?"

He looked back at me smiling, but before he could say anything, I cut him off, saying, "Ben, I know that look and I know what you're going to say. But my response is going to be tough. You can't come."

Ben just sighed, saying, "It's my job, Lila."

"So take the night off. You know I can protect myself . . . so please, as a friend, just trust me," I said, begging him.

Ben looked down at the floor then stepped backwards into the elevator as Matt walked back over-excited saying, "Max let us use his Lamborghini. This night is going to be amazing."

When we arrived at the Golf Club's function centre, Matt's friends were waiting outside for him and were cheering as they saw the Lamborghini pull into the driveway.

Matt excitedly handed the key to the valet and introduced me to his friends, pointing to each one of them. "Lila, this is Harry, Sam, and Chris," he said, "and this is my wife, Lila." I think they were a little too excited, seeming almost giddy to re-live old memories. As we walked into the centre, I overheard Chris, saying quietly to Matt, "Damn . . . you scored a good one."

Matt must have forgotten that I had really good hearing as he replied, "I know, right."

I wasn't sure how I felt about the phrase scored, but I just shrugged it off as we walked into the function room.

We all stood at the bar as we ordered our respective drinks, and Matt asked Chris, "Hey, where's your wife? Didn't you get married last year?"

Chris sculled his first drink then answered, "Ex-wife now. She only married me for the money."

I interrupted and asked, "What do you do?" as Chris ordered a second drink and answered again, "I'm a mechanic . . . She left me for some lawyer guy."

Sam then tapped Chris's shoulder, reassuring him and saying, "Not all women are as heartless as your ex. Take Lila for example . . . I bet she wouldn't chase men for their money. Would ya', Lila?" he asked.

I was unsure what to say, since Max pays me nearly three times as much as Matt's salary and included living expenses.

"Um," I mumbled.

But Matt quickly interrupted saying "No, she loves me too much for that."

Harry just snickered, "Says the guy who just rolled up in a three-million-dollar sports car."

"You're not jealous, are you, Harry," Matt said jokingly.

I was beginning to see how this night was going to go, and my suspicion was confirmed as

Matt took me around introducing me to the rest of his old classmates. The conversation tended to circle around the fancy car he rocked up in and how he scored an amazing wife.

There's that word again, scored.

While Matt was busy talking with his friends, I snuck away from the group and sat down at the bar. Not surprisingly, Matt didn't seem to notice.

While I sat nursing my drink, I surveyed the room and noticed another man who was making the rounds talking to everyone and boasting about his amazing career.

Great, another one.

The man then made his way over to the bar to introduce himself. "Hi, I didn't realise we had an angel in our year level . . ."

Unfortunately, at just that moment, I was in the process of drinking, and I laughed so hard, struggling to hold the drink in. As I swallowed to clear my throat, I commented saying, "That has got to be the cheesiest opening line I've heard tonight."

He then ordered me another drink and smoothly said, "I know, but I still got you to laugh!" as he smiled at me, asking what class I was in.

I tried to correct him, explaining that I was a plus one, when he interrupted saying, "A plus one . . . Please tell me you're my date?"

But just as I was about to answer, Matt walked up, saying, "Actually, Eddie . . . she's mine."

Matt and Eddie looked at each other with a tense stare, as Harry, Chris, and Sam walked up and stood behind Matt in a defensive standoff.

Eddie broke the tension, putting his arm around Matt and patting him on the shoulder. "Matt, buddy, tell me then, who is this stunning woman?"

Matt pulled away from Eddie and put his hands around my waist, holding me close and replied, "This is my wife, Lila Winters."

In disbelief, Eddie turned to me saying, "You married this loser?"

I could tell Matt wanted to say something snide and inappropriate, but I quickly responded to Eddie's derogatory comment and said, "I'm pretty sure the loser here is the man checking out the breast of a married woman, seeming, oh so ridiculously desperate."

Eddie quickly averted his gaze away from my breast and grabbed a drink off the bar as he readied himself to leave. But turned back to me saying, "How sweet, a woman defending her man's honour. Looks like we know who wears the pants in your family."

Matt didn't take that too well as he grabbed my hand and led me away from the bar, saying a not so nice goodbye to Eddie.

As I was being pulled towards the buffet table, I tried to apologise to Matt, saying, "I'm sorry, Matt . . . I didn't know he wasn't your friend."

He then glared at me and explained, "It's not that . . . it's what you said. I don't need you to defend me."

I wasn't overly sure what to say. I mean if I remembered correctly, it was me he was ogling. So instead I just nodded as we walked over to his real group of friends.

As the night went on, we sat down to eat dinner, and I started to feel like the obvious plus one again and made an excuse to go outside and get some air.

I thought outside would be the safest for me, considering everyone else was inside, I wouldn't run the risk of embarrassing Matt again.

I sat outside in the outdoor dining area, and thankfully it was empty. It was the middle of autumn and not exactly outdoorsy weather for the normal and sane people. Luckily for me, my metabolism was so high I didn't feel the cold like the others did, so I sat and watched the stars in peace . . . until Eddie walked out and sat next to me.

He even did that gentlemen thing and placed his jacket over my shoulders before he sat down next to me and said, "You look lonely out here."

Please, lord, don't tell me he was going to be that guy who just wouldn't take the hint.

I figured I would take the high road and politely hand his jacket back, saying, "I'm not a crowd's person, and I was actually enjoying the peace."

I then stood up moving away from him and leaned on the ledge bordering the outdoor dining area overlooking the golf course. That was a clear and obvious hint. But he didn't get it, as he stood to lean on the ledge next to me.

"You know, most women are usually charmed by my handsome good looks and devilish demeanour," he boasted.

I rolled my eyes and snickered, "Vain much?"

Eddie just took it as a compliment and agreed with me saying, "Only a little."

Well he was persistent. I tried changing the subject and asked, "So what do you do for a living?"

Eddie replied with an answer I never would have guessed, saying, "I work in the astronomy lab in Sydney."

I looked at him in disbelief and sighed, as he said, "I'm serious. I get paid to look at stars all day."

I decided to test him. "All right, dazzle me with an amazing astronomy fact," I demanded.

Eddie accepted my challenge and moved in closer to me and pointed up to the stars, whispering, "See the star with the reddish tinge?" He stood behind me, resting his head close to mine and used my hand to point to the star.

I tried not to respond in a negative way and snickered, "Yes," as I subtly moved away.

Eddie just smiled seeing fully well what I was doing and explained, "That's not a star, that's Mars."

I pretended to be amazed as he continued to tell me more facts.

"Over there is the Southern Cross and just a little lower is the fake Southern Cross, and would you believe that straight up there . . . the big thing, that's the moon," he continued.

"Okay, I believe you. You're an astronomer," I said jokingly, hinting for him to stop. He nodded and looked at me as he finished his drink and placed it on the ledge and made the stupid decision as he leaned in and tried to get a kiss from me. What an idiot.

But it got worse. I pulled away and asked, "What are you doing?" and he replied, "I'm seizing my moment . . . just go with it," as he tried to kiss me again.

This guy clearly had too much to drink because he went from idiot to insane in two seconds.

"You must be imagining things," I snapped back, walking out onto the golf course to get away.

But he started to get frustrated and grabbed hold of my arm tightly, pulling me closer to him, smugly saying, "Aww . . . come on. You know you can't resist me. Just one kiss—"

I asked him to stop and to let me go, but he wouldn't. Instead he started kissing my neck. I took a deep breath, resisting the urge to use my super powers and throw him across the field. Instead I turned to him and looked him in the eyes seductively, lulling him to relax his guard, then kneed him in the groin and punched him in the face.

And while he reacted to the pain I tried to hurriedly walk away.

And you have no idea how hard it was not to use any of my super powers, because trust me, this guy was asking for it.

Eddie looked down at the blood on his hands and was fuelled with rage as he shouted, "You little #*&%#," and tried to grab hold of me.

That's when Ben ran up next to me, pushing Eddie to the ground and pulling me closer to him, protectively wrapping his arm around me and just stared at Eddie.

The commotion must have drawn the attention of Eddie's friends as they came out to see what was wrong. And they must have assumed Ben had given him a bloody nose as they circled around both of us, seemingly itching for a fight.

Ben held me close and whispered quietly "Are you okay?"

I just nodded still trying to assess the scene, and I was admittedly thankful, confused, and angry at Ben's presence.

I was pretty sure I told him no.

Eddie stood to his feet and looked at Ben probably realising it wasn't Matt and asked, "Who the hell's this guy?"

Ben replied trying to keep it professional saying, "I am Ms Winters' bodyguard. Now I need you to please walk away."

But we both knew Eddie was beyond walking away, especially now that his friends were there. Eddie just snared back at Ben, "No, your little whore led me on, then gave me a bloody nose . . . So now I want an apology."

Ben and Eddie both clenched their fists as they readied to punch each other. But instead, I intervened trying to avoid a massive punch up.

I grabbed hold of Ben's fist and pulled it down and tried to gently and humanly kick Eddie backwards, but as I did, Eddie caught my foot mid swing and smugly grinned back at his friends. He was probably thinking, As if I'm going to let a woman beat the crap out of me.

So I used this to my advantage. Using Eddie as an anchor and still holding Ben's hand I spun horizontally in the air and with my free foot, kicked Eddie's face—thus, freeing my other foot. Eddie was forced backwards and held his face in pain.

By that time, we had gained the attention of the rest of the reunion as they all came out to have a look.

Matt walked out with the rest of his friends and saw me holding Ben's hand as he stood protectively next to me.

Not the best timing . . .

Matt just looked at Ben, then looked at Eddie's bloody nose and now bruised eye, then back at me and the large red handprint mark, left from when Eddie grabbed me.

Eddie just looked back at Matt and chortled as he began to walk out towards the car park.

It must have set Matt off because the next thing we saw was Matt tackling Eddie to the ground and punching him repeatedly.

Eddie defended himself, overpowering Matt and pinning him on the ground. But before Eddie could get a punch in, Ben pulled him away.

Matt stood to his feet still in a fighting mood about to punch Ben as well, until I shouted, "Matt, stop," and grabbed Matt's arm, trying to pull him away, but he was too fuelled with rage as he turned and pushed me, causing me to lose my balance.

Keep in mind I was in high heels.

I ended up tumbling down the golf course slope into the lake, getting a few nasty cuts and bruises along the way.

Ben ran down the hill so quickly, leaving Matt to slowly realise what he had done and make his way down as well.

He helped me out of the water and sat me on the banks and saw a massive gash starting from the top of my forehead across my right eye and cheek, and my grazed and grassy hands from my attempts to slow the fall.

"Lila, Lila, look at me," he demanded in a worrying panic.

I looked up at him with teary bloodied eyes and leaned in to hug him as I cried.

The sirens of police cars appeared in the background and as Matt came closer, Ben quickly turned to stop him and pulled him away from me.

Matt stood back with his hands in the air, agreeing with Ben to stay away. He stood and looked at the damage he had caused me and fell to his knees with deep regret.

"Honey . . . I'm so sorry. I swear, I didn't mean to!" he said trying to get my attention. "Lila . . . just please tell me you're okay, please."

But I couldn't look at him, and I couldn't answer him. Honestly, I didn't know if I was okay. All I could feel at that moment was disappointment.

Ben pulled me to my feet and walked me back up the hill.

Matt walked behind us calling my name trying to explain himself, saying "I was just trying to defend you . . ."

I stopped and looked back at Matt, with such disappointment in my eyes, "No, you were defending yourself." He looked at me in denial, as I continued to say, "All night you've been parading me around, like some trophy you'd scored."

Matt argued back. "So I'm proud of my wife—what's wrong with that?"

"I'm not some trophy or prize you can fight over. I can defend myself," I exclaimed trying to hold back the tears.

Ben walked with me up the golf course slope to a waiting ambulance, as the police officers came down to arrest Matt.

CHAPTER 33

HARSH REALITY

Journal entry by Alex Woods

We arrived back at the hotel in the early hours of the morning of yet another failed mission. The site we raided looked like it had only just been abandoned, and all the evidence destroyed.

I don't get it. They are clearly cleaning house, but we only seemed to be just that little bit too late.

Max was waiting for us as we pulled into the basement car park. He greeted Adela as she walked past, then looked up at me and Chase, looking frantic and flustered, saying, "I need you two to come with me."

He didn't say much after that, as we drove through the city of Melbourne out to a police station in a small town just past the airport. As I got out of the car, I saw Ben hugging Lila as she sat next to him on the steps outside the police station. I rushed over to see if she was okay, but she wouldn't even look at me.

Max walked up behind me and said, "Lila, are you okay?"

She nodded, still refusing to look up at us, then Max asked, "Have you given your statement?"

Lila nodded again as Max walked into the police station with Chase.

I knelt down and brushed the hair from Lila's face to see the butterfly stitches holding her face together, and grazes on her hands as well as a nasty hand-shaped bruise on her arm. I tried to control my emotions and breathed out slowly, while Lila just stayed quiet and still refused to look at me.

"Lila, please, just look at me . . . talk to me—anything," I whispered.

"I don't want to talk," she mumbled, crying on to Ben's shirt.

I tried to hold her hand to comfort her, but she moved it away. I could feel her pain as I knelt in front of her, as well as fear and a great sadness. Something had happened, and it's something that couldn't be fixed easily.

I didn't know what to do. I wanted to know what happened and who did this. I wanted to beat the crap out of them. But then I also wanted to sit with her and comfort her—all while respecting the keep-your-hands-off-her rule that Matt demanded of me.

Then I saw Matt coming out of the police station and walking towards Max's car. He glanced over at Lila to say something.

That was when Ben stood in front of Lila protectively and stared at Matt. I watched as Lila ran at full speed away from the police station while I slowly put the pieces together.

I sat on the steps still moving at full speed watching, unsure what to do or how to feel, as Ben, Matt, Max, and Chase all realised that Lila had gone.

Journal entry insert by Terrence Connors

I walked along the Yarra River today in the Botanic Gardens of Melbourne, plotting my next moves, when I felt a disturbance amongst the tree. I could feel there was an overwhelming sadness and I went to investigate. I moved at full speed and hid up in a tree as a woman sat at the base of it, crying.

It was her . . . it was Lila.

It was the perfect opportunity to make my move and grab her.

But I was stopped as a tree branch had wrapped itself around my foot. I watched as a small green vine grew up from the ground next to Lila and wrapped around Lila's hand and a small blue rosebud blossomed from it. Lila wiped the tears from her face, looking up at the rose.

That's when I saw her injuries.

She sniffled as she tried to smell the perfume of the rosebud and attempted to smile but stopped upon feeling the pain of her cheek. I watched in amazement as Lila's injuries healed instantly and as she felt her cheek again, she smiled with a grateful look on her face.

No Nature Guardian has ever been able to create an instant healing remedy—not for hundreds of years. And she did it without even trying.

I leaned on a different branch to get a closer look and started breaking the branch. As it crackled, Lila stood to her feet in fright, so I hid amongst the branches and leaves.

Lila looked around the empty gardens then disappeared at full speed.

CHAPTER 34

NYMPHS

Journal Entry by Alex Woods

Journal entry insert by Maxwell Eden

It's been two weeks since the golf course incident. Lila had requested some time off to recover and sort out her family life. And in that time, she had been staying in the guest bedroom of her apartment. She didn't talk to anyone and only came out to train when she thought everyone else had gone to sleep.

But with her absence from the search party, things started to get worse. They started to feel like they were going around in circles. Alex especially was getting distracted, worried about his friend and probably feeling a bit helpless.

Not only that the hotel was, let's just say, looking a little dreary, as all of my indoor plants were wilting and starting to die. Even the rooftop garden looked sad. Given Lila's abilities, it was safe to assume there was a connection between the two. So I have organised a surprise team-building exercise, and called Lila to the office to talk about it.

And for the sake of my plants, I'm not giving her any choice.

Original journal entry continued by Alex Woods

I have not had a great past few weeks, and I admit I've spent way too much time at the bar. I woke up again, wallowing in my misery of self-neglect, next to two naked ladies still sleeping and hugging me. I was sure I'd remember their names by the time they woke up.

Unfortunately, that time was sooner than I had hoped. Lila had stormed into the apartment on a rant of how inconsiderate Max was, sending us away at the worst possible time, especially her. While she ranted, I tried to get in to a more decent position and pulled away from the ladies.

Lila finally stopped her rant and looked at me for a response, realising my current predicament, as she looked at the two ladies and the state of my horrifically messy room. She turned away embarrassed at what she had done and apologized as she walked back out of the room.

I quickly chased after her and wrapped the bed sheet around me, running at full speed to stop her from leaving.

"Wait . . . please—it's not what it looks like," I said desperate for her to stay.

She looked back at the two ladies as they finished getting dressed and walking out of the apartment; they smiled back at me.

Lila looked back at the empty unmade bed and my clothes on the floor and said. "I'm pretty sure it's exactly what it looks like."

She tried to leave again, but I wouldn't let her go. I needed her to stay, so I could explain myself. The last thing I wanted was for Lila to think less of me . . . so I held onto her wrist and said, "Lila, I can explain."

She looked down at the hand I was holding and took a breath as she looked up at me and replied, "You don't have to explain. But you do have to let go."

I begged her again saying, "Just don't leave, okay?"

She looked down at her hand again, then stared back at me waiting for me to let her go, as she stood in silence.

I let go of her arm and realised I was holding it way too tightly, leaving a large purple mark where my hand once was. "I'm so sorry," I gasped as I rushed to get some ice from the freezer.

She just shrugged it off saying, "It's fine." But I knew she wasn't fine. I could feel her anger and frustration. And as I tried to ice her wrist, she looked at the door and gritted her teeth.

"So you came in upset about something Max has done. But I couldn't quite understand the rest. Did you want to say it again this time a little slower?" I asked, cautiously grinning.

She let out a great sigh as she explained again. "Max has organised a get-away for the team and masked it as a team-building exercise. According to him, we all seem to be stressed . . . So I came down here to tell you to pack your things, our flight leaves in two hours."

Lila could see on my face that I was agreeing with Max on the idea and started to walk out of the apartment, jokingly commenting, "Oh and if you hurried, you might be able to catch one of your girlfriends to invite them along."

She closed the apartment door as I tried to respond and shouted, "They're not my girlfriends!"

Well that's just great. Lila finally came to open up to me about her feelings and I screwed it up.

Max had arranged for us to travel on his private jet to a fancy hotel with hot springs, run by a Buddhist monastery in China.

The flight over was long and awkwardly silent as Lila and Matt sat in separate seats and only exchanged pleasantries when they had to.

And as we pulled up to the monastery, we were all greeted by the monks as they bowed their heads. But when Lila stepped out of the limo with her two kids, all the monks stopped and either looked shocked or surprised, whispering to themselves, and all knelt down on their knees to bow to Lila.

Lila unsure what to do whispered to Adela, "Um, do they know who we are?"

Adela the one who had picked the location of the trip seemed to have been here before as she answered, "In a way, yes," as she walked off into the hotel.

We all followed Adela into the hotel to get more information about the hotel. "Don't worry," she said. "This is the safest place for us. It was originally built for the Guardians as a safe haven hundreds of years ago. The monks just live here as the caretakers."

You know that would have been a nice fact to know before we arrived at the hotel.

Journal entry insert by Matt Winters

Lila and I unpacked our suitcases while the kids had a snack at the table. It was really tense in the silence. So I tried to make small talk by asking what happened to Ben, who seemed noticeably absent since last week.

Lila just kept unpacking and answered, "The General had a mission that only Ben was qualified for . . . so he called him back temporarily."

"Good . . . I mean, I don't know. I'm just glad he didn't get into any trouble from what happened." I eventually muddled out the words. I sat down on the bed and tried to figure out the best words to say. Then just looked at her saying, "Lila . . . I can't possibly say sorry enough for what I did . . . but I'm just hoping you might be able to give me some hint as to what I can do to make things right between us."

Lila then sat on the bed next to me and said, "Honestly, honey . . . I don't know. But it's not just you I'm angry at—I'm upset about everything and sad about how things could have been, you know, if I wasn't . . . me."

I knew exactly what words I had to say then, as I knelt down in front of her and looked her in her eyes saying, "You know, a very wise woman once told me, You can go through life wondering what could have been and get nowhere, or you can accept what life has dealt you, and strive to get somewhere. Only one will make you happy."

Lila chuckled knowing what I had done and whispered "Using my own words against me—that's so not fair!"

I was nervous as I hugged Lila. I was so worried she might pull away. But instead she just relaxed and hugged me back. I had waited to do that for weeks, and I was almost in tears when it finally happened.

Original journal entry continued by Alex Woods

The next morning, Lila was in the garden practicing her yoga, and Matt was reading a book, watching Danny and Ruby as they played in the garden, jumping on the rocks.

Jennifer had walked into the garden at the same time as me and said to Lila, "I thought you were supposed to be relaxing."

Lila stood up and watched as Jennifer set up a comfy reading spot for herself, then giggled replying, "I am relaxing." She then turned to me as she stood in the sparring position and smiled saying, "Are you ready?"

I was over the moon and I readied myself for a fight and replied, "For you.... always."

Lila then reminded me of the rules of public sparring: you know no super powers and try not to hurt each other too much.

If I am correct the last time we did this, I ended up with the bloodied nose, not her.

Jennifer and Matt watched in suspense as Danny and Ruby cheered us on. Ruby was cheering for me, and Danny was cheering for his mum.

Both of us tried to hit the other's shoulders, then we both dodged each other's punches. We ended up using the entire court yard trying to both tap each other's right shoulder. It almost looked like we were dancing as we dodged the kicks and punches, until Lila gained the higher ground on one of the rocks summersaulting over me and tapping me on the shoulder.

She boasted to the audience, "Score one for me."

I turned and quickly grabbed her hand before she pulled it away and pulled her closer to me as I wrestled her to the ground. I ended up lying on top of her to keep her hands pinned to her body as I tapped her right shoulder and smiled, saying, "Score two for me."

Lila struggled to break free without the use of her hands then looked at me with a massive grin and said, "I know that smile, you cheeky little cheat."

She was totally right and did use my super speed but only a little. She then yelled loudly, "Sick 'em, Danny."

Danny ran down from the rocks screaming and jumped on my back trying to wrestle me to the ground. I pretend to lose as Danny pulled me to the ground and tapped my shoulder.

Lila then declared victory for Danny, announcing to the spectators, "And score three goes to Danny. Wooooooooo!"

Max, Adela, Jessica, and Chase had all come out to watch as well and cheered as Danny took his victory lap around the garden.

But Lila and I hadn't noticed that Matt had walked out of the garden while we were sparring.

Journal entry insert by Matt Winters

It was hard to watch Lila having so much fun with Alex. My jealousy was getting the best of me again, and to avoid me making a scene, I went for a walk along the trail towards the hot springs.

I was throwing pebbles into one of the hot springs when Lila came looking for me.

"Hey . . . are you okay?" she asked.

I just shrugged my shoulders and kept throwing the pebbles.

"You're upset about Alex, aren't you?" she asked again pushing for some sort of response.

I threw my last pebble into the waters angrily, causing it to splash back at us as I explained, "Kind of . . . it's just watching you fight . . . I could see it."

I looked at Lila hoping she would understand what I was talking about, but she just looked at me still lost in what I was trying to say. "I see the passion you feel towards him when you're training with him," I explained.

"Matt, you've known me since I was 16 years old. You used to watch me train with Ben and cheered me on from the sidelines. You should really know by now that I get passionate about any strategic game. I love the game, not the opponent."

I nodded and pouted a little as I picked up another pebble. "I don't know. I just wish I could do the same thing he does with you."

Lila stood on the footpath and said, "Well, it's about time," then readied herself to fight me.

I looked at her baffled at what she was doing and said, "Lila, I don't know how to fight you."

She dropped her shoulders and let out a loud huff saying, "Have you learned nothing from all these years watching me? When I first met Alex, his fighting skills were very minimal, and we spent days playing the shoulder tap. Why? What's the whole purpose of the game?"

I took a moment to think and took a wild guess, "To learn how to dodge."

"Correct!" Lila shouted excitedly. "To learn your opponent and dodge their attack. Find their weak spots while still staying alive. Now let's begin . . . I'll go first," she said trying to tap my shoulder.

I dodged her several times before I got tapped. She nodded and smiled because it was now my turn. I tried and failed to tap Lila's shoulder again and again.

Lila stopped in panic as she watched a large wave rise up from the hot springs and land on me, pulling me into the water. It felt like it had a strong grip around me as I struggled to swim up to the surface. I was being pulled farther and farther down into the hot spring . . . until it all went dark.

Original journal entry continued by Alex Woods

I was playing go fish with Danny, Ruby, and Chase while we waited for Lila and Matt to return. But they seemed to be taking a while.

Suddenly Lila appeared next to me in panic, pulling me at full speed away from Danny and Ruby to the other side of the garden and started speaking in a shaky voice.

"He's . . . he's gone—I can't find him. Something-something took him."

I tied to follow along, but I had to stop Lila and get her to be more specific, asking, "What took him?"

She just looked at me with tears in her eyes and replied, "The water took him. He was pulled into the water and disappeared."

Jennifer was listening in as Lila tried to explain and interrupted asking, "Why, what was he doing?"

Lila glared at Jennifer suspiciously, asking "What do you mean why? Do you know what took him?"

Jennifer then rushed out of the garden, frantically looking around the hotel, we followed behind her waiting for an answer. She shouted, "Adela! Adela, we need you."

Adela appeared next to us looking just as confused and asked, "What's up?"

"Matt's been taken," Jennifer said anxiously, "and I think the water nymphs might have done it?"

Adela looked at Lila and pulled the "oh crap" face, saying, "Oh, no! That's not good!"

Lila's heart began to race, fearing the worst and asked, "Why? What are they?"

Adela then walked us to a large and very old wall painting in the hotel, pointing to a picture of a water creature that looked human, kind of.

Adela then explained. "Legend says that they are the descendants of a Water Guardian who attempted to become one with the element. The Water Guardian was the original creator of this temple for her and her family to live in peace."

Lila was still confused and asked, "What's this got to do with Matt."

Adela shrugged her shoulders, saying, "I don't know. All I know is that the legend is where all the other legends of water creatures like sirens and mermaids began."

Lila studied the painting staring at it, then ran at full speed out of the hotel. Adela and I followed behind her as she led us to the hot spring where Matt disappeared.

While we were running, I was thinking back to my history classes from high school. And we stopped at the hot springs and asked, "In every story or legend I've heard about, the creatures are always female . . . luring men to their unsuspecting deaths."

Adela just looked at me then over to Lila who seemed to be examining the rock face wall at the edge of the hot springs in a fluster.

I then tried to make my point a little faster saying, "Well, they've been around for several hundreds of years . . . How do they reproduce, if they're all female?"

That's when I had gained Lila's attention as she ran back over to us at full speed and angrily exclaimed, "Are you trying to tell me that my husband has been kidnapped by water nymphs . . .to . . ." Lila struggled to get the words out, either due to anger or just the thought of it.

So I finished her sentence saying, "to mate with him."

"Well that's not happening, not with my Matt," she said, pulling her hair back into a ponytail and climbing into the hot spring.

Adela climbed up onto the rocks of the hot spring but instead of getting in the water, she walked on the surface of the water—super cool!—to where Lila was and asked, "So what's your plan?"

Lila explained that the wall art was a painting of the temple resting on the side of a mountain, just like this one. And that the water creatures swimming in the water came from inside the mountain. "I think there might be a cave inside the mountain, and there must be a water channel that leads into it from this hot spring."

Well, looking on the bright side, at least we're not fighting a fellow Guardian trying to brainwash us. Nope . . . these were just sex-crazy water nymphs.

Adela and I both jumped into the water and swam over to Lila. Adela then pulled us down under the water where she created—well it's hard to describe—it looked like a giant bubble that goes on your head so you can breathe. So, I'm going to call a water, no, a breathing bubble. She made one for each of us, then we all made our way down towards the bottom of the hot spring.

I will add, this hot spring was deceptively deep. As we swam to the bottom of the spring, Lila stopped, looking around at the darkness.

As she turned to me look for me, a group of creatures swam out of the shadow, circling around Adela and Lila like they were praying and bursting their breathing bubbles. Lila attempted to fight back using the water plants to attack some of the creatures, and Adela created a whirlpool. But there were too many of them and they swam so fast, knocking both of them unconscious and pushing them into the shadows. I swam to help them, but the creatures grabbed me and pulled me into this tunnel at the bottom of the spring.

Journal entry insert by Adela Eden

I woke up in a dark water cove, gasping for air, after one of the scariest moments of my life. I never thought the water would be where I died, but this was a close one. I opened my eyes and coughed out a significant amount of water, and looked over to see Lila still unconscious. A creature that looked like a tree, kind of, but also looked like a young woman, was hovering over Lila, holding a flower in her hand. She squeezed out the fluid from the bud of the flower and dropped it into Lila's mouth.

I didn't know what she was doing, so I shouted at the tree thing to stay away from her and stood in front of Lila to protect her.

The tree thing dropped the flower and hid in the corner of the cove, watching as Lila woke up gasping for air and spitting out water.

"Lila . . . are you okay?" I asked kneeling down next to her.

She was still gasping for air as she answered, "I hate water . . ." She picked up the flower and looked at me saying, "A magnolia stellate, how did you know to use that?"

I shook my head telling her it wasn't me and pointing to the tree thing hiding in the corner.

"Oh my," Lila said absolutely astonished. She then looked down at the flower and said thank you to the creature.

I whispered to Lila in a very quiet voice, "Do you know what that is?"

She whispered back, "No, but I've seen one before . . . in the dreamland." Lila stood to address the tree thing and asked, "Are you a wood nymph?"

The tree thing slowly crawled out of her hiding place and answered, "Yes, I am. My name is Wyala, you met my mother once."

Lila moved closer to the creature saying, "Your mother? Your mother's name is Agatha?"

The tree creature nodded as Lila continued to question, "You saved us, right? But how did we get here? Is this the dreamland?"

The tree creature pointed to a long tunnel hidden by the shadow, then answered, "This is the entrance you seek. We have been following you since the temple, and I know what we did was forbidden . . . but I thought that if we helped you . . . You would not be mad, yes?"

Lila looked up at me, hoping I had an explanation. I shrugged my shoulder, unsure of the answer. To my knowledge, nymphs weren't allowed to do anything that risks their exposure. But up until now, I thought they were just a scary bedtime story.

Lila looked back at the tree thing, "We're looking for our friends . . . do you know where they are?" she asked.

The tree thing stood up and walked into the dark tunnel looking back as we followed her.

She led us through the tunnel entrance, into a large underground cavern filled with trees, waterfalls, and flowing rivers leading towards a large lake in the middle of the cavern.

Lila and I both looked around the cavern in awe and amazement as the tree thing stood and pointed down to the lake and said, "Your friends would have been taken to the lake, that's where they take all their men . . . but this is as far as I go."

Lila thanked the tree thing as it walked back through the tunnel. And we slowly made our way to towards the lake.

Original journal entry continued by Alex Woods

My head was pounding with a massive headache when I woke up. Matt was sitting next to me, staring at the lake.

I looked around and asked, "Matt . . . where are we?"

He just sighed and answered, "We're in a cavern, deep within the mountain, accessible only by water, with no chance of escape by any human thing."

"Human thing?" I repeated confused at the bleak description he made of himself. Until he explained that, that was what the water people called him as they demanded him to stay and not touch anything. Matt then pointed to a water nymph who was standing guard not far from us, saying "That one's name is Sira, and apparently we are waiting for something."

Remembering what I was discussing with Adela and Lila before I ended up here, I was almost afraid of the answer when I asked, "Wait here for what?"

But Matt answered with a very surprising and unexpected response as he answered, "Their mother."

Great, just what we needed. I have never had a good experience meeting a woman's mother. Even when I wasn't dating the woman, her mother still hated me.

Matt started pacing, and I casually looked around for any possible escape routes. I stood up to stretch and commented, "Well, this vacation has been really fun. Did Lila ever find out whose idea this really was . . . I mean, she knows it wasn't Maxwell's idea."

I tried to hold back a laugh, when I saw Matt look at me feeling really guilty, then continued pacing.

"Wow, you're going to be so dead when Lila finds out," I said really struggling not to laugh.

Matt, snidely replied, "You didn't have to come on this vacation!"

Matt's pacing morphed into a storming march, when I commented, "I didn't want to go on this vacation, and from what I gather, neither did Lila."

Matt snickered back. "I was only trying to get her away . . ."

"Away from what?" I asked.

Matt stopped and angrily shouted, "Away from you. Ever since you showed up in town, there has been unending trouble. Because of that, I hardly ever see her, and every time I do, you show up—or Max or Ben or Chase."

I quickly realised why Matt was getting so worked up; it was all this pent-up territorial frustration he had. All humans have it; he just hadn't found a good way to vent it, yet.

Matt continued his rant saying, "Lila's not the type who made friends, or at least ones that came over for dinners, and now she's constantly surrounded by men, who have so much more in common with her than I ever will. Can't you see my point yet?" He finished his rant and sat down at the lake's edge, throwing stones into the water.

And I sat down next to him and said, "Look, mate. I'm going to level with you. Lila's my closest friend. And trust me, it's not easy being just friends with someone like her. But I respect her and I respect you. And I know you probably would never trust any man around Lila, and if I were in your position I'd probably struggle too. But you got to put all that aside and trust your wife. The one thing I learnt from my parents was that a good relationship is built on trust—not with the world, but with each other."

Matt began to calm down, but before he could say anything else, our tender moment was interrupted by the loud roar of what sounded like . . . a dragon.

Suddenly we were surrounded by water nymphs. Sira walked towards us; she looked at the lake and said, "We are ready for you. Come."

She held out her hand to Matt and I, but—and this is the best part—Lila ran at full speed standing in front of us, and damn, she looked angry. Adela appeared standing next to her, both ready for a fight. I heard Adela whisper "I think we might be a little outnumbered."

But Lila was confident and angry and she said, "I can take 'em."

She raised her hand over the ground as she watched several of the water nymphs running towards her. And as they readied to fight her, a long solid stick rose from the ground and into Lila's hand; Lila swung it like a baseball bat, throwing the water nymphs to the ground one by one.

Adela joined in the fight and started using hand-to-hand combat. I pulled Matt back to a safe area and protected him from the stragglers, but I started to get this strange feeling from the nymphs, that they seemed to be more concerned about protecting us from Lila and Adela—almost like they were protecting their prey. Every time Matt and I tried to escape they'd stop us, and every time we got closer to the girls, they'd stop us.

Almost half of the water nymphs had fallen to the ground, unable to fight, when the loud roar again filled the cavern. All the water nymphs stopped fighting and ran back to the tree line, cautiously watching; then they started to hum in unison.

Lila, Adela, and I all covered our ears struggling to cope with the noise, but it didn't seem to affect Matt who was standing, watching in—I think, shock staring at the cave walls.

Adela shouted to anyone who could hear asking, "What are they doing?"

But considering she was the Water Guardian on the team, we were hoping she had the answer, which didn't fill us with much hope.

Matt then shouted answering Adela's question, "I think they're calling for their mother."

"What mother?" Lila screamed baffled at Matt's response. We all stood to our feet absolutely horrified, as Matt pointed to the lake and watched a large water dragon emerge and rested on the surface of the water. It stared at us, letting out another mighty roar, then it started running towards us.

Lila turned back to us and screamed, "RUN!" as she ran at full speed, grabbing hold of Matt's hand towards the tree line with Adela and I following behind her.

But the dragon breathed an icy breath, shooting large icicles at us. They shot into the ground, creating large explosions beneath us, separating us all, and sending us flying.

We slowly made our way back together asking if we were all okay until we realised Matt wasn't with us. We looked around to see Matt struggling to stand at the edge of the lake where the water dragon was standing, looking at him.

Lila screamed Matt's name, which infuriated the dragon which turned its head breathing its icy breath, bombarding us with large shards of ice again. But before the icicles could hit us, large tree roots sprung up from the ground, creating a not very sturdy looking shield, blocking the icicles in their path.

Adela and I both looked shocked at Lila at the fact that she could create something that large, with just a thought.

Lila seemed busy concentrating on the wall as she screamed, "It would have been nice to know that dragons existed."

Adela replied just as confused, "They don't any more. They died in extinction thousands of years ago."

So I couldn't help but sarcastically point out the massive and obvious dragon that was still alive in front of us.

"They said that's their mother, right," Adela asked, slowly getting to her point as she looked over to the water nymphs and asked, "Why aren't they dragons, as well?"

Lila looked at the water nymphs then back at their supposed mother, and shouted "I've got an idea . . . but I need a distraction."

Before I could comprehend what they were doing, or even ask what the plan was, Adela had jumped out, standing to the side of the shield screaming and running to get the dragon's attention. She held out her hand towards the lake, creating several waves and pulling them up onto the dragon, crashing down on it.

The dragon then lifted its tail and swung it towards Adela, who was now trying to help Matt to his feet. They were both sent flying, but were quickly caught by an extended tree branch and gently placed back on the ground.

I looked back at Lila to see her right hand stretched out towards the nymphs who were watching from the tree line. They were too busy watching their mother dragon to notice the tree roots and branches wrapping around them trapping them where they stood.

Lila took a deep breath and raised her left hand out towards the dragon. The shield of roots and branches then broke apart and wrapped around the dragon pulling it to the ground. The dragon managed to break its head free, raising it up and preparing to breathe its icy breath again, but stopped as it looked at Lila and her outstretched arm, pointing towards the tied-up water nymphs, struggling to break free.

Lila yelled, "I'll make you a deal. You calm down or I'll squeeze tight on both hands . . . and we'll see whose bones break first, yours or theirs."

The water dragon stared at Lila, probably trying to guess if she was bluffing or not, then lay its head on the ground, looking at the nymphs.

Lila lowered her hands and the tree roots and branches retracted back into the ground, freeing the water dragon and all the nymphs.

I wasn't overly confident with Lila's plan to free the dragon, and I'm guessing neither was Adela and Matt when they ran up to stand next to us and both asked, "What are you doing?"

They were both immediately shushed by Lila as she walked up to the dragon's head and said, "Well, now that's over. Let's talk, Guardian to Guardian."

She stood and stared into the eyes of the dragon as it transformed back into an old woman. I overheard Matt whisper to Adela, "Now that's weird."

Adela looked back stunned and replied, "An old woman is weird, but a dragon isn't?" He stayed quiet after that.

The old woman introduced herself as Ji and apologised to Lila for taking her property, pointing to both me and Matt. Matt didn't take that so well, but stayed quiet, listening to Lila as she explained, "They are not my property, no man is, but that does not give you the right to take men against their will."

Sira walked up to stand with her mother and interrupted, snapping at Lila, saying, "We need them to survive, and you weren't using them."

"True, I wasn't using them. But that still doesn't give you the right to just take people. That's not how the world works anymore. In the real world a man and woman fall in love, and then they invite them back to their underwater caverns."

Sira looked at the other water nymphs confused then back and Lila and asked "What is love?"

"Um . . . it's an emotion and a bond you share with each other," Lila answered, but she seemed to struggle with that definition. She even got flustered when Sira asked if she loved us, like she described. I tried so hard not to laugh and to be honest I think Adela was holding back laughs too.

But before Lila could answer, Ji interrupted shouting, "Enough! My daughters are forbidden to love. They are of no use to us in that way."

"You can't forbid love—it's a natural part of our lives. You can only ignore it . . .," Lila shouted to Ji as she began to walk back into the lake. I could see Lila was getting to the water nymphs, she was convincing them, slowly. But Lila knew if she couldn't convince the mother, there was no hope for the children.

She ran at full speed to stop Ji and whispered, "Children cannot learn from your mistakes, if they do not know about them. The choice should be theirs to love or not to love."

I didn't fully understand what Lila meant, but clearly Ji did, as she turned to her daughters and told them a story of her pain.

She was one of fourteen wives to the Emperor; the wives were all Guardians used for their abilities to entertain the Emperor and his guests. As a woman she was treated terribly—all the wives were. But Ji had fallen in love with one of the palace guards. He was so nice to her and made her feel special. They hid their love for each other, and for a while Ji was happy . . . until the Emperor found out and ordered the guard to be executed in front of her, to make a statement to the other wives and palace guards. So Ji ran away and fled here in the caverns, building this sanctuary and vowed never to trust a man again.

Adela was teary-eyed as she sniffled saying, "That's so awful. I'm so sorry", to Ji.

But Ji didn't want pity as she yelled, "No, no more excuses. No more questions. Take your men and leave. Now!"

Lila looked back at Matt, holding his hand, getting ready to leave but saying one final word, "Okay, we'll leave . . . but know this: a life without love is no life at all, even if it's safer." Then we all ran at full speed out of the cavern.

We swam up out of the lake and slowly made our way back towards the monastery, making jokes about what just happened and what could have happened. Our laughter was quickly broken by the sound of Sira and a group of her sisters running after us, shouting, "Wait . . . please. We wish you to teach us more about love!"

I could hear Lila sigh and she rolled her eyes as we all turned to greet them. But before the water nymphs could say anything, a young female tree nymph ran out of the trees and hugged Lila, and was so very happy and ecstatic that Lila had survived. She was followed by two older male tree nymphs. The young tree nymph's name was Wyala and those were her older brothers Lin and Par.

Sira and her sister stood back in shock looking at Lin and Par. Apparently, they had never seen a male nymph before.

Lila started walking back to the monastery and said semi sarcastically, "Yes . . . well, why don't we discuss the males and their attributes of love over dinner, my first meal for the day."

The rest of that night was, let's say, very interesting, and I can definitely classify this as the weirdest holiday I have ever been on.

And Lila's emotions didn't kill a single plant while we were there.

CHAPTER 35

SECOND THOUGHTS

Journal entry by Terrence Connors

It's been a few days since I had seen Lila roaming through
the halls of the Eden Hotel. But my contacts tell me she is
due to return tomorrow. I took this as the perfect opportunity
to confirm my suspicions about her.

I let myself into her apartment and had a look around at the
trinkets and memorabilia she owned. I eventually found what
I was looking for in one of Lila's old photo albums. It was
a picture of her when she was 6 years old, playing on a park
swings with a young boy—that was me.

I knew it . . . I had been searching for her for a long time.
I was devastated when I was taken away from my family, and
she was the only friend I had. The day before I was taken,
our families were at a picnic. There was an accident; Lila got
hurt and she lost her necklace. I pulled the necklace out of my
pocket to compare it with what Lila was wearing as a child in
the photo.

The necklace had a small wooden pendant carved into the shape of a white oak tree, with a small ruby stone resting in the centre of the tree trunk. Symbolizing the heart of the tree.

I placed the photo album down on the dresser and placed the necklace on top, in the hopes that when Lila sees it, she would remember me.

CHAPTER 36

A TEAM OF CRIMINALS

Journal entry by Alex Woods

When we finally got back to Australia, the team had grown a whole new level of respect for Lila and her leadership. Not everyone can slay a dragon.

But while we were gone, the Eden Hotel shopping district was the victim of multiple robberies. The odd part about it was that the robbers never took anything. Security footage shows three men storming into a shopping outlet, packing the merchandise into a bag then leaving without the bag.

Police suspect it's just simple thuggery, trying to scare shopkeepers and customers to drive down sales. Nonetheless, Lila had a plan, and today we were going to catch a criminal, or two.

The security teams were divided and assigned to potential targets in the shopping district. I was assigned to watch the jewellery store with Lila, but for some reason she never showed up.

I was distracted looking around for her when two masked men walked into the store, wielding baseball bats and screaming, "Everyone on the ground now!"

All the customers dropped to the ground, except for me, of course. This seemed to aggravate them. "Didn't you hear me, old man? I said 'on the ground'!" one of the guys yelled.

I remained standing and asked, "Why?"

It was a clear and obvious stall tactic that these guys seemed to miss. "Why should I get on the ground?" I asked again.

"Um, 'coz we're like robbing the place, and we'll hurt you if you don't get on the ground!" one of them answered.

"Yes, but why are robbing this place? Out of all the jewellery stores you could have robbed, you chose a store inside a hotel filled with security guards, and other patrons. So my question is, why choose this store?" I asked again.

By this time, I had gotten close enough to stand right in front of one of the robbers. My next move was to disarm him, but I was also waiting for my backup.

The robbers looked around the store and confidently boasted, "I don't see any security guards, do you?"

I smiled back and answered "I don't, but you do." The robber looked out the store window for any signs of security guards, and while he was distracted, I pulled the baseball bat out of his hands and elbowed him in the face, knocking him to the ground.

His partner ran up behind me and took a swing at me with his baseball bat. I ducked out of the way, turned and kicked his legs out from under him.

While they tried to regain their bearings, I handcuffed them with zip ties and waited until Adela and Chase ran in to "help".

I leaned down to unmask our robbers to realise they were just kids, probably no more than 15 years old.

While I gave my statement to the police, Jessica and Adela were working their PR magic on the shaken customers and shopkeeper. And within the hour, everything had returned to normal . . . except for one thing—Lila was nowhere to be seen.

We all met back up in the conference room with Maxwell, Chase, Jessica, and Adela all waiting and going over what just happened. Apparently, Adela had a suspicion she wanted to discuss with the team. But still no Lila. Adela asked me where she was, but I thought she was up here with all of them.

Adela discussed her theory then asked if I'd go check on Lila. As I made my way down to Lila's apartment, I thought about what Adela had said. Her theory was that the robbers weren't there to rob the place, that instead they were looking for something or waiting for someone, who each time never showed, which was why they were only targeting this hotel.

Remind you of anyone . . .

What if they were looking for Lila? Why, what could a couple of teenagers want with Lila? It seemed odd that a teenager would commit a crime all for the sake of getting to Lila or any of us for that matter.

When I got to Lila's apartment, no one was home, so I called Matt on his mobile. He said that by the time he woke up in the morning Lila had already left.

That phone call did not end well. It just made Matt worried and organised to come home early. I walked through Lila's apartment looking for any clues as to where she might be. I called her mobile, only to find she had left it on her bedside table.

My heart almost stopped when I walked out onto the balcony and saw an overgrown pot plant with vines hanging over the side, leading down to the ground.

Lila, where did you go . . .

I wasn't sure if Lila wanted me find her, but I was going to anyway... and damn the consequences. I ran at full speed to grab one of Lila's jumpers and climbed down the vine following her scent. It's a good thing I was an Animal Guardian.

The scent led me to the Carlton Gardens to a very large, very old tree. I looked around to see if anyone was watching and waited for a couple to walk out of sight and with one jump, I landed on one of the highest branches of the tree. I spotted Lila lying on a large hollowed area in the centre of the tree, asleep, in her pyjamas with tree branches wrapped around her.

I gasped and whispered, "No! Not again . . ."

I climbed down, unsure of what to do, remembering the last time she was bonded with the trees. I placed my hand on Lila's chest to feel her heartbeat and chest movement. "Come on, Lila, wake up . . .," I said with a panic, then I tried shaking her, saying loudly, "Lila! Wake up!"

She woke up in a fright looking at me confused, and I was relieved to see her alive and conscious and hugged her so tightly. She looked around at the tree and asked, "Alex . . . where are we? Why are we in a tree?"

"I don't know," I answered, "After you didn't show up at the store this morning, I got a little worried. And followed your scent here. I was beginning to fear the worst . . . that you'd been taken by- by him. Do you want to tell me what you're doing in a tree?"

But she was at a loss for answers and said, "Honestly, I don't know. The last thing I remember was watching the late-night movie on TV. I've been having trouble sleeping since we got home. Maybe my subconscious thought I'd be safer here?"

I could tell Lila wasn't being completely honest, but I couldn't understand why she would hide anything from me. I gave Lila her sweater and helped her jump down from the tree, and as we walked back to the hotel, I filled her in on this morning's escapade, while casually questioning her about hiding in a tree.

She eventually caved after I agreed to buy her lunch, in her case, breakfast, and we sat outside a café explaining everything, but it just left me with more questions.

"Wait, I'm lost. You're saying Darkman, I mean, Terrence has been invading your dreams? How long has this been going on?" I asked.

Lila was also left with questions after explaining about the robbery, so she answered, "Since we got back from China . . ." then asked, "The baseball bat did it have any initials on it?"

"Yeah . . . P.H.S.C . . . But stop changing the subject!" I said frustrated, she clearly didn't take the invasion of her dreams seriously.

And what's worse she ignored me, continuing to focus on the baseball bat, as she explained, "I've seen those initials before It's a high school . . . and I think I know which one."

Lila quickly finished eating her lunch and started rushing down the street towards the hotel.

"Wait, Lila. You're changing the subject again!" I yelled as I rushed after her.

As we walked into the lobby, she turned to me just as frustrated that I wouldn't let the subject go and made a deal with me.

"I'll tell you what. I will discuss more about these dreams and maybe a plan going forward, while we are driving to the high school. I don't have time to argue with you. It's Friday with only an hour left of school, which gives us the perfect opportunity to question the baseball team about their missing baseball bats," she explained.

I agreed to pull the car around while she ran up to her apartment to get dressed. And as we drove through the streets of Melbourne, I got all the answers I needed and we formed a plan, that if Matt was okay with it, it would happen tonight.

When we arrived at the school, the bell had already rung and the children were walking out with their parents. Lila looked at me, as if she had a plan that I might not have liked. She was right, I didn't like it.

She asked me to turn into a dog and use my hunting skills to track down the baseball team. She had a theory that the group we were looking for would have made a plan to meet up after school to check on the progress of their fellow arrested teammates and most likely form a new plan. She also convinced me that being a dog would be the perfect cover for her wandering around the streets, looking for a group of teenagers.

While Lila went in and borrowed a baseball bat from the school gym, for me to get a scent, I morphed into a dog and sat in the car waiting for Lila. When she returned, she laughed at the sight of a dog wearing human clothes as she helped me out of them. We walked the street following a trail I had picked up and it led me to a large sports oval not far from the school.

"Bingo," Lila said as she looked at a group of thirteen teenage boys talking near the batting cages and practicing. Lila looked at me and smiled as she whispered, "Go fetch their ball, Alex."

I ran through the middle of their practice and caught their ball mid-air and ran back to Lila, forcing the group of boys to chase after me. Lila grabbed the ball out of my mouth and sarcastically apologised to them as she handed it back.

One of the boys grabbed the ball off Lila, staring back at her in shock, gasping, "It's you—it's really you!" he said turning to his friends and smiling. "It's the chick from the video."

Lila calmly asked "So my team was right, you were looking for someone, when you robbed my hotel."

I started growling, feeling very protective of Lila, fearing we may have walked into a trap as I recognised one of the boys from the robberies standing at the back of the group.

But Lila just scratched the back of my ear to calm me down. Which, in my opinion was an unfair move . . . However, it did scare the group of boys who took a few steps away.

"We were hoping to see you this morning at the store, but you weren't there. We wanted to prove it was you . . . in the video," one of the boys said pulling out his phone and showing Lila the YouTube video of her fighting Adela in Bendigo.

"That's you, isn't it?" the boy asked, looking back at Lila, who was now lost for words.

"Let me get this straight. You boys committed three crimes, all to prove that was me in the video . . . ? What makes you think that's me?" she asked, trying to laugh it off.

Her laughter quickly stopped when she saw Matt's nephew Jake walk up from the back of the group, shouting, "Because I recognised you. I even compared one of the photos I have of you! And don't even try telling us it was fake because Steve was the one who recorded the video."

Jake pointed back to the boy holding the video and explained that he and a group of the baseball team were all up in Bendigo camping that night; they all saw her.

I began to growl at Jake and his friend Steve as he glared at Lila waiting for an answer. Lila called my name and told me to sit, and I reluctantly did as she asked.

Jake looked down at me, shocked, "Wait, you don't have a dog named Alex, that's your friend's name," he said, starting to piece things together.

Lila smiled, not confirming anything, and asked "So why commit the robberies? Why not just call your uncle Matt and arrange a meeting?"

"I did," Jake answered, "but when I called, he said you were busy. And then I found out it was you who was kidnapped from the zoo by a raving lunatic who thought you were a fairy."

Steve then interrupted saying, "That's when we formed a plan to force you to use your powers, we wanted proof. So why don't you quit stalling and changing the subject and show us your powers."

I barked at Steve to scare him away from Lila then started tugging on Lila's sweater to give her the hint to leave, but she wouldn't; she had another plan in mind.

"It's true I am changing the subject because I'm good at that," she said grinning back at me. I huffed rolling my eyes agreeing with her statement as I stood next to her and looked at the ground.

"Look, I can't deny that that's me, the evidence is there, but I also can't have you going around committing felonies trying to expose me. I will agree to show you what I can do as long as you all promise never to commit any more crimes. And you must keep this a secret, and never tell a soul what you see. Deal?" Lila said, then stood waiting for the group of boys to discuss their options.

I just stared at her, hoping she was kidding, but she wasn't.

All the teenagers nodded their heads in agreement and followed Lila as she walked over to one of the freshly planted trees on the side of the oval. She placed her hand on the tree and asked the boys to do the same. All of them hesitantly followed the instructions and placed a hand on the tree. Their hands all glowed, and the tree grew into a large fully grown tree, overshadowing all of them.

All the teenagers looked around at each other and smiled impressed at what they saw. And while they were all distracted checking out the tree, Lila and I ran out of the park at full speed back to the car.

When we got back to the apartment, our security team was all there, waiting for us, worried about Lila and hoping for some news.

We sat and discussed our discoveries over a dinner that Maxwell and Jessica had made for us as a thank-you. Lila also asked Maxwell to ensure that no charges were made against the boys, as a gesture of good faith that the boys would not pursue their criminal activities to find the truth.

When everyone had left that night, I stayed back to discuss with Matt the other plan Lila and I had organised in regards to the invasion of dreams. We both theorised that Lila wasn't dreaming as such but more being pulled into the dreamland somehow. The plan was for me to morph back into an animal and remain in the dreamland, shadowing her as she dreamt.

Matt tried to take it with a brave face as he agreed, on the condition he wasn't losing his spot in the bed.

So it was agreed. Lila and Matt put Danny and Ruby off to bed and I transformed back into a dog.

When we finally got to sleep, both Lila and I were pulled into the dreamland. But it was different—there were no trees or animals. We were in a nightclub surrounded by people dancing, with music blaring and lights moving all around. I turned to Lila and shouted, "I don't think this is right. This doesn't seem like something you'd dream about."

Lila agreed with me and shouted back, "That's because this isn't my dream. I've never been to a nightclub, and I don't recognise any of these people. Plus, I am pretty sure I wouldn't dream of naked women." Lila then pointed towards three semi-naked women all staring seductively at me.

Oh my . . . This was a nightmare . . . my nightmare. And I didn't know how to get out of it. Until Lila grabbed my hand and we were pulled out of that dream into another.

We were standing on a tropical beach with both me and Lila in our swimsuits standing just in front of the water.

"This is relaxing," I commented looking around at the water. But Lila didn't agree as she held her eyes tightly shut and said, "We're still in your dreams." I looked at her and asked how she could know whose dream it was. She so kindly reminded me that if this was her dream, it would be a nightmare and held her eyes shut trying not to panic. So I held Lila's hand again as we were pulled out of that dream into another.

This dream was definitely Lila's. We were standing in the middle of a beautiful forest surrounded by blossoming trees and flowers, with a hiking trail leading to a small clearing with a picnic basket set out on a blanket.

"Now I know this isn't my dream," I said, pointing to the picnic basket and whispering, "I don't do picnics."

We sat down and ate, looking around at the trees and listened to the animals frolicking around in the trees.

"Okay, I have a question for you," I began to ask, "Why are you still afraid of the beach? I know about your friend and what happened to him, and I know we haven't had much luck around water. But we're dreaming, the waters not going to hurt you."

Lila looked up at me and explained that so many bad things had happened to her around water. So why take the risk. I sighed kind of understanding what she was talking about but stood up, pulling her to her feet. I held Lila's hand and pulled her out of her dream and back into my dream of the beach.

She closed her eyes and took slow controlled breaths.

I turned to her and said, "Lila this is the perfect opportunity for you to face your fears and create one good memory of the beach. I promise nothing will happen to you while I'm here."

Lila took a moment to think, then opened her eyes looking around at the beach and smiled.

We started small and stayed in the shallow parts of the water as we swam around, splashing each other and laughing. Then Lila pulled closer into me as she felt something brush past her leg. She looked around, I reassured her saying that it was just a fish.

Lila stared into my eyes and smiled. I hesitated for a second then lost control of my urges and kissed her.

The amazing part was, she didn't pull away. She kissed me back, it felt amazing and I swear my heart skipped a beat as I was overjoyed. We continued kissing as we slowly made our way back to the shore and we lay down, kissing her so passionately.

We were abruptly interrupted by another hand tapping me on the shoulder. I looked up to see Lila staring down at me, kissing a dream version of herself.

Damn, so far, my dreams were not making the best of impressions about me. I looked down at dream Lila, who looked so amazingly beautiful and happy, waiting for me to kiss her again, then back up to the real Lila, who just stood there smiling at my confused face and said, "I think I might give you some privacy," as she walked through a glowing portal that appeared next to her. I tried to explain myself and stood up and rushed after her through the portal.

I appeared back in Lila's dream and looked around to find Lila. But I couldn't see her. I called her name and she answered in a panicked voice, shouting mine. I looked up to see Lila being held captive by one of the blossom trees, as the branches wrapped around her, tightening each time she struggled.

Terrence appeared standing next to the blossom tree, looking up at Lila and he glanced over at me.

I screamed at him and demanded he let her go. But Terrence looked unswayed by my threats and casually replied, "Actually, Alex, I think it might be time for you to let her go. Kissing a married woman, what will her husband say? I think this would be the best time for you to go find out."

He raised his hands towards me and a gush of leaves pushed me back through the portal. I woke up back in Lila's apartment, back to my human self. I found myself tied up amongst the now overgrown indoor pot plant Lila had in her room.

Matt was already awake, caring for Lila, who looked like she was having a nightmare, sweating, and scared, trying to break free of something. He rushed to help me break free of the plants by cutting the vines with a kitchen knife.

I fell to the floor and saw another vine wrapped around Lila's hand. I quickly grabbed the knife off Matt and severed the vine. And as I did, Lila woke up in panic, gasping and looking around the room.

I hugged Lila so tightly, whispering, "I'm sorry, Lila . . . I'm so sorry, Lila . . . You're safe now."

Matt cleared his throat as he looked at me and highlighted that I was still naked hugging his wife. I quickly stepped away and got dressed at full speed and rushed into the kitchen to bring back a glass of water for Lila.

Matt and I both sat on the bed, speechless, as Lila explained, "He wants to meet . . ."

CHAPTER 37

I ALWAYS KEEP MY PROMISE

Journal entry by Lila Winters

The sun had only just started to rise when we had called for a team meeting.

We convened in the lounge room of my apartment to discuss what our next steps should be, after discussing what had happened during the night. Matt didn't seem to be taking it so well, while he paced back and forth across the lounge room.

"I knew this was a bad idea. I should have told you from the start that this dream thing wasn't going to work, and that this whole thing was a terrible idea? And now some evil Darkman wants you to meet him in the middle of nowhere, and do God-knows-what!" he stopped talking and pacing and took a second, then asked, "What exactly is he planning to do at this meet?"

I didn't really know. He said he was going to bring a peace offering, to show that he meant us no harm, but that could be a trap. I shrugged my shoulders and smiled and added, "But he did give me another clue about my necklace that has reappeared after so many years. Apparently, he was the one who returned it to me," as another show of good faith probably.

Chase piped in with an idea saying, "For all we know, it's a trap, right? So why don't we set a trap ourselves?"

We all agreed to the idea except for Matt who seemed very much against the idea of using his wife as bait. Understandably.

We all stood around the dining room with a printed-out map of Terrence's chosen location. Surprise, surprise, it was at a national park, surrounded by his element. But it was also mine so we were going to make the most of it.

We spent all morning going over the plan, and Matt watched and got more and more upset then eventually stormed off into his bedroom.

I gave him some space to calm down as we finished planning out the trap. Then sent everyone out to prep. I also had a few things I needed to do in order for this plan to work.

I packed up Danny and Ruby's day bags and made arrangement for Jane, Matt's sister to look after them for the weekend. I wanted to keep them safe, if anything were to go wrong. I was confident it wouldn't, but it's better to be safe.

And I couldn't ask my mother to look after them without tipping off the General that I was up to something.

Journal entry insert by Adela Eden

I met up with Alex in the lobby after grabbing the last of the items I needed for our plan to work, and I made sure someone else was able to cover mine and Jessica's shift. We usually cover the front desk on the weekends.

It was odd though. While I was down at the front desk, Matt came down to pick up a parcel that was left at the desk for him. He looked really nervous when he opened it then quickly rushed back upstairs to his apartment.

Alex and I made our way up to Lila's apartment, carrying lunch for everyone as we reconvened to go over the plan one last time. We met Jessica, Chase, and Jennifer, who were waiting outside the door of the apartment. Alex used his key card to let us all in as we waited in the dining room, serving out the lunches. The day was going quite well, until we all overheard Lila and Matt arguing in the bedroom.

"Since when is it okay to risk your life on crazy ideas with people you've known for less than a year?" Matt yelled.

"They are my friends, and I trust them!" Lila replied.

Matt's voice got louder as he yelled, "Some friends they are! Two of them abducted you and flew you to Sydney to beat information out of you, two of them tried to kill you on multiple occasions, and one of them clearly wants to get into your knickers!"

Alex cleared his throat, looking down at the ground as he heard that last part.

"I'm guessing we're going to keep 'Nature girl' out of this one," I commented trying to break the tension in the room.

Alex sighed and replied, "Unfortunately, for this plan to work, we need Lila . . . and Matt on board."

Journal entry continued by Lila Winters

I was trying to make Matt see reason as he continued to argue with me. I made a promise to help find Jennifer's family and this was the best way for me to keep that promise. If we were able to get our hands on Terrence, I was positive he could lead us to the missing Guardians.

I sat down at the end of the bed next to Matt, who was trying to calm down as he said, "Sweetie, put yourself in my shoes. A year ago, we were an average normal family. Then Alex showed up out of the blue and whisks you away on all of these missions and adventures. And I'm left to watch from the sidelines, hoping you come home in one piece."

I started to understand why he was angry and whispered back in a kind of reassuring tone, "I agree . . . we're not your average family anymore, and I'm sorry I can't promise you, I'll come back in one piece. But I've had a bit of luck so far, just a few bumps here and there . . . " I turned Matt's face to look at mine and pleaded with him. "For this plan to work, Matt, you definitely cannot sit on the sidelines. I need you right there with me."

Matt let out a large sigh of annoyance at the fact that my pleading had gotten to him, and agreed to come along with us, as he said "You make your potentially impending doom sound so comforting."

We walked out of the bedroom to the smell of what was left of lunch to see Agent John standing in the kitchen. My eyes glowed as I looked at the nearby potted plants and caused them to grow large enough to trap Agent John against the wall and shouted, "What is he doing here!"

Agent John tried to answer but struggled as the plant tightened their grip. "A little birdie told me you guys were going after Terrence. So, what's the plan?" he said, and looked over at Adela, confidently greeting her, saying, "Oh hey, Del . . . glad to see you're back on our side now."

I interrupted his cheery reunion stating, "You are not welcome here."

He tried to respond gasping for air, saying, "I'm here to offer my help . . . I have a lot to offer."

I loosened the plants grip around him and gently placed him on the ground as I walked closer to him. He didn't notice the plant moving behind him to open the front door.

I then spoke very calmly and answered, "Agent John, I don't want what you have," my eyes glowed, again the plants grabbed hold of him and threw him out of the apartment, landing on his pompous self-righteous ass. "I will never work for you, and I will never work with you," I said, happily slamming the door.

Journal entry insert by Alex Woods

The final hour had arrived and we were all in position. I hid in the bushes and watched Lila and Matt as they waited for Terrence to arrive.

Matt still didn't seem overly keen to do this as he turned to Lila and said, "Are you absolutely sure you still want to do this? There is still time to turn back."

Lila just laughed it off and replied, "And waste the trip out here? Come on, let's have some fun!"

Suddenly Terrence dropped down from one of the trees, landing in front of Lila and Matt, and said in a smug tone, "I couldn't agree more . . . Let's have some fun. I will admit I was half hoping you would come alone. Where's the rest of them?"

"Around," Lila replied back in a smug tone.

Terrence started to circle around Lila and Matt, as if they were his prey. It made me nervous, but I knew that if I moved now, it would ruin the whole plan.

So I sat patiently and listened as Lila talked to Terrence. "Look this has been a great walk in the park, but why exactly do you want me here?" Lila asked.

"I have come to protect you," Terrence responded still circling her and occasionally looking around at the trees.

She laughed and said, "The last time I checked, you were the bad guy."

It was a horrific sight to watch, but as Lila was busy focusing on Terrence, she didn't notice Matt who had pulled a cloth out of his pocket and smothered it with some kind of liquid, taking Lila by surprise, smothering her face with the cloth. I was about to rush to Lila's aid, when I was pulled from the bushes by my elder, Mr Hooper.

I begged Mr Hooper to let me go as I watched Lila fall unconscious and be carried away in Matt's arms, following Terrence back up to the car park. I tried to fight Mr Hooper, to break free of his grip, but he responded by throwing me to the other side of the tree line.

Here, Adela and Jennifer were also taken by surprise when a woman appeared behind Jennifer and said, "Hello step-mother," pushing Adela into a nearby tree and throwing a fireball, that surrounded her, trapping her inside. The woman then held Jennifer by the throat up against another tree and glared at her.

Jennifer looked over to see her husband appear at full speed towering over me and gasped for air as she chokes out the words "Henry . . . Katie . . . please . . . we're . . . family."

Journal entry insert by Matt Winters

As I carried Lila's unconscious body up towards an empty car park with one black van in the middle of it. I remembered back to when this all started.

It was just after Maxwell's birthday party. I just finished dancing with Lila and excused myself to go and relieve the babysitter. Lila was still technically working as security with Chase, so she stayed behind.

I met Terrence in the elevator; I didn't know him at the time, but he eventually introduced himself.

Now I see Lila's world a lot differently, as I carried her unconscious body towards the black van. I stopped for a second to catch my breath. I guess Terrence forgot I wasn't super strong like them.

He rolled his eyes and let out a great sigh of frustration as he walked back to me, agreeing to carry her the rest of the way.

As he leaned in to take Lila off my hands, a tree root sprung up from beneath his feet, trapping him and pulling him to the ground.

Lila opened her eyes and at full speed reached behind me to grab the tranquiliser dart I had hidden under my belt and shot Terrence in the arm. Terrence struggled to stay awake and looked up at me and Lila baffled and asked, "How?"

Lila leaned down to Terrence's level and smugly whispered, "One thing you've got to know about my husband. He has a tell-tale sign when he lies . . . and a wife would pick that up in a heartbeat."

It was true, the morning after I met Terrence, Lila had cornered me and questioned me for information. I don't remember what I did, but I gave it away while I was eating breakfast.

After she administered the treatment, she asked me to continue the ruse—and feed Terrence false or partial information.

When Terrence finally fell unconscious, we were quickly joined by Jessica and Chase, along with his team of security, who were all now pointing their weapons at me.

"What the hell happened back there?" Chase asked suspiciously. Lila quickly stepped in front of me protectively, saying, "Stop, this is all part of the plan . . ."

Jessica lowered her weapon and looked down at Terrence asking, "Whose plan are you following?"

Lila looked back at me and said confidently, "Plan B," then turned to Chase and demanded he call the fire department, then she ran off at full speed to help the others.

Jessica watched in a huff as Lila disappeared and muttered to herself, "I'll never get used to that."

Journal entry continued by Lila Winters

I ran through the trees at full speed. Looking for Alex and the rest of my team and it wasn't hard. All I had to do was follow the path of destruction and fire. I found them in a small clearing. Alex was fighting Henry Hooper and by the looks of it, Jennifer was fighting Katie, the step-daughter she reluctantly told me about six weeks after I had promised to help find her husband.

The problem was Jennifer and Katie were both throwing fireballs at each other and missing, so Adela was busy trying to put the fire out using the water from a nearby lake, all while dodging stray fireballs.

This plan of ours was going perfectly . . . not.

I ran at full speed shoulder, tackling Katie and pushed her to the ground and turned to do the same to Henry. As they both lay on the ground, I raised my hand and pulled up the root from a nearby tree—trapping them.

Adela and Alex ran over to see if I was okay and stopped just in front of Henry and Katie. Alex shook his head, looking around and said, "What's going on? We saw you being carried away by Matt."

"It's a long story," I replied. I looked at Adela and asked, "Will you be able to put out the fire?"

She shook her head apologetically, "Not without help . . . it's too big. So whatever you're going to do, I suggest you hurry," she said looking at Alex and me.

Henry and Katie were starting to break free of the vines, so I had to use two hands to pull more roots up and hold them down as Alex pulled the lily seeds from my back pocket and threw them down in front of Henry and Katie.

My eyes glowed as I tried to concentrate on growing the lilies large enough to absorb the toxins from both of them. Henry and Katie eventually stopped struggling, looking down at what's binding them up, to see Jennifer.

"Jenny," Henry said still confused, "what's going on?"

Jennifer leaned down to hug Henry then looked up at me and nodded, giving me the all clear to release them. I dropped my hand and relaxed as the tree roots retracted back into the ground.

Alex looked at me in fear and worry as he wiped away the blood, dripping from my nose. I tried to brush it off and said, "It's just a nosebleed, don't worry about it."

I helped Katie and Jennifer to their feet after they finished hugging and asked in hurrying tone if they could assist in putting the fire out.

Journal entry insert by Terrence Connors

Why? Why do women have to be so difficult? And why didn't I see this coming? I knew Lila wouldn't trust me, and I knew they would have set a trap for me. But I wasn't expecting Matt to play me like this. It explained why Lila and her team were constantly eluding my patrols.

One thing Lila probably didn't expect was for the sedative to wear off so quickly. I pretended to be unconscious while the humans discussed what they should do with me. I overheard them getting more and more nervous about the imminent fire threat and the sirens of the fire engines made them more unsettled, concerned about what to say to the police about my unconscious body and their missing team members.

But I was more nervous about what was still out there waiting for Lila. I wasn't the only one given the assignment to bring her in. There were others from different sides of the playing field. When my superiors found out just how powerful Lila was, there was a bidding war as to who gets first crack at her.

And the race was on . . .

I didn't lie when I said I was here to protect her. I knew if I got Lila to my superior first, I could convince her to let Lila stay under my protection.

While the humans were distracted no one noticed that I had loosened the tree roots and retracted them back into the ground.

I ran off at full speed, leaving them clueless.

Journal entry continued by Lila Winters

The fire was getting larger, and it was too strong for Katie and Jennifer to control, and Adela was just barely keeping it at bay with the water.

I was assisting Henry and Alex to get some of the wild life to safety, when Katie yelled to us, "It's too strong. We're losing control! We have to pull back!"

Katie and Jennifer started to run across the clearing, away from the fire, and Adela dropped her hands and ran behind me as the water from the lake fell down on us, like rain. I stopped, quickly turning back to make sure she was okay, as she screamed, "Lila, look out!"

I turned to see tree roots spring up from the ground behind me, wrapping around me, twisting into a cocoon, trapping me inside, and pulling me down into the ground. I could feel it pulling me somewhere . . . and it was pulling me fast.

Journal entry insert by Alex Woods

I watched as Lila was snatched up by tree roots and disappeared into the ground. I screamed her name and started digging with my hands to find her. Adela ran up to help but after finding no success, she pulled me away screaming, "Alex, she's gone, we need to go . . . the fires coming."

We ran at full speed with Adela up to the car park where the rest of the team was waiting, surrounded by fire engines and police.

Matt ran up to me, asking "Where is she?"

I vented out some of my anger on the now abandoned black van, giving Matt a very clear answer that I lost her. Matt started running back through the trees towards the fire only to be stopped by two firefighters, telling him to go back.

"My wife. She's still out there!" he yelled.

The firefighters told Matt that they would look for her, but demanded he stay with the group. He walked back to me and whispered demandingly, "We have to do something. You can track her, right?"

I nodded and held on to Matt as we ran at full speed out of the car park, and stopped at the edge of the lake at a bridge crossing to the other side. Matt tried to get his bearing and hold back his vomit as he asked, "What's wrong? Why'd we stop?"

Before I went any farther, I needed to clear my suspicions and asked, "What happened back there? I saw you attack Lila and carry her off. I thought you were playing on our side."

"I am," Matt replied.

But I didn't believe him and shouted "Then why didn't you follow the plan?"

"Because Lila asked me to do it. A few months ago, I was attacked in the hotel elevator. But Lila found out and cured me. She told me to keep it quiet and continue to feed Terrence bad information. This morning, Terrence left instructions for what I had to do. Lila knew if I didn't keep up the act, Terrence would know and disappear. This whole thing was Lila's idea . . .," he explained.

It was hard to believe that Lila didn't trust me enough to tell me what had happened. How could she not tell me?

Matt started to cross the bridge and looked back to see me hesitating and pleaded with me, saying, "Look, I know you have no reason to trust me right now, but my wife is somewhere in that fire, and she needs your help . . . Please."

I nodded and followed Matt across the bridge, looking around, screaming Lila's name.

Journal entry continued by Lila Winters

The cocoon of roots eventually sprung up out of the ground, releasing me and throwing me to the ground in front of Terrence. I was scared and struggled to believe it was at all possible to do that and gasping for air.

He knelt down to help me to my feet and said in a calming, slightly creepy voice, "It's okay, I've got you."

I pulled away from him, ready to fight him, saying, "You just don't give up, do you?" and spin-kicked him into a tree as I ran away at full speed.

I ran through the woods, trying to avoid the fire; but everywhere I turned, I could see the fire and I couldn't slow down because Terrence was right behind me. I was quickly pulled to a stop when a tree vine swung down, grabbing my foot and pulled me into the air.

I hung upside down as Terence stopped and stood in front of me smiling. "That should hold you," he said.

But he was wrong. I reached my hands to the ground as my eyes glowed, pulling the tree roots up and wrapping them around him and throwing him into a large tree trunk. He fell to the ground wincing in pain, as he nursed what I can only guess is a now a broken rib.

And while he was busy getting used to the pain, I grabbed the dagger from my boot holster and cut the tree vine, somersaulting down to the ground. And running off at full speed again.

Again, I ran into the problem of fires everywhere I turned. I stopped running, looking around for a clear path. But there wasn't any. I was surrounded, and the smoke from the fires was starting to affect me as I struggled to see and started coughing as I fell to the ground.

Terrence appeared next to me, holding on to me tightly and pulling me to my feet, shouting, "Come on. We've got to get you out of here."

Suddenly I heard Matt and Alex's voice calling my name from the fire. I pulled away from Terrence trying to run to the sound of their voices screaming, "Matt! Alex! I'm here."

Journal entry insert by Matt Winters

I could hear Lila calling through the wall of flames. As we looked over the fire and through the smoke, I could see Lila trying to get to us.

She was surrounded by flames, but she finally saw us and screamed, "Matt! Matt, I'm here!" She was pushed backwards as the fire moved towards her, burning her arms.

As she looked down to see the burns, Alex and I watched as she was shot in the arm with three large tranquiliser darts.

Lila looked at her arm and wiped the blood away as she pulled one of the darts out. She looked back at me and Alex, looking so scared and sad as she began to stumble.

I screamed her name as she fell to the ground and tried to find a way of getting to her, but Alex held me back.

We both watched as Terrence appeared, standing over her unconscious body. The wall of fire got bigger, blinding us with its bright flames and pushing us backwards. It was if it had a mind of its own.

"Lila! Lila!" I shouted as tears filled my eyes.

Adela and the rest of our team were running through the woods, looking for me and Alex. Adela took one look at me being held back by Alex, fighting to break free, with tears streaming down my face, and just knew something had gone terribly wrong.

Something must have fuelled her powers because she looked back at the lake, reached out her hand, and created an enormous wave, almost emptying the lake and pushing it across the fire—smothering the flames and putting the fire out.

I looked back at Adela almost drained of energy then around at the burnt and charcoal-black trees and broke free of Alex's hold, running to where Lila last stood.

But there was nothing . . . nothing but burnt trees and ashes.